T0197151

The
Wildly Irish
Sextet

The
Wildly Irish
Sextet

Dick Wimmer

Soft Skull

Library of Congress Cataloging-in-Publication Data

Winner, Dick.
The wildly Irish sextet / Dick Wimmer.
p. cm.
ISBN-13: 978-1-59376-181-3
ISBN-10: 1-59376-181-3
1. Men—Ireland—Fiction. 2. Fathers and daughters—Fiction. 3. Painters—Fiction.
4. New York—Fiction. 5. Ireland—Fiction. 6. Humorous stories, American. I. Title.

PS3573.I4785W55 2008
813'.54—dc22
2007051836

Cover design by Luke Gerwe
Interior design by Maria E. Torres
Printed in the United States of America

Soft Skull Press
New York, NY

www.softskull.com

CONTENTS

CONTENTS

Wildly Irish

May 1979

One

Aer Lingus lifting me away from Erin's green and fragrant shore and that insane media blitz, paparazzi galore, of Paris and London, Munich and Rome—all those cities, eleven in seven days, twelve in the last month, as I wobbled and skidded, staggered and groaned back to dear, dirty Dublin and my castle by the sea. Landleaper me finally wending my way by and by home to Jaysus, that strange, unfinished painting—with no idea whose features they were or where the hell it was leading—like a blazing shaft of sunlight easing and peeking a path through stormy seaclouds to fiendishly taunt and tease me with a familiar face—but damned if I could recall, quite see it all—as I continued wildly swirling and layering on the coarse and lumpy, pulsing lovely gleam of the paint—

And Laura appeared behind me, with a wifely kiss on the cheek, in a flowery yellow sundress as I kept tracing and erasing the creamy sheen of that haunting face that I just couldn't quite get right!

"Who is she, Boyne?"

"I don't know, but it's driving me up the wall!"

"*You* don't know?"

"No I don't!" jamming my brush back in that cracked water glass, "Though I'm sure I've seen her before."

"Here in Ireland?"

"I just told you—"

"A former lover?"

"*Laura!*—Sorry, sorry—No, but I'm almost positive I've met her before."

Then later that night, all of us playing poker, Poldy, my great white Samoyed beast, asleep at my feet, four paws in the air, and my blonde-haired daughter, Tory, still feisty at twenty-three, asking, "So what've you got, Dad?" "Three queens." "Come on! Three queens?" "All right, how 'bout one queen and two effeminate jacks?" "OK, that's it, I'm outta here! You can't play poker with him." "Tory!" "He's always goofing around!" "Where you going?" "Up to the attic." "Just one more hand?" "No, I want to go through those boxes." "Why?" "I'm intrigued by our past." "But they're all so dusty, Tory." "Fine, Mother, I'll wear gloves and a mask." And she then shouting from above, "Hey, guys, come on up, hurry, hurry!" and showing me that love letter from my father, Tim, to Gillian Shea—and that faded photograph, *the face in the painting!* Looking so like my mother, with her dark Asian eyes, oval face, brown pageboy hair—

And now rereading my father's words once more as this plane drones steadily on across the pond:

```
                                    July 16, 1942
Dearest,
There's always one profound fear in our
childhoods that serves as the basis for our
love relationships.
              Meeting After Long Parting
    Like overlapping images, words intertwined,
                  We blend again,
    Such sweet affirmation, unique combination,
                  You and I,
    As your laughter's jubilation dazzles my heart,
    Trampolines it into a somersault grin
    With the wonder of your eyes,
    Childish sheen or root beer gleam,
    O how I treasure our Celtic dreams!
```

And that sent me skying off on this quixotic quest back to my childhood home, first to Boston for this Gala Retrospective at the

Museum of Fine Arts, the old MFA, and then to Valhalla, New York, with this ancient photo and strange letter to the love of my father's life, nearly forty years ago, tucked in my vest. Tory and her hubby Gene already back there on Long Island, with my grandchild snug in her belly, and me alerting my horde of lawyers to endless annuities, paragraphs in the will when the bab pops out in a blaze of glory!

One of these pale, polished girls looking a bit worn beneath the eyes, but nevertheless prim and voluptuous in her tight stewardess green, her agile rump just aching, I'm certain, to be stroked or painted. Out the window: Green breast in a graygreen sea and the gulls far below, tilting on the winds. *Exquisite echoland, hush! Dyoublong?* And so drowsy now, my eyes fluttering, slowly sliding closed, feigning sleep like I used to when I wanted to hold onto a dream. A sunrumpus of shapes of my second wife Ciara's moist bluestone eyes ringed with shadow and her just-washed, just-now-dry blonde hair. Then Laura again, whom I've married twice, making passionate love last night, after mollifying her jealous Gillian-fears ("She's a bloody painting, you're real!"), leaning down between the sleek heat of her thighs to nuzzle and kiss her soft floral labia, vibrating my tongue like a tuning fork over her clit, she thrusting hard, quivering against my lips, swiveling her hips faster and faster, squeezing her knees round my ears, then rolling to the side as she sighed, settling back and stroking my eyes, my lips, and kissing my briny fingertips.

"So, my Love, now you can tell me what women really want."

And she smiled, still licking my fingers, "The deed . . . to the castle."

Clouds through the window. The sea down there a bit choppy, spilling with whitecaps. A lone ship cleaving the water. The shadow-dappled, gull-wheeling, green-shimmering sea. This droning 747 Viscount St. Paul rising now, and the swift thought that below in the summer morning while I dozed lay Killarney and

Galway, Glengariff and Cork, the rough coast of Connemara or Donegal Bay. Or who knows? Another plane off course. Last year's Alitalia crash into the sea still looming like a dark, ominous cloud over me: as well as my mother perishing on that Pan Am flight when I was twelve: *Ladies and gentlemen, this is the Captain speaking*—No, never happen. Too young to die now that I'm fifty and finally got the world by the bollocks! Anyway, the pilot's probably an old R.A.F. man. Leftenant Kelly, of the doughty heart and roguish wit, flying the lead squadron alongside Niven and Errol Flynn, a gallant Irish lad. Down below, *the blue chasm of the waves, a fresh sea saltness in the teeth,* lifeboats bobbing on the cold and icy brim. Awaiting the Coast Guard cutter, if the Irish happen to have one—probably some Bawneen or Aran Island curragh. And hell, I should've taken the Concorde from London like Laura said, been there by now, three-and-a-half hours door to door. Or sat at the back like that fellow told me to do on my last flight from Paris. Last two seats on the aisle the safest, he said, and he should've known. Been through it before in Spain, lost one of the landing wheels, and they nosed over into the reeds. Strange fellow, Brian something or other, he looked exactly like Scott Fitzgerald. And when I told him, he said, Scott who? Sorry, don't know who he is. Doppelgängers abound.

And *there's always one profound fear in our childhoods that serves as the basis for our love relationships.* For me, it was losing my mother's tender cuddling while she crooned Bach's "Sleepers Awake," and then deserting me and my father when I was nine. The message so loud and so clear: If you love 'em, you'll lose 'em.

Still, no stopping me now heading back to my childhood home, or, as Tim used to say, the last possible spot when all else has been forsaken—

"Ladies and gentlemen, this is the Captain speaking." *O Jaysus, NO!* my heart in my throat! "We've encountered a bit of turbulence and there's more up ahead, so fasten your seat belts, please."

Brightness falls from the air, Inishfallen, fare thee well! The woman across from me, eyes closed, mumbling Aves to herself and massaging her rosary beads as the fiercely buffeted plane begins a violent bumping and shaking.

A fine fume of rain driving in from the sea as I continue wolfing down a Jacob's biscuit, licking the sweat from my upper lip, and depositing this cellophane in that crinkling pouch, seat belt sign flashing and blinking on this roller coaster ride, thunder and lightning and—*WHAP!*

What the fuck was THAT?

Zigzagging bolts striking the plane, fracturing the sky, people shrieking and weeping, and we're plunging down, down, down in a supersonic death spiral!—a jolting, grinding sound of the landing wheels being lowered—Why? Explode when we hit the ground, water, Atlantic Ocean! Holding my breath, only seconds left—and we're suddenly, *O Christ,* leveling out through this raging storm, beaded silver streams coating the windows—

"Ladies and gentlemen, this's the Captain speaking. No cause for alarm. We should be arriving shortly at Boston's Logan Airport, so please keep your seat belts fastened."

Two

Merry-go-rounding shirt-sleeved Beantown at a breakneck pace of meetings, interviews, and calls—then slamming that phone book closed at the Ritz last night, the papers all headlining my terrifying flight, after finding no Gillian Shea, G. Shea, or any other bloody Shea in Valhalla, New York—and waiting now at the MFA—as this tall and bony Don Quixote in his rumpled seersucker suit and polka dot bowtie comes dashing breathlessly across the courtyard with prissy little sidling steps:

"—O Mr. Boyne, so sorry I'm late, I'm Basil Quinn, and I can't tell you how delighted I am that you survived your flight, we were all so mortified, glued to the tube, it must've been positively dreadful—"

"Right, and I'm never flying again!"

And following him through the Retrospective wing, with my paintings as far as the eye can see brilliantly lit and leaping off the walls as I add, "And all of them forgeries, I'll bet."

"O no-no-*no*, Mr. Boyne, no—O don't *say* that, please! Not these, among the finest paintings of this or *any* century! But what's happening with that?"

"Interpol called just before I left to say they've narrowed the search for the forger down to the States."

"Ah, that's marvelous!"

And I pause before these glittering portraits: and, so strange, superimposing Gillian's face in my mind over Ciara's lips, Laura's nose, and my mother's Asian eyes.

● ● ● ● ● ●

Then later in the evening dining alone here at Locke-Ober's on their savory oyster stew (a favorite of my father's and JFK's, and he a favorite of mine). Met him only once in '62 on East 76th sneaking out of the Carlyle (where soon I'll be staying) and away from the Secret Service, he and brother Bobby approaching me down that empty consulate street, and I bellowed, "Up the Republic!" and Jack flashed a blinding smile and, flicking back the hair from his tanned brow, quickly nodded and hurried on—only to die in less than a year!

● ● ● ● ● ●

Flooring this rented Lincoln Continental along the Bronx River Parkway under radiant May sunshine—and passing all these slower cars—And what the hell *am* I seeking, searching for that makes me keep painting her haunting face, like wandering Aengus, some secret cord, silver thread (*silver apples of the moon/ golden apples of the sun*) that embraces my father's past and my own? I was thirteen in 1942, my mother, Aideen, having perished the year before, been to Ireland many times—So could it've been at Carnaween? Or maybe in Brittany before the War, when my father and I bumped into Joyce and Nora? No—weaving by that traffic stall—so it's back to this old address on my father's letter, while I keep rummaging my brain all night and day to try and recall who she is and where I met her—and veering swiftly off at the Valhalla exit, skirting the Kensico Dam—and, Jaysus, my heart skipping a beat, since I haven't been here in over a decade! Down this same main street, one block long, with that old railroad caboose now a restaurant, by the station, toward my childhood home—and abruptly struck with a rush of emotion, the losses flooding back:

O my father, with your Van Gogh eyes and gentle, tapering hands—and, as I've said before, you don't love anyone *but* yourself if you're afraid to love your father! He a short-order chef during the Depression at the Empire Diner in White Plains, so we never lacked for food. Loved to watch him flipping flapjacks high in the air and deftly catching them on his spatula, while frying up bacon strips sprinkled with sugar—and that smoky aroma still sizzling in my brain, dear, sweet father of mine, who hung early work round his kitchen, the great Timothy Patrick Boyne!

And blowing my nose and drying my eyes as I turn down our old street—

And what the hell *happened?!* This *is* Madison, right? *O Suffering CHRIST,* they've torn down our home, paved it over, and thrown up a three-story brick office building in its place!

Stopping sharply and swerving to the curb to gather my breath—then letting out a long Lear-like *howl!* Some dog howling back—no people around, call the town council, have them erect a shrine! Good God, is there *anything* sacred left?

A kid on a skateboard whizzing by—

And I'd better find Gillian Shea's! Probably a McDonald's now or a forty-lane bowling alley, who the fuck knows! as across the Taconic I go.

Checking Tim's letter again: Harding Avenue. Here it is, a quiet, tree-shaded street filled with neat front lawns and small, middle-class, clapboard, stucco, and Tudor homes, more dogs barking, women with baby carriages—and there's number 10.

Not familiar. And what should I say? Do you remember me? Followed my career? Eyes peering out with a root beer gleam, childish sheen, from an oval face with pageboy hair?

And up the narrow path—feeling anxious, licking my upper lip—to this worn screen door, weather strips, a rusty buzzer. Ringing once, twice, holding my breath and staring in. Not home? Doesn't seem so. Should I go?

No, try the neighbors. Past her mailbox with no name on it. "The Deveres" on this one carved in wood as I keep shifting out here from foot to foot. Not home, either. How 'bout the other side? Rapping the black brass knocker.

The door swings wide: a fat, middle-aged woman with her hair in curlers, her vacuum behind her.

"Yes?"

"I'm trying to find a Gillian Shea."

"O, she hasn't lived her for years," fanning herself with her hand and blowing the hair from her eyes, "She's in a nursing home."

"Really? How long?"

"O, must be a year, few years now."

"Would you happen to know which one?"

"I believe it's Saw Mill River, but I wouldn't bet the farm."

And pulling off the parkway and bumping past these red Texaco pumps. This dented phone booth without a door, torn styrofoam cup on the shelf and all sorts of graffiti scrawled on the walls: "Pat 194—" under a huge pair of balls as I find the number and, dropping in my coins—ringing, ringing, ringing:

A noisy clatter of shouting in Spanish—"Saw Meel Reever."

"Is Gillian Shea a patient of yours?"

"*Who* jou say?"

"Shea, Gillian, with a 'G'."

"Shea with a '*G*'?"

"No, Shea with an *S*: S-H-E-A."

"O *Shea,* jou say! Wait jus' a minute . . . Yeah, she here. I put you t'rough, OK?"

Waiting, waiting—

A faint female voice, "Hello?"

"Gillian?"

". . . Yes?"

"This is Seamus Boyne."

"Who?"

"Seamus Boyne. You and my father, Tim—"

"O dear Lord! O my—Seamus! O my Lord, where, well, where *are* you?"

"In Valhalla."

"You're still there, never left?"

"No-no, I live in Ireland now—"

"O I'm so excited, I can't believe you called me! O I have to tell my son, only child, have to call him right now! Maybe you can help him, he's a painter, too, lives on 482 Broome Street, fifth floor, and my sister, Fiona Dolan, lives in Bronxville on 296 Pondfield Road—"

"Yes, well I thought I might come visit you."

"O Seamus, that would be wonderful, so wonderful! And I'm in Yonkers—"

"I know."

"—at 1188 Saw Mill River Road. But when?"

"Whenever you say."

"Tomorrow at noon? Is that all right, convenient for you? Give me time to freshen up, look my best, show you about."

"Fine, I'll see you then."

"I can't wait. And I'm at 1188 Saw Mill River—Seamus?"

"Yes?"

"O you're still there. I thought I'd lost you, we were cut off. Well, thank you again, thank you, thank you, thank you. 'Bye-'bye."

"Gillian? *Gillian?!*"

"Yes, yes, I'm still here," she giggling, "haven't left."

"Good. One quick question: When did we first meet?"

"Don't you remember? In Ireland, I was over for the summer, I was a student at the Rhode Island School of Design, in my salad days, and you had that home outside Dublin, by the sea—"

"Carnaween."

"Yes, yes, that's the one. And I spent a week or two with you."

"When was—?"

"And we had a picnic at Kilcoole, you were a little boy—so long ago since Kilcoole—"

"What year was that?"

"—And then I saw you again back here. O but listen, listen, we have so much to talk about, so much to say, so when I see you tomorrow, I'll tell you more—remember, 1188 Saw Mill River Road—ta."

And driving away, back to the city, with my mind spinning and straining hard to see Erin's green and fragrant shore or Kilcoole's lonely shingled beach—but I *still* can't recall, blocked it off!

And Suffering Jaysus, so wondering what my father had done. What did he do? Pleaded, begged, cajoled, my flower of the mountain, believe in me? And she did, loved him whatever and the hell with guarantees, as they left from Kingstown Pier—No-no, what am I *saying*? That was Joyce and Nora, his common-law wife, fleeing *to the woods and waters wild* to share their hazardous life—mind such a bloody muddle now—and what'll I find tomorrow?—far from the ould sod, where, once upon a time, they raced through the park to embrace in their glade, nimble swirls of hair flaring and cascading, milling her mouth with laughter and fondling the soft plump squeeze of those jiggling breasts—And *Christ* no! that was Ciara, *my* second wife, dead now eight long years ago! For these days, I'm so filled with joy since Laura came back, conquered her cancer under the care of Irish doctors—and next year, God willing, we'll be doting grandparents besides! Tory and Hagar, who would've believed? Gene and I having come so far from those madcap days when we whirligigged and ran our heedless ways.

On through smoggy Yonkers on this Saw Mill River Road—got to call them later—and so long since Kilcoole and that picnic by the sea—

Wait, wait, *swimming* in the sea, the Irish Sea, and she *saved* me—*Yes, yes, YES!* pulled me onto a sand dune when I was ten, while my father was off mending a curlew's broken wing: Her shining wet face, dark hair dripping, first kiss, can still feel the warmth of her lips on mine, giving me mouth-to-mouth—so embarrassed I was aroused, blocked it off—O Gillian—all those years ago!

Three

Approaching this nursing home, vine-covered prison, antiseptic mausoleum, a tomb with a view, and on inside by these wheelchaired patients grotesquely twisted in sleep, or moaning and groaning, a black nurse screaming, "She peed all over the hall!" *La Bamba* blasting off the walls, visitors signing in at the front desk or receiving a pass, phones ringing—and this receptionist breaking free to lean toward me.

"Gillian Shea?"

"235, that way. Next."

Forget the pass and signing in, up the stairs and by the Bathing Area and open bedrooms: withered geriatrics, their toothless mouths agape, Dachau skin and bones, those Puerto Rican nurses, and arriving at 235, the beige door closed.

Softly knocking—and what'll I see: dark Asian eyes and gray pageboy hair?—before knocking softly again.

"Gillian? . . . It's Seamus Boyne. . . . Gillian?"

Try the door—"Hello?"—then peeking in.

Covers and quilts loosely piled around her, only her pale brow showing, must be sleeping—breeze from the open window—won't wake her, and backing out—

"Ah, sir!"

Nearly *leaping* out of my shoes! as this reed-thin cadaver, "Millichap" on his nametag, gives me a pat on the shoulder.

"Haven't seen you in quite a while."

"Seen *me?* But I've never been here."

"Not lately, I know—"

"Yes," moving off, "well she's sleeping, so I can come back later, call her—"

"As you wish, Mr. Shea—"

"No, *her* name is Shea, mine is Boyne."

"Uh, yes, well, you sure you don't want to wait?"

"No, as I said, I'll come back later, call her first."

"But—"

"Thank you."

"Sir—?"

"'Bye," past the wheelchairs.

"As you wish, Mr. Shea, er, Boyne."

And down the stairs—Christ, even the staff here's gaga!

Four

Cursing cab drivers flipping me off as we go screeching through Central Park—and I pause for this light under these tall, conforming cliffs of glass—the radio reporting multiple shootings up in the Bronx and Staten Island, too—*it's lovely going through the zoo.* 12:40 now, drumming my fingers rapidly on the wheel, tapping my toe. Call Gillian in an hour, return at 2:30 or so, after I meet her son. And what was that station Hagar liked, near the middle of the dial, QXR? Ah, *Semiramide's* stirring overture! And such fun getting behind the wheel again. In Ireland, I'm usually chauffeured all around. More checkered cabs crowding me in, revving their engines, ready to drag, and—

WHEEE!! taking off, pedal to the metal, *EEE-YAH!!* like Mario Andretti at Le Mans, breezing in and out of traffic, allegro vivace, and narrowly making lights, missing cars, passing those cursing cabbies and pointing to myself and mouthing, "My fault!" as I go grinning dementedly down Broadway at 60, 65—releasing my anxiety of finally seeing Gillian—past Greenwich Village and West Houston (pronounced How-ston) Street to ease into SoHo, TriBeCa below—and out my window, those cowed, hunched men keeping close to the walls of the city's side streets, reminding me so of Irishmen clustered along the Dublin quays in shiny black serge suits and worn checkered caps, a cigarette stub stuck in the corner of their chapped lips, and who, transplanted here, politely nod and press the proper floor, escorting the posh up and down the elevators at Sutton Place or Gramercy Park. Kowtowing yes-men giving you the weather with a hearty brogue and still waiting for that windfall of quids this country was supposed to offer, while collecting their Christmas tips for that return trip when the weather eventually improves.

Turning right now into Broome's one-way street, a marvelous expanse of cast-iron façades, and let's see the numbers: 488, 486—ah, 482, and parking round the corner on Wooster, paved with Belgian blocks, far smoother than cobblestones.

Identical women gliding by with high-gloss make-up and black heels clacking in echoing synch as I enter this twilit vestibule. Fifth floor, she said. Name scrawled on the wall: Donal Tuohy.

Donal Tuohy? Who's Donal Tuohy? Her son? Took his father's name? Gillian must've married again—Sure never married my father, at least as far as I know.

And aloft in this antique elevator, which stops and slackly sways as the cage clatters aside.

That blue door open wide, where inside, a tiny man, wearing overalls—rather old for her son—is tightening some pipes behind the radiator.

"Hello? . . . Hello?" Must be deaf. "He*llo?*"

He slowly turning, with his Chaplin moustache, and breaking into a lopsided grin, "O, Mr. Tuohy, welcome back!"

Blind as well? "Tuohy? No, I'm—"

"There was a gas leak in the building and I just this second found it," gathering his tools, "So no more problems, sir, no more cares."

"Who's Tuohy?"

But he limps past me, clumping into the elevator and muttering, "Whole place coulda exploded, an accident waitin' to happen."

This's starting to get crazy, first I'm called Shea, now Tuohy, who next? And looking around this pillared loft, just one of those faces, glancing in that ornate mirror: my grizzled/snowy beard, appearing older here, my wrinkles out of place—and through this kitchen clutter, Ajax and a pile of dirty dishes, chipped teacup, loosely made bed, paintings stacked in that far corner, and this color postcard of Renoir's dancers: girl in a red bonnet; man, with my bearded face, sporting a slanted straw hat—and these photos tacked to a cork board:

Of *me?* Me and my *father?* Can't be, these are places I've never been! Then who the blazes—what the hell is going *on?* And there's Gillian, a younger Gillian, with the spitting image of me—or him, *whoever* he is! A flyer from my Retrospective—

Suffering Jaysus, *what is this,* Boyne in Wonderland?!

And moving across the loft toward the paintings.

And *Christ,* what are *THESE?*

MY work? Coming closer, looks like—but I never painted this or this, though not too bad—

O GOOD GOD, these are the bloody forgeries!!!

Faces east in a sort of serene Georges de La Tour style of creamy candlelight, trying more for a Vermeer glow—and nothing at all like my work, unless the buyer was stoned out of his mind!

And what'd Tory tell me last night: The forger sells only to private buyers, one got suspicious, phoned Interpol, who's tracked him here to the States. And now I've *GOT* ya, Donal Tuohy! as I keep on gleefully pacing.

But those photos? Stalking me all these years? Better phone Interpol fast! No, 911:

Phone ringing forever—New York's finest, right! Could be dying here, happens all the time—

"Police Emergency, Operator 1123. Name, address, and where ya callin' from?"

"This's Seamus Boyne calling from (212) 925-6679—"

"Hey, slow down, slow down, take it easy."

"Sorry. And I'm at 482 Broome Street, fifth floor, and I've found all these art forgeries—"

"OK, sir, stand by at your location, 482 Broome Street—"

"I'll meet you out in front."

"Fine, we'll be there right away. And what's the name again?"

"Boyne, B-O-Y-N-E, Seamus Boyne. . . . Hello?"

"Yeah, I'm still here. We'll be right there, sir."

Great! And let's see what else I can discover about this Tuohy, who may be back at any second. Smoky motes of sun pluming down from the dusty skylight, this scarred wooden desk littered with bills from Con Ed, AT&T, the Pearl Paint Co., a ceramic blue owl, envelope addressed to Fiona Dolan, albums in a brick-and-board bookcase of the Clash, the Doobie Brothers, and on that nubby red plaid sofa, copies of the *Post* and *Daily News* spread open to pictures of me arriving at Kennedy.

Better find the landlord now! Wow, my heart kettle-drumming wildly away—take a deep breath—and down to the cellar. Remember he's deaf, and blind as well—I'm still breathing hard—

And shouting, *"Hello? Hello?!"* then searching for ten minutes through this murky maze—

There he is, limping along that dark corridor (but not twirling a Chaplin cane) and stepping out into a narrow alley reeking of scattered garbage, before dropping something into that can and closing the lid as I come up behind him, "Listen, sorry to bother you, but could you please tell me who is Donal Tuohy?"

"What?"

"Who's Tuohy? Donal Tuohy?"

"Tuohy? Why *you're* Tuohy! Whatta you playin' some kinda game with me, Mr. Tuohy?"

"No, no, just tell me who lives here and painted these—"

"What?" and he continues along the alley, a mangy gray cat dashing out.

"Tell me about Mr. Tuohy."

"Tell you about who?"

"Jaysus! About Tuohy, Tuohy, Donal—"

"Tell you about yourself?"

"Look, read my lips, I am *not* Donal—"

"O you in trouble, Mr. Tuohy?"

"I'm *NOT* Mr. Tuohy!"

"Then whatta ya a cop? Drugs?"

"*No*—"

"Well, he was strange, a very strange sorta guy, sure looked a lot like you," emerging from the alley onto Broome Street, "rarely saw him, paid by mail—" just as the cops, thank God, finally arrive in a shiny black and white and approach the landlord.

"Seamus Boyne?"

"No, he's Mr. Tuohy."

"Who're you?"

"Me? Alvin Cobb. Why?"

"And you're—?"

"The landlord. But—"

"You Seamus Boyne?"

"Yes—"

"Well yer under arrest."

"*Me?* What're you *talking*—But the *forgeries!* Look, just come upstairs—"

"No, you come on with us. You can come easily or we can just cuff ya."

"But arrested for what?"

"Murder."

"What're you *talking* about? Of *who?* Come on, will you!"

"Gillian Shea."

"*Gillian Shea?* But I just *saw* her—I mean I never actually *met* her, she was sleeping, so I left—*MURDERED?*"

"And you were the last person to see her alive, the director saw ya, the last person to come outta her room, so, sir, would ya come wit' us."

"But I only *spoke* to her! And furthermore, why would I *call* you, bring you down here? To *arrest* me? This's crazy, insane! At least let me call my lawyer."

"Ya can do that down at the station house."

"No, no, listen, wait, I swear, promise I'll come with you, but please, first, just come upstairs with me and at least *see* these forgeries!"

"Hey, buddy, I don't give a damn about any forgeries—"

"Two minutes, just one look is all I ask. You can even cuff me if you want, but two minutes to verify you saw them and then we go, please! You must know I'm a world famous painter—"

"Yeah, so?"

"Whatta ya say, Tone?"

"Hell, I don't know. Yer not plannin' on doin' somethin' stupid, are yuz?"

"Guys, believe me, two minutes is all!"

"Mr. Tuohy—"

"Right, Alvin, right. You'll come with us, let us in."

"Why's he keep callin' ya Tuohy?"

"*God* only knows!"

"But ya are Seamus Boyne, ain't ya?"

"I swear I am! Here, in my wallet, passport, license—"

"OK, but two minutes and that's it."

"Thank you, officers, thank you so much."

"Where we goin'?"

"Back upstairs, Alvin."

"But why?"

" 'Cause you have the key."

"O, right, sure."

And up we go, wedged as I am between officers Bombasi and Santiago. The elevator swaying to a stop, and the cops letting Alvin limp out as he fishes about for his key, followed by Bombasi and—

KABOOM!!!

Flying wood and falling plaster, all of us knocked flat, gas fumes and clouds of dust—*SUFFERING JAYSUS*, what the roaring blazes was *THAT?!* Can I move my arms, my legs? *YES*, unbelievably! Not dead yet—cushioned by Santiago and beefy Bombasi—as I slowly rise to one knee, then stagger on up—no pain—and lean against this wall—door blown right off its hinges, black, acrid smoke pouring out, fire raging inside—and Santiago groaning, Bombasi out cold but still breathing, and Alvin—feeling, fumbling for a pulse—can't find one—O Christ, poor guy!

Helping Santiago—easy, could have internal injuries—into the elevator and down, holding him up, and gently guiding, lugging him outside, a small crowd forming, this skinny black kid in a Bob Marley T-shirt, dreadlocked teenager, "Whot hoppened, mon?" "Who knows, gas leak—but give me a hand here, would you?"

Both of us easing Santiago into the squad car's back seat, "Thanks a lot. And there's another cop up on the fifth floor, needs help," before I reach over the front seat to grab that hand-held mike—

How the hell does this work? Button, right, press the button:

"Hello, hello?? Police officers hurt, police officers hurt on 482 Broome Street, send an ambulance right away! Ten four. Out."

More people milling about. "Stay with him, will you, till they arrive." "Sure, mon, sure," and I take off—all of them still gazing up at the smoke and shooting flames—and keep on walking: Someone framing me, now trying to *kill* me, so I've gotta get away, can't call the police, who want to arrest me, put out an APB (all this TV lingo), and find out who's doing what to whom, poor Gillian Shea, Donal Tuohy, Alvin Cobb—and this killer, forger, Good God, could be watching me right now!

Around the corner into Wooster, swiftly over these Belgian blocks, and into my car, starting it up and peeling out at top speed, don't need an accident—sirens rapidly approaching, along Broome, then zooming uptown amid this teeming New York traffic, checking my rearview mirror and glancing left and right—*O MOTHER OF CHRIST!* Nearly hit that old lady, sorry, sorry, my fault—They'll be looking for this car, have to ditch it, then call Tory—No, just switch it, switch my plates—but then the guy'll report it and they'll find me in a blink—

Wait a sec, there're two 3s on mine—*that's it!* Pull in somewhere, turn my 3s into 8s! All I need is a magic marker—14th Street coming up, there must be a place, and swinging right and still checking behind—*There!* Delsemme's Artists' Materials.

But where can I park? Who cares, anywhere will do—No, don't call attention, get a ticket. That Volvo pulling away from the meter. I'll slip right in—*Whack!* Sorry, black Caddy behind, dented bumper. Try again—*Whack!* Christ, haven't done this in years, my bloody car the size of the Titanic! O fuck it, leave the rented prow sticking out?

And back in a mo with these magic markers. Starting my car, the radio blaring Bach, soft rock, hard rock, Spanish music, world news—*"Reports now confirm that three died and thirteen were injured in that terrorist bomb attack outside Jerusalem. Israel has vowed to retaliate. In Britain, Prime Minister Margaret Thatcher—"* and nothing as yet about me, so I shut it off.

This side street practically empty. Hopping out, few deft strokes of the marker—There. Standing back to admire my work, which now reads: ZWT885. Be worth a bloody fortune someday, Boyne's license plate, like Warhol's cans of Campbell soup, Oldenburg's clothespin, or Jasper Johns's Ballantine Ale. Sotheby's beginning the bidding at three and a half million—

And I can't go back to the Carlyle, sure to be waiting. Striding south now, 10th Street, 9th—and there's a phone on the corner, call my daughter. Dialing 516-751-7954: outside this booth and down the street, numerous vendors, festoons of colored balloons, and that huge banner reading "Beaux-Arts Spring Festival"—

"Hello?"

"Tory."

"O thank God! Where *are* you? What is going *on?* Gene just heard it on the radio, it's all over the news, you took off, on the lam, accused of murder, nearly *died—"*

"The undiscovered country, from whose bourn/ No traveller returns, puzzles the will."

"What're you *talking* about?"

"Just felt like a little *Hamlet*, lass. But listen, I'm coming out to Stony Brook, so keep your eyes glued for any suspicious characters lurking about, they may be bugging the phone, and I'll see you soon."

"No, Dad!"

"What no?"

"One of the first places they'll look is here, definitely be under surveillance, phones've been ringing non-stop."

"Yes, yes, you're right. So what should I do?"

"Well, remember Gene has that writer's cottage, bungalow, out on Crane Neck?"

"Perfect, Tory!"

"And I'll meet you—Where, where? OK, look, there's a cheese shop, Elmo's Cheese Shop—"

"Elmo's?"

"Yes, Dad, as in St. Elmo's fire. Take Northern State all the way and it's on the corner of Main Street and 25A, you can't miss it. At what time?"

"What time is it now?"

"2:20."

"Well, say, 5, 5:30."

"Fine, see you then. And Dad?"

"What?"

"This must be devastating for you, with Gillian and all."

"O it is, and I didn't even see her, talk to her, she was sleeping. Did they say how she died?"

"Suffocation."

"How'd they know?"

"The broken blood vessels in her eyes. Peticiae, it's called. Means she was straining to breathe."

"O Jaysus!"

"Should I call Mother?"

"No, I will. Love ya, lass, thanks, 'bye."

And stepping outside into this festive throng, cheek to jowl, shoulder to shoulder, with lurid masks and garish attire, sawhorses blocking the streets, and these sidewalk vendors hawking sausages, ices, pizza, and gyros, rock music clanging from lamppost loudspeakers, arts and crafts, clothing and jewelry, jugglers and toddlers, and mounted police—

"*Hey, you, STOP RIGHT THERE!!*" O Suffering *Christ!* Striding on—

"*That's BOYNE!!*"

Hoofbeats and shouting exploding behind as I dive into the swarming masses, dashing in and out, "*Heads up, coming through!*"

more cops joining the fray, gaining on me—and sprinting along 8ᵗʰ Street, with my heart madly hammering away—have to get back to my car—"Seamus?" *Now* who? "It's Laetitia!" This gaudy gray-haired lady in a spotted leopard caftan flinging her arms around my neck, "Laetitia Marengue!" and giving me a long French kiss. "How *are* you? From London, remember?" "Yes, yes—still have your gallery?" "It is *here* now. But where are you running to?" "Can't talk, tell you later!" "Well call me, here is my card, my number—"

"Sure, 'bye!"—and bounding off with a ragged sigh, my nimble feet dodging and weaving—and that sleek brown horse tethered to a fire hydrant on the corner, cop/rider nowhere in sight—some guy jamming a rubber pumpkin over my head, "Here ya go, like the Headless Horseman!" which I can't get off, barely see out the peep-holes—as I untie the reins and scramble aboard, *"Go! Go! Hi-yo, Silver!"* and he gallops away like Secretariat winning the Belmont by thirty-one lengths!—*"Hey, he's got my fucking horse!"*—people scattering before me like the Red Sea, down University Place and into Washington Square Park, galloping under the arch toward baby carriages and mothers scurrying left and right—through the splashing fountain and vaulting over these gaping, gasping chess players on my trusty steed—that other cop now coming into view as I veer left across the grass and slat benches toward NYU—and slide off, hit the ground, and tie him to a tree, "Thanks, old son!" casting aside this pumpkin, kissing the horse's nose, then go scampering down Waverly and, throwing caution to the winds, sprint flat out back to my car—

Still there! Marvelous! Fast look over my shoulder and whip across to the East Side, onto FDR Drive, and *out* of this blasted city!

Five

"Boyne on the run, Boyne on the run!" raucously singing my own sardonic version of McCartney's tune as I keep flashing by this slowing

traffic, left hand shading my face, and under those darkling clouds, droplets now falling—my story all over the news: *Be on the lookout, could be dangerous, Boyne sightings as far away as Topeka, Kansas and Martinique*—and leaving Nassau County and Great Neck (Hagar's hometown), Port Washington and Roslyn far behind on tree-lined Northern State as I cruise through Suffolk County, munching away on my third Jack in the Box cheeseburger while sipping Dr. Pepper through a straw—*the media having descended on his daughter and Boyne's Irish estate*—my darling Laura, call her immediately, put her mind at ease, get to the bottom of this, replay my every move, and figure out who, what, and why someone is *doing* this to me!

This slanting rain coming across the sea from Ireland—and any second expecting the road to be blocked off up ahead, bull-horns blaring, lights glaring, awaiting my arrival with weapons drawn—No-no, don't get too paranoid, since I'm sure I appear to the average driver as just another commuter heading home for the weekend, tooling merrily along five miles under the speed limit—

O JAYSUS! coming up behind me like a bat out of hell with those headlights blazing, that state police car—*pulse racing, body bracing*—and he zooms on by and is gone round the bend, then a blue Corvette goes shooting past on this slick road and swerving straight for a little dog crossing—*"CRAZY BASTARD!"*—who disappears in the rain onto that wide verge of grass, trees behind it, as I wheel abruptly off and skid to a stop, hopping out (Seen by passing cars and cops? Screw it!)—Where'd he go?—the traffic roaring past—searching over the damp grass—*There*—a wet Welsh Corgi. Still alive? Yes, but terrified.

"Easy, doggie, easy, I'm here." He trembling and panting, though seems to be OK, as I gently palp his sides, red-brindled coat with white flashings. And nothing appears to be broken, his tail cheerfully wagging. No collar, must've fallen off, never find it. He probably ran away, lives near here, or was abandoned. Call a vet, an animal shelter? "Come on, boy, let's get out of the rain." But he remains rooted to the spot. "Come on, let's *go!*" He still unmoving, so I carefully pick him up, cradling him in my arms, carry him to the car and ease him into the passenger side, his wide, brown eyes staring up. "Hey, no need to worry, boy—here, have a cheeseburger with Russian dressing—'cause you're in good hands now, I swear!"

Six

"*PSSST*, Boyne!" Whipping wetly about in these sheeting gusts of rain, "Over here!" as trenchcoated Hagar appears dripping out of his Mustang and the streaming shadows of Elmo's free-standing Cheese Shed—and I jog splashing swiftly under this awning.

"Where's Tory?"

"Back at our house with the media circus. They're camped all over our street! It's the lead story on every TV channel, Cronkite, Chancellor, Wawa, Peter Jennings, you name 'em!"

"Fucking Yahoos, like vultures waiting to pounce!"

"So we thought it best if *I* left and Tory stayed by the phone."

"You sure you weren't followed?"

"No, I zigged and zagged, kept checking. Anyway, more things have come to light."

"Like what?"

"Like no one has come forward to claim Gillian's body yet, and they can't find her son."

"Really?"

"Also, it seems not all the paintings in that loft explosion were lost."

"And, Gene, *those* were the forgeries!"

"I know, that's what they're saying. They've got experts coming in from Boston—"

"Basil Quinn."

"—and Interpol to authenticate them."

"Right. So what's *our* plan?"

"You follow me out to Crane Neck, garage your car—you can use mine if you need it—then figure out a plan."

And off we go through this blustery downpour, few cars passing, by those harbor lights and, above that grassy rise, a crescent of white Colonial shops, the Corgi's ears perking up at that mechanical post office eagle flapping its wooden wings as the clock strikes six, past the Three Village Inn, filling up with Friday night diners—and keeping Hagar's car in my sights—up Christian Avenue under these hazy lights as Bach's ethereal Air from Suite No. 3 comes floating over the radio to soothe my frazzled nerves, "Ah, that's God's music, doggie, Johann Sebastian," petting and stroking his head, and down the slope of Mt. Grey Road beneath this canopy of thick, arching oaks, with the rain still slashing and—*O CHRIST!* another car coming up fast behind, tailgating me, *jig is up!*—but no sirens or flashing lights—and he flies past me with a squeal of tires, and by Hagar, too—as I let out a sigh, "Just a false alarm, doggie, we're almost there."

Into heavily treed Old Field through this misty haze, the rare car passing, and left down a dark, winding curve behind his Mustang, by inland marshes and bulrushed meadows, Long Island Sound dim in the distance, then up a dirt path, crunching pebbles, and a quick left again into a sheltered drive of high hedges to this trim little saltbox completely secluded by a cluster of cliffside trees, and no other homes in view.

Hagar hustling across the uncut lawn to lift the garage door—and doing a comic double take as he spots the Corgi when I pull inside.

"What is *that?*"

Dousing my lights, "A dog," and stepping out.

"I can see that! 'Cause he's sure not your Samoyed, Poldy."

"Right, someone nearly killed him on the parkway, so I picked him up. Come on, doggie, let's go."

"Is he OK?"

"I think so, but he doesn't respond too well, probably still frightened. Come on, boy, hop out."

"Or maybe he doesn't understand English."

"You know, Hagar, you just may have something there. Let me try a bit of French before I carry him in: *Venez ici tout de suite!*"

The dog doesn't move.

"Then try Spanish," Hagar leaning in, "*Venga aquí!*"

Still nothing.

"How 'bout: *Kommen Sei herein, mein herr!*"

The Corgi keeps on staring as Hagar throws up his hands, "Can you believe this, the whole world's out there trying to nail you for murder and you're standing here talking German to a dog! But hold it, wait a second, Seamus, I've got an idea. This's a New York dog most likely."

"So?"

"So then how 'bout *Move your ass, muthafucka!*"

And the dog jumps out.

Laughing as I follow them both inside, "How many acres have you got here, Gene?"

"Nearly four," and he hits the lights and closes the door, the rain still rattling down outside this wide picture window, "That's Smithtown Bay and Long Island Sound's around the bend, Connecticut's straight across, Bridgeport and Stratford, and my own private beach, 300-feet-long."

"Jaysus, I'm never leaving!"

"Anyway, lemme find you a towel, and I just stocked the fridge with Guinness and your favorite, Stouffer's Welsh rarebit. Phones're all over, if you wanna call Laura, bedroom's upstairs, TV's in there, and I'll be right back."

Around me in this cozy cottage strewn with books, a rustic slew of New England furniture and a large hooked rug with the look of a patchwork quilt as Hagar reappears in a moment, and I towel off the Corgi, who loves his belly rubbed. Then hoisting a brew, the bitter brown foam of an almost cold Guinness, I settle down on this three-cushion sofa, stretching my tired legs, and the dog hops up beside me, blue paisley setting off his red-brindled coat.

"So, Seamus, really, you sure you don't want to just give yourself up?"

"No *way*, Hagar, no *bloody* way!" draining my bottle of stout, "Jaysus, Mary, and José, boy, *no way!*"

"But you didn't *do* it," and he sits across from us in a white wicker rocker.

"Of course I didn't *do* it! That's the point—I have to clear my name! 'Cause once you get tangled up in that spidery legal web—"

"But you'd be out on bail in five minutes."

"Right, that's what you say now," gently stroking the Corgi's head, "but you never *know* what can happen!"

"So what'll you do?"

"I'm not sure yet. Gather my wits about me and see what my options are."

"Yeah, well let me ask you this: Could the explosion at the loft have been a gas leak?"

"Could have, but that's what I've got to determine. And if not—"

"Then who do you think might've done it?"

"Haven't a clue—No, that's not true, but first I want to find her son and then this Donal Tuohy. Look, Gene, we'll talk in a minute, but now could we turn on the news? And I want to see Tory."

"How? You can't get to our house. It's totally surrounded."

"So we'll meet on the beach or some secluded rendezvous—" leaning forward, "Hold it, hold it. What is this? O, ABC, and hey, there's my old pal, Baba Wawa—Good God, she looks awful, doesn't she?"

"She *always* looks awful."

"The face-lift is slipping, looks more like a Shar Pei now. And watch these interviews: She'll always start by asking, 'Well, how do you *feel* about that?' "

"—*Well, how* do *you feel about that?*"

Shaking my head and switching to CBS, for a jump-cut documentary of my career: the '67 Tate break-in; subsequent MOMA shows and awards; the '73 kidnapping of Tory; and a hand-held home video of today's Ichabod Crane ride through Greenwich

Village—then to NBC: "*NYPD Chief of Detectives Frank Ladesma said that Mr. Boyne seems to have been troubled lately—*"

"Troubled my Irish tit! Why, 'cause lately I've taken to painting nudes *in* the nude again?"

"*—formed a Task Force and established a Hot Line. Any information leading to the arrest and apprehension of Seamus Boyne, please contact the number on your screen,*" then switching back to Wawa: "*—Police are exploring the possibility of a revenge motive, that Boyne was after her son, Padraic Shea, became enraged and tried to kill the forger—if, in fact, he is the forger. But at this point, this is all speculation.*" Peter Jennings breaking in: "*Barbara, sorry, but apparently there was another sighting of a man resembling Boyne in Yonkers, who escaped capture, and yet another on Staten Island turned out to be a baritone at the Met by the name of Garibaldi, who was also bald and bearded—*"

"Jaysus, I'm like Padre Pio, Hagar, in two places at once! Now if you find Christlike wounds, stigmata, on my hands, feet, and side, then you *know* I've been troubled lately!"

And more reports on the other channels:

Massive manhunt—famous fugitive eluding capture—"*Use caution. Suspect may possibly be armed—*"

"Right, armed with a Welsh Corgi muthafucka!" and snapping off the set and standing, "I've got to call my wife."

"Sure, go ahead."

"By the way, you have any dog food?"

"I'll get some. Phone's over there."

"Have to call the shelters and vets as well."

"Seamus, wait a second, listen, they'll probably have a tap on your line in Ireland and then they'll know you're here."

"You think so?"

"Definitely. So let *me* call and convey what you want to say."

"Right, right, good thinking, Hagar, very good thinking. Here, I'll dial the number." Punching it out, then silence, no clicks, ringing once, twice—

"Mr. Boyne's residence." My butler's elegant English tones.

Handing the phone to Gene and pacing back and forth.

"Symes, it's Mr. Hagar. Would you put Mrs. Boyne on? Thank you. . . . Laura, it's Gene. I know, I know. He's all right, not to worry, and he said he'd speak to you—Yes, I know it's crazy. No, not yet, but I'll keep you posted. When? Why don't you wait? You can always get a flight."

"Gene, let me speak to her."

He vigorously shaking his head and turning away, "Definitely, I will, I promise—Tory's fine—O of course, and I'll talk to you soon."

"What'd she *say*?"

"The media've been hounding her all night and day—and remember, it's nearly one in the morning there."

"Did you hear any clicks?"

"No, but—"

"Maybe I should call."

"And say what?"

"Just let her hear my voice."

"Seamus, please, just relax."

"How can I *relax*? Now they'll trace the call to here, won't they?"

"Not necessarily, it just pays to be safe, listen, maybe I should stay, in case—"

"No-no, Gene," still pacing, "they'll notice your car's missing."

"Well, look, we're only five minutes away."

"And my Corgi here will protect me."

"There's a softball bat in the closet."

"The same Big Daddy?"

"From our championship days."

"Ha-ha! You still playing?"

"No, over the hill. But if you need it—"

"You forget, boy, I'm a master of judo, karate, kung fu, haiku—"

"Yeah, you can rhyme the bastards to death!" and he heads for the door, the rain still clattering down, and not a light in sight.

"Hagar?"

"What?"

Bear hugging him, "Thanks, boy, for being here."

"My pleasure," and he heartily slaps my back.

"O, and tell Tory to meet me at 5 A.M. on the beach below."

"Will do. 'Bye."

And he drives away as I release a sigh and move toward the fridge to find some canine yummies.

• • • • • •

—Along Erin's green and fragrant shore, with her darkly glittering Asian eyes—if you love 'em, you'll lose 'em—and now I might be losing it all, work, family, life, unfairly imprisoned, killed by this crazy—or was I *always* jealous of Gillian? Coming between my father and me? And visiting her Harding Ave. house as a teenager and shocked to see all those photos of *ME* tacked to her wall—my profound childhood fears of my mother disappearing—But Tim and I growing so close together, "the most feared twosome west of Macao," he always making me laugh, an amateur actor, voracious reader, supporting my talent, and hanging my early work round his diner—

One Indian summer, I took Laura up to Rhode Island to show her that grim brick asylum, founded in 1849, where my father died O those many long years ago when I was seventeen. And telling her, even at the end, when he was ranting and denied all cigarettes and liquor, he could make me laugh, propped up in his sterile bed, his gaunt and jaundiced frame reddened with bedsores as he unwrapped the aftershave I'd brought him and sniffed it with a devilish grin.

"You know, of course, boy, all American toiletries are made from the same ingredients, one product does for all: as a hair tonic, mouthwash, underarm deodorant, to brush your teeth, kill athlete's feet—" and suddenly swigging it down with a wild-eyed glee, "—and rather bracing too as an aperitif! And soon as I escape, we'll have ourselves a real gargle, a right proper pub crawl, I swear!"

"Escape?"

"Leaving these loonies behind!"

"Where you going?"

"O, who knows. Find myself another island, Staffa, Sark, Tierra del Fuego. Build myself a submarine, one of those little one-man subs like the Japs used during the War and go cruising round the world, pop up anywhere."

"And what if you're caught?"

"O, locked in irons, off to the padded cell, or the lethal hypodermic, some cruel and unusual punishment. And I forgot how they do it in Ireland, firing squad or cut off the head?"

I was grinning then, "I thought it was the penis?"

"No, no, boy, they do that *months* before."

"They don't quite take to it, do they?"

"Of course not. The Irish think of them only as excessive protuberances to vacate through!" And following his raucous guffaw and yet another swig, he suddenly leaned forward and took both of my hands in his, "But seriously now, you're an *artist*, Seamus, and always have been—at age four, you could draw anyone who came into our house, exactly, unerringly, and at nine, you loved art so, after your mother left, you'd take your meals at your easel and pee in a plastic bowl—no time to pause for bodily functions, just painting merrily away, driving creatively on! O believe me, boy, you're *sui generis*, unparalleled, unique! Hell, you've already, in my unbiased opinion, surpassed Degas as a draftsman who can hold a form implacably within a line and yet not cramp it. O there's no question, no question whatsoever, you'll ultimately be recognized as the extraordinary talent you are! So proud of you, boy, so very,

very proud! 'Cause, Jaysus, face it, nothing's going to get anybody out of this world alive, but sometime before we die—No, no, listen to me now, Seamus," as tears began filling his glinty eyes, "if we're able to create something, be it food for me or art for you—I mean except for disease and decisions, life just lets you *do,* until it kills you—but the one way to beat it, to *really* beat it, is to make something last. And this, God love you," the tears were now spilling out of those Van Gogh eyes, "is *exactly* what you're doing! For how few of us, how very, very few, have the pluck and audacity to carry on like you?"

And two weeks later, in the autumn of '46, he was dead of liver cancer—sharing his last meal with me—and I felt like Turner when he lost *his* father, that I'd lost an only child!

Seven

Up at the crack of dawn and along this lovely, secluded beach with pregnant Tory and my frisky Corgi, the torrents of rain having dwindled to a soft, metallic patter around three-thirty or four as I fitfully tossed awake, then were washed clean this morning by a keen ocean breeze.

Her straight, tousled hair a blonde shaft of light as Tory strides past those boulders in a white Irish sweater, green sweatpants, scuffed Reebok sneakers—and my father's lilac eyes—while I follow close behind with my grizzled/snowy beard, sunglasses, and dark beret, and stopping abruptly along the sand—"What, Dad? Is somebody here?"—to glance down the beach at that Rubenesque woman running out of the surf to towel herself off. Her hair glossy and the loose folds of skin shimmering pinkly in the haze as I continue appraising this bosomy Irish-looking lass, and Tory grins.

"You interested, Dad?"

"Aesthetically, yes. Her flesh appears to be shaped in a rather interesting fashion, especially around the natal areas."

"So I see."

"O, well *you* know, in Ireland they disrobe right on the beach. Makes for some rather marvelous early morning viewing. Quite refreshing, in fact, when you've just woken up, clears the head, believe it or not. Well, hell, your mother frequently did it."

"*My* mother?"

"O absolutely, when she was pregnant with you."

"In the *nude?*"

"Ask her about it some time. But the flesh over in Ireland is fantastic, like strawberry shortcake, really pink and beautifully smooth. Blue under the skin."

"*Blue* under the skin?"

"O sure, the blue line and all of that, the classical idea. That's quite true. 'Cause over there, they never wash, rarely take a bath. And the air there's so clean, it does the job of soap and water. O, the weather there's the best thing in the world for you, makes the skin glow."

"Do you ever go swimming yourself?"

"Me? O Jaysus no! I haven't been swimming in years, except when I fell in once, almost drowned. And you have to have a regulation bathing suit, so I can't wear my Guinea underwear. But if you want we could pop out tomorrow, if the weather holds. O and by the way, Tory, you feeling OK, the baby, I mean?"

"Seems to be."

"And I meant to ask you, are you planning on having more?"

"O sure," she smiling, then chafing her puggish nose with the heel of her hand, which she's done endearingly since she was three, "it was enough that I was an only child."

"Exactly, lass! Though there are positives, of course, to being an only child—as Freud said, you think you're special for the rest of your life—but drawbacks as well, loneliness, for one. But *you* need a brood, bouncing babs around, surround yourself with a family!"

The gulls high-wheeling, riding the wind, and Tory's blonde hair tossed and blown, sweeping it from her eyes. *Nipping and eager airs.* And the waves: *Whitemaned seahorses, champing, brightwind-bridled, the steeds of Mananaan.*

"What's over there, lass, across the water?"

"Straight across is Connecticut, Stratford and New Haven. But anyway, Dad, how long are you gonna search for this killer before you turn yourself in?"

"Till tomorrow noon. My show opens on Monday, and if I haven't cleared my name by then, I swear I'll call my lawyer and walk into police headquarters."

"I really wish you'd do it today," she slogging across the damp, pebbled sand, " 'cause I'm still scared of what might happen."

"I know, Tory, but I have to play this out."

"And in disguise, right?"

"How else? Shave my head and put on that fright wig."

"You're gonna look like Harpo Marx! Well at least let me style it before you take off," and she gives me a playful shove.

The Corgi romping along, skipping beside the lace fringe of the tide, then stopping and sniffing, before lifting a hindleg and pissing as I smile and gaze across to the pastel haze of the Connecticut shore, Stratford and New Haven, Yale and . . . Gillian Shea? Where? When? By the water's edge, again. But *where* precisely? Mystic! *Yes, yes!* with those swaying clipper ships, and she held my hand as we strolled about the harbor and my cheek grazed her jiggling breast—

"But why, Dad, would someone kill her? I mean they had to've known her."

"Not necessarily."

"Or maybe she was a nag, a harpy, a suffocating Jewish mother."

"*Gillian?* Not bloody likely."

"Well, you never can tell. But you know the difference between a Jewish mother and a Rottweiler? Mother told me this."

"No."

"Eventually the Rottweiler lets go."

"Funny, very funny. But it could've just been some loony. That's why I need to talk to the people around her, have you call her sister Fiona—"

"Or maybe your father left her a fortune."

"I doubt that—and find out how come I look the spitting image of her son and this Donal Tuohy, 'cause those photos are truly amazing! Come on, doggie—Sorry. Muthafucka—before you get pinched by a crab. And, Tory, don't forget to call the shelters and vets as well."

She kneeling and scratching his doggie chin, "I'll take him back to *my* house now."

"And find out if anyone's lost him."

Eight

The phone stridently ringing—Who the hell's calling? Padraic? Tuohy? Santiago? Pick it up or—?

"Yes, hello?"

"Dad—"

"Tory!"

"—were you just here?"

"Where?"

"At my house?"

"When?"

"A half hour ago?"

"No. Why?"

"O my God! 'Cause there was this guy here with the reporters who didn't *quite* look like you, but his eyes, steely—well, he must've been in disguise!"

"Is he there now?"

"No, they all left—at least he did, 'cause the next time I looked, he was gone."

"O Jaysus, it *must* be him!"

"Who?"

"The killer, Tuohy, her son! Where's Gene?"

"He's on his way over, took my car."

"Well if anybody can lose him."

"I know, I'm glad he's driving. O and, Dad, the wig looks great. Did you hear about the Polish man who bought his wife a wig because he heard she was getting bald at the office?"

"Tory!"

"All right, but please call me later."

"Sounds like a plan. And don't worry, I'll be OK, wrap this up today."

"I sure hope so, 'bye."

And a few last scrapes of Gene's Gillette blue blade down my silken cheek, now smooth as a stripper's arse, and a bracing splash of his Aqua Velva.

And, if I do say so myself, I don't look too bad, lopping off fifteen bearded years in one fell swoop—like those clean-shaven photos at Tuohy's SoHo loft.

And I'd better call Santiago. Don't care if they trace it now, since I'm not coming back:

"Major Case Squad, Cusimano speaking."

"Detective Santiago, please."

"Yeah, hold on. (Where'd Reuben go—Reuben? Reuben around? Reuben? O here he comes. Line two)."

"Santiago."

"It's Seamus Boyne. How are you?"

"I'm fine. Where're you?"

"On Long Island. But you feel OK, back at work?"

"Gettin' there. Why ya callin'?"

"Well, first off, you know I'm not guilty."

"I don't know that."

"Come on, why would I save your life?"

"So why ya callin'?"

"To find out what you've learned."

"Whatta ya plannin' to do?"

"Clear my name, and I thought you could help me," keeping one eye out the window, "Any news?"

"Well, we interviewed all the staff and directors at the nursin' home."

"Millichap?"

"The director, right, and nothin' much there, nobody seemed suspicious."

"How 'bout other patients?"

"Nothin' so far, but we're still checkin'."

"And Tuohy?"

"Tuohy?"

"Donal Tuohy?"

"O, he died three years ago."

"*What?*"

"Yeah, he was an art collector, his death's never been solved."

"And Padraic Shea?"

"Can't find him."

"Right, well he may be here—" Hagar's horn blasting outside. "Look, detective, could you meet me in the city? I may need your help."

"Sure. Where?"

"You name it. But come alone, no set-up, you understand?"

"Of course, of course. How 'bout Twenty-fourth Street Park, by Bellevue, that OK? It's quiet there, nobody bother us, by Peter Cooper Village. At what time?" Hagar's horn loudly honking again.

"Well, let's see, take me a while to get in. It's nine, almost ten now. Say two?"

"Two it is."

"And remember, just you."

"Ya got it."

Rushing out to Hagar, behind the wheel of Tory's red TR7, her bumper sticker reading "I'm out of Estrogen AND I HAVE A GUN," as I jump swiftly in, "Not followed?"

"No."

"Let's *GO!*"

Nine

Hagar speeding down the L.I.E., with me beside him in this curly brown wig—that makes me look more like Hedy Lamarr than Harpo Marx.

"You know, boy, just 'cause I'm paranoid doesn't mean the whole world's not trying to *kill* me!"

"I think I've heard that before, but relax, Seamus, will you."

"But Tory saw—"

"'Tory saw'! She wasn't positively sure, and as you say, doppelgängers abound, all sorts of false sightings still going on in Tuckahoe and Nyack."

Breezing along, the traffic fairly light for a Saturday morning, and clouds overhead billowing in surreal profusion like a school of blue whales in the brain of "Billy" Turner, sunbursts firing the passing chrome and—

"*Uh-oh!*" checking my sideview mirror once more.

"What?"

"I think we're being followed. This powder blue Buick's been behind us ever since we got on the Expressway."

"Yeah, there he is. Lemme gun it, see what he does."

Roaring by an Audi, Civic, and four-door Dodge.

"Still there, Hagar, might be an unmarked police car."

"All right, give him the old zig and zag."

Cutting ahead of a pickup, that van, and nearly scraping the guardrail—

"*Christ,* he's right on our tail! Can you make out his face, boy?"

"No, too much glare. Can you?"

"Not really, just a dim silhouette. Better give it the gas!"

VAROOM!

And he goes shooting past this eighteen-wheeler, weaving between a Winnebago and a huge semi—the Buick still behind!

"Hold tight, Boyne!"

"What the hell does *that* mean? Don't give me old movie lines! Like if I hold tight, I'll be all right in a crash?!"

Just missing a Jeep and green and white Camry filled with kids—and swerving into the left-hand lane, Hagar spinning about—

"Think I lost him—"

"No, here he comes *again!*"

Traffic merging, slowing round that bend as we rocket in and out—and I grip the headrest tight with both hands, heels jammed forward—and Hagar pushing it now past 80, 85—then back to the center lane, a narrow crevice between two big rigs straight ahead, and I shut my eyes—an adhesive whoosh—and open 'em, blinking, as we whizz on by—and a *thunderous crash!* clanging metal behind, tires squealing, jackknifed semis, broadsiding pickups—

And the Buick? No sign of him? Killed in the crash? Or miraculously escaped?

By Deer Park Road, Melville up ahead, black smoke rising in the sideview mirror—

"O *Jaysus,* I hope that Camry with the kids is safe!"

"I know, I know," Hagar now slowing below the speed limit, "Yes, yes, they're OK—and at least we lost *him*—"

"Or killed him!"

"Right, but just in case, I'm gonna drop you off at the Great Neck train station and I'll keep going, just to throw him off."

"Good idea, boy."

"You know, I'm just thinking, if he's still alive, he might go after Tory and the baby."

"But he wants *me*."

"To *get* at you."

Ten

This longhaired Chinese conductor in his light blue shirt and black pillbox hat punching my ticket as I flop back on the cracked vinyl seat and the train gives a slight lurch, then goes easing away from the station—those passengers looking impatient, but paying me little heed as we rattle along on the 12:16, plenty of time, will be in New York at 12:47, if nothing untoward happens. For the killer might be on board. No, relax. And Tory's OK, meeting Gene for the day.

"Flushing next, Flushing."

Passing these squalid back gardens below the cinders of the clickety-clack railroad tracks—Monet felt *his* garden was a far greater creation than his paintings—my wig slipping a bit, giving it a furtive tug—And that sunburst out there igniting the circling of gulls, fringing their wings with a border of gold—like those summers with my father along the shore, observing the Blue Grosbeak, the Western Meadowlark, and the flight of the Black-legged Kittiwake. Gillian so adoring him, waiting on him hand and foot, and kind to me as well—but catching, from time to time, a strange look in her eyes, that amorous root beer gleam.

Around me, the nicotine stain of old people's hair, their vacant stares, and the nasal twang of that voice at the end of the car: Hagar's Great Neck friend? Yes, right, right, first base, Shelly Levitas—doesn't notice me as he babbles on to a buddy:

"—And this painter Boyne, who's all over the papers and TV now, played softball with me three years ago, I swear to God! But anyway, what was I saying? O, yeah-yeah, about this guy I met the other day who said he was from Rye, but when I told him I came from Great Neck, everybody went crazy! *Still* the place they all try to get to!"

That plump, peroxide-haired lady two seats down staring at me—recognizing me?—or merely flirting? as I promptly glance away and—

O Jaysus! Here she comes, holding onto the seat back, and gaining her balance, "Sorry I forgot your name, but we met at Bruce Weintraub's briss—"

"Bruce who?"

"Their first child. And I don't know if you heard the news—"

"Madam, I'm sorry—"

"—but Blanche had to have both breasts removed—"

"Look, I'm—"

"—and Ben, her ex, the beauty, ran off with his student from Adelphi and—O my, but you're not—O I'm *terribly* sorry, I thought you were someone else, please forgive me, my mistake, I'm *so* embarrassed, but you look exactly like the *moyle.*"

"I know, I have that kind of face."

"Woodside next, Woodside."

Eleven

Forehead shiny, cheeks flushed as my reflection goes flickering past the glittering array of arcade shops within Penn Station's jostling crush and I pause before this bank of phones—that mousy little man staring hard at me, then whisking off—a cop approaching—I turn aside—and he continues by.

Rummaging about for Laetitia's number. Where? Ah, here. And I'm starting to feel like Richard Kimble, *an innocent victim of blind justice, freed to hide in lonely desperation, to change his identity, to run from the relentless pursuit of*—while the phone keeps ringing, ringing away. Click. And Rachmaninoff's Second Piano Concerto booming scratchily out on the answering machine, followed by Laetitia's breathy Zsa Zsa Gabor voice: "Darling, please leave me your precious message." *Beep!*

"Laetitia, Seamus Boyne. I may see you soon."

And upstairs and out to the street into a thick blast of heat and this waiting cab:

"Twenty-fourth Street Park, by Bellevue and Peter Cooper Village."

• • • • • •

Dark gleams rustling the trees and the underside of leaves catching the light, people scuffing soles over shadowed paths—and that looks like him, sitting on a park bench alone, in a neat white shirt and tie, his black jacket draped across his thigh.

"Ah, Santiago, good to see you, thanks for coming," and gazing quickly around at the mothers and kids, old people and snuffling dogs on the grassy lawn.

"Yeah, and ya lost your beard, grew a hairdo—though I gotta tell ya, liked it better the old way."

"So did I."

A brief grin, within his five o'clock shadow, "And thanks for helpin' me out the other day."

"You're welcome. How's Bombasi?"

"Comin' along, thanks. He's home now, still pretty shaky. Anyways, I got some good news for you. Most all of the paintings have been identified as forgeries, though two are still in doubt and could be real—"

"'Real'? How could they possibly be 'REAL'?! That's UNBELIEVABLE!!"

"I know, and Quinn said no, but Interpol wasn't so sure."

"Sure of what? Where their arseholes reside? Those swine-eyed Yahoos couldn't tell a Picasso from a Playboy crotch-shot!"

"Yeah, well we found a device in the loft, remote control device."

"Figures. But why have the place rigged?"

"Don't know yet."

"Look, detective, let's say Padraic, her son, killed Gillian just before I got to the nursing home, ducked out the window, then waited for me to arrive, and followed me downtown to his loft, which was rigged if anything went wrong?"

"But what's he got against *you?*"

"I don't know, except he was out at my daughter's this morning, tried to run me off the road—"

Santiago standing, "Ya sure 'bout that?" and looping his jacket over his shoulder.

"No, not really, we didn't see his face, but who else *could* it be?"

Cabs pulling away from the V.A., and that Acne Painting van parked, with a ladder atop it, across the road, gleaming sunlight shrilling down.

"Yeah, well the question still remains, why would her own son kill her?"

"How the hell should I know! And who says *he* did it?"

Santiago leaning closer, "Yeah, well why would *anyone* kill their own mother?"

"She's not *my* mother—Hey, who are those guys in the *van?* And those parked cars? This's a *trap,* isn't it, you set me *up,* you son of a bitch!"

"No, listen, they're just my buddies, routine procedure—"

"And you're probably *wired* as well—"

"Boyne, *wait!* Where you *goin'? BOYNE!*"

Sprinting under these leafy trees and down 25th Street—one hand holding my wig—and Santiago puffing behind, no doors or entranceways in sight—right up First Avenue, others joining in hot pursuit, 26th, 27th—assassinated like Kennedy in broad daylight—*Here!*

And darting swiftly into Bellevue, with all these loonies thrashing about, see me as a fellow inmate, Harpo without the harp—snack bar to the left—along this wide hallway and through a narrow door into the main building, sliding across the highly polished flagstone floor, large planters and couches, doctors and nurses, staff and patients milling before the Information desk, and out onto a small lawn, following this path, down a tiny staircase two-at-a-time—and back out to 26th Street!

Flagging a cab, driven by a turbaned Sikh.

"Where to, sir?"

Slamming the door, "12 Beekman Place—and floor it!"

And off he roars, with me sinking low, only my eyes showing over the seat: cops collecting back there, looking left and right—and the driver studying me closely in his rearview mirror, then speaking in that lilting Indian accent and nervously giggling with glee:

"O, sir, please forgive me, but I must tell you that I am most honored to have you riding with me as my fare."

Streaking past 34th Street, "—What?"

"And, Mr. Boyne, if I may say—"

Snapping around, "You *know* who I am?"

"O, indeed, sir, indeed, *and* your splendid achievements. I have dutifully followed your career from the outset and consider you the finest artist now living."

"*Do* you now? The finest, you say?"

"O positively the finest."

"Then I guess I won't be needin' this any longer!" and flinging the wig out the window, signs to the Queens-Midtown Tunnel flying by, "And what, may I ask, is your name?"

"Manjit Singh O'Rourke, sir. Irish father, Sikh mother."

"Hey," laughing, "why the fuck not!" The U.N.'s flags flapping in the breeze.

"And I, too, am a painter."

"Is that so?"

"And quite a good one, if I may be so bold. But I, as you see, sir, have to drive a taxi by day and wait for my ship, as you say, to come in. But believe me, as far as your predicament is concerned, your secret is safe with me."

"I greatly appreciate that, Manjit."

Down 50th Street and into Beekman Place as he hands me a card over his shoulder, "Here is my private phone, sir, should you have further need of my service."

"Well would you like to come in?"

"O, sir, that is most kind, but if you don't mind, I will, as you say, take a raincheck."

"You sure?"

"Yes, sir, but again, should you have need, please do not hesitate."

"I will. And thanks again, my friend."

Twelve

Knocking once more on the fire-breathing dragons of this mahogany door and anxiously licking my lips—a few rhine-stone-collared poodles out for their constitutionals across the street—one lock after another springing free inside: and a thin Japanese man wearing gold-rimmed glasses and a long checkerboard apron over white linen slacks swings the door wide with a squinting grin.

"Ah so, Mee-sah Boyne. Your shoes, preez?"

"Seamus darling!" and Laetitia comes sweeping grandly out from the rear of this pink and black art deco duplex, "I am so happy you have arrived!" dressed in silver lamé palazzo pants and a sheer aqua silk blouse, her silver hair now swathed in a chignon, "And you have met Hiro Sumi, I see, a former chef at Benihana. But have you eaten yet?"

"Matter of fact, no—"

"Well, Hiro was just preparing a delicious repast. And of course you like tempura?"

"Yes, I—"

"But you have caught me, alas, right in the midst of rushing off, I am chairman—or, sorry, chair*person*—of the Decorating Committee of tonight's Beaux-Arts Ball in Greenwich Village. But here, darling, follow me a moment."

And into a lush bedroom of silky frills and taffeta, and mirrors on the ceiling.

"I cannot tell you how delighted I am that you have made this your safe haven, escaped capture, though I was certain you would—and I love you without your beard. You look so—so *youthful* without it!" she adjusting her scalloped bra, "Seamus, please, would you be so kind as to button me up?" Her freckled back tanned by the Hamptons. "And you still—O *still* have such marvelously gentle hands. It has been so long, darling." She staring down at my pants.

"Since when?"

"Since we slept together."

"But we never—"

"O details, darling, details!"

Light knocking on the open bedroom door, and Hiro peeking in, "Mees-ah Boyne, preez, you like eggplant with your tempura?"

"That's fine."

"White mushroom, green pepper?"

"Thank you, Hiro, that sounds divine! But tell me, darling, you are not *really* a murderer, are you?"

"No, of course not."

"I didn't think so, but these days—And I cannot get over how *youthful* you look! At that party in London, I adored the way you capered about like a satyr on a Greek vase!" She stroking my arm, my shoulder, "You are so uniquely you, in what you are and in what you do! And all of you is so—so immense, have such extraordinary hands and feet, and especially this, down here," and she wedges her knee between my thighs.

"Laetitia—"

"And still smell so delicious," tickling down my sides, over my arse, "kootchie koo!"

Knock-knock.

"Excuse preez, Mee-sah Boyne, but you like pineapple, too?"

"That'll be all, Hiro."

"Pineapple's fine."

And she suddenly squeezes my behind as though she were testing honey dew melons, "Laetitia, what're you *doing?*" and I twist rapidly away as she starts chasing me round the bedroom, with me dodging and weaving, then leaping shoeless onto her bed and bouncing across to the other side, kicking silky pillows, and Hiro knocking again:

"*Dashi* sauce, Mee-sah—?"

"Not now, Hiro, please!" she pausing, smiling, and still panting, "—O Seamus, that is my exercise for the week! Though I really must go, we can continue later this evening, but you stay for as long as you like, *Ciao.*"

And slipping on a pair of silver pumps, she exits out the front door and I move toward Hiro's repast.

Thirteen

Nibbling and dipping this fabulous feather-light tempura, then washing it down with frosty Kirin beer, I collapse in a heap, now so sore and exhausted . . . before waking in a fog at 5:45 and punching out Tory's number:

"Hello?—O hold on a second. (Gene, let me climb over you.)"

"(Here, I can move.)"

"What's going *on* there?"

"(Tory, it's becoming rather hard now to concentrate. Matter of fact, it's becoming rather hard.)"

"Suffering *Christ*, she's *pregnant*, Hagar!"

"(He should've been here five minutes ago.)"

"I heard that! Well at least be careful."

"Dad, where the hell are *you?*"

"In the city."

"*Which* city? Sorry, sorry, but you keep turning up on every channel of the evening news! Anyway—(Gene, will you *move!*)—I just got off the phone with Fiona Dolan, Gillian's sister—what an incredible conversation!"

"How so?"

"Well, I could hardly shut her up, she went on and on, but I learned all these outrageous things!"

"Is Fiona aware of the murder?"

"O of course."

"And where's Padraic?"

"Staying with her."

"He's there NOW?"

"No, he was out running errands."

"Right, like trying to run us off the road!"

"So I heard. She said he should be back by nine. But, Dad, maybe he's *not* the murderer, just someone who looks like him and you?"

"Could be, but that's what we've got to determine."

"Anyway, we're supposed to meet up at her place at eight."

"You *told* her that?"

"Yes."

"Tory, what if he's *there?* Obviously Fiona doesn't know he's killed his own mother. We're talking about a possible psychopath, homicidal maniac, you know?"

"So should we call the police?"

"I can't trust the police, can't trust Santiago. But, anyway, if she talks to him before, he may *not* show or be there waiting—though if he's exactly my size, Gene and I can probably subdue him."

"Even if he has a gun? Dad, look, why don't we just call the police and have him arrested?"

"You mean we all meet there early and I give myself up *before* they go in?"

"Exactly."

"Right, right, well that might be a whole lot safer, lass. And the address again is?"

"296 Pondfield Road in Bronxville."

"At 8?"

"Make it 7:30, and Gene and I'll meet you across the street. (Will you stop!)"

"Christ, Hagar, is that all you do?"

"(No, I write, too.)"

"Gene!"

"I'll see you there, Tory."

"O and Dad?"

"Now what?"

"Mother's flying over, have to pick her up at two-thirty tomorrow, 'bye."

Fourteen

"Sir, I must tell you again how delighted I am that you have chosen me for your driver," he grinning with those glinty silver fillings as he tilts back his turbaned head and we go zipping up the Hutchinson River Parkway, the luminous, milky glow of a full moon above those passing trees.

"You know Westchester, Manjit?"

"Not very well, sir, I must admit." Careening round this leafy curve.

"Well, I've brought a map."

"Good thinking, Mr. Boyne, sir, very good thinking indeed. But if I may observe, you are very *much* like a cat."

"A cat?" smiling and stretching back against this maroon, cushioned seat.

"In light of your splendid escapes. Your nine lives, sir?"

"Ah, right. And you're not worried about harboring a fugitive?"

"Not at all, O not in the slightest. It is, for me, sir, a very great privilege."

"Thank you, you're very kind, Manjit." More trees and shrubs whipping by, traffic fairly light for a Saturday night.

"Do you know this area well, sir?"

"I grew up not far from here, so it's like riding back through and time." Past familiar parts of Pelham and Mount Vernon. "Though memory, like art or this childhood landscape of mine, always stands still—we just see more into it and from different angles."

"How wise, sir, how very, very wise. And if I may be so bold, Mr. Boyne, might I ask, have you always been a painter?"

"Always."

"Never held other jobs?"

"A choice few."

"For instance?"

"Well, let's see, before I got into the wine business, I was down on my luck, looking for work, needed something fast, and found a position as a window dresser in New York."

"A window dresser, sir?"

"Right, I lasted a week. Placed the mannequins in obscene positions and got the old heave ho."

Manjit's high-pitched giggle, "O that is good, sir, very, very good!" as we approach this exit. "And now, sir, where to?"

"Let me check the map," switching on the overhead light, "Ah, here we go, get off up ahead, at Cross County Parkway, then right at Exit 12, North Columbus Avenue, and straight into Pondfield Road."

Where they all should be waiting—and I may be forced, God knows, to call Santiago.

Fifteen

A gusto of hugs and kisses, followed by handshakes all around, "Tory, Manjit. Manjit, Gene. And Tory, you're sure Fiona's inside?"

"Should be, at least her lights are on."

"Any sign of him?"

"None, but we just got here, Dad, ten minutes before you."

Manjit's cab and Hagar's Mustang parked on Argyle Place, diagonally across from Fiona's home, an old white, two-story Dutch Colonial, on this heavily treed, sparsely lit street.

"Well, I think we should wait till Padraic arrives, Dad, keep out of sight."

"Assuming *he's* not inside."

"But in the meantime, you call the police."

"Right, right. . . ."

"There's a gas station on California, off North Columbus—"

"*OK, Tory, OK!*"

"Look, we're not going in without—"

"I know, I know. Manjit, let's go."

"Sir?"

"We'll be right back."

And down to this brightly lit Mobil station, hopping out and feeding my change into the outdoor phone, then shifting from foot to foot as it keeps on ringing—

"Santiago here."

"It's Seamus Boyne."

"Hey, you run pretty good for an old man."

"I want to make a deal."

"Yeah, what kinda deal you wanna make?"

"I believe I know who the real killer is."

"And who's that?"

"Padraic Shea, who looks exactly like me."

"And where will you be?"

"Bronxville. We're parked near his aunt's house. And he's either in there or'll be here shortly."

"So you want me to come and meet ya?"

"Right, 'cause I'm sure you know by now I didn't do it."

"Yeah, and what's the exact address where you're at?"

"296 Pondfield Road."

"296 Pondfield, OK. And the phone number there?"

"I'm at a pay phone down the road."

"Then you'll be in a car or what?"

"I'll be standing across the street."

"OK, fine, and listen, it should take me 'bout twenty-five minutes, half an hour, to get there, so you be waitin' outside."

"And no more fast ones, Santiago."

"No, I'll just meet ya there."

"See you soon."

And back into Manjit's cab.

"Everything all right, sir?"

"I'm not certain."

· · · · · ·

Nervously pacing over forty minutes now, with no sign of Padraic *or* Santiago, Fiona's light still burning—and *that's it!*

"Dad, where're you *going?*"

"You wait here!"

"Dad, *stop!*"

"I can't!" rushing across the shadowy street, "She may be in danger in there!"

"So what're you gonna do?"

"Mr. Boyne, sir!"

"*Seamus—Christ Almighty!*"

"Gene, *get* back here! O God, come on, Manjit!"

"Yes, of course, madam, and I have my dagger."

Up this dark, concrete path to knock on the ebony door.

"Dad, will you *please*—"

"Quiet, quiet, no noise." And waiting, glancing around, then knocking again. "Hello, anybody home? Hello?" Not a sound as I knock once more, then ease open the door and slowly step inside under this pale hall light. "Fiona? Hello? *Fiona?*" The rest of the house pitch dark.

"Dad, let's *go*—"

"Shhh! Look, we'll fan out. Tory, you take the upstairs, Hagar head to the left, through the living room and that screen porch, and Manjit, you try the cellar."

"Cellar, sir?"

"Basement."

"Ah, yes, yes. Cellar, sir, of course," he grinning with his glinting silver fillings.

"Should be through that door, unless it's a closet. And I'll go to the right."

Cautiously feeling my way through a dark dining room—can't see a bloody thing—and searching, fumbling for a light, the smell of musty curtains and a trace of some strong, sweet-smelling perfume—*CRASH!* Manjit downstairs—"Sorry, sir, storage chest"— then taking a deep breath before bumping myself into these chairs, that table—"EEEEE!!" *Christ!*—a blur of fur goes squealing past.

"Dad, you OK?"

"I'm fine, fine. Dumb cat!"

"What?"

"*Cat, cat,* stepped on a stupid *cat!*"

Tory moving upstairs from room to room, the floorboards creaking—"Hey, guys, look what *I* found!"—as I slowly edge toward what should be the kitchen, a hall between, "Hello? . . . Fiona? Hello?" and, finally finding a light switch, trip and nearly fall—"*Holy JAYSUS!*"—over a foot sticking out in the hall!

A white-haired woman sprawled on the linoleum as I reach for the pulse near her ear—

"Hands up, over your head!" his gun drawn, "Get away from the body, Boyne, or whoever you are, you're under arrest!"

The other cop, Fred Flintstone in a suit, shoving me against the wall and about to snap on the cuffs—"But I just *found* her—"

"It's true!" Tory coming through the door.

"Who're you?"

"His daughter."

"And I'm his son-in-law."

"And I, sir, am his friend."

"What the hell *is* this? And who's on the floor?"

"We assume Fiona Dolan."

Santiago checking her pulse, "And you never met her?"

"Never." Flintstone still gripping my wrists. "Is she dead?"

"Yeah, suffocated, looks like."

"O Jaysus!"

"And Padraic Shea?"

"No sign of him."

"But, detective, I found this upstairs," Tory handing him a letter.

"What is it?"

"A suicide note."

And Santiago, putting his gun away, reads it aloud: "I, Padraic Shea, freely admit to the murders of my mother, Donal Tuohy, and now, in great despair, my dear aunt, Fiona. I won't even attempt to discuss the reasons, except to say shortly I shall end my own life and take my sins with me. Don't try to find my body, for you never will."

"Suffering Christ! But why would he kill *her*?"

"She was probably onto him, Dad."

"Right, right. And are you going to search for his body?"

"Yeah-yeah, we will," Santiago gazing around the kitchen, "but we still gotta bring you down to the station house."

"*Me*? What're you *talking* about?"

"Detective, you've got *her* body, a suicide note confessing the crimes, what more do you want?"

"Hey, ma'am, what can I tell ya, it's standard procedure, shouldn't take too long."

"So I'm *still* under arrest?"

"No, you're not bein' charged."

"And I can leave if I want?"

"Yeah, ya can, but I'd appreciate—"

"OK, OK, I'm coming," and I let out a deep sigh as I follow them across the street and back into the cab, "Manjit, my friend, thank you so much for your help."

"Always my pleasure, sir."

Sixteen

"O, and one final thing, Mr. Boyne, make sure we have your number where you're gonna be at. And do me a favor, don't leave the state, 'cause I'll probably be checkin' in with ya every day, OK?"—and still hearing Santiago's parting words as we go racing through lower Manhattan with Hagar's Mustang leading the way, running interference to escape the insane media blitz of zigzagging zanies—and end up at Keen's Chop House on West 36th, with its vast churchwarden collection, dark paneled walls, polished wood tables, and cracked leather banquettes, for a celebration treat of savory Welsh rarebit and a seemingly endless supply of bitter brown Guinness.

• • • • • •

My lawyer, Isadore Toal, assuring me that I'm basically free on all charges—except for a host of unanswered questions, such as: Where is Padraic's body? And why this murderous rage at me, his mother, Tuohy, and Fiona? Obviously he wasn't killed on the L.I.E. And so many bits and intriguing pieces left to be explained about the forgeries and his life with Gillian as we arrive back in Stony Brook at two in the morning—and find that my little Corgi's run away!

The three of us splitting up in weary agitation—how he got out, not really sure—and wandering through the woodsy dark, under that shaving of a moon and the rustling pin oaks and shrubbery—Tory driving alone along Mount Grey Road, Hagar stalking north, while I head down to the park at the center of Old Field South, a few houselights on, insomniacs reading or watching TV, and stumble over a log, calling out for my motha-fucking Corgi—if you love 'em, you lose 'em—

What was THAT?!

And spinning about—a huge, looming shadow, *O JAYSUS!!*

No, just a swaying branch that looked like—heart in my throat, swallowing hard—and trudging on. No sign of him—can't lose him now. Maybe he ran back to his home? as up this road I scuttle, Guinness-reeling, my knees still thick with stout. And so miss my Poldy, only dog I know who rides on the back of a Harley.

And Laura arriving tomorrow afternoon, my wife twice over and a woman lovely in her bones, completing my family, and usually so exhausted from the flight, her thighs twinkling with wet desire as my tongue kisses her lips awake, like the light falling and filling my canvas to the brim from a quick, splashing stroke that trembles at the edge yet does not flow over, or like love, which is not love until it's vulnerable, vulnerable to loss, to profound fear—and *she,* Gillian, saving my life, pulling me free, with her shiny wet face, full, warm lips, and my erection blooming on Kilkoole beach for her to obviously see!

Her raw, sexual heat, always there, coming back now—as I keep shouting for the Corgi and scuffle through these swirling leaves, a driftwood wind blowing me hither and thither, sealegs a bit wobbly—and that time at age thirteen, fourteen, as guilt-ridden, I blocked it off, couldn't, wouldn't recall when I awoke in a panic one Valhalla morning from that recurring nightmare of so missing Aideen, my mother, and was about to enter my father's bedroom, his door ajar, and saw him humping furiously away beneath a single sheet—not sure what game they were playing or was he hurting her—but her eyes, those sensual Asian eyes, were smiling straight into mine as Tim kept grunting and groaning, unaware of me, while she kept smiling while and licking her glistening lips, a beauty mark on her chin.

O *Christ,* Gillian! Was I your love object as a teenage boy as Tim grew steadily sicker, all shoulder blades and ribs? She always praising my talent—Yet needing my approval, attention, and the worship of her womanly charms?

And this she conveyed to Padraic? He a surrogate me, the spitting image, as she forced him to become what he never could, never would be, and drove him into raging psychosis?

O who the hell knows! Curious, though, he an only child, *I an only child. Think you're escaping and run into yourself. Longest way round is the shortest way home.*

Returning now to Tory's house, Hagar there, also empty-handed, then driving me out to Crane Neck at 3:15 in this groggy morning—

And *Jaysus, Mary, and José!* who should greet us with a waggy tail and licking tongue as I give his belly a vigorous rub!

"How'd he ever *find* me?"

"Followed your scent. Amazing! Listen, Seamus, I'm totally beat, I'll talk to you in the morning, man, get some sleep. Night, Mutha."

And the Corgi and I knit *up the ravelled sleeve of care* under a tumble of covers and quilts and pass out together.

Seventeen

—*Quilts and covers loosely piled across her bed, her pale brow showing, and he, me—breeze from the open window—violently stuffing pillows over her face till she finally stops her breathing*—as I wake with a terrified *howl,* rapidly blinking and gaining my breath, the Corgi nuzzling my fist, "—It's OK, boy, it's OK!"

A hot blaze of sun burning the fog off the water at a quarter past twelve on this Sunday morning—as I sigh once more and, planting both feet on the floor, briskly massage the nape of my neck, then rise unsteadily and pop open the fridge to feed my shimmying dog three slices of Danish ham and some crumbled-up Wonder bread—

"Hey, easy, boy, easy—"

The phone ringing. Santiago with news? Or Laura? No, she already took off.

"Yes?"

"Morning, Dad. How'd you sleep?"

"Not too well. And you?"

"Not too well, either. They started calling at 8 this morning. Unbelievable! Does the press *ever* sleep? O, and Symes called, Mother's flight's been delayed, so she'll be here around 5, 5:15."

"You coming with us? Maybe you should rest, Tory."

"I think so. You and Gene can go."

"Good idea. So we should leave about 3?"

"Or sooner."

"Right, Tory, I'll be waiting."

"You hear from Santiago?"

"Not yet."

"Well go outside, Dad, take a walk. It's such a glorious day."

"You know, there's a thought."

And feeling that gnawing painting ache again as I take a midday stroll round the hilly grounds, missing it so, to finish Gillian's portrait, add that beauty mark on her chin. This marvelous view overlooking Smithtown Bay and Long Island Sound, sailboats tacking by through a bedlam gust of wind, and eventually back inside to turn on the TV: news about the gas shortage and my harrowing escapades, Eamonn Coghlan winning the mile at a Pepsi Invitation meet—and switching channels to *The Flintstones*, ha! dancing detergent commercials, and—great!—*Duck Soup*, with the Marx Brothers ransacking Fredonia with glee, one of my all-time favorites.

Eighteen

Signs for Kennedy Airport now appearing as Hagar goes sharply veering and bumping off Southern State, wheeling through this traffic maze, and nearing International Arrivals.

"We're early, Seamus, made good time."

"Then let's have a drink."

"Why, you worried?"

"I'm *always* worried, boy, especially about flights."

• • • • • •

This dark airport bar crowded with businessmen and hookers, backpackers and wives, clinking glasses of Bud on tap and chomping pretzels from a bowl, Hagar off in the loo, that TV above, angled in a corner—and what do you know, there I am at the MFA—must be old footage.

"Bartender, could you turn that sound a bit louder, please?"

"Sure. Another round?"

"Absolutely."

"—*And Mr. Boyne will be returning later tonight to the MFA to do, as he said, some last-minute touching-up of his paintings*—"

"*HOLY JAYSUS!*" and screaming into the bathroom, "HAGAR," guys jerking their startled willies and spraying pee off the walls. "*HE'S ALIVE!*"

"Who is?"

"*PADRAIC!* He's *NOT* dead! I had a feeling—and I've gotta get up there!"

"Where?"

"To Boston!" hustling out, "let's see, when's the next flight?"

"Seamus, whatta you *talking* about?"

"There!" scanning a TV monitor, "United has a 5:20 shuttle that gets me in at 6:32, and I can buy a ticket on board."

"But what about Laura?"

"I'll see her before I leave, still got time."

"Look, please, will you call the police and let *them* handle it?"

"No, I can't, Gene, I've gotta do this. Come on, Laura should be landing any minute now!"

Waiting within this waving crowd of well-wishers, limo drivers holding up signs—and here she comes with her regal stride, stunning in a green shantung suit and short platinum hair, as I burst forward to embrace her, "O my dear!" squeezing her hard, kiss-kiss, "Good flight?"

"All right. Gene, good to see—"

And I step between them, "Listen, I'm leaving."

"You're what?"

"I have to fly to Boston."

"But why?"

"Padraic, the killer, is still alive."

"*Alive?*"

"Alive!"

"So what're you going to *do?*"

"I don't know, but I have to go, have to get to him first!"

"But why is he in Boston?"

"To destroy my work."

"Then call the police."

"That's what I said, Laura."

"No, if they get there first, they'll kill him or he'll clam up, and then I'll *never* know!"

"Never know what?"

"Know *why?* Laura, please, I *have* to go!"

"But Boyne, this's crazy! You're putting yourself in great danger."

"No, I'll be fine. He won't kill me face-to-face."

"Who says so?"

" 'Cause he's sending me a message."

"What message?"

"To come to him. Look, don't worry, dear, I'll be careful."

"You want me to come with you?"

"Not on your life!"

"Boyne, you're mad!"

"But you already know that! And by the way, you look *terrific!*" giving her a passionate kiss.

"—And I also know when you get like this, I can't change your mind, but—"

"Be back soon."

"You want me to drive you to the United terminal?"

"No, Gene, I'll grab a cab, be faster. 'Bye!"

And I go sprinting toward that staircase.

Nineteen

"To the tables down at Mory's, to the place where Louie dwells—"

And you believe this? I'm sitting strapped in here on this jam-packed shuttle flight, rocketing down the Kennedy runway and—*JAAAY-SUS!!*—into the wild blue yonder, where it's white-knuckle time, even though the evening skies are clear, there's wind shear on my mind, the "Whiffenpoof Song" in my ears, and this freckled, pigtailed girl right off the farm beside me belting out for all she's worth, *"We're poor little lambs who have lost our way: Baa! Baa! Baa!"*

Still so bloody scared, licking the sweat from my upper lip, and trying to gain my breath, "—Excuse me, miss, but why is the whole plane singing?"

*"Little black sheep who have gone astray—*We're rehearsing for the Barbershop Quartet Contest in Boston."

"O lord," lifting my eyes to the skies, "there's no *way* I can die now!"

"Are you French, sir?"

"Me, French? Why?"

"'Cause you're wearing a beret."

"O, no, that's just to cover my bald dome."

"Well, you look very elegant, I must say."

"Thank you, that's very sweet. But I don't *feel* very elegant now," as I keep breathing hard.

"Do you sing?"

"Only in the shower."

"Well, then please join in."

And she pries my fingers free from the padded armrest to hold my hand in hers as I raise my off-key tenor for some airborne harmony:

"Gentlemen songsters off on a spree, doomed from here to eternity, Lord have mercy on such as we: Baa! Baa! Baa!"

Twenty

And bidding adieu to the jolly pigtailed girl and her band of barbershop singers as I hop into this waiting cab, no Manjit at the wheel, rather Horace Flato, a hairy Red Sox fan.

"The MFA."

"You got it, man."

And we're off with a rasp of gears at 6:49, his baseball cap tilted back on his brow—And Christ, what *is* my plan? First get inside—Posing as Padraic? Well, he got in as me, but not, I'll bet, in a green beret, black windbreaker, khakis, and new white Nikes!

The sun going down over the fiery Boston skyline, past Hancock Tower and down Commonwealth Ave. And am I truly mad? Committing suicide? Or being drawn like a fly into his spider's lair? My time to die? Never see my grandchild alive? *No bloody way!* Like Laura, after being told by her American doctor three years ago she had just a few months to live, today is fine, still going strong, and now her doctor's dead!

Damn! into this honking traffic jam, leaning forward on the edge of my seat:

"Isn't there a faster way?"

"Not at this bloody hour."

Buses lumbering out to Beacon Hill, Kenmore Square, and Mass. Ave. as I release another sigh, and still hearing that music in my mind, *Sing the Whiffenpoofs assembled with their glasses raised on high,/ And the magic of their singing casts a spell.*

Twenty-one

Church bells tolling and the smell of fresh-mown grass as I go strolling up this dark crescent path toward that portly, lobster-eyed guard waiting in a navy blue suit between ionic columns and before the polished doors of the MFA.

"Sir, the museum's closed, so—O, Mr. Boyne, sorry, didn't see you leave, and you've changed your clothes."

"Uh, yes, well, just popped out for a little snack."

"Ah, must've been on my dinner break," he inserting his silver key, and the door swings free as in a fairy tale. "Just let us know when you're through for the night. O and by the way, good luck tomorrow on your show."

"Appreciate that, and thanks again."

And I waltz right past with amazing grace, and round the Information desk—expecting Padraic, or Basil Quinn, to come dashing down these stairs at any moment—No, sure he's patiently waiting in the Retrospective wing to snare me in his lair as I creep silently across the courtyard on my Nike soles to ease behind this entrance for a fast peek in—No sign of him. And not a sound. No other guards in sight. He's probably down the far end—

"Well, well, look who's finally here!"

And spinning around, I stare aghast into a mirror-image of

myself a few years back, though his glinty blue-black eyes and crooked grin are wide and wild, like he's been gnawing on an electric line. And he's bald as well, with no beret, having shaved his beard, and clad in a red plaid shirt, dungarees, work boots, and pointing that copper pistol in his paint-stained hand straight at my pounding heart.

"So, Boyne, we meet at last. And you made good time, I must say. Though you look much older in person than I thought you would."

"Yes, well, and you're somewhat younger than I expected. How old *are* you, Padraic?"

"Thirty-four. Born in 1945, just before your—our father died."

Glancing quickly over my shoulder—"Our?"

"O, but you don't *know*, do you, old son?"

"Know what?"

"That I'm your half-brother."

"My—*Good God!*"

"They forgot to mention that, eh? Well, apparently they were lovers for five or six years, then he took sick, so I was raised by my mother in Valhalla—raised, of course, to be envious of you, in addition to looking almost exactly *like* you—"

"That's 'cause Gillian looked so much like my mother."

"O did she now? Well, well, well. But enough of this journey down memory lane, Boyne. Would you care to see *my* work?"

"Your—O yes, yes, by all means," and lurching forward—

"Easy now, old son, I'm most adept with guns, knives. And then once you've seen what I've done," those parched fissures in his crooked smile, "then I'm finally going to do you in."

"But *why*, Padraic?" slowly moving between the gallery walls— hasn't touched the Ciara paintings, thank God! "Your mother *saved* my life!"

"Yes, and now I'm going to *take* it."

"But how can—I mean I'm your half-brother!"

"With delight, I assure you. And after I kill *you,* I will kill your daughter and her unborn child."

Blinking hard as I fight back my rage to rip out his heart!

"You ruined my work, so now I'm ruining yours—or actually improving it, Boyne, if I do say so myself."

"But what did I *do* to you?" still glancing anxiously about—

"What did you do to me? What did you *do* to me? Now there's a laugh! Well, let's see, shall we? You stole my father, you stole my mother, and essentially stole my childhood as well!"

And not a bloody guard in sight—"But she loved you, Padraic."

"Loved *me?* And how could *you* possibly tell?"

"'Cause I talked to her and she was proud of you as a painter, she told me so."

"And did she also tell you how I was always taken for you, always compared to you, that I had the same talent as you, but was never as good as you? She looking like *your* mother, me trying to *be* like you—All of it so *sick!*" and he sighs, his jaw muscles twitching, "Though I must admit, I was rather awkward at sports, an ungainly runner—but you, old son, were the sprinter, of course."

Nodding, "And you went to college?" just keep him talking—

"Hunter, yes, for a year. But I also have to tell you how delighted, delirious, actually, I was when I heard you'd died in 1973, then took to forging your work when you resurfaced, and I kept struggling, you grew even richer, more famous, saw you on TV, my mother went into that nursing home—"

"But how was I to *know?*" Or make a dash for the door?

"I used to stare at your picture for hours on end, and at his picture as well, trying to make some sense of it all—Ah, but now tell me, Boyne, what is it like to be famous?"

"To be famous?" Or make a grab for the gun? "Can be a crown of thorns, Padraic. Though I wish I could've known you as a boy."

He blinking his glinty eyes, "O you do, do you?"

"No, really, not just competitively, but to take that awful burden *off* you."

"Yes, well now I'm going to show you that I can paint even *better* than you! This way," and he heads toward an open wooden carrying case on the floor filled with brushes, tubes of paint, rags, jars, palettes—then stops before this early landscape of mine—*Good GOD!*—as whirl in a fluttering vortex of light—and *ruined* by these streaks and slashes of mauve and white!!—as seething inside, I swallow hard, trying to stay calm, and he picks up a brush with his free hand and begins painting an owl—a dreadful *blue* owl!—over my lush green hedgerows—

"But you don't approve," he wickedly grinning, "do you now?"

"—Uh, no-no, on the contrary, Padraic, no, it's—it's really, really quite interesting, in fact, only wish *I'd* thought of that."

"O I knew you'd try to flatter me, just knew you'd never see—"

"No, I mean it, but don't stop, Padraic, keep going, don't stop now! It's really quite good, most inventive, actually."

"O I'm *sure* you think so!"

"No, I do. But look," and bending toward a brush, "here, what if I expand your aviary, toss in some meadowlarks and loons—"

"Stay right where you are!"

"—Kittiwakes and hawks? 'Cause I'm seeing all *sorts* of possibilities now, you breathing new life into this tired old landscape."

"All *sorts* of possibilities, eh?"

"O absolutely, Padraic, got my creative juices flowing, that tingle going, hair at the back of neck, you know what I mean?"

"Yes, Boyne, I *do* know."

And I pick up a brush and reach—

"*NO*, don't *TOUCH* that! My owl is perfect!"

"O yes, yes, of course, you're right, but you haven't finished this one. And I'll bet you were going to add a few more feathers here, weren't you now?"

"Well—"

"See, I *knew* it!" and I begin—lightly—to desecrate my own painting with a swirl of mauve—hate mauve—and green, "Just following your lead."

"Yes, well . . . all right, but remember I'm watching you, Boyne, and one false move—"

"Of course," loading up my brush and delicately stroking along the borders of the canvas—waiting for just the right moment. "Come on, Padraic, join me—There, in that corner, *love* your marbling, that enamel marbling, like Pollock's *Lavender Mist*—but don't stop, Padraic, don't stop, keep on going!" and I pluck a tube from the case as he places his gun on the floor. "O you've got some aurora yellow, I see."

"And why wouldn't I?" Uncanny, he cocking a wicked eyebrow just like my father, same shape of his head, bald dome, and *my* hand and facial gestures: We two, same and not-same, as I dab my brush again—and an unexpectedly tender rush of feeling now for him flooding over me, he, my brother, half-brother, kid brother—

"And you're only thirty-four, Padraic? Amazing! So sad you never met Tim."

"Tim?"

"Your—our father."

He blinking once more, his jaw still twitching, and earnestly painting away—with pretty good technique, really, a certain raw talent there—

"But tell me about your mother, Padraic."

"My mother? What do I have to tell *you*? My mother *adored* you—you knew that—and I was left with the crumbs, the crumbs of a lonely life."

"I'm sorry, I really am."

"You were the great love of her life, not me *or* our father. But what do you need to know, you slept with her, didn't you?"

"*SLEPT with*—? *NO! O Jaysus, no!* I swear—Why, you think *I'M* your father?"

"Well, *are* you?"

"*No!* I was sixteen when you were born!"

"So?" And he flashes that crooked grin again as I sigh, "Touched a nerve there, didn't I?"

Suffering *Christ*, I could've been this maniac's father! "And Donal Tuohy, who was he?"

"Tuohy? O, Tuohy was nothing, a collector, filthy rich philistine, whose name I took when he threatened to blow the whistle. Pedantic little pest, who also looked like us—he *deserved* to die!"

"And your mother?" as I keep on painting—

"She called me, told me you'd spoken to her and were coming up to the nursing home, everything was closing in, she wouldn't listen—"

"And your aunt?"

He pausing, staring off, "I adored her! But after she told me she'd spoken to your daughter, well—then I wrote that suicide note confessing, and suddenly everything came clear and I knew precisely what I had to do!"

"Right, right—and I like those overlapping feathers of yours, very nice, very nice indeed. Though I must say your color there's a bit harsh against my green."

"*Harsh? HARSH?* What the devil's *harsh* about it? Hell, *your* green, YOUR green is absolutely *RIDICULOUS!*" and he flings his brush aside, "Should *never*'ve let you join me! You have no *idea* of color, Boyne, no idea at *all!*"

"*I* have no idea of color?"

"No, not in the slightest! You slobber on those sickly greens, bile greens, slimy greens, 'cause you think it looks so, so *Irish!* I mean even your hero, Turner, *HATED* your slimy green!!"

And he fires his palette at me—glancing sharply off my cheek—as I let out a roar and go ramming into his gut, slamming him into the wall, my painting falling, the two of us sprawling across the floor, rolling over and over, same and not-same, red plaid on black nylon, dungarees on khaki, half-brothers locked in a warring embrace, he stronger, younger—and fiercely kneeing him in the face, he groping for the copper gun—then stunning him with a karate chop to the throat, I vault to my feet and take off running—bullets ricocheting, pinging off the marble above—and down this hall flat out like Eamonn Coghlan winning the mile, more shots zinging by—*Christ!* one nicking my side—and that portly guard appearing, Padraic dropping him with a bullet to his thigh—as I scramble up these stairs to the second floor—restaurant to my right—and into this wing, past Renoir's *Dance at Bougival,* red bonnet, yellow straw (man's face: Padraic's now, mine then), and Gauguin's *Where Do We Come From? What Are We? Where Are We Going?* Jaysus, but isn't that the heart of the matter? Swiftly on through—don't hear him now—another guard shouting below—and he's shot him, too!—by Turner's brilliant *Slave Ship* and Picasso's awful *Rape of the Sabines,* the gall to compare him to me!—and breathing hard, need a place to hide, across the Tapestry Gallery, of skylit space—another shot shattering that vase!—and ducking posthaste into this loo—

Holding my breath! Hear him stomping awkwardly by on those clunky boots of his—and now what? Sounds like he's heading down the stairs—Got to ambush him, cut him off at the pass, then knock him cold.

Darting fast glances left and right: Coast is clear, alarms must've sounded, cops on their way!

Under this rotunda dome of lovely Sargent murals—I'll make a commotion to lure him up, then drop him on his arse!—by these Grecian urns, *Thou still unravish'd bride of quietness, foster-child of silence and slow time*—and into the Medieval Room, grab that halberd? which I fumble and let fall, clattering, to the floor! Chop to the neck or left to the jaw'll have to do. Wonder if he has any bullets left? A second clip? Heard, I think, six go off. Taunt him before this narrow window? Down below, that small fountain in the empty courtyard—

And here he *comes! Nowhere* to hide! And this's how I'm gonna die? Unlike Rothko slashing the veins inside the crooks of his arms or Gorky stringing himself up in his studio barn, but shot by my mad half-brother in the MFA! *O Jaysus! Holy Mother of God! Please be out of bullets!!*

"Well, well, well, you can run, as they say, old son, but you can't—"

"Padraic, listen, there's no way out, so let me help you—"

"Help *me*? I hold the gun, Boyne, you may have noticed."

"No, *wait*, I'll spare no expense, medical, legal, you name it—You're my *brother*, for God's sake!"

"Marvelous, you know, after all these years, to have, at last, the power in my hands! But enough blathering, brother of mine, just say bye-bye, short and sweet!" And he pulls the trigger—I blink.

Nothing.

Another click—I stare.

"DAMN you, man!"

And with a banshee shriek, he snatches up the halberd and, swinging it wildly from side to side, charges across the room with a battering clatter, pinballing off those toppling urns—and tripping awkwardly over one, grasping out for me—goes crashing through the windows—*Suffering Christ!*—into the fountain below!

My side bleeding, staining my shirt and khakis as I stagger down these polished stairs—*crazy fucking bastard!*—to find him still alive and groaning, and barely lifting his face from the shallow fountain.

"—*Help!*—*Please*—think I broke—broke my back—can't, can't breathe—" and his face falls into the bubbling water.

"Right, Padraic, well, neither could they!"

And I watch him flail a moment longer, then reach in and gently pull him free . . . just as Gillian pulled me.

Boyne Roaring

July 1981

Part One

One

Old Poldy, my snowy white Samoyed beast, healer, caretaker, and canine Hell's Angel, lying beside me at 6:55 of a foggy Irish morning in my big brass bed, his head upon the pillow, all four paws in the air, and lightly snoring.

He hopping up last night after sensing my panicky state as I went tromping and stomping blindly about the castle, grieving the loss of Laura and my temporary sight.

And now deeply sighing, grunting, and blinking awake, he rolls onto his right side and snuffles back asleep as I ease free of these silken sheets and slide silently off the bed—bloody dog hiding my Elavil and Tullamore Dew!—to totter into the loo and stand swaying over the bowl in my shamrock boxer shorts, patiently waiting to pee with my huge wee-wee hard-on—still standing, waiting, then straining—far too tense, relax the muscles of the pelvic floor—ah, yes, a steady, glinting stream and—

O SUFFERING JAYSUS! Can't *SEE* anymore!! *Fucking Amaurosis Fugax!* Total visual loss for seconds, minutes, an hour or two, or maybe next time, evermore! as I keep peeing all over the walls and floor—then bumping and stumbling out, fumble my groping way helter-skelter down the hall and lurching—has to be here—into my skylighted studio, smashing into my easel, *"GOOD GOD!"*—knocking over paints and tables as I crash to my knees, and Poldy now feverishly licking across my face, eyes, nose, and beard—

"Leave me *BE*, dog!—*Symes! SYMES!!*"

Echoing footsteps hurrying along as I continue flailing like a windmill and spitting out wispy Samoyed hairs—

"Sir?"

"I can't bloody *SEE!*"

"So I see."

"I know *YOU* can see, damn it! Help me to a chair."

"Certainly, sir."

"Where's Poldy?"

"Right before you, sir."

"Come here, doggie. Sorry I yelled at you, snapped at you."

He licking briskly over my beard again and blind, blinking eyes—that now begin clearing to pastel blurs and Seurat-dots, and, finally, butler Symes and my panting Siberian beast.

"How long this time, sir?"

"Few minutes, I'd say, though longer than the last three. And Hubert, thank you so much for your support."

"My pleasure, sir."

"But now," as I slowly rise and go dizzily padding down these curving stairs toward my kitchen and breakfast nook—fighting off despair—and Symes behind me with his bloodhound jowls, rheumy eyes, and elegant livery of black jacket and striped tie, dark gray trousers, and fiddle strings of thinning hair brushed across his scalp and drooping over his left ear as he releases Poldy onto the front lawn, then reappears in my vast, green-and-blue tiled kitchen.

"Sit with me, Symes."

"Sir?"

"Here, in the breakfast nook. Have you eaten yet?"

"Well, not quite yet, sir."

"Right, then I insist. Come on, sit, sit, I'll serve *you* this morning. Cereal, Symes?"

"Uh—Fine, sir."

Opening this metal food bin, I shake out the remaining grains of Puffed Rice from three separate boxes, then peer inside my brightly lit Frigidaire.

"Ah, the milkman's left a couple of pints, so we've at least got that. Do you like the Puffed Rice, Symes?"

"Not particularly, sir."

"Well, that's about all we have, I'm afraid, only one choice this morning—O, wait a second. There's part of a skinny chicken leg back here. A tad bowlegged, it seems. Want that?"

"I'll just have the cereal, sir."

"Right, and here, let me join you." Trying to get a grip, but betrayed by my hand's erratic tremor. "More milk?"

"No, that's quite sufficient. So what will you do, sir?"

"Do, Symes?"

"About your condition, sir?"

"Well I won't have that bloody operation yet, that's for damn sure! Even Dr. Hafiz said I should wait."

"But this is your fourth episode, sir."

"As well I know, Symes, as well I know."

"And the last in the car, sir."

"Symes, I'm watching my diet, taking my aspirin and blood thinners." Yet still so bloody stressed! "Anyway, more cereal for you?"

"Thank you, sir, but I think I shall share mine with the dog."

"Right, and I think I'd better get dressed."

"Want me to assist you, sir?"

"No, I'll be fine. Hafiz said the episodes are usually days, weeks apart. Take myself a walk down by the sea. Though I think I'd best put something else on before I chance the air, pop upstairs, get my sunglasses. Wouldn't want the Irish to see me unclad, you know, bad publicity there."

Swiftly back to my bedroom for a hot, needling shower and a fresh pair of boxer shorts, then slip on this new green windowpane-plaid suit from my Dublin tailor—Poldy out the window ravenously gnawing on a beef marrow bone, silky white fur on mowed green grass—and my hand starting to shake again—so a fast belt, *Sláinte!* from my hidden stash of Tullamore Dew—shivering, burning through my tripes and spine—before tripping lightly down the stairs.

"Symes?"

"Sir?"

Posing in the doorway. "So, what do you think?"

He casting a hooded eye at my attire. "Well . . . a trifle sudden, I'd say, sir."

"Yes, 'sudden,' right, most apropos."

And off I go, Poldy abruptly leaving his bone and scampering beside me, plume tail swishing down the garden paths, my sight restored—but never knowing for how long—and flooded now as it is with a floral bouquet of rustling colors, hawthorn and kerry lily, marsh pea and scarlet pimpernel as I inhale another briny whiff of Wicklow air and lope on by my boxwood maze, through the white wooden gate, and down to the silvery shale, sand, and pale blue Irish Sea—Poldy flushing out a fluttering grouse and barking at its frenzied, whirring flight—around Broad Lough and The Murrough's strip of land.

No one else about at this early morning hour—And why *now*, in the prime of my life? Bach going blind in the last years of *his* life, but ten days before he died, miraculously regaining his sight— or Joyce having eleven operations for iritis, acute conjunctivitis, cataracts, and glaucoma—Beethoven losing his hearing and still composing—But that's music, writing, and this is painting—as I brusquely snap my sunglasses off but fail to prevent—*JAYSUS FUCKING CHRIST!!*—a sudden scald of tears, my shoulders convulsively shaking, leaning back against this seaweedy rock— with Poldy, my hairy old caretaker, playing tag with the foamy surf, and not noticing my distress. Or perhaps it was lead poisoning that caused it: all those years of working in the nude, my body dripping and splattered like a Pollock mural, or like Goya, with his middle-aged intestinal woes, or Van Gogh, with his near-insanity, who actually *ate* some of his leaded paint—

No, Hafiz saying it's more likely caused by my high blood pressure, but, and here's the *big* but, if I don't have that operation eventually, that carotid endarterectomy, those blood vessels could throw an embolus up to the central retinal artery, no blood'd reach the eye, and *I'd go blind for life!*

O Laura, Laura, so needing, missing you now! For what'd Blake once say: "You never know what is enough unless you know what is more than enough." Sniffing and drying my eyes, then tracing my snowy, grizzled beard, I continue treading slowly along the shoreline. The odd moo cow in those farm fields far below the rolling green and purple hills of Wicklow, Stag's Leap way down there, *a day of dappled seaborne clouds*—And Laura's final days: dying an agonizing death from lymphoma, aging twenty years, couldn't breathe, spleen too large, coughing and vomiting non-stop—

NO, DAMN IT!! Just recall the good times, nearly five years of recapturing bliss: the two of us in our old Toyota van wheeling over the walled, narrow roads of Ireland, bringing back the dance, the old romance, and breathing in, after I'd spilt my lusty seed, her intoxicant sexual odor: "So now, Boyne, you're sowing your wild oats all over again?" "No, not me, my dear, for as Oscar Wilde once said, 'I have never sowed wild oats, though I have planted a few orchids.'" Or that fall morning when Poldy and I were playing frisbee on the front lawn, I felt the warmth of someone watching me and turned to see up past the castle's ivy vines, Laura at the full-length window, with a smile of loving mischief in her eyes, as, almost in slow-motion, she unbuttoned her white dress down the front to reveal blushing breasts, down came her dress, then down her rosebud panties—and up the stairs I rushed! "You know what I love most about you, Laura?" "What?" "Your rosy arse after sex. Renoir claimed he'd always caress his lover's arse for days on end before finishing a canvas." "And you know, Seamus, what I love most about *you?*" "That I'm stark raving bald?" "No-no, though I do like to rub my hand over your 'polished dome,' as you call it, and your elfin ears. No, I love your huge extremities."

And our lovely daughter Tory—that waiter in New York last month saying she looked like a young Stevie Nicks—flying skyward on her

Stony Brook swing, rising higher and higher, the chains creaking—I so afraid they might break—as she, gripping them tightly and grinning brightly, her sun-blustery hair streaming behind her, soared far above the ground, close to the overhead bar, to touch the rim of the clouds! And now raising Shay, that two-year-old towheaded grandchild of mine—whom I may never see again!!

Poldy trotting briskly toward me with his wet paws to nuzzle his moist muzzle against my hand. This driftwood wind blowing me hither and thither, sealegs a bit wobbly in my green plaid suit, as I shade my eyes, a mariner's pose: that glinty light. Someone signaling from those hedgerows? Strange. Who knows—my Gaelic beard tossing in the breeze, surf groping up the shore, islands of opalescent foam—spent hours sketching the sea. And what was that comment about me in this week's *Time* by Robert Hughes: "Boyne's most recent seascapes are so vast in scope, so deep in feeling, and so authoritative in their intensity—" then comparing me to Turner with Matisse's remark that he fantasized Billy had lived in a cellar and once a week threw open the shutters to "what incandescence, what dazzle, what jewelry!"

And *Suffering Jaysus,* now *my* shutters *closing* at fifty-two! Everything spinning topsy-turvy, world going crazy, Reagan getting shot in March, the Pope in May, Bobby Sands dying from that hunger strike—and I'm going *BLIND!* No, no fucking way!

"Come on, Poldy!"

Hurrying home across the dunes, crushing crackling wrack and shells, to work on my huge portrait of Laura—one of the best things I've *ever* done, rushing now to complete it with my high-octane energy, like some near-hallucinogenic single malt—and later, ring up Flynn, drop on in for dinner and a brew and stop thinking about it, take my mind off it, and just keep painting her, green shadows, golden gleams, using Turner's tinted steam, my evanescent, airy dream and—

O MOTHER OF CHRIST!! Blind once *AGAIN!* My terrified

heart—heavy, labored breathing—standing here stock still on this woodsy path, tears spilling . . . as Poldy starts licking my hand—

Two

"Evenin'. Mr. Flynn's residence."

"Is Himself to home?"

"That he is, sir, but he's into his shower now. I'll get him to call ya straightaway, soon as he emerges. Otherwise he'll soap the phone."

"No, Conor, I'll be over in a jiff."

"Well he may be takin' a nap then. But ya *are* Mr. Boyne?"

"The one and only. And leave the door ajar."

"As ya wish, sir."

Poldy and Symes outside now playing hide and seek in the boxwood maze, so another quick taste of the Tullamore Dew, and away in my XJ6.

Three

Entering Flynn's gray Gothic castle stealthy as a pard and up the winding stone stairs, under the painted plasterwork ceiling (with those cherubic satyrs I modeled on him still performing in lecherous glee), to steal silently into his bedroom, little he snoring, orange beard and curly locks raw umber in the dark, as I retain my green bowler, before deftly stripping off this new plaid suit, shirt, underwear, socks, and shoes, then gently shake his shoulder.

"Flynn . . . Flynn? . . . *Flynn!*"

"—Huh? Who? *Wha?*" He blinking, squinting, and switching on the lamp, ". . . Holy Mother of God, Boyne, yer bloody fuckin' *nude!*"

"Well I was wondering now if you had the name of a good tailor?'

"What're ya daft, man, or've ya become a streaker in yer dotage?"

"No," grinning, "but I've always wanted to do that before I expire."

Four

Roaring along the Stillorgan Road toward dear, dirty Dublin, flashing me famous incisors, and raising a voice in boisterous Celtic song, *"I've been a wild rover for many's the year, and I've spent all me money on whiskey and beer—"*

"Boyne, yer a bit hammered now, are ya?"

"Not yet, but I'm well on me way, hardly eaten all day but for a puffed rice or two and a quick glass of lunch—but I had to escape from that bloody dog!"

"Not the loveable Poldy, is it?"

"The very beast. Out from under the watchful eye of my canine lord and master! He's drivin' me up the wall!" Swerving in and out of this evening traffic and splashing past buses and rattling lorries. "Ever since Laura died, he keeps me under lock and key, strict surveillance, like house arrest, can't drink, smoke, pop my bloody pills! Hell, he's worse than Dr. Hafiz! So tonight, when he wasn't looking, I dashed out the back door and sped over to you, so I could drink to my heart's content and imbibe till I die!"

"And where the hell're ya takin' me now—*WATCH IT, MAN!*—Christ, didn't ya see that horse'n wagon?"

"To this brand-new restaurant that's all the rage, the Friary Mews, for a freedom feast, and tonight it's totally my treat!"

"Now there's an offer I could never refuse."

Into Leeson Street, and park my Jag round the corner.

Gray aftermath of rain gurgling down the sewers and lacing these latticed windows with intricate webs and woven designs, buses rumbling by, as we cross this cobbled courtyard and down the steps, through an oaken door, into a posh eatery of faux abbey decor packed with nattering people and waiters in flowing monk's attire.

Flynn, with his plump, Buddha belly and shoulder-length orange curls, impishly grinning, "Look familiar, Boyne? O and talkin' about that, I had to go to a funeral this Monday past."

Standing by the shiny brass bar, "What, another rocker die?"

"Ah, yer a funny man, y'are, a funny man. No, remember my Aunt Coddle?"

"From the nursing home out in Bray? Sweet woman she was."

"And forever grateful to you fer placin' her in that grand facility in Terenure. Well, last Saturday she passed away."

"O I am sorry."

"Gentlemen?"

"Boyne, party of two."

"Of course. Right this way."

And blinking, I follow a vain and lanky headwaiter, with the bespectacled chicken face of Eamon de Valera, through this room of golden lantern light and shamrock stained glass, beamed ceilings and red carpeting, to a cozy black banquette in the corner, where he hands us these tassled leather menus.

"A drink, gentlemen?"

"Half a Guinness and a small for me uncle here, and I'll stay with the Tullamore Dew."

"Certainly, sir," and he glides away like a true-blue politician.

"Should ya be drinkin' so much, Boyne, what with yer blood pressure'n all?"

"Not to worry, drink up, get our money's worth, we're here to savor and enjoy! But how're *you* these days and your recording biz, still sex, drugs, and rock 'n' roll?"

"Can't complain. Just signed two new groups, The Fourskins from Galway and JJ and The Epiphanies from Rathgar—O and did ya hear the one about the servant in the Galway hotel who brought a telegram to a guest's room and was asked to shove it under the door, and he replied that he couldn't because it was on a tray?" Flynn and I both guffawing—people at the next table, woman with lacquered hair, man with a monocle—glancing over and whispering at recognizing me. "Ah, but Sufferin' J, Oy'm in danger, Boyne, of becomin' a professional Oyrishmun, Oyrishmun, Oy am, very lepri-corny, as Dylan would say—Ah, but here we are!"

This chubby French waiter, with a mole on his florid cheek, now serving us our drinks and—*Good God!* spilling Flynn's over his knee—

"O *excusez-moi, monsieur, excusez-moi,* I get you another— sorry, I am so sorry, be right back," and he scurries away in his brown monk's robe.

"Here, Flynn, use my napkin. Don't think it'll stain."

The other diners looking askance, faking smiles, pretending it never happened, still nattering on.

"Boyne, are ya all right?"

"Why?"

"Well yer wound so bloody tight and yer hand keeps on shakin'."

"Well blesséd are the cracked, 'cause they shall let in the light—"

"Here you are, *monsieur,*" the waiter nearly tripping over his robe and flapping sandals, "—O I am sorry, very sorry."

"Not at'all."

Flynn and I clinking glasses, "*Sláinte!*"

"Have you gentlemen decided or—?"

"Another round of the Dew."

And taking a moment more, we order mock turtle soup, cognac-laced liver paté, Chateaubriand for me, medium rare, and for Flynn, "I wonder now could I have the deep fried scampi?" "Certainly, sir." And a bottle of Chateau Lynch-Moussas. "Originally, the vineyard of an Irishman," I add, "Mr. Lynch was mayor of Bordeaux."

"Is that so, *monsieur?*"

"I never lie. The Irish, of course, lie like crazy—"

Flynn smiling, "I know I do."

"—only the Chinese are greater liars." And the chubby waiter waddles off.

"Anyway, Boyne, how's yer paintin' of Laura comin' along?"

"Best thing I've done in years, Flynn, using green shadows and golden gleams, been painting it with tinted steam, like Constable said of Turner, made it, God willing, like an evanescent, airy dream. And I think next I'll do one of Ciara."

"Grand idea, yer sensual second wife."

The waiter returning now with French bread, a bowl of paté, and the mock turtle soup, then leaving as I take a steamy spoonful—"*O Good CHRIST!*" grimacing, "This tastes like Valvoline! How's yours, Flynn?"

"10W-40. But relax, man, relax, we'll order somethin' else. Yer so bloody edgy tonight."

"That I am, Flynn, that I am—and with damn good reason."

"Ya want to talk about it?"

"Not now, later, 'cause this place feels like they're doing *us* a favor serving subpar food, day-old paté, and no one ever complains— you won't let *me* complain, make me hold my tongue."

"All right, all right, tonight ya can complain to yer bloody heart's delight."

"Really? You've given me the green light?"

Froggy hastily returning on his flapping sandals, "The soup was not to your liking, *monsieur?*" and tilting his tonsured dome.

"No, it was dreadful, so was the paté, but forget it, we'll just have our entrees."

"But of course, and the wine, it will be here very shortly."

Anxiously guarded stares from the other tables as I toss off another Dew, and the headwaiter nowhere in sight.

"Sir, the Chateaubriand for you, medium rare."

"Right, right—and another round, if you please."

"Certainly. And for *monsieur,* the deep fried scampi."

"That's grand, and I'll have me another round as well."

Slicing through my meat, chewing hard, then wincing, *"Suffering Christ!"*

"Tough?"

"Try rigor mortis! And that's *it!*"

"Boyne, what're ya goin' to do?"

"I'll show you what I'm going to do!" signaling for the head-waiter, "O I say, you? Yes, *you,* my good man."

And geeky de Valera, reeking of spurious savoir-faire, comes gliding across the red carpet. "A problem, Mr. Boyne?"

"You call this steak?"

"Yes, sir. Why, what would you call it?"

"How 'bout equine haunch, dobbin's rump, or glue factory reject? I mean do you truly believe this poor flogged and indigestible nag is worth, let's see here, thirteen bloody pounds? Do you? 'Cause if you do, sir, you're even more venal than I assumed."

"Would you like me to—?"

"And nothing I have had in this establishment thus far has been worth the price, the soup, the paté, this suet!"

"Sir, I'll speak to the chef—"

"But perhaps it is only *my* jaded palate. Let's ask the other diners here their opinion, shall we?"

"Boyne—"

Standing and chiming my wine glass with my fork. "Ladies and gentlemen—I say, ladies and gentlemen, may I have your attention?"

"Please, Mr. Boyne, sit down—"

"Excuse me, your attention, *please!*" Still chiming my glass, with more heads turning, mouths gaping, and sauces drooling from fleshy lower lips. "Pardon me, good people, but I wonder now if I might have your attention for just a moment. Most of you've been served—"

"Mr. Boyne, I must protest—"

"Ah, you're being served as I speak, ladies. Sorry, go right ahead, I'll wait till you've had a taste, dig in."

"Percy, who *is* that man?"

"Now, all of you, do you really believe—you, for example, madam, that that slice of dover sole you just sampled is worth—let me see that menu there—thank you, Flynn—ten pound fifty p.? Is it *that* delicate, *that* buttery? Not nine pound fifty p., mind you, nor eight pound fifty p., but a full ten pound fifty p.? And you, with your veal cordon bleu, does that fully measure up to twelve pound fifteen p.? 'Cause I must say I doubt it, I really do. And if it doesn't, is even a ha penny less in value, then why in hell should you pay?"

"Sir, let me get the chef—"

"Why, in fact, should any of us accept the second-rate, or shy away from protest, or should we demand full and equitable value and never, *ever* settle for less?"

"Heah-heah!" barks an elderly gent from the rear.

"So I propose that if you feel as I do that the value *is* subpar, that you're truly not getting your money's worth, to lay down your utensils now and leave without paying."

"Sir, please, I beg of you—"

"Otherwise we're just surrendering like sheep, accepting inferior quality at inflated prices—and there's no bloody need for that, no bloody need at all!"

"He's right!" "Well said, I quite agree!" "He's that famous painter, isn't he?" "Boyne? Could very well be." "The one on TV—"

And the entire restaurant, some with a bit of urging, muttering and mumbling, "We don't have to pay?" rises en masse and heads for the door, past a dazed and pleading de Valera, our chubby French waiter, and a host of grinning busboys, up the small stone steps and out into lamplit Leeson Street under a misty orange moon.

The nun with the monocle mincing over to me, "You are Seamus Boyne, are you not?"

"No, I'm only posing as Himself. Anyway, good people, thank you all, and, look, no need to go, dinner tonight's on me, wherever you choose, Le Coq Hardi, Patrick Guilbaud, Snaffles, the Shelbourne, or Mickey D's—no, no, I'm only joking!"

And they decide by a narrow vote on Le Coq Hardi, an ass's roar from here on the Pembroke Road.

Escorting all of them over to greet owner and chef John Howard, leave him my gold card, then politely beg off. "Maybe another time, but all of you enjoy. And again, thank you so much for your support, God bless."

"Where're we goin', Boyne?"

Hopping back in the Jag, "I can have Symes rustle something up or we can stop off for fish and chips. Sorry, Flynn, but I'm no longer in the mood for food," steering hellbent down the Pembroke Road, past Jury's Hotel, "Always wanted to do that, too," through Ballsbridge, along Anglesea, "And Good God, it made my day, changed my mood!" Everything suddenly dark—"O not *AGAIN!*"

"Boyne, what is it?"

Sharply swerving, veering, "Can't *SEE!*"

"Then fer the love of Jaysus stop the fuckin' car!"

—and slamming headlong into a splintering phone booth!

"Boyne, ya OK?"

"—People die in Ireland all the time!"

"Fine, but what *was* that? What's goin' on? Can ya see *now?*"

"No, still can't."

"Are ya goin' *blind?*"

"Just for a few seconds, comes and goes."

"You're serious, aren't ya?"

"Of course I'm *serious!*" Cars and buses honking as they go whooshing by.

"How can ya paint?"

"Ultimately I can't."

"But what *is* it?"

"Amaurosis fugax."

"What?"

"Amaur—"

More drivers cursing and streaming past.

"Ah, and yer mother, too! Well how long have ya had it?"

"Couple of months. The previous episodes lasted ten, twenty seconds each, after waking in bed, and a totally terrifying one driving alone down to Cork, pulled onto the shoulder and stopped when I heard the gravel crunch, lasted a minute and a half. And another this morning, two this afternoon."

"So what can ya do about it?"

"Live with it, pray to St. Raphael."

"Who?"

"Patron Saint of Eye Diseases. Or go under the knife."

"And you're horrified of that?"

"Absolutely! One slip and I lose my sight! Ah, Flynn, it's coming back, my sight's returning! Sorry to put you through this."

"Want me to drive?"

"If you would." Gingerly sliding out to switch places in the Jag.

"Boyne, hold on just a tick."

He checking the damage first: not too bad, one mashed phone booth, "But ya've bashed yer front fender all ta blazes"—and Christ, this *can't* go on much longer!

Five

Poldy waiting at the front door last night like a stern Dickensian headmaster, the stormy petrel of my life! And Flynn saying, before he left me in Symes's comforting hands, "I'll give ya a shout tomorrow, maybe pop over half twelve or round about," as I lope slowly through my morning kitchen, head still reeling, limbs achy and stiff, and up the curving stairs into my paint-littered studio. The skylight's sunshine steepling dimly down from a sudden rent in the pre-dawn clouds. Poldy now sleeping, four paws, as usual, in the air. And picking up this tube of Winsor-Newton and staring at my huge portrait of my first wife, whom I ended up marrying twice, on unprimed duck, eight-and-a-half-feet high—which now I'll never finish, finish anything ever again, even working as fast as I usually do, like Turner adding, erasing, drying, glazing, or Van Gogh, with his passionate speed, using that heavy impasto, sometimes close to a quarter of an inch, and, like me, exaggerating the essentials, so you can actually *feel* the chrome yellow sunflowers in your hands, the coarse stamen cushions on your fingers (the rosebud silk of Laura's cheek)— And Vincent's last letter to Theo: *In my own work I am risking my life, and half my reason has been lost with it*—And soon *I'll* have no reason, no art, and no life!

My heart sharply pounding, trying desperately to catch my breath!—My fierce, lifelong goal to be not just a man with a useful trade but a man with a blazing vision! A promising artist in my teens, a successful one in my twenties, and today, they say, a great one in my middle age. Or maybe, like Braque once said about Picasso, "He *used* to be a great artist, but now he's only a genius." Suppose I could always sculpt or carve in stone—*No*, who the hell are you *kidding!* Matisse losing his sight near the end of *his* life but producing those brilliant paper cutouts.

And the public wanting the same or better from me, but not different, only accepting masterpieces. And lately, with fame and fortune, growing fearful of the spontaneity I used to have—to just paint whatever flew past in a flash of growing mastery, drawing, sketching anything I saw—and now so reluctant to let a painting go, consider it complete, striving for perfection rather than excellence, always adding those last few touches and not slinging it Pollock-like onto the canvas!

O JAYSUS, and there it goes *again! Dark, so dark!!* flinging my brush behind me—*No!* rapidly blinking, it's just the sky growing dark, ominously dark, like El Greco's *View of Toledo,* thunder rumbling, coming closer, wind swirling, thrashing the trees, lightning bolts jaggedly streaking and firing the skylight, then suddenly—a cascading cloudburst, teeming Old Testament showers loudly sheeting down—my heavy, labored breathing, Poldy skulking by out there in the hall—Call Tory and get her advice—as I hastily punch out her number in the States—then hear her lovely voice on her answering machine after the seventh ring:

"For Tory and Gene at the beep. Thank you."

And replacing the clattering phone without a reply, Poldy trotting down to his breakfast, barking at the bowling-ball thunder—

And I have to get away, elude Poldy again for the day, take the wine-colored Jag out for a spin and my mind off all of this chaos— soon as this storm begins abating.

But where should I go? Dublin? No. Cork? No. How 'bout Joyce's tower? Right, that Martello Tower in Sandycove. Never actually seen it. And pop into the Pipers Lounge in Bray for old times' sake as well—if I don't total my car in the process!

Six

Sandycove's surging sea down there, the whitemaned steeds of Mananaan, and brisk winds out of the east, west, or who knows where. Slabs of rock in the harbor and sailboats, sleek trippers they are, veering on the horizon, one tacking by the Muglins. Eyes that once watched me as I passed long ago on the Groote Beer: And that first morning of land, the gulls cawing madly, balanced as they were on air, then swooping down the long slide and back to their tentative, poised hover. Spontaneously a thin shiver of earth out of the pitching sea, a lighthouse winking: Ireland. Green slice in a graygreen sea and I was so excited to be returning again, ten years after my father's funeral in '46, drunk and awake all night with the gulls spearing my stale bits of cake that I let out a wild call from the side rail, my free fist pumping the air and shouting, "God bless Ireland!" while I pointed my erection toward solid land, "There're only two countries left in all this barbarous woe—Ireland and Israel—and they'll fight it out between 'em!" when tiny, heeled feet began descending the stairway above, a white, pleated skirt coming slowly into view as I spun about, hard-on in tow. She blinked. A startled gasp. She paused. Then fled up the stairs in the wake of my laughter— and two months later she became my wife!

O Laura, what a bewitching summer that was, no money nor cares, just living on air with my Sarah Lawrence grad, posing bare for my paintings again and again, before I chased her round my studio! Or making love atop that hill in Kilcoole after watching a herd of ponies woo one another, nuzzling about and running down a glade with such exquisite freedom and ease, and a month later, when she found she was pregnant, she couldn't remember our lovemaking at all or where Tory was conceived, just those ponies running along.

Down these narrow, walled roads, warm sun merrying over the churning sea, and *Jasyus*, just breathe that briny air after the morning's passing squall. A lovely salt-snap to it, laving my face and ruffling my hair as Joyce's tower, Martello Tower, rises into view— with that slim, slackjawed man darting behind a tree—Who the hell is he?—then disappearing on *lightshod hurrying feet.*

And a young girl on a white pony down by the beach, who looks, I imagine, like my second wife, Ciara, did at that age. Three dogs milling along the shore, getting forepaws wet. One of them hers, I suspect, keeping near at hand. The pony slowly stepping out into the shallows, cooling its fetlocks, Dun Laoghaire in the distance, old Kingstown Pier—where, in due course, I shall pop into the Purty Kitchen (if I still can see!) and continue my day-long pub crawl.

Within the walled circle of this Martello Tower and through the slow iron door. A cold, domed room, daylight falling across the dark flagged floor, these whitewashed walls, a souvenir map of Joyce's Dublin and other displays. Items of memento, his wallet and cane, and moving up the winding stairs. *Stately, plump Buck*

Mulligan came from the stairhead. Over the parapet toward Dalkey: a dim blue sea, Bray Head's blunt snout of a sleeping whale. And Joyce, with his sight all but shattered, having to write with three magnifying glasses on large colored cards with different colored pens, or taking cocaine to relieve the pain.

And back down these metal steps, along the path to the Forty-foot. Mulligan capering, nimbly leaping, hands fluttering above the brow of the cliff. A black sign declaiming, "Dogs and Bicycles prohibited from entering Forty-foot." No ashplant to let trail lightly along, squealing my name behind me: Shaaay-musss. And looking back at the tower, hell of a place to live. Dank, bleak in the winter, far too claustrophobic for me; need windows, not high barbicans to see.

But my own tower, castle of Ballyduff, fast becoming a solitary tomb by the Irish Sea, with no Laura or Ciara around! My sneakers stepping down to these sloping rocks, dabbling a bold toe in the slow lap of lacy foam. Souvenir pamphlet, *Ulysses* map of Dublin, held in my hand. Bluemassing clouds in the distance, another storm soon appearing over *the scrotumtightening sea.* Joyce's brilliant images. Have my own brilliant images—that soon I'll never see! The Ciara-girl on her white pony having come round now by the Dalkey side, the white swell of his belly, nibbling grass by the seaside path. And how quickly images fade, loss swiftly arrives. Sun dimming, slowly lowering over the crest of the tower. Time now for a foaming jar, then I'll head on home.

Seven

Darkly cascading cloudbursts, those rattling sheets of rain, outside my pitch-black den or solitary cave—

"Mr. Boyne? . . . Are you in here? . . . Mr. Boyne, sir?"

". . . Yea-ah. . . ."

His silhouette framed against the lighted opening door and finger-brushing over his thin memory of hair, pomaded fiddle strings no longer melodic, as I lean back in my recliner before the dead TV screen.

"It's Symes, sir."

". . . Ah, and how *are* you, Hubert?"

"Fine, sir, fine. But what are you doing sitting in the dark?"

And he turns on the light—as I look up, blinking and squinting, one hand raised to shade my eyes from the glare, this half-filled bottle by my chair.

"Did I wake you, sir? You just wake up?"

"O, I don't know, Symes . . . ," adjusting my tilted beret.

"Or have you just arrived home?"

"No, I've been home for some time, Symes. . . .Well, you ready for a late evening Guinness?"

"No, not for me, sir."

"You're not much of a drinker, are you, Symes?"

"Not much, sir."

"No, I knew you weren't. Well, your loss is my gain, haha, half a crate to go!" Staring at the dead screen a moment longer before taking another fast pull on this bottle, then laughing a short laugh and leaning back a little more, my legs crossed, and removing my free hand from the pocket of my pants and giving my snowy, grizzled beard a piano-tuning scratch, a quick trill of the fingers. Looking over at him out of the corner of my eye and smiling, "So, here we *are*, Symes, just the *two* of us. Tell me, Hubert, what do you think of this *green jewel* in the sea, eh?"

"I mostly enjoy it, sir."

"You '*mostly* enjoy' it. Yes, well, and why the hell shouldn't you 'enjoy' it? It's given you everything it has, hasn't it? Depressing, bloody Ireland, all of it green emerald *crut!* Well, hell, it may be over now, so what does it matter? I may be leaving soon anyway."

"*Leaving*, sir? Where're you going?"

"O, I don't know . . . find myself another island, Staffa, Sark, the Alpine Passes, Singapore, *Bombay* maybe—always wanted to go to

Bombay—or build myself a submarine, one of those little one-man subs like the Japs used to use and cruise around the world, pop up anywhere."

"But *why*, sir?"

"Or maybe I'll go to Cairo, or Dakar, and become a sheik. Who knows, 'cause I've got this Egyptian friend of mine living there. Half-Egyptian, half-Irish, his parents met at Gallipoli during the First World War. But I don't really care about the where, the what, *or* the how, Symes, 'tis only the *why* that interests me. Do you understand, Symes? Just the *why*. . . . Every day we're given the opportunity, you see, of making someone happy and we flub it, *fuck* it up! We have to be reminded, by ourselves, about concern. Jaysus, Hubert, have something to *drink*, will ya, man?"

"But why are you leaving, sir?"

Another fast swallow of my stout, and I turn, blinking, to him with glazed eyes, staring at a point somewhere to the left of his chest. "Tell me, have you had many *women* in your life, Symes old thing?"

"Not many, sir."

"I see. But a *few?*"

"Yes, sir. Listen, is there something I could do—?"

"A *choice* few. And where was this? England, I assume, Chipping Norton? . . . But you don't like to talk about it, do you?"

"No, it's fine, sir, only—"

"No, I can see it *bothers* you, Symes."

"No, sir, only it may bother *you*."

"Bother *me?* Good *God*, nothing *bothers* me, Hubert! I just want to do my work, my art, my Laura and Ciara portraits—and now, I don't *know*. Though listen, if you don't want to *talk* about this—"

"No, if you'd like, sir."

"You're sure? I wouldn't want to step on any toes, a great deal of latitude there, Symes, a very great deal. You might regret it. No, no, we can do without the details. I understand. Wouldn't want to make you too uneasy, or press you. I know what these things are like, old man, feisty wives gone poof."

"You're not in very good spirits, are you, sir?"

"Fan*tas*tic spirits, Hubert, simply superb!" Uncapping another Guinness, belting it down, and drying my mouth on my sleeve. "But hell, there's no need to wait for things to happen, we have to *make* them happen, have to act *now*, Symes, this moment, no more mucking about before the bloody lights go out—And you're absolutely certain you wouldn't care for a cocktail, a last gargle before sleep—or what passes for sleep these days, up at all hours to pee or lie awake with panicky visions eating at my innards?"

"No thank you, sir."

"All right, whenever you're ready, Symes. But I was only offering a little friendly advice here, 'cause I do know about women, you don't have to tell me anything about women, not now, anyway—O Suffering Jaysus, I know all about them, the loss of them. But whatever happens, Symes, you're always welcome here—with or without a woman. And you're sure you won't have a last Guinness? Hell, you might as well, I paid for it, you know?" Chortling, chin bridled, laughing into my chest, as I reach for one of the few remaining bottles, then switch on the tube. "Ah, ad for Disney, Symes, Coming Attractions. Christ, will you look at the *size* of that cat! What's the name of this one, this particular show?"

"'Survival of the Animals,' sir."

"Yes, fan*tas*tic the way they move. Cheetahs. Jaysus, to be a cheetah—Good God, you'd be *holy!*—with their amazing sight. Well which do you identify with, Symes?"

"I don't have a preference, sir."

"You *don't?* But every conscious person in the world is identified with some member of the animal kingdom. I, of course, identify with the quickest, with those who *do* survive. But of all the animals, I suppose I feel most closely associated with the ibex."

"The ibex, sir? And why is that?"

"Why? Because of its courage, I suppose, its natural cunning. It knows how to get in and out of things very well, how to maintain its freedom. Here, have the last one, Symes, please!"

"No, it's yours, sir."

"Of course it's *mine!* And don't worry, I'll take it if you won't. I'm still aware of what *is* and *isn't* mine—O, the program's over. Have to wait till next week. They just lure you on, you know. That's the American Way. End up with 'The Adventures of Brer Rabbit' or that praying mantis, what's his name, Jiminy Cricket? 'Due to circumstances beyond our control, the previously scheduled program has been . . . *removed.*' Like the animal after the camera leaves him. Remember years ago, I did all those pencil sketches of Poldy, my great Samoyed beast. You know, of course, he saved my life?"

"Indeed I do, sir."

Tears suddenly coursing down my cheeks.

"Sir?"

Sniffling and swallowing hard, "But have you ever—ever seen any of those old sketches of mine?"

"No, sir, can't say that I have."

"Ah, well, then I'll have to *show* you some sometime. Poldy snuffling asleep, dreaming of Siberian wastes or pulling sleds across the frozen tundra. Later, perhaps, when this is over—"

"But it *is* over, sir."

"So it is, isn't it, more Coming Attractions. Or is that the program? Can't tell anymore. Well, Jaysus, Hubert, you really want to *see* my Poldy sketches, don't you now, those lovely doggie sketches? Yes, well most of them are packed away, probably never find them."

"Would you like me to help you look, sir?"

"—No, no, I'll go."

Getting up slowly and trudging, a bit wobbly, out of the den, and on toward the storeroom. A rattle of papers, unwrapped, boxes dropped, as I stumble about, rain still falling out there—and coming back, holding them in both of my hands.

"These are the only things I could find at the moment. Sure more are around, but they're all over the bloody castle." Handing him a sheaf of Poldy sketches in assorted poses. "These were done some time ago, his rather blithe period as a puppy, his first days in Ireland. The head of this one's not quite finished yet, needs a bit more work round the muzzle. See, here?"

"Yes, but these are truly brilliant, sir, if I may say so. And you've never shown them, tried to sell them?"

"These? No."

"Why not?"

"Well, all sorts of reasons," sitting down a bit unsteadily and picking up my bottle of Guinness again, "Too close to the core, I guess. And now I'd *never* sell them, don't *want* to sell them. Though here, Symes, I'll *give* you one—"

"No, sir, I couldn't—"

"But I insist, give you, my trusty retainer, a distinguished service gift. 'Cause you can't *buy* anything off me, nobody can *buy* me, I'm not *selling* anything anymore, not to anyone! You know what I mean, Symes? *Eff* it! *Up* it! Bugger off!"

"Yes, sir, but there's no point either in hiding these. You're not going to *give* them away."

". . . O I just might," tipping back my bottle of stout, "'specially if I lose another wife—*or* my bloody sight!"

"Sir, if I may, it might be a good idea to get away tomorrow for a while, get some air—"

"O I got my air today, Symes, *and* my rocks. King of the Bloody Rocks, haha!"

"Yes, but I shouldn't want you to crawl under one."

"Well, sometimes you *feel* like crawling under—"

"But there's always somebody *ahead* of you, sir."

"Right, Symes, quite right, exactly! Hell, I'll drink to that!" and swallowing the last dregs of the bitter brown foam of an almost cold Guinness.

"Sir, you might feel better if you went to bed, got some rest now."

"Indeed, Symes, indeed, knit up the ravell'd sleeve of care. Thank you, Symes . . . and thank you for listening, for being here." Feeling another wave of panic flooding over me—

"My pleasure, sir."

"And would you, could you turn off that light on your way out?"

"Of course, sir."

"Thank you, Symes. Good night."

"Good night, sir."

His footsteps heading up the stairs as I stand and begin pacing round my den—And I can't keep *living* like this—*can't live without painting!* Georgia O'Keeffe in her seventies finding a hole in the center of her vision, or Mary Cassatt, with her cataracts, stone blind the last twelve years of her life! And there's no *way* I could tolerate that! So now I'll take my old patron Sligo's advice, when, back in '67 and so desperately poor, I came begging at the door of that wonderful, white-haired and mustachioed Irish rhino of a man, the Viscount L.C. Sligo-Moeran, who told me, *"The best thing to do, Boyne, is die."*

"Die, sir?"

"Die, die, m'boy! Give them what they want! A living artist is worthless, but dead—Aha! Now there's the rub! Alive, m'boy, they consider you a hopeless dreamer, a member of the arrogant elite. But dead? Ah, dead, they'll claim you were a genius, a prophet who spoke with the Lord. Alive, you're a burden. Dead, you're the stuff that myth is made of. So I say die, Boyne, for your own good! The more horrible the means, the more grisly the demise, the more appalling the gore: the greater the legend! Die, and you will surely become an icon. Die, and your price will leap tenfold overnight! To death! Which will give you life eternal, bathe your name in glory, and fill your coffers with gold!"

"But I'm not dead, sir—"

"That can be corrected, m'boy!"

And shortly before I tried and failed, he took his own life with an ancient duelling pistol. And now *MY* time has come!—reeling round the room, Poldy and Symes sound asleep—just hop in my car and drive through this storm to the top of Stag's Leap, then speed off into the sea!

Eight

Gray rain insanely lashing my Jaguar sedan as I go splashing and swerving round my circular drive, the radio reporting these hazardous squalls thrashing all across Ireland and—

"Woof!"

O MOTHER OF CHRIST! "Poldy, what're you *DOING* back there?!"

"Woof!"

"Woof, my Irish *ARSE!* How'd you get *in* here? I know, don't ask! Well you're going home right *NOW!*"

Swinging a skidding and sliding U-turn—and dropping him off, shooing him into the vestibule, then drying my face with a beach towel from the loo . . . before flooring the Jag once more down the drive—

"Woof!"

"O by the crucified fuckin' JAYSUS!"—and screech to a shuddering halt, sighing and leaning my head on the steering wheel, my hands and stomach shaking—"Won't let me do it, eh, old doggie? Not in the cards tonight? Knew what I had up my sleeve, what I was planning? Then OK," and turning around again, "you win. Home to the castle—and maybe I'll take up sculpting, do a bust of you just by the feel of it—But you won't tell me how you got back in the Jag, right? No, I didn't think so."

Escorting my soaking Samoyed inside the main hall and toweling him down, with Symes holding his collar, then off to the pub in Rathnew, this raging storm abating.

Nine

Slow, slow, just take it slow—with my rotating head of Guinness—rain now reduced to a windy, sideways drizzle as I leave the pub behind and, swerving and sliding again, up my drive I go—

Stumbling out of the Jag, on through the vestibule and—*GOOD GOD!* Symes, by the foot of the stairs, lying trussed up in duct tape—and Poldy across the hall, as I fly to his side, with a gaping wound near his rib cage, gory lacerations exposing tissue and muscle, duct tape wound round his paws and muzzle.

"Easy, doggie, easy!" gingerly removing the tape—he whimpering, yelping in pain, trying to lick the wound—"Easy, boy," holding and stroking his head, then turning, "Symes, be right there," carefully untrussing my man, "What *happened?*" his rheumy eyes wincing and blinking.

"They robbed us, sir."

"Who?"

"Two men, knocked me down. Poldy attacked them, but they threw him against the wall, must've hit his head, then wrestled him to the ground and taped him up as well."

"But that wound—?"

"He was struck rather hard, sir."

"What were they after?"

"Your paintings, it would appear."

"Could you tell who they were?"

"No, both wore ski masks, long black macs, one slightly larger than the other, and neither talked."

"When did this occur?"

"Shortly after you'd left, sir, the third time."

Symes standing, still blinking and slowly finger-brushing his fiddle hair back in place as I return to Poldy, who struggles to his feet—but quickly sinks back down.

"Symes, get Dr. Gilroy in Greystones on the phone, emergency service, and tell them I'm on my way!" racing full-bore up to my studio: at least half a dozen paintings gone, maybe more—but they left the one of Laura, thank God—And what's this? I didn't paint it—Left one of their own? By mistake? Figure it out later. Now, galloping down the stairs, get Poldy to the vet posthaste!

Ten

Gilroy sewing him up, with the last, fading drizzle still falling, the sutures to be removed in ten days or less, and treating a head wound as well—as now the rehab begins, nursing him like a baby.

Though Poldy is so bloody lively, I have to dope him up, knock him out, with Ketamine and injectable Valium—which only slightly slows him down. And Flynn saying, "But drugs never worked fer you, either, did they, Boyne, me ould darlin'?"

"Not really. They gave me brilliant images in the mind but took away my *desire* to paint—Ah," and glancing around as the Garda's vast bulk darkens the entrance to the den, "time to talk to the Serious Crimes Unit."

No clues as yet. Six paintings and four drawings stolen, and the odd one left in their wake. The local sergeant asking if I have any ideas whose work it might be. Padraic's perhaps?

"No, not his style at all, far too amateurish. And he's still in Sing Sing last I heard, up in New York state."

"Could there be some sort of message, sir, in all of this?"

"Such as what, Superintendent?"

"Well, you broke into the Tate a while back and left your work. Now they break into your home and leave their work."

"Never thought of that, might very well be."

And for the rest of the day, Symes, Flynn, and I clean up after the storm, which killed at least seventeen people and injured dozens more across northern Europe and the British Isles, as those gale-force winds toppled trees and construction cranes and caused, says the TV, damage in the tens of millions.

And later, after I've talked to Tory in the States, assuring her I'm all right, Flynn forces me to drink a fruity concoction frothed in my Waring blender of blueberries, raspberries, rose hips, and chickweed, which his health guide highly recommends for the eyes.

And then it's time for Poldy's dinner, a gourmet selection that Flynn and I take great delight in ornately describing in restaurant critic's prose:

"A delectable hillock of chunky Alpo and Pedigree Chum sautéed in fragrant Worcestershire and barbeque sauces, and ringed with a Stonehenge of beef marrow bones."

Eleven

Poldy showing tentative signs of recovery, albeit with yelping residues of pain, as I hoist him, my canine Hell's Angel, cautiously aboard the Harley to sit behind me, his paws upon my shoulders, in that specially designed basket-seat, and we cruise on down to the beach.

He belching contentedly, then hopping off onto the sand, before lapping at the freshly ruffled surf. A pale slant of fleeting sun trying to peek through those bluemassing clouds—when suddenly his ears prick up, head snaps round, nose twitching—and he takes off, paws flung out, like a champion bloody greyhound—

"Poldy! Where on earth are you *going?*"

He bounding flat out toward those distant forms, looks like a woman, with a small white dog—

"*Poldy!*" jogging after, huffing and puffing, across the sand, still littered with the storm's flotsam and jetsam, and drawing closer, the dogs sniffing each other, vagina, butt, and bollocks, the woman smiling—

Lovely she is, Rubenesque with melonous breasts and rosy, wind-bussed cheeks, a full-lipped cupid's bow mouth, and long, auburn hair flowing down to her taut-high, exquisite arse, and clad in a tight black sweater, black jeans, black sneakers, and a silky green Book of Kells scarf cloaking her sloping shoulders—

"Poldy!" He now chasing the Spitz into the border bushes and swiftly mounting her—"*Poldy!*"—as I dart past the woman, "I'm sorry, really sorry—Poldy!—He's recuperating—*POLDY!*"

"No, it's all right. Let them be."

Stopping short, "It *is?*" turning, "You sure?"

"Of course, they're just doing what comes naturally. And Tara's past the age."

"Yes, well—You're American?"

"Canadian, actually."

"From where?"

"Well I was born in Vancouver. British Columbia."

"Ah yes, never been there, but I hear it's lovely. So what do you do in Vancouver?"

"Me?" She, with a twinkle to her graygreen eyes, still watching the furiously happy humping, "I'm a nymphomaniac." Tara and Poldy really going at it. "And my dog is, too."

"Right, and mine's well on the way to Satyrville. No, but really, what else do you do?"

"That's not enough?"

"No-no, that's fine."

"Well I'm also doing research over here on the sexual habits of the modern male."

"Is that so?" Poldy still pumping, eyes closed. "And what've you discovered?"

"O all sorts of fascinating things."

"Such as?"

"O, let's see, that contrary to popular opinion, black men are not the most well-endowed."

"Who are?"

"American Indians."

"And what else?"

"What else? Well, that the best lovers are not Italians but rather Jews."

"Jews is it now?"

"Indeed it 'tis. But tell me, sir, who are you?"

"Me?" grinning, "Well, I'm Tonto Goldstein."

Her glorious laugh, green eyes gleaming, "You knew the joke, didn't you?"

"Yes, and I'm Seamus Boyne. And that lusty rascal's Poldy."

"I'm Tiki Wines." Shaking my hand with a firm, warm grip.

"Tiki? As in Kon?"

"Wow, you're the first person who ever said that. No, I'm being feisty, sorry. It was just a nickname that stuck. My given name is Hilda."

"You don't look like a Hilda."

"Hilda Lydia, in fact."

"So how'd you get to Tiki?"

"I couldn't pronounce my mother's name, Trixie, as a child. It always came out Tiki. So they called me Tiki."

"I love it!"

"So do I. But actually I'm a movie producer."

"You're making a picture in Ireland?"

"A fil-um, as you say. At Ardmore, yes."

"What is it?"

"O some dumb comedy with Ronnie Corbett and a crazy cast of thousands. Thankfully, we're almost done."

"And so is my dog." Poldy slumping off, then sitting down and panting, as I gently kiss his nose, stroke his head, "It's OK, doggie, OK, you were great, bloody marvelous in fact—it's these nymphos you've gotta watch out for."

Tiki smiling and petting Tara, who comes wagging up beside her.

"Come on, Poldy." But he stays, doesn't move, still heavily panting, as Tiki leans close to his sutures.

"How was he hurt?"

"Long story, but I think I'll have to carry him home. And may I ring you, Tiki, see you again?"

"Well . . . I suppose so."

"You live in Rathnew?"

"No, I'm staying in Ashford."

"Ah, know it well. So tomorrow morning at—what time is it now?—say, 9, 9:30?"

"Fine. O wait, tomorrow, tomorrow? No, that's OK, we're shooting at night."

"Marvelous. Tiki, I thank you, my dog," lifting him high, "thanks you—even more than I, and I'll see you tomorrow at 9."

"I'll keep the whole day free."

Twelve

And next morning at 8, following another of Flynn's fruity "blindness shakes"—Symes having skillfully handled last night's media circus, limiting me to a single statement, and the press estimating the loss of my work at well over 12 million pounds, I furiously burst from the loo, tripping and nearly falling headlong over Poldy as I scamper for the ringing phone, "—Yes, hello?" and Symes leads my doggie toward his bubble bath.

"Ah, Boyne, there y'are!"

"Right, Flynn, and thanks to you, I never get off the throne! But tell me, what've you found?"

"Well I'm only after just arrivin' back meself, followin' an all-night recordin' session with those bloody Fourskins—whore's melts, the lot of 'em! But that was after I'd had a bit of a gargle with me Irish Mafia and Liam Coddle, who's just out of Portlaoise, and who still thinks cunnilingus is the Irish airline."

"Right, right. So?"

"So he'd heard about the burglary, he did, but, thus far, doesn't have a clue who did it. Still, he figures it to be a local job. The thieves usin' the storm fer a cover and not triggerin' yer infrared system by knockin' on the door. Or, says he, maybe 'twas the infamous tattooed Yakuza."

"Don't discount it, Flynn, 'cause did you know that art ranks behind only drugs and munitions in illicit international trade and is growing faster than any other form of larceny? The Garda said there are currently some 100,000 stolen works floating around the world and 90 percent of 'em'll never be found."

"Right, that's what I heard as well. But then why, I ask ya, leave their own work as a callin' card?"

"God only knows. But when I catch that bastard who beat up Poldy, no mercy, Flynn, I swear I'm gonna tear his bloody eyeballs out and stuff 'em down his gob!"

"And so ya will, so ya will. Well at least it's given ya a new lease on life."

"But a hell of a way to get it! That and your fruity, loony concoction—still got these bloody chickweed seeds stuck in my teeth!"

"And ya haven't had another episode either, have ya now?"

"No, but—"

"No-no, no buts, Boyne, that's the long and short of it, man—O hold on a tick—(I'm just on the phone, Conor!)"

"What's going on?"

"He says *he* may have some news. Hold on."

Pacing about the hall, hearing the bathwater running, and still thinking of sensual Tiki, meeting her at 9, first woman since Laura died—a nymphomaniac fil-um producer from Vancouver—who made my plasma race, heart flutter—with her blazing graygreen eyes—

"Boyne?"

"Still here, Flynn. And what'd Conor say?"

"O, just the Fourskins were on the telly. Anyway, as fer the burglary,

I'll check all me snouts (informants to you) and get me Irish Mafia on it straightaway."

Thirteen

Bewitching Tiki, clad today in a forest green jumper, black Canucks baseball cap worn backwards, and I strolling along the blustery shore with shafts of slanting sunlight pouring down, Poldy and Tara sniffing each other once more before scampering toward the sea. A blue rim of sea frilly with whitecaps washing over the rocks, and a wave of surf leaping high and crashing in. "Careful, doggies, careful."

"My God, Seamus, what a day!"

"Yes, usual swell, I'd say, rather choppy down there. Here, we can walk above the shale. Aren't you cold, Tiki? Want my windbreaker?"

"No, I love weather like this. It's like fall back home, those gusty Octobers."

"Right, well you might want to put it on later."

"What's over there, Seamus? Across the water?"

"Straight across would be Wales, think the town is Caernarvon, near Holyhead, Holyhead or Nefyn."

"And way down there? That mountain?"

"Christ, you can *see* that far?"

"Yes."

"Bray Head. And behind it, the town of Bray."

"It looks like a forehead."

Squinting, straining, "Does, doesn't it. It's best with the sun on it. Here, come on up, Tiki. We'll walk this way, along the marram grass."

"And what's down there?"

"Way down? Well that would be Wicklow. You can follow the railroad tracks past Stag's Leap into Wicklow town."

The two of us still strolling side by side—and so drawn to her voluptuous heat, glorious smile, and breezy redhaired brio.

"And this area, Seamus, is all part of Rathnew?"

"It 'tis. Though Rathnew actually runs inland a bit more. My home, Ballyduff, is an exception. But the whole coastline's changed, much of it's been washed away by fast-rising tides."

"And Ballyduff? What does that stand for?"

"Well, the homes, towns here all have names, usually for directional purposes. Wicklow, for example, means Viking's Meadow."

"And Ballyduff?"

"That's a hill somewhere in Donegal, I believe, where the original owner supposedly was born. It sounds more like a prize pig, though, doesn't it?"

"You're chock full of local lore, aren't you?"

"Better than nuts."

"What?"

"Chock Full O'Nuts. Bad joke, sorry, sorry."

"That's OK," she striding on, then glancing over her shoulder, a roseate blush to her Nordic cheeks, "I like you, Seamus Boyne."

"And I, you, Tiki Wines. Are you hungry?"

"That I am."

"Well, would you have time for lunch at me castle?"

"Sounds like a plan. Come on, Tara, Poldy."

The dogs panting across the sand, pink tongues lolling, paws dripping and studded with shimmering spindrift.

"So Wines was your married name?"

"Yes, spent time in Alberta, then Holland—"

"Holland? My first wife—no-no, second wife, Ciara, was Dutch—I married my first wife twice. She died five months ago."

"O I'm so sorry. Where in Holland, Seamus?"

"Delft, I believe. Yes, Delft. Been so long since I've thought of that. Ciara was Dutch-Irish actually."

"Like Audrey Hepburn."

"Is that so?"

"Yes, few of them around."

"But continue with Mr. Wines, Tiki."

"Well, I'm a widow as well. Of three, nearly four years now—but unlike you, not at all upset about it."

"How come?"

"It was a marriage made in Hell. My late husband—I do like saying that—my late husband, among other things, collected art, but awful art that I hated, so right after he died, I'd already filed, I stripped bare the walls and sold the lot at auction. Didn't care how much I lost, and now, won't even *look* at another painting!"

"Well I can show you some art, some you might even enjoy."

"By whom?"

"Me, of course."

"You're a painter?"

"No, I'm a plumber. Of course I'm a painter! You've really never heard of me?"

"Sorry, but like I told you, I avoid *all* art now like the plague."

"No, it's OK, I didn't mean to sound pompous or uppity, but in certain circles, they tell me, Boyne is still a small gem in the diadem of Ireland."

"O I'm sure."

"And you didn't hear about the burglary?"

"Burglary? No, I've been so busy with the fil-um. But, believe me, I'd love to see your stuff."

"My 'stuff'?"

"Oops! Another faux pas, eh? OK, OK, I'll shut up. Just lead on, McDuff, to Ballyduff, and the dogs and I will follow."

The three of them padding behind me, across the solitary dunes, and Tiki now removing her cap and shaking out her lustrous mane of auburn hair, offsetting her pale, lightly-freckled skin—and so wanting to slip my arms around her, but still uneasy, feeling fiercely guilty over Laura.

" 'I love all waste and solitary places; where we taste the pleasure of believing what we see is boundless, as we wish our souls to be.'"

"That's lovely. Did you write that, Seamus?"

"No, that was Shelley. I wrote 'Clouds billowing in surreal profusion like a school of blue whales in the brain of Billy Turner.' "

"Turner the painter?"

"Turner the painter. Joseph Mallord 'Billy' Turner, the finest painter who ever lived."

"Really? Well, at least we agree on that. I once used Turner as a footnote on a college essay I wrote about David Lean."

"Turner as a *footnote*? Which college was this?"

"University of British Columbia. And I also remember Mark Twain, who had little regard for Turner's work, comparing it to 'a tortoise-shell cat floundering in a plate of tomatoes.' But what did he know?"

"Not much about Turner, that's for damn sure. Poldy!" hurrying toward his barking as he bolts briskly into a hedgerow, Tara pausing to watch, "*Now* what's he found? You'd never know he'd been injured, would you?"

"No."

He emerging after a moment, his muzzle covered with dirt and leaves, and holding a Milky bar wrapper.

"Maybe I should've got myself a pet lobster instead."

"Why?"

"Like Gérard de Nerval, the nineteenth-century French writer, who dragged his lobster through Paris on a leash of blue ribbons. Called it the perfect pet, 'cause it knew the mysteries of the sea and never barked."

"You realize, Mr. Boyne, you're impressing the hell out of me. I had no idea you were so well-read, so verbal."

"Verbal? Good God, Tiki, I'm so bloody verbal, I can make a syllable wince or engorge a vowel into a tumescent howl!"

And broadly grinning, she now skipping like a ballerina gracefully on ahead, Tara nipping at her heels—and the more she skips, the more graceful she becomes—hardly daring to take my eyes off her, hoping my sight won't go again. Seagulls shrieking above through that eerie, ethereal light, heightened sheen of a "blue altered sky," as we all come up the tree-lined path—

"Wow!" Tiki stopping short as my Georgian castle rises into view.

"Wow?"

"Wow! What a place!"

"You sound just like my daughter."

"How old is she?"

"Tory's . . . let's see, Tory's twenty-five now."

"Does she live with you?"

"No, back in the States with her husband, Gene, and my grandson, Shay. You have any children, Tiki?"

"No, never wanted them with Mr. Wines, and now it may be too late. But we'll see."

"How old are you?"

"Forty-three. And you, Seamus?"

"Fifty-two."

"You look much younger."

"So do you."

"Compliments, sir, will get you everywhere."

Up the flowered drive and through the front door as the rain starts softly falling.

"And this is Symes. Symes, meet Tiki Wines."

"The pleasure is all mine."

"I like him already."

"And I, you, miss."

"Any calls?"

"The media, as usual. Superintendent Gillespie and Sergeant O'Day. Nothing to report. Will you be having lunch, sir?"

"We'll make it ourselves. And you can take the rest of the day off."

"Thank you, sir. That's awfully kind."

And Tiki and I decide on croque monsieur, grilled ham-and-cheese sandwiches, made with a nutty-sweet Emmenthal and Grey Poupon, and a '78 Bâtard-Montrachet. Followed by a leisurely tour of the castle as up to my studio we go, Poldy and Tara curled together below.

And Tiki, eyes wide, "Wow! . . . O wow *wee* wow!" closely examining what works of mine remain, "I've regained my faith in painting! Especially this one here. Is that your first wife?"

"Yes."

"She's absolutely lovely."

"Thank you."

Then telling Tiki about the burglary—holding off about my eyes, not the right time—as we move down the corridor and into my bedroom, vast tiled shower, and coming out. She pausing.

"Seamus?"

"Yes?"

"Could I ask you a favor?"

"Of course."

"Well, I've never kissed a man with a beard before—would you mind if I kissed you?"

"Not at all. Take your time."

Been a month of Sundays since someone new—as she smiles, gazes up, and gently takes my face in her hands—my heart hammering—to kiss my eyes, my cheeks, and, at last, sensuous and lingering, my lips within my whiskers. And I'm now rock-hard, my thumbs and fingertips grazing, kneading her sensitive nipples through her forest green jumper as she sighs, still passionately kissing, her fluttering tongue slipping slyly inside, and my hands cupping, stroking, gliding downward, unbuttoning as I go, tracing the lacy scallops that trim her bra and flicking the hook that holds it free, I let the jumper fall and surround her within the harbor of my arms, nosing into her scented, auburn hair and brushing it from her brow, her fingers caressing my wooly chest, squeezing my nipples erect, my cock straining hard against my shorts, against my pants, then against her massaging palm as I suckle her index finger, shuddering, bucking against her, about to explode, throbbing against her grip—and she trips, stumbling, losing her balance—and we go toppling onto my big brass bed.

"—You have such great hands, Tiki!"

"Thank you, I used to be a masseuse in my younger days."

"Really."

"That's how I put myself through college."

And still throbbing as I quickly shed my clothes—she her panties, a true redhead, luxuriant fleece—then reach beneath her silky cheeks, "Good God, Tiki, you've got an amazing arse!"

"Yours isn't so bad, either."

"No, I mean it, I could rub these forever."

"And I could let you."

Still teasing, licking along her lush curves, "And you know what else I like about you?"

"No. Well, mmm, yes."

"That's what else I like about you!"

"I know."

"Tiki, can I kiss you . . . here?"

"Yes."

"How 'bout here?"

"O yes," she trembling, "yes!" arching, pleading with her slick lips, "O please, Seamus, come inside me now!—*O God yes!* You're so *big* and—and there, right there—" as our limbs intertwine, pumping faster now, side to side, and raising her higher, "O please, Seamus, make me come, make me come, O please make me come!" she shuddering and writhing, her head tossing wildly, whimpering, then deeply sighing, "—Enough, that's enough. . . ."

"Enough?"

Her spasms subsiding—"Yes, O yes."

—as I keep on pumping, "Enough?"

"Yes."

"You sure?" Still pumping.

"O *no!* O don't stop, Seamus, please don't stop! O my God!'

"Enough?"

"Enough, enough."

Still pumping, "No more?"

"No more, no—O no, more, more!"

"You sure?"

"Yes, yes, just fuck me, fuck me harder—O dear God in heaven!"

"Done?"

"Done."

And slowly sliding out, "No more?"

"Yes, yes, no—O no, O please, please—"

"Please what?"

"—just once more—O I can't stop it, Seamus, love you inside me—God, you're driving me *crazy*, going to come again—O there, there, right there, right there—don't move—*O GOD,* right *THERE!!*"

She still quivering, the sweat glistening on her lightly freckled skin, then collapsing and snuggling, warmly cuddling in, "That never—wow!—that never happened before—multiple wows!—one right after the other! Well I told you I was a nymphomaniac. Did *you* come?"

"Not yet."

"Well, here," twisting round, "I can remedy that."

Both dogs sitting, smiling at the foot of the bed.

"*O JAYSUS, Tiki!*"

"What?"

"Can't *see!*"

"Tara and Poldy, were you watching all this time?"

"First they *rob* me blind, now you *fuck* me blind!"

"Seamus, what're you talking about?"

"*I can't SEE!*"

"At all?"

"*At all!*"

"O my God! Is there anything I can do, anything you can take?"

"No, just more blueberries and chickweed."

"Are you serious?"

"Who the hell knows…O there, there, it's coming back again," blinking, sniffing, and Poldy, now coming into focus, licking my rigid toes.

Fourteen

Finishing up my painting of Laura on this windy, overcast morning with a frenzy of background brushstrokes, using a smooth Rubens madder, a reddish-orange glaze—and, for me, the sight of paint finely applied has always been like food to the eyes of a famished man!—while making scores of lines in the air before I lower my brush to the canvas.

And so hoping my stolen paintings are found in one piece, after last night's call from agents John B. McPhee and Charles T. Spitzer, who oversee the F.B.I. National Stolen Art File, a computerized list of more than 4,000 stolen art works, informing me they're now on the case as well, since I do hold dual citizenship—and that certain thieves will cut up a painting and sell the parts separately: a hand here, a flower there, a face in another place. Or paint out backgrounds or key details so it can be resold on the open market as a different work by the same artist. Some of these bunglers even rip canvases off their support stretchers so they can roll them up. When Vermeer's *The Letter* was stolen in Brussels in '71, the thief not only rolled it up, they said, but ruined it by sitting on it in the back of a bloody taxi!

What the world's coming to with this booming art market, so that all I can do is rage on with the only weapons at my command—touching, retouching, repainting this glaze—yet living, too, in this great state of terror, fighting this black despair with my "fierce tears"—Dylan holding forth at the White Horse, his father blind at the very end in that loving villanelle about "Grave men, near death, who see with blinding sight/ Blind eyes could blaze like meteors and be gay" (gay in the old, true sense of that word). *And by the crucified fuckin' Jaysus, I will not, NOT go gentle now into that good night, but "rage, rage against the dying of the light"!!*

The phone *shrilly* ringing! O right, Symes still not back yet—as I rush past Moira Feeney and her country minions, here to scrub my castle clean, "Yes, hello?"

"So, my dear Seamus, how do you feel today after making crazy, wild, creative, totally exhausting, and multi-orgasmic love?"

"Tiki, listen—"

"Seamus, are you OK? How're your eyes? You sound—"

"—I don't think I can see you anymore."

"Really? O you mean—that's not a joke? . . . Wow! . . . Too close to your ex?"

"Well, yes, I guess so. O I don't know, my sight, Poldy, the burglary—too bloody much! Tiki, look—"

"No, it's all right, easy come, easy go."

"No, that's not what I meant. You're a marvelous girl, woman, wonderful lover—look, give me some time, will you?"

"How much time? I'm only here three more weeks."

"I'll ring you. I promise."

"And here I was going to ask you out to the studio, thought you might like—"

"I would. But please, let me ring you."

"No, I'll ring *you* on Friday."

"That'd be fine. And I'm sorry, Tiki, really."

Fifteen

"—Sir, sir, come quickly." Symes urgently shouting from below.

"*What?* What is it now?" as I go cantering out of my studio and down the curving stairs:

He sprawled on the gleaming hardwood floor, his back flat against the mahogany-paneled wall, "—Sir, would you kindly remove your oversexed beast from my knee!"

My dog humping away at a furious pace, "*Poldy,* get *off!*" and hardly batting an eye, "Poldy, *OFF!*" as I ease him aside, he panting, with a petulant glance, out the front door, and Symes, struggling to his feet, finger-brushes his hair back in place, "I am not accustomed, sir, to such amorous advances," then dusts off his gray, pinstripe, double-breasted suit as I head toward the kitchen—

"Sir, a word, if I might?"

Turning, "Certainly, Symes."

"Well, the other night you asked me about the women in my life—"

"O please, Symes, I didn't mean to pry, had far too much to drink."

"Not at all, sir."

"But you've never married, have you?"

"Never, sir. But there have been several amours."

"Amours, eh? Current?"

"Well, sir," he glancing at the open door.

"Do I know her, Symes?"

"Indeed you do, sir."

"Not Mrs. Wines?"

"*Sir!*"

"Sorry, sorry, forget that I said that."

"I shall, sir."

"Then who?"

Another sidelong glance, "In strictest confidence, sir?"

"Cross my heart."

". . . Moira Feeney."

"Our *char?*"

"Precisely, sir."

"How long's this been going on?"

"Three years, six months next Wednesday."

"Good God!"

"Yes, well, though in some circles I might be considered a woolly mammoth, in that regard—"

"Of course, Symes, I had no doubt whatsoever."

"Thank you, sir, that's extremely kind," and he slowly mounts the stairs.

Symes such a gem, a jewel among men, even at a spry and gallant sixty-three, his numerous virtues forever emerging, like not allowing me to venture forth till he's ironed any rumpled folding money of mine—the phone now ringing, and I pluck it up.

"Hello?"

"So, Boyne, are we still on fer today at Bewley's?"

"Indeed, Flynn, we are."

"Well then I'll just whip on some togs, keep the beef tea simmerin' on the hob, and sniff the bouquet of a freshly rolled spliff before leavin' ta meet ya fer a sip of café latté!"

"Fine, but I can't stay too long, 'cause I'm seeing this woman out at Ardmore."

"Which woman is this?"

"Canadian woman, but I'll tell you about her later. Any further news?"

"Well, me Mafia may've tracked 'em down."

"Who?"

"These two swinish brothers, Brian and Brendan Coffey. Word's out that they may've been hired to commit the crime, and were last seen in Fumbally's Lane, off Clanbrassil Street, but now may've fled to France."

"Hired by whom?"

"Might've been Padraic behind 'em, or Irish gangs here fer gunrunnin', fund-raisin' and the like. But more to the point, Boyne, how's yer sight?"

"Comes and goes, still mainlining your fruity, loony shakes every night—though I'm becoming addicted to rose hips now, I think—but no new episodes for the past few days."

"Ah, well that's grand news at least—and I'll see ya at Bewley's at the stroke of noon."

· · · · · ·

Toward the huge stone arch of Stephen's Green, under these rustling trees that overlap the road, as I go striding swiftly for my parked car, Tiki waiting—A shout! I glance about to where a cluster of children, rosepolished from all the summer showers, balance over the last damp fringe of those paths, daisies strewn across the grass, and on past the duck pond, a blizzard of gulls soaring, sunlight suddenly pouring down through quaint mazes in the wanton green, furry squirrels scurrying—Flynn hurrying off to a studio recording—and these little girls with giggle eyes munching away on their Milky bars. The Irish so love their sweets, crosses, and black-pointed shoes. Dolly Mixture, Liquorice Comforts, and Savoy Pastilles—And I can't *wait* to get my hands on Poldy's assailant, pummel the life out of that thieving bastard! Revenge still firing my rage like my morning's Tullamore Dew—

And as for Tiki Wines: too much too soon, have to go through the mourning process, can't say hello till you say good-bye, Irish Catholic guilt right up there with orthodox Jewish guilt, been a mere five months, though it seems like only yesterday—And she's not Laura, no, but nobody will be, either—and, to be fair, it took me the second time around to get close to her, growing together these last few years till the lymphoma overwhelmed. And anyway, Tiki would wear me out! I mean, Mother of Jaysus, it reminds me of Flynn's old line: "Me cock's so worn to the bone, it's currently on loan to the Smithsonian!" But who is she? And what does she really want? Not a groupie, that's for sure, never even heard of me. But she just appears on the beach, out of the sea, like Venus on the half shell—Botticelli's alive and well and living in Wicklow!

Sixteen

And Tiki's flaming auburn hair flowing down to her glossy arse, absolutely stunning now in those tight black slacks and a red tailored shirt as we move arm-in-arm through Ardmore Studio, meeting Ronnie Corbett and the cast, who keep fawning over me, then blinking in and out of one Sound Stage after another, past lavish sets for *Excalibur,* a TV series about leprechauns being filmed, through a fluttering eruption of pigeons, and into this cul-de-sac—she suddenly kissing me and grasping *my* arse in both of her hands—as I come up for air:

"Tiki, what am I going to *do* with you?"

"Enjoy me while you can! Tempest fugit," she leading me across a parking lot, "or whatever the phrase is that I used in my essay on David Lynch," the green Wicklow hills in the distance.

"I thought it was David Lean?"

"Sorry, I meant Lean. My mind's such a jumble today."

"Right, and I'm the Elephant Man! Tiki, come on, come clean, who *are* you, what's going on?"

"You *know* who I am."

"No, I know who you *told* me you are. And the more I think about things lately: the glinting lights on the beach, the burglary, leaving that painting, then meeting you by chance—"

"And mistaking Lynch for Lean? OK, I did it, I confess! I robbed you, seduced you, to gain entrance to your castle—"

"Look, you have to admit, it does seem mighty coincidental, I hardly know you—and you never heard of me but heard of Turner!"

"Sorr-ee! Art wasn't my major and I just happened to read this thing about Turner."

"And your husband just happened to conveniently die. How, by the by, *did* he die?"

"Stroke, on the eighteenth green, after missing a three-foot putt."

"And you got all his money?"

"Most of it. And now, having run through his, I'm after yours."

"Well, there is a lot going on here, you must admit, that doesn't quite—"

"Add up?"

"Right."

"Seamus, please believe me, I never heard of you—a major gap in my education, I do admit—but I had no idea who you were or where you lived, I was just out walking Tara—who goes and gets shtupped by your horny Samoyed. Really, I swear on *my* dog's life, this is true. And if anything, I'd like to help you, if I could, get your paintings back and find the asshole who beat up Poldy!"

"Yes, well, me, too, it's just with everything going on—"

"I know, I know—" both of us glancing now at the sky as a skein of geese go flapping by. "O and, Seamus, that reminds me, I meant to tell you—I looked this up the other day—and it's not a *school* of whales."

"It's not?"

"No, it's a *gam* of whales, g-a-m, and a school of *fish*."

"Ah, yes, you're right, absolutely right, I stand corrected, Tiki. And here I thought I knew all the animal collectives."

"Collectives?"

"Groups, pairs, aggregations."

"Like a pride of lions or a flock of sheep?"

"Precisely! But keep going. How many more can you name?"

"More? Well, let me see, a colony of ants, a covey of quail, a school of fish, said that, uh, a . . . let's see, a gam, a skein—What else? Bears, tigers? I can't think of any more. Your turn."

"A sleuth of bears—"

"Sleuth?"

"A husk of hares, a grist of bees, a drift of swine, and, my all-time favorite, an *exaltation* of larks!"

"Incredible, Seamus! You're just brimming with minutiae! I'm going to sign you up for *Jeopardy!* And besides, I've been meaning to tell you, you look positively smashing today in that Irish sweater and beret."

"Well, thank you, miss, that's very kind—"

"So, would you mind—?"

"Another favor?"

"Well, yes, in fact. Follow me."

"Where we going?"

"Shhh, you'll find out." Into this white office building.

"Tiki?"

Down the empty, carpeted corridors, "Just come on!"

And side by side through these two swinging doors—into a vacant bathroom, "But this is the Ladies—?"

"Nobody comes in here."

"What about your office?"

"It's always crowded, people coming and going—" and Tiki—no shoes under those stall doors—fervently kissing me again, then unzipping my fly and fondling my swollen shaft.

And after she releases me throbbing from her mouth, I drop to my knees, her black slacks and panties now accordioned at her feet, and her ruddy fleece and warm, convulsing loins beneath my licking, suckling lips, tip of my probing tongue—she twisting round, her hands flat against the tile as I stand and wedge myself deep inside, doggie-style, "O that's good, Seamus, *so* good, so big!"—then reach down to the pendulous heft of her melonous breasts, splaying my fingers and weighing their jiggling sway, she bending, stretching back, and—*Good Christ!*—gently squeezing, stroking my balls—and no one, not even Ciara, knew how to stroke and tease, cup and please a man like this—as I keep moaning and pumping—But why *me?* *Positively smashing*—and now, banner headlines: *Caught screwing in Ardmore's loo*—Tiki tightly pressing her silky cheeks flush against my thighs and, leaning forward, "Seamus, don't move!" starts riding my cock hard like a female jockey or winner of the Irish Derby!—footsteps approaching!—as I join her bucking thrusts, "O Mother of God, Tiki, I need—need much more room for the *size* of my passion!"—and we come gasping and groaning together—before swiftly scrambling to button and zip, "hide behind that door, I'll handle this," wedging my foot against the left corner, a woman pushing to get inside.

"Hello? Is someone in there?"

"Yea, I'm afraid the door's stuck, be just a minute." And whispering to Tiki, "(I'll let her in *here,* then you dash out *there!*)"

"But why are you, a man, in there?"

"To repair the door." Signaling to Tiki, "(Ready?)"

"(Ready.)"

"Ah, there we go."

And in comes Miss Marple, the door swinging back, blocking her view of Tiki, who goes dashing out—with me right behind her—and quickly down the hall, around this corner, she giggling, leaning against me, the wall.

"Are you all right, Seamus? I didn't hurt you, did I, by pulling away so fast?"

"Not a chance. 'Tis a veritable caber!"

"I know, and you're the world sexiest Irishman!"

Seventeen

Sitting alone this morning in my skylit studio, Tiki still asleep, sipping a tall glass of ice water with its slice of lime (reduced as I am now to hailstone cocktails!), listening to Bach's sublime *Air* from his Orchestral Suite No. 3, brilliantly played by Marriner and the Academy of St. Martin-in-the-Fields, and closely examining one more time this painting that was left behind the night of the burglary and Poldy-bashing. Cobalt green and cadmium yellow, and a small triangle of pewter sky. Good brushwork here for these trees—at least it's not a Keene or a velvet Elvis—but withholding the bold stroke or slashing display of color. And this is—Yes, Stephen's Green, it seems. Wanting my opinion, my expertise? Well why else leave it? Not like dropping a calling card or a cufflink, you know—as I chew this thin slice of lime down to the rind. And maybe I should advertise in the *Irish Times,* praise his work, offer to meet and discuss it with him, so as to flush him from his lair or beard the lion in his Dublin den.

And pausing before my portrait of Laura again, now finally complete. Though what'd Valéry once say, "An artist never really finishes his work; he merely abandons it." And I *can't* stop now, however terrified I may be by my blindness fears, just keep raging against the dying of the light and start in painting my second wife!

Ah, Ciara, my Dutch-Irish sweet, long-dead darlin', you were even lovelier than I'd ever imagined when first I saw you in the summer of '67! A nymph in the flesh! Wondrous and golden like Leda and the Swan, Deirdre of the Sorrows—and Good God, now here I am, totally bald and mostly snowy-bearded, painting you again, never going to *stop* painting you again! Paint you *forever* in the nude, like the *last* time I saw you, with your rosy arse in the air and a host of shamrocks laced through your hair, so you'll never die, will always stay alive—before you went waltzing off without me to the Douglas Hyde Gallery to be blown to bits by an IRA bomb meant for Louis Mountbatten—who never *did* arrive!

Applying another shiny coat to this mile-high canvas of you in the shower, the creamy sheen of your silken skin and those keen bluestone eyes with their flaxen lashes—But the noose of fame kept crowding us in on that dark March evening a decade ago, with me absolutely refusing to attend that Douglas Hyde show, couldn't stand another bloody moment of fame and fawning—but you said no, someone had to be there to represent us, so—"*O HOLY MOTHER OF CHRIST!*"—tears now welling and clouding my sight—

"Seamus, what on earth are you shouting about?"

"—What? Shouting? O, Tiki," quickly drying my eyes, "you're up, didn't even hear you come in."

"*Now* who are you painting?"

"Uh, Ciara, my second wife."

"I see," and smirking, she turns sharply on her heel, "Well I'm already late to the studio," and I hear her canter down the stairs, Poldy and Tara barking, as I take another lengthy sip of this tall glass of ice water . . . then continue painting, my hand still shaking—And the

London Times calling those early Ciara portraits of mine, "some of the most important works painted by an artist in the present century," and Kenneth Clark echoing my father, Tim, that I'd surpassed Degas as a draftsman and Vermeer as a—

O Jaysus, Ciara, such a luminous tumult you were! What a wondrous woman! Marvelous lover! And what a desolating, soul-shattering demise! as I bloody well cried myself dry for three days straight—as long as I did for Laura, Lennon, and JFK—then lay prostrate in my unmade, rumpled bed, all my defenses demolished and strewn, a deep, searing wound, before I began walking alone for hours on end along the Wicklow shore from sunrise to sunset while talking out loud to you.

And I never would've survived without Poldy by my side. He saved my life, he damn well did, my most favorite doggie, bless his precious Hell's Angel's heart! as I keep blinking lovingly back at Ciara toweling herself off from the shower on this seven-foot-high canvas, thirteen-meters long, and making her skin, mmmm, like strawberry shortcake, pink and beautifully smooth. My own growing slack over this armature of bone. Though still retaining most of my strength throughout an outrageous half-century of living. Ciara once saying, "Seamus, your hands are the strongest I've ever seen, twist open ketchup bottles, unscrew lugnuts, throttle chickens, hogs, and sloats!" But not nearly as strong as Tiki's, a former masseuse, who never loses when we arm wrestle. And how do I get back in her good graces? She jealous of me painting Ciara—Ah, I know, got just the thing, organize one of my elegant surprises!

Eighteen

Sniffling Tiki sitting up in my bed, three pillows propped behind her lustrous head of curly auburn hair, and reading that *Time* cover story about Alzheimer's Disease (which, of course, I keep assuming that I'll soon receive). And she still so lovely and Rubenesque, with her wind-bussed cheeks and cupid's bow grin as she frowns, sighs, and casts me a sidelong scowl with those blazing graygreen eyes.

"What, Tiki?"

"Nothing," lowering her lids.

"Are you really jealous of Ciara?"

"Well, why shouldn't I be?"

" 'Cause she died ten years ago."

"So?"

" 'So?' What the hell does 'so' mean?"

" 'So' means—just means 'so'. Why, was she *that* good in bed?"

"Who?"

"Mother Teresa!"

"Look, the point is, OK, she *was* rather passionate, but we were only together for three and a half years, and, hell, you're different—"

"Different how?"

"Ah, Tiki, come on, *enough* of this now—"

"No, tell me. I'd like to know."

"Look, you have your specialties, she had hers."

"Such as?"

"Hey, I'm not going to go into graphic detail, that's a definite no-win situation. The fact of the matter is—"

"Tell me her specialties."

"You really want to know, don't you?" She nodding, still sniffling. "Well, let's see . . . well, she was very good at sixty-nine, OK?"

"And I'm *not*?"

"Didn't say that, never said that—O Jaysus, Tiki, *enough* with this now!"

"And *my* specialties?"

"Yours? Well . . . for one thing, your fingers are far more imaginative, love how you caress my bollocks, for no one, not even Ciara knew how to stroke and tease, cup and please—"

"She never did that?"

"Not like you."

"Go on."

"No-no, now you, Tiki. Tell me what *I* do that *you* like."

"Well, all right, fair is fair, I suppose. Let's see, I like . . . O, I like how you take your time, and I like your 'huge extremities,' as your first wife, Laura, called them, like when you're hard when I awake, or when you come up from between my legs and I taste myself on your lips. But what else do *you* like, besides me playing with your balls, your bollocks?"

"Well I liked what happened in the Ardmore loo."

Tiki smiling and sniffling again, then sharply breathing in and closing her eyes—before suddenly exploding with a head-blasting sneeze! "Sorry," and sliding naked out of bed, hurrying toward the bathroom, her auburn hair bouncing softly down her back, above her roundy arse.

"You OK?"

"Fine. Just my allergies."

"Right. Well, I'll tell you one thing, my dear, even at forty-three, your delectable, roundy arse is even better than hers."

"You know, Seamus, what you are?"

"Don't say it!"

"You're a bloody pygophile!"

"O is that what I am? Always wondered. And pray tell what is that when he's at home?"

"Someone who savors buttocks."

"Well 'looked at simply as form, as relationship of plane and protuberance,' as Kenneth Clark significantly said, 'it might be argued that the back view of the female body is far more satisfactory than the front,' especially a nice, roundy arse." Tiki now returning, after taking a Sinutab, and slipping gracefully under the covers once more. "Though I still can't believe you were awkward as a girl."

"Well believe it, 'cause I definitely was, unattractive, overweight, with facial skin that had to be peeled. O that's the truth, and it stays with you all your life. And no matter how much you change outwardly, you *remain* that ungainly sixteen-year-old longing to be glamorous and sexy and self-assured."

"Well you'll always be that for me."

"Thank you, that's very sweet."

"And so is this," nuzzling down her buxom body and lustily gnawing these sleek, melonous swells.

"Such a pygophile y'are."

"Just an old gluteal fool!"

Nineteen

And watching delightful Tiki on this bright and glinty Irish morning deftly pick and choose this food and that for her usual homemade sandwich. Arranging like a decorator with shapely fin-ger-pluckings all those red pepper strips in parallel rows along the piled-high turkey breasts, lettuce duly centered, before dropping the top slice of Russian rye, slathered with Grey Poupon Country Dijon, then licking her thumbs, her lips, and taking a trencher-man's hearty bite.

O I could watch her forever, I could, I could! but I'm late as it is, so I must take my "dotage cocktail," all these bloody pills—Diovan, for high blood pressure, statins, for high cholesterol, shark carti-lage, Bayer aspirin, and a Ginseng chaser to boot—before I leave for Dublin and the Garda who are waiting.

Ah, 'tis so lovely growin' old!

Age may be fine for some elephants and whales, those who survive till ninety-nine, but it seems all *I* keep doing these days, besides going blind, is taking forever to come, with less and less sperm emerging, forever to heal, my mouth filled with implants, arse with flaming hemorrhoids, and a prostate that takes me forever to pee, or frequently three times a night, as well as occa-sional vertigo, dizzy spells when I rise too abruptly from the throne, and unwanted hair sprouting from my ears and nose, though not a single strand ever appearing on my polished dome! So what kind of woman, I ask, falls for a blind, suicidal painter?

Twenty

And later, lurching back through my thick front door, my stomach still rather queasy as I pass my man on the way to my den—what am I doing in here?—and slowly upstairs to my studio—

"Suffering Jaysus, Symes, sometimes I feel as though my brain were a sputtering flame! Can't remember why I walked into a room or just stand there like a pummeled cow, on the bloody road to Alzheimer's!"

"Then I'll leave you alone, sir."

"Mrs. Wines isn't back yet?"

"No, sir, still, I assume, over at Ardmore."

"Thank you, Symes, and, please, hold all my calls for now."

And forcing myself to sift through these voluminous police reports, following that two-hour meeting with Supt. Gillespie and Sgt. O'Day. And here are the slim, slackjawed Coffey brothers, with their long list of arrests, terrorizing in the south as well as in Derry, and still at large; last seen in August of '79 after the bombing death of Lord Louis Mountbatten. And finally, this latest photo and report (a possible connection) about my doppelgänger, half-brother, Padraic Shea, still safely imprisoned in Sing Sing, and looking the spitting image of me at thirty-six, with his bald dome, graying beard, and piercing blue-black gaze—as I shove these files aside and reach for my splattered palette, add some stale beer, just like Billy, to my paints—for hell, one good Turner deserves another! And plunge headlong back into the past to preserve Laura and Ciara on canvas and avoid my suicide—

The phone's single, piercing ring! "I've got it, Symes," and I fumble the receiver up to my ear:

"Yes, hello?"

"Dad?"

"Ah, *Tory,* my lass, always delighted to hear your voice!"

"You all right?"

"Why do you ask?"

" 'Cause I been trying to get you, kept ringing and ringing—"

"Well I told Symes to hold all my calls, and, anyway, I usually keep the phone in the oven, since it rarely serves a useful function."

"You ever forget it was in there?"

"Only once. Slapped in the odd roast and burned the bloody thing to a crisp."

"Right, well a Sgt. O'Day just called here from Dublin."

"O did he now? About the recent burglary?"

"Just seeing what I know. So what's happening with that?"

"Got our own investigation going. But how're you, Tory?"

"Fine, busy."

"And your hubby?"

"O, Gene's still writing, teaching summer school, with all his adoring co-eds."

"And your fairhaired, obstreperous son?"

"Shay's still a joy—no terrible twos for him. And Stony Brook's hot and sticky. But please, Dad, let me know—"

"O absolutely. Though, listen, I have to go."

"Go where?"

"To organize a surprise."

"Surprise for who?"

"Well it wouldn't be a surprise, would it now, if I told you?"

"Guess not. Anyhow, love you, Dad."

"Love you, too, Tory."

"And be careful. Promise? I don't want to lose you."

"I promise. God bless."

Twenty-one

"Seamus, where on earth are we going?"

"You'll see, Tiki, you'll see."

"But what shall I wear?"

"Your finest, your favorite—that frock! Like 'native woodnotes wild.'"

"Yes, Professor Higgins, but you really want me to wear this out to dinner?"

"Definitely! Love you in that, your green shamrock A-line dress, regal and elegant in strapless attire!"

"But I feel like I'm back in the fifties, when everything had to match, shoes and purse, gloves and hat, lipstick and fingernail polish, and underwear as well."

"Then why don't you wear those electric red panties under that sheer silk suit you wore the other night and we'll scandalize the local gentry?"

"Never you mind. And you won't tell me where we're going or why?"

"No, not yet. Symes?"

"Sir?"

"Bring the Jaguar round."

"Immediately?"

"Give us twenty minutes."

"I'll need thirty, Seamus, at least."

• • • • • •

Symes speeding south in the wine-colored Jag and along these winding, leafy lanes, with me in my beret, green bow tie, and blue windowpane-plaid suit, as I knot this blindfold firmly round Tiki's head.

"Seamus, what the devil are you *up* to?"

"No damn good, as usual."

And arriving in short order at the appointed border at 9:35 on a dark and moonless night, then down this gravel path, past those hoary sand dunes spiked with grass, the hoot of a cargo ship on the slate-gray sea, and the long vowels of wind through the slenderly swaying trees.

"Can I take this damn thing off yet?"

"In a moment, my dear, in a moment."

"Smells like hawthorn or fuchsia—"

"Now we're here!"

Tiki removing the blindfold and blinking, "Seamus, why are we on a golf course?"

"Because instead of crystal or china to celebrate, I decided on alfresco."

"Celebrate what?"

"Our one week together."

That trio of Viennese fiddlers, like a scene out of a Billy Wilder film, striking up as we exit the car and tread lightly onto the slightly damp kidney-shaped green, past the flapping flagstick, where a table is set with a golden candelabrum, Waterford and Belleek, and I hold out Tiki's padded chair. "Happy anniversary, my dear."

"Seamus, you are truly unique!"

The trio now fiddling madly away as Symes fills our glasses with a piquant Chardonnay, and I raise my voice of rusty thunder, to combat the wind and sea, "Here's a wild rose from a wild man," when he returns with a silver salver.

"O thank you, Seamus, it's lovely."

"Wine and garlands for your kindness and Canadian passion."

The trio now launching headlong into "Humoresque."

"Victor Hugo once said, 'Forty is the old age of youth.' "

"And fifty?" she brushing a stray hair back from her brow.

" 'The youth of old age.' "

"That's very good. And have you had many women up here?"

"O Jaysus," broadly grinning and trilling my snowy, grizzled beard, "acres of female pulchritude done to a turn in the Irish sun!"

"Yes, well I quite believe it."

"Spilt my seed and fathered children hither and yon. Well you know what my old friend Augustus John used to say?"

"No, but I'm sure in a moment I will," and taking another sip of her Chardonnay and looking off down the throat of a dark and narrow fairway.

"That when he walked along the Kings Road, he patted all the children's heads in case one of them was his own."

"And Laura or Ciara?" Another foghorn lowing far out at sea.

"Never brought them here."

Symes now turning from that metal folding table, holding several chafing dishes, and serving us an appetizer of grilled salmon steaks sizzling in hazelnut butter.

Then rising a few moments later, I bow from the waist and extend a courtly hand, "Tiki, may I kindly have this dance?" And she joins me for a spirited Strauss waltz. "Twirl you and whirl you like Rogers and Astaire—who, when asked how he danced, replied, 'I just put my feet in the air and move them around.' "

Twenty-two

And the following morning, blissfully grateful for her nightly loving and our terpsichore, I'm serving her favorite breakfast in bed of shirred eggs with Swiss cheese, ham, and scones with raspberry jam—while outside, that hazy flame of sun through the latticed panes is already so ox-roasting hot that even the Swiss cheese is sweating profusely—as stepping over Poldy, I stumble, trip—"*O MOTHER OF CHRIST!*"—and nearly fall.

"Seamus, you've lost your sight again?"

"—Yes, *goddamn it!!*"

"Here, take my hand and sit down on the bed. Dogs, out, out!"

"Happening much faster now, far more often—"

"Well then I'm going to run you a bath."

My sight gradually, partially returning. "O, so you want to get in my pants?"

"No—"

"You want me to get in *your* pants?"

"Seamus—"

"You want to wear the pants?"

"Look, enough with your pants already!"

"Tiki, I was only trying to lighten the mood."

"You're *always* trying to lighten the mood. And this isn't funny! Do you have any oils, bath oils?"

"Ask Symes. He has a whole cache in the pantry."

"Brilliant!"

And she goes pattering down, returning shortly to run me a bath in my huge Victorian tub with its brass claw feet, then gently guides, lowers me in, adds ten drops of jasmine, a tablespoon of sesame, and a mixture of milk and honey to this soothing, steamy blend.

"How're your eyes now, Seamus?"

"Still a bit blurry."

She sitting on that bath stool, "So how long can you—?"

"One more attack, and I'll see Dr. Hafiz. But anyone ever tell you, Tiki, what a wonder you are?"

"Just a Hollywood agent long ago."

Sinking lower as my eyes keep clearing, "Tell me about that," and blowing bubbles from below.

"What do you want to know?"

"How'd you get into show biz?"

"Well, briefly, I'd just come out of a totally dysfunctional affair with a stuntman, was very, very vulnerable, and I met this seemingly settled export-importer by the name of Myron Wines, who treated me like a princess for four months, and then I hardly ever saw him again, while he was jet-setting to and fro."

"Were you faithful?"

"In actual fact, I was, believe it or not."

"Why's that?"

"Because I surprise even myself now. Though *he* wasn't, not bloody likely! And nothing drives me crazier. But as I told you, I was planning to leave him, when he died."

"Have you any brothers or sisters?"

"One older brother, who plays hockey for the Vancouver Canucks. Anyway, fil-ums came about as a lark, did some bit parts, invested in one or two Canadian movies, and *voila,* now I'm a full-fledged producer. More hot water?"

"No, it's perfect," sighing and staring deep into her eyes, "Tiki?"

"What?"

"I'm getting an Irish toothache."

"Can I get you anything?"

"No-no," smiling, "that's British slang for an erection," which bursts through the surface like a shiny circumcised missile.

"Must be the milk and honey."

"So come on in."

"No, I've got to get going." She standing. "You ready to come out?"

"Not quite yet." And leaning back, my arms along the sides of the tub, "Listen, Tiki, I've been thinking."

"Yes?"

"Don't go back to Vancouver."

"And do what?"

"Stay here with me."

"Seamus, how can I now? I have to cut this picture. Maybe in the fall."

"But I may be blind by then!"

"I know, I know—and I don't want to leave you now, especially if you have this operation."

"Then don't."

"It's not that simple."

"Why not? There's another man? Wines is still alive?"

"No, it's just, O just some things to tidy up, finally put aside."

"Well keep me posted."

"Believe me, you'll be the first to know."

"And what else are you up to?"

"Up to my ears with you! Anyway, Seamus, I have to go. I'll call you from the studio."

And now what to do? Pray again to St. Raphael to save me, see me through? as Poldy, his plume tail swishing, comes trotting up to the tub, and I stroke his snowy ruff, "So what've we gotten ourselves into, old doggie?" as he keeps on nuzzling in, his cold nose urging more.

Twenty-three

And the phone keeps ringing off the hook for the next few days as edgy Tiki (over my Ciara painting?) leaves early for Ardmore in her scarlet Targa, and I hustle up to my skylit studio and this seductive Ciara portrait: She drawing me back like a siren day after day to her golden, nymph-like image, whenever Tiki's away. Then later, placing on this CD of James Galway playing Bach's Concerto for Flute and Strings, I pause for a needed break and sink down with a ragged sigh into my rickety cushioned chair.

Far too old for all of this, Poldy beating, paintings stolen (like losing children), and now Garda protection to boot from Detective-Sergeant Flato, a froggy little man, here on increased patrol ("Flato, you say? You wouldn't happen to have a relative over in Boston?" "I do. A cousin, who drives a cab." "He gave me a ride some years ago." "Is that a fact?")—as bloodhound Symes appears at the door.

"Mr. Flynn is on the line, sir, returning your call."

"Thank you, Symes. O, and did Mrs. Wines say when she'd be back?"

"No, sir. But she was followed again by that Flato man."

"O good, I'm glad."

"Yes, well, if I may say, sir, and this in no way casts aspersions on his competence, of course, but the detective does give off a rather peculiar odor."

Grinning, "Yes, I know, Symes, a certain underarm Beaujolais tang."

"Droll, sir, most droll."

And picking up the phone as he leaves: "Flynn, any news?"

"News? Ah, well, Boyne, me ould flower, let's see, I got paralytically drunk today followin' a liquid lunch and commenced singin' lewd roundelays to a most appreciative group."

"No, from your Irish Mafia!"

"Ah, right, right. Well, while you've been there ridin' the baloney pony, the Coffeys, in actual fact, have fled to Paris, with yer work supposedly stuffed in a pair of golf bags."

"Mother of Jaysus!"

And I continue painting Ciara's splendid body with my beery palette and, later, such wanton desire that I'd so love to run my tongue between her girlish cheeks, taste her heat, and inhale the fragrance of her wet sex as she pleads for penetration!

And stepping back now from this shimmering canvas as I capture for my soon-to-be-stone-blind eyes the silken sun of her golden hair (scraping away these darker flecks) while, on her toes and fresh from her shower, she holds aloft that fluffy towel. My brush smearing these scumbled highlights along her lush, buttermilk rump, too much strawberry pink, should be softer, gentler, so I'll try the palette knife—No, not quite. What it needs, I believe, is a quick lick of my tongue—

"Seamus, what on earth are you *doing?*"

And whirling into her blazing graygreen eyes, "Ah, well, just a touch-up, Tiki," as she comes up behind me.

"With your *tongue?*"

" 'Tis only beer, some stale Newcastle Brown."

"O you *are* impossible!" she striding back into the hall. "And that's *it!*"

"What's it? What're you talking about, what're you doing?"

"What I should've done days ago!"

"Which is?"

"Leave!"

"Tiki, come on, it's only a painting!" following her into the bedroom, "Look, I've always said I want people to stand *close* to my paintings—Rothko's preferred distance was eighteen inches—so they can *feel* the color, *feel* the texture as a physical sensation, even break down and *cry* when they confront it."

"As well as lick her butt?" She hastily grabbing her few clothes out of the closet and tossing them on the bed.

"Tiki, trust me, I'm not *that* kind of pervert!"

"O of course not, Seamus—and I'm going to have the world's smallest fiddle play you the world's saddest tune!"

"Bet you can't say that in Irish."

"Like hell I can't. *FUCK OFF!* You never did get over her, did you?"

"No, Tiki, listen—"

And I try to turn her around—but she twists my hand hard till I give.

Twenty-four

Calling Ardmore and her Ashford flat over and over—But she doesn't, won't answer the bloody phone! Or maybe she's gone back to the States or home to Vancouver—as I keep marching anxiously round my castle—with Flato still keeping an eye on her. 'Cause I'm sure she'll be back soon (*has* to be back soon), so I'll just finish painting Ciara and fervently pray I don't lose my sight even sooner.

Twenty-five

The following morning, I awake under a tumbling smother of pillows with my throbbing pate and, stumbling into the bathroom—"*Suffering JAYSUS!*"—nearly jump out of my skin as I stare into Padraic's aging face staring back from this three-way mirror!

And the phone shrilly ringing! Please be Tiki—

"Have ya heard, Boyne?" No, just Flynn again.

"Heard what?"

"Their plane crashed, was headed fer New York."

"What happened?"

"Well, they think a flock of birds, which'd been causin' problems at De Gaulle fer years, flew into the 747's wings, and it barely got into the air, strainin' to gain altitude, before it slammed into the ground and exploded."

"And the golf bags?"

"Lost with the Coffey brothers. . . . Boyne? Boyne, ya still there? . . . I'm truly sorry, old friend. O, and one more thing, Brian Coffey turns out was an aspirin' artist who once studied with dear old Padraic and apparently left his work fer you to admire."

My nerves now so bloody raw!—'cause an hour later, Flato (whose last day this is) informs me that Tiki emphatically told him I should *never* call her anymore. The temperature out there soaring, and Symes leaving at four on a well-deserved holiday in Chipping Norton with Moira Feeney—"Sir, you're certain you're all right?" Nodding and glancing away. "Well, call me if you should need me."

And the heat wave finally breaking as this gusty afternoon shower comes spooling and swirling down, oaks and evergreens swaying and crazily shaking, and I drop Symes and his lady off at the airport, then go wheeling back to Rathnew, in desperate need of a dark and foamy jar of Newcastle Brown to calm my nerves, slake my raging thirst.

And splashing up my foggy castle drive, swiftly on inside, I hurry up to my studio with Poldy behind, the air conditioners all roaring away full blast—and come to a screeching halt before my completed Ciara portrait—

But *ENOUGH* of Ciara now! Black despair filling me up, everything slipping away, my sight, Tiki, and aging life—so I'll do one more, one last painting, and make *TIKI* the *center* of a triptych! 'Cause I've lost two wives already—and now a possible third! as I begin furiously sketching and painting her huge portrait: switching from Cadmium Lemon and Winsor Yellow for Ciara's golden hair to Venetian Red and Burnt Sienna for Tiki's lustrous mane. And yes, yes, I'll paint her as when I first saw her on the Rathnew beach below, a majestic, towering, Rubenesque portrait, with her melonous breasts and wind-bussed cheeks, full-lipped grin and flaming auburn hair, and wearing that tight black sweater, black jeans, black sneakers, and the silky green Book of Kells scarf I adore, beside the surging steeds of a whitemaned Irish Sea. . . .

Nearly finished, *GOT* to finish, one last brushstroke before my eyes fail—*O SUFFERING CHRIST!!*

And I drop to my knees, blindly flinging my palette aside! Lost her, and now, like Dylan said, my "blinding sight," episodes far longer, much closer together—now blind, *BLIND FOR LIFE!*

And finally sitting up, feeling, fumbling my way to my rickety cushioned chair—Know what I have to do—and clumsily down these curving stairs to grope and slip on my orange, hooded slicker—*O JAYSUS!* That clap of house-rattling thunder!—*"POLDY!"* and, kneeling before him, kiss and hug my precious doggie one last time, he lovingly licking my whiskers and nose—then, standing and swaying, close the front door and, teary-eyed, step sightlessly out into the dusk's showery bluster and stumbling, lurching down the sloping garden paths, know the route by heart, inhaling briny whiffs of Wicklow air, by my boxwood maze, past marram and scurvy grass, and—*ah!* tripping, tottering onto the silvery shale, blowing fans of sand, around Broad Lough and along The Murrough's strip of land, whitecaps crashing, seething in, soon be in the teeth of a raging storm, dizzily slogging across the dunes, crushing crackling wrack and shells—and, *Christ,* panting and nearly pitching forward, my hands clasping at air—and hearing Sligo's distant voice in my mind: "Die, Boyne, and you will surely become an icon, give you life eternal, bathe your name in glory"—joining him and Rothko, or plunging in like Virginia Woolf with rocks stuffed in her pockets—

More earsplitting thunder as this shower keeps slashing and hissing into my face, imagine a savage sky growing surreal, like El Greco's *View of Toledo,* stormy cauldron of the Irish Sea far below Stag's Leap—my snowy, grizzled beard wildly lashing in this breeze—like old Lear on the heath—as I go staggering farther out along the high, wide spit of this deserted beach—

"*SEAMUS!*"

Heart leaping, spinning about—my eyes fluttering—and abruptly clearing, blurring, regaining my sight—as I keep squinting left, blinking right—

"Here! Up *here!*"

"Tiki?" Atop Stag's Leap! "What—What're *you* doing here?"

"I missed you, *really* missed you—"

"But how—Jaysus, how'd you know?"

"Saw your car at home and searched around—But hurry, get off that spit! The water's rising fast!"

Good God, the tide behind me now halfway up the bluff! And I'm marooned out here! Tiki frantically waving, "Come *on!*" as I stare, keep staring, start—stop—then go sloshing, splashing across the tidal pools toward those steep wooden stairs—broken below, never hold me, nearly knee-deep in brinewater—and reaching the sandy bluff, Tiki some forty feet above, and begin crawling, scrabbling up, up, up, like an ibex—my heavy, labored breathing—clinging to roots, rocks, and thorny shrubs, any toehold, handhold to secure a purchase, sand spilling, soggy shoes slipping, nearly a third of the way, the tide still rising, more lightning fracturing the evening sky, and—"*O JAYSUS, TIKI!!*"

Sharply sliding, clutching and grasping onto this damp, sandy bluff, the roiling waves lapping higher, fierce rain whipping into my eyes and beard—

"Seamus, you all *right?*" Her lovely, glistening face brightly lit by lightning flashes as she leans over the ledge, wearing a green U2 sweatshirt and her brother's black Vancouver Canucks cap worn backward with its streaming bill.

"Yes, just catching my breath—Where's your raincoat?"

"Back at your castle."

"But you're getting soaked, Tiki!"

"I'll be fine. O, and I saw your new painting."

"And?"

"Well, Ciara is nude, and I'm, I'm wearing clothes."

"*Suffering Christ,* is there *NO* pleasing you? I nearly lost my sight—"

"No-no, Seamus, I'm sorry, you're right, I'm wrong, sorry for being so bitchy—It *is* brilliant! It truly is. But I was just so shocked, so flattered, really—Actually never *looked* that good in my life!"

"Right. Well where're the dogs?"

"In my Targa, behind me." She glancing around in this sheeting, slanting squall, Poldy and Tara now raucously barking. "Seamus, can you make it the rest of the way?"

"Not without your help."

"Then I'll go get a rope! There's one in my boot. I'll tie it to the car and lower it down to you. Be right back."

And, God, what a *ridiculous* way to die, being swept out to sea! More terrifying bolts of lightning fracturing the sky.

"Seamus, here, here's the rope," Tiki leaning far over on those clumps of slippery grass as I try to squirm, wedge a bit higher against these sharp, thorny shrubs—the rope coiling down through these blasts of sheeting rain—"Got it?"

"Got it, got it! You attached it to your car?"

"All attached."

"OK, let me just tie one last knot across my chest—And, Tiki, go slow, *real* slow!"

Lifting myself up as far as I can go and squinting, blinking hard, sweeping these rainy gusts from my eyes—can't see over the ledge, assuming she's reached her Targa, parked on the grassy slope—the

rope slowly going taut, then a sudden lurch—the rope snapping—
"*TIKI!*"—and I go sliding violently down, down, down into the
churning sea—can't *breathe!*—and wildly flailing—and rising,
coughing, spewing salt water like a drowned rat and—"*GOOD
GOD, I've lost my sight forever!!*" Tiki shouting from above:

"Seamus, it's OK, Poldy's on his way, he's swimming toward
you! Just keep paddling, treading water!"

"—Tiki, I can't *SEE!*" Blindly blinking, bobbing farther out—

"Hold on, he's almost there!"

Poldy's nose bumping against my cheek, "*Yes,* old doggie!" and
reaching out, gasping for air—where'd he *go?*

"Seamus, he's paddling around you, wants you to grab his tail—
GRAB HIS *TAIL!!*"

Awkwardly groping and splashing—"Poldy, *here,* over *here!*"—
then grasping his wet plume tail! And he starts steadily swimming
through the churning waves, nearly losing my grip—

"Great, Seamus, you're just about at the cliff, and here, here's
the rope!"

Tara now barking above through the slanting rain—as I hold onto
panting Poldy with my right hand, the rope with my left, twining it
round my wrist—and a few moments later, I hear the Targa starting
up, this rope tightening, drawing taut once more, and we go slowly
bumping and scraping up, up—*DAMN!*—banging against jagged
rocks and roots—before I feel Tiki lift Poldy onto the cliff—Tara
happily whimpering—"Seamus, take hold of my hands!" And Tiki
yanks me, slipping and sliding, as my fingers grasp and grope, onto
this slick, grassy slope—where she holds me, hugs me tight—

"Seamus, promise me now you'll have that operation."

"—Right, I promise, I promise!"

Twenty-six

And five days later, after my successful carotid endarterectomy, restoring my blazing sight, and flinging out all of Flynn's rose hips and chickweed, Tiki flies back to Vancouver to cut her movie, while I, stitches in the side of my neck and still somewhat sore, prop myself up now on this sunny Irish morn beside Poldy, with fluffy pillows tumbled behind us in my big brass bed, as Symes enters with the mail on a silver tray.

"Sir?"

"Yes?"

"A postcard for you."

A color photo of Vancouver Island. I turn it over:

```
Seamus,
I've got some news.
Tara is pregnant.
And so am I.
```

Tory on Edge

August 1981

One

"What do you mean she's having your baby? Who *is* this woman? How long have you known her? And how do you know it's even *your* baby?"

"Well, because—"

"Dad, come on, wake up and smell the roses! She could be the biggest gold digger this side of Zsa Zsa Gabor for all you know! You just recovered from serious eye surgery. Mother just died—I mean, really, how long, total, have you known this, this *Tiki Wines?*"

"Hold on, Tory, let me move the phone—Not that long actually."

"Actually *how* long?"

"O, six or seven weeks."

"Terrific! Look, at least get a blood test. I mean, who *is* she? Tell me about her, what's she like, where'd you meet her, how old is she—?"

"Forty-three."

"—and what's the attraction—"

"Well she did save my life—"

"—that she's got big boobs and is great in the sack?"

"Hey, watch your mouth, lass! You're still my daughter."

"And you're still my father! Dad, please, listen, I love *you* deeply, but you're extremely vulnerable now after all that's happened, dealing with the police, Padraic at the MFA, so I think you might want to step back and take a good, hard look at this, not rush into anything—"

"Tory, she's pregnant!"

"So? Women get pregnant all the time last I heard."

"OK, look, I understand your concern, I really do, and I appreciate it, and that you're upset 'cause it sounds like I'm just doing this on the rebound, and you think, Tory, she's taking your place—"

"Wow, how perceptive of you, Dad!"

"That's what she always says."

"What, how perceptive you are?"

"No, 'Wow, multiple wows.' "

"Good, I'm so glad. And I don't think she's 'taking my place,' Dad, I bloody well *know* she is!"

"Will you at least give her a chance, try and get to know her?"

"No, I *already* know her!"

"How the hell can you possibly know her when you haven't even *met* her?"

" 'Cause you sent me 500 pictures of her!"

"Come on, Tory, try thinking about me, *my* feelings."

"That's exactly what I *am* doing, and all I see is you being roped into a match made in LaLaland! She's a movie producer, right? Well? Duh!"

" 'Duh' what? I'm her next picture?"

"You better fucking believe it! And with her hitting it really big at the box office!"

"Look, she's flying in from Vancouver, and me from Dublin, and we'll be in New York this Friday, the fifteenth, so why don't you and Gene join us for lunch on Sunday, OK?"

"No way!"

"Why?"

" 'Cause a) I have a birthday party that Shay has to go to on Sunday, his best buddy's Terrible Twos birthday party, and b) I usually plan on enjoying my Sundays and not sitting there grinding my teeth down to the gumline."

"Come on, Tory!"

"Dad—"

"Fine. Be stubborn."

"O look who's talking! Anyway, I've gotta go. And *I* still love you."

"Well you've got a hell of a way of showing it!"

"Dad—"

"Just forget it. You know how much it means to me, how important it is, how deeply I care, but no, just forget it—"

"OK, OK, *fine,* I'll *meet* her, *we'll* meet her. You happy now? And this is where, at the Carlyle?"

"Right."

"What time?"

"O, I don't know, let's say 2:30, 3, make it a late lunch. How's that sound?"

"Hum a few bars. No, terrific, I can't wait!"

"Tory, you're impossible."

"I know, I'm your daughter."

"How could I forget!"

Two

"Gene?" watching him slap on his bracing Aqua Velva. "What time did I say Shay's birthday party was supposed to start?"

"Noon, I thought you said."

"But you're not sure?"

"Tory, relax, will you. We've got plenty of time, it's not even 10:30 yet—"

"Mommy?"

Towheaded little Shay in his blue denim shorts and white Bullwinkle T-shirt waddling bowlegged into our bedroom.

"What, sweetie?"

"Me go?"

"Soon, very soon."

"Get baboons?"

"Yes, baboons, lots of baboons," and I give him a monster hug as Gene comes blinking out of the bathroom.

"Baboons?"

"Balloons."

"Ah, right, right."

And no terrible twos here, the sweetest, gentlest child ever there was, there was, as I keep smoothing down his blond, curly hair, "And I must say you look positively spiffy, my dear."

"Spissy?"

"No, spiffy, spiffy. A very handsome young man."

"Spissy."

Gene hoisting him high in the air—"Da-deee!"—then setting him atop his shoulders.

"And you can stay at Jason's as late as you want, have dinner there, watch TV—"

"TB."

"—and we'll be home before you know it—and Gene, don't get him dirty, 'cause he looks—"

"Why, what's wrong with a quick roll in the mud, mud, glorious mud? *Nothing quite like it for cooling the blood!*" and off they go with Shay still squealing, "Da-deee!"

And what on earth'll *I* wear to meet the buxom Tiki? 'Cause I look awful, hardly slept a wink all week, with these dark smudges under my eyes, a saddle of freckles on my nose, peeling brow—Nothing here for Ms. Tiki Wines! (Or was that Tiki Whines? Heehee!) How 'bout this frilly Twenties number? Zelda Hagar, with her cloche hat and high heels, a ditsy Fitzgerald flapper? Not quite, my dear. Or this modest little black number? Hot and humid out. And why am I even going? 'Cause he's my father, that's why! Be nice, Tory. Yeah, right! To this flaming-haired hussy with the boobs of life!

Why're men so taken with our chests, pendulous mounds of flesh? Mommy's milk. Shay suckling for all he was worth, nearly drained me dry. Most women's boobs, face it, are unappealing, floppy or saggy or totally gross, quickly lose their shape with the pull of gravity—A boob job? Never! Not *this* twenty-five-year-old. What you see, gang, is what you get. Shifting right, left, smoothing down my hips, tummy, black sheath modest to a T, no cleavage—There, tugging the bodice down, slight trace of cleavage to my 34 Bs, chest and legs nicely tanned. No lipstick, light mascara, and loose, blonde, shoulder-length hair. Got to cut it soon. My Psychology prof, horny Aaron Pendragon, saying how good it looks. Creep! Hitting on any student younger than menopause. Like his guru, Carl "The Pervert" Jung: "Is goot for mine patients to sleep mit zer shrinks." Hello, I don't *think* so!

Irish earrings, these tiny Celtic crosses. And smile, Tory, smile, your bestest phony smile, 'cause you're on *Tiki's Camera!*

Three

Northern State Parkway so lovely this time of year, evergreens, roses, and mountain laurel in rustling summer bloom as I sigh again and adjust my silky hem. Should be in the city by 2, 2:15 at the latest. And Gene looking really handsome today (my mother thought a shaggy Paul Newman) in that powder blue turtleneck and navy blue blazer, his hair getting grayer by the day, love that distinguished silver fringe—and I'm still so on edge! as I ask:

"How's your class going?"

Sinatra on the radio now with "Witchcraft."

"What? Sorry."

"Your class, Gene, at Stony Brook?"

"OK. Same old same old. *So we beat on, boats against the current.* Probably not as good as your dance class."

"No good-looking chickeepoos ogling Professor Humbert?"

"Not bloody likely. Just the usual summer crop."

" 'O, Professor Hagar, can you take a look at my work—and my sexy booty?' "

"Never quite that brazen."

"And what's your course called again?"

"Love and Lust in the Modern Novel."

"O, right, right. And your novel, how's that coming?"

"You think Shay'll be OK?"

"Shay? Sure. He'll have a great time. We'll probably have to drag him home."

"With his baboons."

"What? O, right, right, his baboons." On by the Huntington exits, a few stray clouds gathering in the sky. "Anyway, your writing, Gene, how's it going?"

"Slow, for the moment."

"Well just wait'll they read your novel. I guarantee the critics go crazy, 'My God, what a talent!' "

"Yeah, one of the best-kept secrets in publishing. 'Where has he been all these years?' "

"Holed up in Stony Brook in his wife's warm womb."

"Or papering his walls with endless rejections. Even the milkman rejected my note."

He squeezing my hand and grinning as we pass the Plainview exit, and I grin back. "But you think today, Gene, will go OK?"

"You mean with your father and his lady?" He now gently kneading my nape. "No problem. He'll be his usual outrageous self."

"But what if—?"

"And I'm sure she's perfectly fine."

"May I finish, please?"

"Sorry."

"Anyway, what if she's a total nut-case, obvious gold digger?"

"Then I guarantee you'll let him know."

Four

"And this is my daughter, Tory."

"I've heard *so* much about you, such lovely blonde hair."

Looking away, then down at the floor, "Thanks."

"Yes, well, listen, all, I've got us a table waiting at an ould butty of mine's pub, Eamonn Doran's, down on Second Avenue and 53rd, so let us not tarry any longer, but rather hie ourselves off for a fabulous Oirish feast!"

This portly, white-haired man with his jolly, wind-cherried cheeks and green shamrock suspenders heartily greeting my dad and Tiki, then me and Gene, before escorting us past the crowded, noisy, hammered-copper bar and under this dark beamed ceiling, maps and insignia on the walls of old Ireland, golden lantern light, a shamrock of stained glass, and an antique jukebox to the dining room at the back with its mirrored walls, tufted black banquettes, beige linen, and a pretty Irish waitress ready to take our orders standing silently behind the venerable Eamonn Doran.

"Today," he begins, with a lilting Dublin brogue, "I can recommend the rack of lamb, steak and kidney pie, and the Muscovy duck 'tis lovely."

And we all nod, as I continue stuffing my gob with this crusty white soda bread studded with black raisins, then proceed to order appetizers of Irish smoked salmon and baked littleneck clams, and Chablis for Tiki, Guinness for my dad, and Bass Ale for Gene and me.

"There was a time when English spirits were never offered here, lass, no Beefeater's gin and the like, but the times they are a-changin'— And easy on the soda bread, Tory, or you won't have room for your steak and kidney pie."

My sullen nod in response, still avoiding meeting Tiki's eyes as the rest of them keep on talking. Though I do sneak in a fast, furtive peek at her now and again, and I must admit she *is* striking, very pretty, and extremely sensual with her flaming auburn hair and pale, lightly freckled skin, in that long blue knit dress and silky green scarf—can see why my father—

"And I hear you have a little boy, Tory."

Grunt, nod, and keep munching on my littleneck clams.

"What's his name?"

Gene nudging me, "Tory?"

"What? Sorry, what'd you say?" Still looking away.

"Your son's name?"

"Shay."

"That's cute. Is he named after anyone?"

Taking another brusque bite of this bread, "Well not Padraic, that's for damn sure!" and washing it down with a frosty swig of ale, "And not the ballpark, either."

"Ballpark?"

Duh! "Shea *Stadium?*"

"S-h-e-a?"

"No, my son's is spelled S-h-a-y."

"Yes, well, she stands corrected, lass—and she should, since she's wearing orthopedic shoes."

Tiki beaming at my father's lame-o joke, "That sounds like something Symes would say."

"He did." And she amorously cuddles—*Yuck!*—into his tweedy shoulder.

Our main courses arriving, clouds of steam rising as I break the light brown crust of my steak and kidney pie and savor this hot, chunky stew, so gamy and strong, and mixed with that flaky pastry. And watching Tiki eat her Muscovy duck, I have to say I'm fascinated, captivated, 'cause she's really a great eater, delicate and graceful, with sensuous but ladylike bites, before engaging Gene about where they went to college. She at the University of British Columbia, and he, with his tour of the Ivy league, at Cornell, Yale, and Columbia, ha ha, ho ho! It's off to Small Talk U. we go! And portly Eamonn returning.

"So, how is everythin' here, all right, I assume?"

"Marvelous, absolutely bloody marvelous! My compliments to the chef."

"He's from County Tyrone, Seamus, just come over. And if there's anythin' else you'll be wantin', just give us a shout."

"Will do, definitely will do, 'cause you know what that Irish proverb says, Eamonn?"

"There was a hermit named Dave?"

"No, the other one, that goes, 'Dance as if no one were watching, sing as if no one were listening, and live every day as if it were your last.' "

Under my breath, "And it very well may be!"

Gene jabbing me once more, "Tory!"

Five

Lawanda Mandelle, my M.A., M.S.W., L.C.S.W. now for the past three months, continuing, as usual, to sit languidly back in her tan Naugahyde swivel chair under her wall of laminated credentials, while I keep leaning forward facing her on this nubby beige love seat and rambling on and on about Gene and my recurring memories of Max Barilla:

"Really, I cried for a week straight when I heard how he died. He was, well, Max was my first guy, boyfriend, who saw me from my point of view, as more than, you know, spunky, perky, or feisty (sounds like a rock band)—and that I also had a brain in my head."

Lawanda nodding with her studied, "soothing" smile, her heavily mascared eyes drifting over my shoulder with a casual flick to the Ormolu clock ticking behind me, and about to launch into another summary of platitudes ("before our hour draws to a close") like a body massage, rubdown at a spa, or salve of psychobabble— when I abruptly sigh, slide forward, and stand, on the verge now of hyperventilating—my purse in my sweaty, trembling hand.

"Tory? Is something the matter? You still have, let me see here, at least seven minutes remaining."

Coming round her chair, "Fine, Lawanda," and catching my breath, "but *I'm* stopping."

"Stopping this session?"

"No, stopping for good."

"Is that so?" she swiveling toward me, "Well I'm not sure that's altogether wise."

Pausing beside her potted plants, "But isn't that *my* decision?"

"Indeed it is, but—"

"You've been telling me all along to take responsibility for my actions, make my own decisions."

"O of course, though I still have *my* opinion, Tory, and I believe—"

"But *I* don't want your opinion anymore," jerking open the door, "and what *you* really want is my money! 'Bye."

Six

Alone at home, waiting to pick up Shay from Jason's house, with a glass of chilled white Zinfandel in my tight little fist, listening to James Taylor, who's seen fire and who's seen rain, seen lonely times when he could not find a friend—and hell, feeling so damn sad and lonely myself, that endlessly sinking sad, losing Mother to that horrid lymphoma, and now holding her hairbrush, missing her so. As a little girl I'd sit on the floor and love to watch her brush out the shine before her bathroom mirror. And after, as I examined those tangled gold threads, I would ask, "Momma, how can you lose so much hair and not be bald?" Then Max Barilla, from Yale (called him Sas, for sarsaparilla), who drowned in some lake in northern Maine, from a cramp? Heart attack? Sudden stroke? No one really knows, since they never found his body. Or our poor little Corgi, killed by a car on Mount Grey Road—and now my father becoming a father again!

O Jeez, just too much! So filled with this aching rage! And I'm taking it out on Gene. Unfair, driving him away, even getting suspicious of him lately, playing around, his students always coming on. Like me with my old teacher, Arlo Biggio, after losing Nina Jaccalone, my best friend, in that head-on collision so long ago.

Another glass of wine before I go? No, enough. Don't want to be reeling when I pick up Shay, but so damn tense, wound tight as a bloody drum!

Bring myself off? O why not? Still got time. Into our bedroom and lock the door. Gene and I . . . been three weeks now, when I said, the words just popping out, "Boy, do I like to make love to you!" "Why?" " 'Cause you care about a woman's body, my pleasure, what *I* feel." His kindness and warmy hugs, my insatiable woolly bear—and crazy, too, liking to put his ear down there so he can "listen to the sea." Licking my inner petals and teasingly kneading my clit, his lips and chin glistening, dripping wet—doing everything a vagina would ever want done to it—as I squeezed his head hard between my thighs, so greedy for his hummingbird tongue that reached my G-spot and drove me right through the ceiling, before he swiveled round to straddle my face—Like that time we went driving out to Mattituck, the Sound glowing like cloudy pewter as far as the shimmering horizon, and few cars on that nineteenth-century stretch of farm road, only bikers in gaudy stripes and harlequin colors bent over and furiously pedaling, and as dusky twilight came settling down, he bringing me off with his hand—nearly as good as mine—before I took his hot, throbbing "lollicock" in my mouth, and he looked like he'd just died and gone to heaven, pinkish, so sensitive tip, and before his thick Irish toothache went thrusting into my moist Irish fortune by the shade of that dusty, unpaved road, and I came shuddering and moaning and squealing—so wet now, rapidly stroking myself side to side and biting my lip to keep from screaming, my body beaded with sweat, hips rising and bucking and grinding—OmyGod!—with ripples of exquisite release—The phone stridently ringing!

Seven

Reaching groping across with my free hand—and the receiver slip-

ping, bouncing off the bed just before the answering machine—
"Hello?"

"... Uh, is Mr., uh, Hagar there?" A sexy, girlish voice.

"No, he's not. Who's this?"

"Thank you." Click.

Well, well, well.

Eight

So, let's see, which disguise shall it be: Mata Hari? A CIA spy? Or
bookish grad student slinking by? O come on, Tory, you can do
better than that! No: *I needed to use the library, Gene, checking
out some dance magazines*—and that's only if he spots me. Otherwise, I'll have a quick look in just after his writing class ends,
see who's moseying around, cottoning up to him, batting their
eyes, shaking their booty, and his reaction—then take off like
a bat out of hell! And he's in the Humanities Building—flipping through the catalogue—Room 320, from 4–5:30. And it's
now 5 after 5, picking up Shay at 6. And this stonewashed denim
jumper should do, hair tucked under this navy bucket hat from
L.L. Bean, horn-rim grad school glasses, not too bad, blend right
in, and out—

The phone ringing. Her again. "Yes?"

"Ah, Tory, me lass!"

"O, Daddy, I can't talk now—"

"So what'd you think of Tiki, eh?"

"Listen, I can't—"

"Isn't she marvelous?"

"Well, look—"

"Though you seemed a bit subdued, like when you were seven
or so in Ocean City—"

"Dad—"

"Remember?"

"Remember what?"

"When you were seven or so and you ate all that cotton candy and got a terrible bellyache?"

"How can you remember?" My stomach really churning now.

"O I remember everything."

"Everything?"

"Everything about you. But look, Tiki and I thought we might come on out—"

"Dad, listen, let me call you in, O, another hour or so, 'cause I've got to get going."

"Where you going?"

"O, I, uh, I have to go to the library, pick up Shay, so I'll call you in an hour, promise, 'bye."

· · · · · ·

Across this sprawling G.E. plant of a campus I stride, with its ongoing, never-ending construction, sandy vistas, sterile, Albert Speer-like architecture, and all these jolly girls with their bouncing bodies still defying gravity—for a while longer—and chattering away, one chirpy, breathless conversation tumbling headlong into another: "They're like so *cute* together, they really are!" "—and then to kind of like add insult to injury, I'm dating this guy who's like amazingly rich—not that money means anything—" "O you gotta hear this, check it out, I mean this's between him and I—" Between him and me! Gene always correcting me when I say, "I could care less," "I thought to myself," or "I feel badly," though I encourage him to do so.

And where's the Humanities Building? Have to ask somebody. "Straight ahead? Thanks." And playing out a sample conversation tonight before dinner in my mind: "Any calls today, Tory?" "Just one." "Who?" "A girl." "She give her name?" "No, just asked for 'Mr., uh, Hagar.' A student?" "I have no idea." "A friend?" "How would I know?" "Yeah, right! Some friend, you sneaky asshole!" Then losing him, too, a whistling void in my gut as I start to sweat, eyes shifting left and right, and overhearing more conversations as I enter this building and head down the echoing halls: "Du-hu-hude, I am sooo faded!" "Yeah, man, I'm like pretty hammered myself." "You wanna smoke-out right now, 'cause I got this really cool dirtweed that's outta sight!" "Right on, bro, pack me a bowl." And up these stairs, one more flight, and my masquerade seems to be working, fit right in as I pass these girls—"Like O my God, I mean, like really, does she look fat or what?" "Try Blimporama!"—and those two older woman coming out of Room 318, "—and everything's got to be his way, *when* he wants it and *how* he wants it! Like this morning, I got back from the beauty parlor at 10 o'clock and there's Milton walking around the house naked, as if that would turn me on, with that saggy, hairy body! It's like he gets an erection and points at it—That's supposed to turn me on? When I have him served with the divorce papers, *that'll* turn me on!"

And stopping at Room 320 as I cast a sidelong glance down the hall, the coast is clear at 5:30 on the nose, and edge furtively round this corner: Gene at his desk surrounded by a cluster of students, some cuties, their tight hip-hugger butts—That's *my* guy, girls! He with his professorial mask pontificating, doesn't see me—all that T and A—but which one, which chickeepoo is offering herself up on a silver platter: "If you'll give me an A, Prof. Hagar, I promise I'll fuck your brains out." Go charging in and, swinging wildly, knock all of them flat?

O Jeez, and here they come!

My rapid skip along the hall, fast glance over my shoulder— Gene still inside—and trotting swiftly down the stairway—" 'That's one small step for mankind . . . one giant leap for man.'" "No, the other way around, dude."—last flight and back outside into this sweaty heat—and my bucket hat suddenly lifted right off my head—

"Hey, what the hell're you *doing?*" staring hard at some stoner guy with the face of Charlie Manson, "Can I please have my hat back?"

"I just wanna try it on."

"No way!" and reaching out to snare it, I watch him wave it high in the air, before slamming him against the building, our noses almost touching, "Gimme my hat back before I *really* get mad, you asshole!"

"Here, here's your damn hat! Man, like you've gotta lighten up!" and adjusting his gray Gap T-shirt, he goes shuffling away, hissing "Bitch!" under his weedy breath.

And I hurry back to my TR7, still no sign of Gene, and, swerving out of the lot, speed off to pick up Shay.

Nine

This Johnson's Baby Shampoo foaming into a fragrant, sudsy lather as my blinking little boy keeps on playing with his Rubber Ducky and yellow submarine, humming and buzzing and making all sorts of sputtering motorized sounds amid the glossy popping and winking bubbles, laughing and splashing—"Mommy?"

"What, sweetie?"

"My ducky drownded."

Plucking it from under the water, "Not quite yet," and handing it to him, "But time now to get out."

"No! Stay!"

"Come on, Shay—"

"No!"

"Enough bath."

"No."

"You have to get out," and I briskly towel him dry, his slippery, rubbery body, then pull on his baby blue jammies, before brushing his shiny blonde hair.

• • • • • •

And some time later, as I crawl under the covers, Gene setting aside those student papers and looking up, "Did you know Tiki used to be a masseuse in her younger days?"

"Is that so? You talked to my father?"

"Yes. That's how she supposedly put herself through college."

"Terrific."

"Why are you so sarcastic?"

"Who, me? O, I don't know, how 'bout this mystery woman, former massage therapist, may be ruining my father's life?"

"But she saved his life, Tory. And it is *his* life."

"You know I never thought of that, sounds like Lawanda's or Lucy Van Pelt's 'Flawless Advice.' "

"Tory?"

"What?"

"Just shut up."

"Don't tell me to shut up! You could at least try and feel what *I'm* feeling!"

"Which is?"

"Anger and pain and fucking—"

"I'm sorry."

"—confusion! And the last thing I need, the very last last thing, is to be told to shut up and not share it with you, the one person who—"

"I know, I'm sorry. Come here."

"No! And it's quite possible, Gene, I just may be right about her, you know."

"You may."

"Well at least give me credit if I am."

"I definitely will, but—"

"You still love me?"

"Of course I do."

"Really?"

"Cross my heart and hope to die, Tory."

"And I'm still attractive to you?"

"You've never looked better."

"Even with these dark smudges under my eyes?"

"Doesn't matter. You still glow."

"So now I'm a light bulb?"

"Come here."

"No, there's more to me than just sex."

"Such as?"

"Such as this girl called here today."

"Which girl?"

"I haven't a clue. Do you?"

"No. What'd she say?"

"Just asked if you were home and hung up."

"Then forget about it."

"How'd she get your number?"

"It's in the book. And who says she's a student?"

"Yeah, you're right. But have you ever been tempted, Gene?"

"Occasionally."

"So you have."

"No! It's just with all these girls coming on to me—maybe it's my bracing Aqua Velva. Look, I have the most beautiful wife in the world, and the last thing I need, Tory—"

"OK, OK. Anyway, Sunday they're coming out?"

"That's what your father said. Is that all right?"

"No, but I'll grin and bear it. Gene, I'm sorry I've been acting the way I have lately. Forgive me, please."

"Sure."

"I promise I'll try to like her."

"Well first like your husband."

And with a sigh, I slide across and snuggle into his arms. "Gene, remember how I told you about the feeling that I got in Dublin's National Gallery when I thought my father had died? The one where my chest felt like it had a hundred pound weight on it, where my eyes flooded with tears, and I just couldn't breathe, the pain coming in waves, like that poem I once wrote, remember?"

"About colors?"

"Right. And black—"

" 'Black is where you slip and fall, build your wall, anguished cry, wait to die, mourn the day, dragon slay, hide away.' "

"How'd you *remember* that?"

"But 'Blue is where you live today, clouds of white, feathery breeze, after night, birds in flight.' "

And I squeeze him tight, wanting so to be kissed, petted, and made love to right this second.

Ten

The phone ringing all day long with those infuriating telemarketing calls and several rapid hang-ups: "Yes? Hello?" Click.

Jeez, wonder who that could be?

Eleven

You know, I'm coming to see it takes a man with a considerable sense of self to confess his insecurities to a daughter, telling me how he'd failed, but also how he'd tried, making himself real to me, not a godlike father figure who was always so *un*real.

Like this past spring in Ireland at his splendid estate of Ballyduff when I woke him early one morning, with his bald pate gleaming, bleary eyes blinking after a beery night out, wearing one pink sock and one green as he sat up slowly, slouched on his couch, grumble, grumble, O so tired, exhausted from his treks to Paris, Venice, and Rome, his faithful Samoyed shimmying at his feet: "Yes, Poldy, yes—hang on, old doggie—get you some food and a pee, just hang on a tick, while I answer that blasted phone." And Poldy, so damn patient—much more than I would ever be—and probably muttering to himself, Come on, Boyne, will you! God, you are sooooooooooooo bloody slow!

But he's *my* father, *all mine,* since the beginning of time—and now with a competing sibling? Having to share him with a baby, kootchie koo?

And then, *God,* that Sunday dinner at the Three Village Inn last night, with Gene and me, Dad and dear, old Tiki:

She positively glowing with radiant childbearing glee and wolfing down her pine nut-crusted rack of lamb, with apple mint jus, fire-roasted veggies, and garlic-whipped potatoes, while I limited myself to only cold plum soup, "Not hungry, Tory?" Wonder why. And my charismatic, buoyant dad as usual regaled us with off-color Celtic tales and amusing bon mots: "Hey, why does it take a million sperm to fertilize an egg? 'Cause none of 'em'll ask directions." Then going on for the umpteenth time about his father Tim's amazing Hong Kong curry that came in infinite varieties of mild, hot, and Krakatoa, and ending with his account of how delighted and proud Picasso was to become a father at sixty-six, his son looking so like him, and even more so as the years went by, same dark eyes, square face, and smooth complexion, and the subject of numerous portraits, many of them with his mother, Françoise. "Did you know when Pablo died in '73, he left nearly 2,000 paintings, 18,000 engravings, and over 11,000 drawings and sketches? And that four years later, the great love of his life, Marie-Thérèse hanged herself in the garage of her house in Juan-les-Pins at age sixty-eight? She said, 'I don't want him to be by himself when he's dead.' Or nine years after that, his last wife Jacqueline lay on her bed at three o'clock in the morning, pulled the sheet up to her chin, and shot herself in the temple?"

And I muttered, "You expect that'll be your legacy, too?"

Twelve

And it turns out, boohoohoo, that Tiki has to go back to Vancouver for a while to post-produce her movie and be present as well when Tara, her Spitz, gives birth to Poldy's puppy. And that's the good news. The bad news is she'll be back in two or three weeks, with her quivering, heaving embonpoint! But enough about the fertile Ms. Wines and her pregnant dog. Have to get out of here now and down to Centereach to pick up those ballet shoes for my class at Marie Brock's School of Dance. Shay with Barbi, his favorite teenage babysitter—and starting my TR7: always running, running, and still seeming a step behind! Me with that ruptured Achilles tendon, can't dance onstage anymore, but at least I can still teach jigs and reels and the boot-scootin' boogie to the kids at the Community Center.

Flashing down Stony Brook Road . . . and an hour later, ready to head on home. But such a lovely day, not too humid, with this cool, feathery breeze, so I'll take a drive through sleepy Centereach, and approaching that dingy movie marquee, a porno house, The Pussycat Theater, never been to one in my life and—*O my GOD!*

CAN'T BE! Gene and a girl going in?! Bringing his chickeepoo *here?* To learn some new techniques—? *DAMN!* Horn blasting right behind me, nearly leaping out of my seat, *"Hey, buddy, stick it in your ear!!"* And wildly veering round this corner—I have to find out!—bumping over the curb and parking my car far down this quiet, leafy street, then hustle on back, nobody out in front, and, ducking my head, eyes darting nervously about, shove four bucks across to the bored and hennaed woman cashier, then hurry in past faded posters, *Debbie Does Dallas, Joy Stick* with Wanda Besh, and through these black velour curtains—*O JEEZ!* The screen filled with enormous genitalia! Humungous weenies looking like blue-veined Titan missiles, huge balls flopping, and that girl's orgasmic groaning so out of synch—as I slide lower in this broken, beside-the-wall seat, shading my face with my hand, a stale, clammy smell in the air, some women silhouetted with their dates down there—*And where's Gene?*—the movie really heating up now at that outdoor orgy, all of them, scrawny guys and zoftik girls, humping and pumping mechanically away, camera zooming in for close-ups of the guys pulling out—*Yuck!*—gushers of sperm shooting over the girls' bellies—

And there's Gene! with, I can't quite see—her hair in a ponytail—Which one of his class? Can't remember—Or maybe one of his old Great Neck girlfriends, "Titsy" Mitzi Weiss or—as I lean forward across this moldy seat—her profile turning now, sort of pretty, not familiar, and he's turning, too—

NO, it's NOT him, thank God! And anyway, what would he be doing here? Needing stimulation? Or maybe it was her idea? But what am *I* doing here? What's *happening* to my life? And glancing and squinting around: Prof. Pendragon three rows down, with his girl? Looks like him, but I can't be certain, as I quickly rise out of my squeaky seat and rush up the dark aisle, tripping over outstretched feet—Terrific, Tory!—and go stumbling through these musty curtains past the bored cashier, fast as I can back to my car—and letting out a rapidly blinking sigh as I roar round this corner into Stony Brook Road, across Nesconset Highway, and on to 25A!

Thirteen

And here I was finally feeling that I didn't always need to be pretty and witty and wise for Gene to love me, that I could weigh 300 pounds—OK, well, 200 pounds (150?)—be self-absorbed, or reveal my flaws—but now, who knows, I may have totally misread him.

I mean even when he strokes the inside of my thigh while we're driving and exclaims how he still loves its silky texture, that I'm "excruciatingly lovely," it doesn't have to lead to sex as it used to.

But maybe it does, with me increasingly pushing him away.

And talking of Pendragon, I had to go to the libe yesterday

morning, and there I was wandering about the university stacks searching for some old book by Arlene Croce, the current dance critic of *The New Yorker*. And always feeling hemmed in by the stacks, like the heavily-laden shelves would suddenly topple over—when, as I rounded a dark and musty corner, I ran smack into Prof. Pendragon (who, I have to admit, did look rather cute, as he leaned toward me with his unkempt, blonde-bearded face, L.L. Bean burgundy denim shirt, and well-worn designer jeans), "Well look who's here!" a goatish gleam to his hooded eye. And out of my mouth came, "Were you at that porno movie the other day?" "Porno movie?" "The, the what's-it-called, The Pussycat Theater?" "May've been. But you know, I just wanted to tell you, Tory, we all, the whole class, really love your presence, comments, your chirpy voice, and me especially," his hand sweeping a strand of hair from my brow, caressing my cheek, and, before I knew it, kissing me hard—and after a moment's pause, I was kissing him back hard— till I finally broke away and sprinted up and out of the stacks.

And I'd better watch myself now—though he *is* much better-looking up close and personal. Still, so glad that I took off then. Even thought of calling money-grubbing Lawanda for another shot of psychobabble.

But phoning my father instead. "Tory, I just bought a goat, fabulous goat named Finian!" "You got rid of Poldy?" "Never!" "Dad, can I ask you a question?" "Sure." "You think Gene would ever stray?" "O no way!" "Yeah, Dad, way! He's still young, good-looking, keeps in shape, plays basketball every Sunday, and I see how women look at him. You really don't think he'd ever cheat?" "Hagar have an affair? Never!" "But you had affairs. All men—" "Not a single bloody one." "None?" "None. But, Jaysus, no one ever believes me. No-no, Tory, never once did I dally, stray, dabble in quim, as they say." "Who says?" "Bounders, macho men. Though the opportunity frequently arose, groupies and the like, even had a Carmelite nun proposition me in the nave. But as far as your hubby Hagar goes, no question he loves you madly, lass, almost as much as I. And speaking of that, I got us tickets to Madison Square Garden this Friday night to see U2, this sensational new Irish group—" "They're not that new." "—and Tiki's flying in for the concert, then flying right back, so we'll all go together." "Yippie!"

Fourteen

And we all had a "fabbo" time at the concert! Could hardly breathe for the pot fumes, hear nary a song for the lunatic shrieking—O you talk about your fun, honey! My phone ringing:

"Yes? Hello?"

"... Uh, is Professor, Mr. Hagar—?"

"No!"

And that's the final straw! Now I'm gonna confront that phone-calling cunt (pardon my French) and get to the bottom of this!

Back to the Humanities Building, swiftly up to the third floor at 5:25, and pausing outside his room, other students passing, and Gene announcing in there, "Anyone who needs to see me, see me after class. And Rocco, I need to see you. And Margot, too."

The rest of them leaving, filing out—then, in a moment, Rocco, I presume, departing—and one drop-dead gorgeous girl, Margot, remaining in black, skin-tight jeans and a yellow scoop-neck jersey leaning her eager breasts (giving him a view from here to Toledo) over my husband's desk and asking (in that same breathy voice!), "So like when're *we* getting together?"

" 'We'?"

She wiggling her inviting bubble butt. "Well you said?"

"Said what?"

"Come on, stop teasing me."

"Look, Margot, enough! I'm married, very *happily* married, in fact, so stop calling my home! And you're still getting a D. Period. End of story. 'Bye."

And grinning from ear to ear, I go boot-scooting along the hall on cushiony, sneakered feet, dash down the stairs, and on out the door— *Very* happily *married?* My wonderful, faithful hubby!—And where the hell did I park? Gene coming? No there's my fender, fire engine red TR7, as I go swiveling between cars, blocking his view, don't run into Manson again, and snagging my keys from my cluttered bag—*O my God,* Gene's coming out, stopping to talk to that older man—get this stupid key in—he's still talking, not looking—There! and hop inside, ducking low, and *easy, easy,* don't draw attention, and glide slowly through this packed parking lot, just the top of my head showing, he's *still* talking—don't back up or severe tire damage—and go skidding onto Nicolls Road, and hightail it home, while loudly singing, "I Will Follow," my favorite U2 song!

Fifteen

Gene now taking a shower after playing tag with Shay and putting him to sleep as I lock our bedroom door, tiptoe toward the bathroom, and peek inside: He turning off the taps with a squeak and slowly stepping out, toweling himself dry and wrapping it around his waist, as I enter with a devilish smile—

"What's going on?"

—keep moving forward—

"Tory?"

—and pinning him against the wall with a long, passionate kiss—

"What's that for?"

—squeezing his muscular butt in my hands, "Why does it have to be for something?" then slipping my tongue deep in his mouth, over his sexy lips—

"But wait—Why?"

"Let's just say I'm a raging paranoid."

"What?"

"Nothing, forget it," ripping off his towel and stroking his growing attraction as I guide him onto our bed and quickly shed my nighty.

Sixteen

And last night, I held him so tight, I'll bet he's never been held that tight in his life—("I've never been held that tight in my life." "All *right*, Gene!")—and then my father calling from Vancouver to announce the birth of Tara's litter of six, half Spitz, half Samoyed, one of which Tiki's giving to Shay as a belated birthday present. With me asking:

"By the way, Dad, are you planning to ever marry this woman?"

"By 'this woman,' you mean Tiki, I assume?"

"None other."

"In fact I do."

"And when would that be?"

"When? When *we* decide. Is that OK with you, Tory?"

"Whatever."

· · · · · ·

And Shay and Sinjin, my father's name for this adorable, elfin puppy, with his mitten ears and snowy ruff, an icy sheen of Siberian fluff, are now instant bosom buddies, who often curl up together and fall asleep, or, from time to time, stare at each other in dazed and wide-eyed wonder.

But later on this evening, under a misty summer drizzle, when Gene, Shay, and I return from Shakey's Pizza in Port Jeff, we're shocked to find Gene's newest short story strewn like a confetti blizzard all across the living and dining rooms, Shay giggling, and Sinjin, with that smiling, panting face, waddling sideways toward me and, head down, white eyelashes blinking, tail wagging, gives me a lick on the nose.

And to his great credit and control, my dear hubby holds his temper as he and I painstakingly scotch-tape the tiny jigsaw pieces back together. When will he finally get a computer and toss out his 1954 Royal Portable typewriter? Never, I suppose.

Seventeen

And today, Prof. Pendragon asking me to stay a moment after class (events now coming thick and fast) and saying under his breath, as he leaned toward me once more, "I was hoping that I'd hear from you again," and I nearly kneed him in his Jungian balls, but said instead (to quote my hubby), "I'm married, very *happily* married, in fact," then turned on my heel and left, with my stomach really churning.

And walking now with Tammy Trujuillo, another, younger student, who keeps praising me to the skies for standing up to "that hairy pervert" who's not much older than I. "Yeah, well now I'll probably flunk the course!" "O no way, Tory. You're like so smart, the smartest one in the class, so much smarter and deeper than me, like I'm in awe whenever I hear you talk—'cause I don't do Deep very well."

And the days flying by: Shay and Sinjin growing inseparable; my birthday coming and going, number twenty-six; and Tiki now taken to wearing muumuus and loosely flowing shifts, the baby due in March (a wedding a month later?); and they're all planning, Gene, Shay, and my dad, to go skiing at Brodie Mountain around that time and stay at her family's cabin in Falls Village, Connecticut, while I remain at home (my choice, and I can't ski anyway with my ruptured Achilles tendon) and catch up on my reading, bask in solitude, and teach my dance class at the Centereach Community Center. O I'm sure I'll be fine and dandy.

Eighteen

OK, let's hear it for masturbation! 'Cause yes, I have to admit, I'm totally bored out of my gourd, the snow out there steadily falling, the puppy dozing at my feet after we played for an hour in the piling drifts (he disappearing, sinking white on white, out of sight), while the rest of my family, I'm sure, is having a marvelous time on the Brodie slopes! Tiki, now big as a house, sending them off with hot toddies and good cheer, and keeping the cabin warm till they reappear, even calling me last night to ask if I was lonely.

And stiff upper lip to the core, I replied, "O no, keeping busy as a bee, have no idea where the day goes, just seems to fly by."

"Did you hear the weather report tonight?"

"No. Why, should I?"

"Well, they're expecting a very big snowfall coming down from Canada at any time, so I'm sort of worried."

"O those forecasters never know. As my father likes to say, 'They're always off by a couple of days, like Stonehenge, still rattling the bones.' "

And at least that made her laugh, a nervous, rippling giggle, followed by more awkward small talk, and that was our little chat—and I'm sorry, truly sorry, but I just can't find it in me to be friendly to that woman.

NBC's 11 o'clock News now reporting a massive, late-winter storm out of Canada is blanketing all of New England, could last for several days, knocking out power, closing down roads, two deaths already confirmed and—

The phone ringing! Not Margot again, I pray! as I hop over Sinjin to grab it and say, "Hello?"

" 'Tis I, lass."

"Are you OK? Gene? Shay?"

"We're fine, fine. But Brodie's completely socked in, no traffic in or out, and I'm worried about Tiki. I just spoke to her, but by the morning, she should be socked in as well. So I'd like you to do me a favor, if you will, drive up and stay with her, 'cause she's liable to pop at any moment."

"Uh, well, sure. But the roads?"

"They're still good down there. I just called Triple A, and if you left now—"

"There're no neighbors nearby?"

"Tory!"

"Her doctor?"

"Please, lass—"

"OK, OK, tell her I'm on my way."

"O, thank you, dear, I love you for this."

"Right, right."

"And it's too late for the ferry, so take the Taconic to Millbrook and cut across, should be clear most of the way."

"Whatever. Can I speak to Gene and Shay?"

"Of course. O and I've picked out a name."

"Name?"

"For the laddie. What do you think of Rory? Rory Timothy Boyne?"

"Yeah, well, that's, that's very nice."

"Tory and Rory."

How sweet! "Right. Well let me speak to Gene."

Nineteen

And after forty-two "be carefuls" and "call us as soon as you get there," from him, I reach Barbi at home to dog-sit for a few days, and go zooming along these icy roads, the radio booming Zeppelin's "Stairway to Heaven," snowflakes flurrying thickly across my windshield, and on up the Taconic Parkway at 1:35 on a Sunday morning, Valentine's Day, the fourteenth of February, weather reports getting worse, not many cars out, snowplows passing, clearing a path.

And what the hell am I *doing?* Florence Nightingale to the rescue? Or maybe Nancy Drew. 'Cause what can *I* do? Hold her hand? Sing that Beatles song while I'm doing it? Or watch the baby pop out? 'Cause, really, come on now, what do I know about this woman, flaming-haired hussy with the boobs of life. Really know? She's what, forty-three, forty-four, from Vancouver, has a hockey-playing brother, makes movies, a dog named Tara as randy as she, claims she loves my father (or his money), and has a cabin in Connecticut. Anything else? She saved his life, stayed for his operation, has a great body. OK, fine. Super hair, supposedly funny.

On past the Poughkeepsie exit, Millbrook next and then 44, snow really falling now, straining to see. And how the hell am I ever gonna find her place—What's that stupid address again? Damn slip fell on the floor. Reaching down for it—*O my God!*—car skidding on the frozen shoulder, slickly sliding—my heart going a mile a minute!—and swerving back onto the road, squinting hard as I grope, flick on the car light: Ah, Undermountain Road. Right. How could I possibly forget?

Twenty

Trudging a path through these blizzardy drifts at 3:40 in the icy morning to pound on Tiki's dark front door, the snow heavily swirling, so damn tired and cold—

"O Tory! Your father told me you were coming—and the phone just went out."

"Terrific!"

"But come in, come in," she rapidly blinking in a crimson, hooded housecoat and fuzzy gray slippers, her auburn curls framing her face, "Some weather, eh?"

"You could say—"

"Are you hungry, thirsty? What would you like? I just put a pot of coffee on—"

"How 'bout a Kamikaze, straight up, with a twist? No, I'm only kidding. Just some tea would be fine."

"Of course. I have some chamomile around here somewhere, had it just the other day. Cream, sugar?"

"Lemon. But Tiki, you sit, I can get—"

"Ah, here we are, there's one bag left."

This large, old-fashioned log cabin with its wagon wheel dining table and other Ethan Allen white-washed pine, country-style furniture, feathery comforters quilted with scarlet and forest green prints draped over rockers, love seats, and that rustic sofa as I cross the polished hardwood floor, Tiffany kerosene lamps and macraméd plant hangers, beams and angular ceiling, a flagstone fireplace of brightly flickering logs, and pregnant Tiki pacing nervously around her kitchen.

"So how was the drive? Awful, I'm sure."

"Not too bad, actually, very little traffic, but the storm's getting worse, really coming down now."

"O I know, I know. This'll be just another minute or so. And you wanted lemon."

"Yes, but if you don't have—"

"I've *got* it!"

Whoa! Irritable, aren't we, Tiki?

"Sugar?"

"Fine."

And she coming out a few minutes later with my tea and a plate of butter cookies and setting it down on the wagon wheel table.

"O thank you. So when's your due date?"

"O, not for another two weeks, but my family's always been early *and* quick, popping them out like blueberry muffins."

"Blueberry muffins?" smirking, "Huh, go figure. Mine was

exactly on time."

"Is that right? You don't really like me, do you, Tory?"

"What? Uh, no, I'm just tired and edgy and—"

"No, be honest, I can see it in your eyes—which are lovely, by the way. Has anyone ever told you you look like Stevie Nicks?"

"Yes, but—"

"Well you do, like soft pastels. Though, really, tell me now, what on earth have I ever done to you? I mean I'm not stealing your father away—"

"Tiki, look—"

"—and I know your mother just died and that you're an only child, but—"

"Tiki," putting my steaming cup down, "I don't think this's the time or place—"

"—I care deeply about your father, care deeply about his work, adore his dog, and I was hoping we could eventually become good friends."

"Well maybe we can," looking away, "find some common ground."

"That's right, O absolutely right—"

"Though I'm not sure about absolutely."

"—but it has to be more than just a one-way street." She suddenly standing. "You know, ever since we met, I've been trying, reaching out to you, and now I'm in no mood, have had it up to *here* with your sarcastic comments, sullen looks, and doing me a favor!"

"Hey, listen, I'm sorry—"

"Nobody twisted your arm, you know, to come up here!"

"Then maybe I should go."

"Yes, maybe you should. This wasn't my idea, you know, and the last thing I need now, the very last thing—" her eyes glazing, "I've had stomach cramps all day, worried about the baby and your father—is some snot-nosed brat with an attitude in my house!"

"Fine, then I'll leave."

"*My God!*"

"What?"

"I think my water broke!"

"*O Jeez!* Here, Tiki, sit, sit, lean back, lean back on the sofa—and let me get you some towels, some sheets!" spinning around like a silly goose, "Where do you keep them?"

"In the closet at the end of the hall!"

And rushing back with an armload of towels and hand-embroidered, eyelet-laced, cream-colored sheets, "Listen, Tiki, I'm sorry, sorry what I said before—"

"Just lay the towels down first—"

"—I was just letting off steam—"

"—and drape the sheets, there, over the sofa."

"—I'm just tired, it's very late, and was taking it out on you, and you don't deserve it."

"No I don't—O Jesus wept, what pain!"

"Contractions?"

"Yes, yes!"

"How many, how often?"

"Just one."

"How long?"

"Ten, fifteen seconds. Your father started having labor pains for me a week ago."

"He *did?*"

"Yes, like Picasso."

"O, fuck Picasso!"

"Yes, fuck Picasso!" she still grimacing.

"Everything's got to have some sort of bloody painting reference."

"I know, Tory, I know!"

"And your doctor's out of town? Is there a hospital, medical facility, near here?"

"Yes, in Sharon or Great Barrington, but we'd never get through the snow."

"And the phones're out. Which doctor is this?"

"O, Dr. McGeehan—had to be an Irishman, of course."

"Of course."

"A pompous pain in the ass, who always wears a monocle, even in surgery."

"That figures. And an old friend of my father's, right?"

"Exactly."

"Tiki, can you stand? Here, take my arm, hold my hand."

"Where we going?"

"Into the bedroom, strip the sheets—"

"I can do it, Tory."

"*I'll* do it!"

And over the next hour or so, her contractions coming every six to ten minutes and lasting roughly thirty seconds.

"O, there's another one. They're coming quicker now."

"I boiled some water and my shoelace."

"What for?"

"To tie off the umbilical cord."

"O, right, yes."

"You care what it is, Tiki?"

"What what is?"

"Duh, like the baby?"

"O shut up, Tory! No, not at all, but your father wants a boy, definitely wants a boy."

"So I heard. Rory."

"Rory and Tory."

"Yuck!"

"O come on, Tory, don't make me laugh—That one lasted longer still."

"We can become a musical duo, like Sonny & Cher."

"Or Simon & Garfunkel."

"Donny and Marie."

"Or the fucking Smothers Brothers—O Christ, that little bugger really wants to get out!"

"And if it *is* a he, he'll spend the rest of his life trying to get back in."

"Isn't that the truth," she squeezing my hand, "O dear God in heaven, they're coming now every minute apart!"

"Don't push, Tiki, don't push! Not yet, not quite yet."

"O sweet Jesus, Holy Mary, Mother of God, this's fucking, *unbearable* pain!"

"Just breathe, keep breathing!"

"Tell me, please, why do only women get to do this?"

"God's plan."

"*Fuck* God! It should come shooting out of a man's ass!"

"Now you're making *me* laugh. Boy, this's fast, too fast. I just hope you don't tear, don't hemorrhage—Push, Tiki, push, harder now, harder, I can feel it, I can feel the head—"

"I'm pushing, I'm pushing—"

"Almost there, almost there—"

"Bloody hell! I'm gonna *DIE!!* Wow, what fucking pain!"

"One more push, here it comes, easy, I've got it, and—he's got red hair and a weenie! We *did* it, Tiki, we *did* it!"

"That we fucking did!"

I'm crying, both of us crying, "And luckily nothing tore! A beautiful fuzzy boy! O Tiki, he's lovely, looks exactly like you. Here, let me snip the cord, tie it off, and clean out the mucous from his nose and mouth," then towel him dry, "And may I present for your approval, ta-da, Rory Timothy Boyne!" placing him gently on her tummy.

• • • • • •

"You know, Tory, I would really love something to drink."

"Coming right up," rising from the kitchen table, the blizzard having finally stopped.

"There's a pitcher in that cabinet, as well as a fully-prepared bottle."

"Of what?"

"Morning with the Leprechauns."

"Is that a drink?"

"Indeed it 'tis. Your father got this new ready-mix at a specialty shop in Dublin, thought it'd be just the thing."

"What's in it?"

"Bailey's Irish Cream, Tullamore Dew, cherry brandy, cold, strong coffee, and you just add crushed ice."

"That'll definitely do it."

"Knock your bloody socks off, Tory. But it's divine and, better yet, goes down so smooth, you don't even realize you're getting smashed out of your mind till you wake up next day in some stranger's bed."

"Fine, but you think you ought to drink, especially if you're breast-feeding?"

"Bring it hither, Tory, just a sip or two, while I'm still in a dither from my three-hour nap!"

Pouring the mix into a Waterford pitcher, the morning sun sharply glinting off the fallen snow.

"And could you put some music on while you're at it, but not too loud?"

"How 'bout U2's 'Rejoice'?"

"Brilliant!"

· · · · · ·

And *wham!* the front door slamming open, and in bound Dad, Gene, and Shay in their woolly ski caps and jackets, wind-cherried noses and rosy-glowing cheeks.

"What're *you* guys doing here, how'd you get through?"

"Just ploughed straight ahead."

"Mommy, we sledded! Daddy and I sledded!"

"That's great, sweetie, great, just terrific!" and I keep giggling uncontrollably.

"But what's going on, what happened? Are you OK? Jaysus, Tory, you're drunk!"

"Like a crazy Irish skunk!" as, dizzily teetering, I hug and kiss Shay and Gene and, with a grand sweep of my hand, escort them into the bedroom, where Tiki, also tipsy, is propped up and beaming as she cradles the baby, and exclaims:

"My dear Seamus, may I present your son and heir, the infamous, four-hour-old, one and only, Rory Timothy Boyne!"

"*O Suffering Christ!*" tears spilling, pouring down his cheeks, into his snowy, grizzled beard.

"I can assure you, love, *he* had nothing at all to do with it!"

And hands trembling, my father raises Rory to the sky, my eyes filming over as I sway off to the kitchen to fill two more glasses to the brim, then returning, lift my crystal goblet.

"A toast. To your son, Dad."

"And to your brother."

"And, Shay, to your cousin as well. Easy there, he's very fragile." Shay now sweetly kissing Rory's forehead.

"And to my precious lassie, whom I can never ever repay."

"And to the wonderful woman you chose!" clinking glasses, "Cheers!"

"*Sláinte!*"

"Ah, *sláinte* it bloody well is, Tiki, and may the hair on Rory's bollocks grow as long as the beard on my horny goat!"

Hagar in Love

May 1998 • L.A.

Part I

So we beat on, boats against the current, Scott Fitzgerald once wrote, *borne back ceaselessly into the past.* But nowhere is the current speeding forward any faster into the future than right here and desperately now as I go racing along the perilous switchback curves of Malibu Canyon, no guardrails, straight drop down— End it all? Finally call it a day? For like my students always say, "Hey, this's where it's happening, baby! Shake, rattle, and roll!"— swerving and squealing onto the Ventura Freeway by the shiny new cars, narrowly missing a Beamer's silver bumper and down the Liberty Canyon off-ramp at sixty mph with Sinatra (who, unbelievably, just died) belting out "April in Paris" with Billy May.

Been in California nearly five years now, turning sixty-two in June, yet I still think of L.A. as a way station, and that one fine day—Tory and I getting divorced in '83 after she ran away with her Psychology prof, Aaron Pendragon, in some panicky rite of passage, seven year itch, needing a younger guy ("It just happened." "Nothing just happens!" Psychobabble bullshit!), and I was knocked for a bloody loop. Though Boyne taking my side at the time for the sake of our son, three-year-old Shay, and estranging himself from his beloved daughter/my wife.

And now, fifteen years later, following a severe bout of cabin fever, here I am all but giving up the "swinging" singles scene (or is it giving me up?) and trying to accept the daunting fact that I can no longer get younger women by going back to four old lovers, my four Golden Oldies—and Trisha, the first, flying down from San Francisco tonight, living alone as I do in my three-bedroom Liberty Canyon home with Nomar, my pure white, two-year-old "Hockney" cat, and still looking like a shaggy (but aging) Paul

Newman, as Tory's mother once said (Newman himself now seventy-three—though few of my students have even seen *Butch Cassidy* or *Cool Hand Luke*), teaching Creative Writing at nearby Pepperdine, trying to get another movie made, and talking at all hours of the day and night to my ex-father-in-law, best friend, and still the greatest painter alive, Seamus Eamon Boyne, over in Ireland, and soon to be seventy himself. Our rambling conversations covering books, film, politics, TV, dance, painting, with me focusing mainly on women, and what to make of them, where to find them, and, lately, why the fuck to even bother.

The bottom line being I feel the clock rapidly ticking toward Medicare and nursing homes, having grown increasingly desperate for a mate, a lover, or at least a traveling companion to end my lonely days—

The phone shrilly ringing as I go sprinting through the door and snatch it up a beat before the answering machine clicks on.

"—Hello, yes?"

"Ah, Suffering *Christ*, Hagar, how the bloody hell *are* ya?"

"O, I've had better days, Seamus."

"Why, what's going on?"

"Well, let's see, for starters, just now, coming back from Pepperdine, I thought again of driving off the cliff."

"Wouldn't it be easier to just cut your wrists?"

"But I can't stand the sight of blood. And if I swallowed pills, I'd probably, like one of my students did, take the wrong bottle and OD on Vitamin C!"

"Tell me, Gene, what's the closest you ever came to actually doing it?"

"Well, when your daughter left, I walked into the bathroom, took out a razor blade, and then said to myself, this is gonna hurt."

"Ah, see, you've lost your Jacobean sense of melodrama, boy. What you *should've* done was driven your car, like I did, onto some railroad tracks and waited for the cataclysmic collision."

"But you changed your mind and were chased by the train, barely escaped."

"Well, the best laid plans. Anyway, seriously now, stop feeling sorry for yourself and tell me what's going on."

"O I don't know, confronting my own mortality, been feeling so alone lately, now that Shay's at USC, just me and my cat—"

"And as James Jones once said, 'Nobody ever lied about being lonely.' "

"Exactly, Boyne, exactly. But look, I can't talk now, call you on Monday, have to pick up Trisha at the airport—"

"O that's right, tonight's the night, the first of your four Golden Oldies."

"Yeah, 'borne back ceaselessly into the past.' "

"And of course I'm pulling for you to choose my daughter once more."

"Well you never know. Anyway, Seamus, I gotta go!"

"So go, go, and I'll talk to you soon, God bless."

Quickly checking my phone messages—nothing here of note, then slipping into my Wrangler jeans, splashing on this bracing Aqua Velva, scarfing down two slices of cold Domino's pizza, before rushing out to Burbank Airport through the 7:30 crush of Friday night traffic in my scarlet Accord.

But the flight's been delayed, turbulence over "the Pacific Rim," and doesn't arrive till 10:05. And the weekend I've been anxiously awaiting for the past several months—since fifty-seven-year-old Trisha had sounded so nurturing, vibrant, and sexy on the phone, she the first woman I slept with after my divorce fifteen years ago, was a great lover then—turns out to be a total disaster now!

"So much traffic, Gene!" "Yeah, and it keeps getting worse with more people moving here." "O, that's probably so. But, you know, this's the first time I've been to So Cal in like, God, sixteen, no, seventeen years—really, I have no desire. And you look the same, Gene, have aged well—" "As have you, Trisha." "Like fine wine, as they say. O listen, could we stop somewhere, a McDonald's or Jack in the Box, just drive on through—my mouth is so parched—just a Diet Coke or raspberry tea, or no, if it's not too much trouble and there's a Starbucks near here, I'd love a sugar-free vanilla soy latte."

"A what?"

· · · · · ·

"But, still, I felt awful for her, Seamus, 'cause she was the one who'd flown down, made the effort, even though I paid for the flight."

"And it got progressively worse?"

"Like an installment of *Entertainment Tonight,* all superficial chitchat, and she constantly worrying what other people would think, eating with her pinky in the air, and voicing these totally banal thoughts as though they were profound insights, like you know who her hero was growing up? Guess."

"Amelia Earhart?"

"No, really."

"Mother Teresa?"

"Come on, Seamus!"

"All right, Audrey Hepburn, Ava Gardner?"

"Try Barbie."

"As in Barbie *doll?*"

"You got it! Puts lipstick on her seven-year-old daughter, but only for special occasions. Gone the free spirit, archaeological digger I once knew. And this's what I've been running into lately, feel my life, like the sands of time, rapidly sifting away through the hourglass."

"Jaysus, you sound like a bloody soap opera, Hagar!"

"Right, *As the Stomach Turns.*"

"Well I'm sorry, boy, I really am, but just chalk it up to experience."

"Fuck experience! I've had enough experience! I'm gonna be sixty-two years old next month!"

"I know, I know, but you still look forty-five."

"Men age better."

"Than who, walruses? Anyway, Gene, age is relative."

"No, my Uncle Hy is a relative. O, and did I tell you about the one I tried to pick up at Barnes and Noble recently, gave her my usual line, 'Were you a student of mine at Pepperdine?' and she says, 'You asked me that last month'?"

"Well at least you've still got your sense of humor, boy."

"Yeah, my cat thinks I'm a riot!"

"Old Nomar Garciaparra! How old is *he* now?"

"Just turned two on St. Patrick's Day. Anyway, Seamus, how're things with you? How's your wife?"

"Tiki's superb as ever, and still, God knows why, tolerating me and my Celtic brio."

"And your son?"

"You mean the new lord of the castle? O Rory's positively brilliant, with the bearing of one to the manner born—while his proud poppa, mad old *moi*, has lately been feeling *his* age."

"How come?"

"O, dealing with wild silence and my perishable fame—like those fading scarves of mist over Dublin Bay—so swiftly out of favor, like being cast away, dismissed, or abandoned on a cliff, after scathing rounds of critical reviews in the leading art journals of today by such distinguished experts as A. Montague Scrotum et al!"

"Well the French still adore you. I just read a review—"

"I know. In France, I'm hot. But so was Joan of Arc. And last month the Tate removed two of my favorite works from their hallowed halls, accusing me of having run out of subjects, that everything I paint looks like me, especially this portrait of Rory I've been doing, can't get his face quite right, feel so distant from him, as I gnaw on, only draw upon, *my* sadly aging image! So I need something to revive, *jumpstart* my career, and I thought what about you, Hagar, making a documentary of me actually painting, like that one about Jackson Pollock?"

"*Great* idea! Matter of fact, Seamus, I was thinking of the very same thing!"

"Ah, well as usual, we're in synch, boy. But getting back to the original subject at hand, let me ask you this, what exactly is it you want from your Golden Oldies?"

"Nurturing, love me back, care about my soul."

"Your soul? You been reading John Donne, Saint Augustine lately?"

"Try Dr. Ruth."

"Hey, don't laugh, Gene. You know the story she tells of the man searching for the perfect woman, who finally finds her—except she's been searching for the perfect man?"

"And on that sagacious note, Kingfish, I gotta go."

"Where you going?"

"I've got to teach a class."

"Right. Well I'm sorry Trisha didn't work out, know how much you were looking forward to it. But you showed her a good time, I'm sure."

"Couldn't have been any kinder, went to Ojai, Santa Barbara, Santa Ynez—"

"So don't get down, you've got three more to go, including my daughter. Just keep rubbing the belly of the Buddha, boy."

"Just the belly?"

"Well who could resist your pick-up line from Pepperdine?"

· · · · · ·

Late at night, after switching back and forth from Charlie Rose to Howard Stern to local news, I put Nomar out in my Jacuzzi room, close the sliding glass door, crawl into bed, and focus once more on my list of four: Trisha (finished); "Titsy Mitzi" Weiss (from high school, with her perfect 34 Cs); Tory (who still calls me all the time); and of course Gabrielle (far away in the Philippines, the elusive love of my life), before I go drifting off into my absurd and crazy dreams (though absurdity's becoming far more commonplace these days, with drive-by shootings, O. J. Simpson, and Timothy McVeigh), back, all the way back, almost thirteen years ago, to Gabrielle when she finally came to New York and made her choice at age thirty-eight.

I'd taken her to a party in Great Neck then at my friend Bucky Friske's house, a reunion bash of our old softball team, and all the guys were there in that three-story, Gatsby-like, brick Tudor home on Ballantine Lane, with six bedrooms, six and a half baths, and a vast, sunken living room. The house was packed to overflowing with our Million Dollar Infield team, their wives and girlfriends, Shelly, Bucky, and Myles Hedon (Lou had died the year before), as Gabrielle and I danced and kissed amidst the spirited whirl of wine and beer and Sinatra swinging up a storm, then later on ducked out through the wide French doors and down the drive to that vine-covered gatekeeper's cottage tucked away in a corner of those flowering grounds. And while she closed the squeaky front door, I stood behind her, flushwarm against her, gently globing the soft heft of her breasts, before sliding one hand down her black watch skirt to her springy hair and slick lips as she sighed and suckled my free ring finger.

· · · · · ·

Awaking with a start at 6:15, feeling so bloody raw and lost at needing to finally put aside the past and accept the present, since Gabrielle had ended up choosing Filipino Paul and gone off to Manila to work and live. But still, wasn't it Churchill who said, "The farther back you look, the farther forward you are likely to see"?

And in point of fact, I've become increasingly fed up with the present, feeling more and more out of synch, and recognizing, for example, none of the recording artists I see later today on the Tower Record walls, wincing at the metallic bird chirp or shriek of car key remotes in the crowded parking lot, and realizing once again as I drive along the tawdry Sunset Strip how much I hate rap, punk, fusion, Jay Leno, Joyce Brothers, crazy L.A. drivers, Chris "Boomer" Berman, O.J. Simpson and Johnnie Cochran, this generation's ignorance of history and literature, cigarette smokers, tobacco companies, college administrators, telemarketers, most corporations, Dick Vitale, cell phones, car phones, make-up, platform shoes, air pollution, noise pollution, the word "like" as in "Like he goes, he goes" or "Like whatever" in every single Valley sentence, the gargoyle faces of Jim Carrey, Whoopi Goldberg, and Rosie O'Donnell on those huge, passing billboards, Bryant Gumbel, Tony Robbins, and the Reverend Jerry fucking Falwell!!

I yearn for purer, mellower, deeper: Paul Desmond and Chet Baker, Keith Jarrett and Jim Hall, June Christy and Sarah Vaughn, the romantic making-out in the backseat of cars, Sinatra or Nat King Cole crooning to the stars—and no deafening L.A.P.D. choppers rattling and clattering low overhead like *Apocalypse Now Redux!!*

This evening, after battling through the zigzag curves of Malibu Canyon once more and teaching my Creative Writing class, I come trudging exhausted through my front door, phone Boyne, who isn't home, and leave a message with his ancient butler Symes.

Later, following a forty-minute nap, I microwave a Stouffer so-called Hearty Dinner of meatloaf and mashed potatoes, wash it down with a bottle of Sprite, give the leftovers to Nomar, his white tail happily swishing, and watch The History Channel's two thousandth program on the rise of the Nazi Era, feeling so burned out in my classes, just going through the motions of the music of language, show don't tell, Joyce, Nabokov, and E.E. Cummings, my mouth moves and I hear my lectures echoing from afar.

And during the succeeding nights, recurring memories of Gabrielle keep haunting my dreams, those *transitory enchanted moments:* suckling her sensual lower lip down by the Seine or nuzzling through the wee small hours as we strolled along the Thames, her hand snug in the back pocket of my jeans—as I thrash around on my sweaty sheets in a hazy half-sleep, till I awake at eight and call Shay down at USC—and get his answering machine: the usual U2 fanfare followed by, "For Shay Hagar at the beep. Thank you."

Beep!

"Hey, man, gimme a call tonight. Hope you're well. 'Bye."

Then I try Boyne in Ireland, punching in all the numbers, eight hours difference, ringing, ringing, ringing—

"Good evening. Boyne residence." Those stentorian butler tones.

"Ah, Symes, so good to hear your Alfred Hitchcock voice again."

"And yours as well, sir. I immediately recognized your New York accent. I'll go fetch your friend."

"Thank you so much."

"*Hagar!* I was just thinking of you, boy, wondering how our filum was coming along."

"So far so good, working on the script."

"Marvelous! O and Tory just left, should be heading for you in the near future, talks about you all the time, says she wants you back, especially when she and Hubby Three keep having problems—"

My call waiting beeping. "Seamus, hold on a second, lemme see what this is—Hello?"

"You still out there in Lalaland, Gene?" Myles Hedon's drawly Jimmy Stewart voice charged with high emotion.

"Hollyweird we call it. But I'm on the other line, so hold on—Seamus, listen, I've gotta take this, call you back."

"All right, boy, and all my love to Shay, and send me your script as soon as you're through."

"Definitely. 'Bye." Hitting the Flash button. "Myles?"

"Still here."

"So tell me, what's up, why the call?"

"I'm getting married."

"You're kidding! To whom?"

"Elysa, that former student of mine."

"The one who's a clone of your high school sweetheart?"

"The very same."

"And how old is she now?"

"She just turned thirty-seven. And you're my best man, Hagar!"

So in June, right before I turn sixty-two, Shay vows to buy me a computer for my birthday ("Enough, Dad, with your 1954 Royal Portable, join the twenty-first century!"), and I fly back to New York for Myles's wedding at the Waldorf.

I dance with all the bridesmaids, drink far too much champagne, toast the groom and his former student with forced humor, then, my head heavy and dizzily spinning, heart aching, sneak out at 1:35 and drive this rented Escort slowly through an early morning drizzle across the Queensboro Bridge and end up, of course, in Great Neck.

The town is dark, Middle Neck Road all but empty except for a solitary cab as I splash by old village haunts, toward Kings Point with its ghostly trees, past the shadowy glow of the Merchant Marine Academy, and down to Bucky's brick Tudor home on Ballantine Lane, tears now clouding my gaze, as I turn off the engine of this compact rental car.

Squinting, I step gingerly into the mist. The sloping lawn now overgrown, the large house looking so desolate and strange, and a "For Sale" sign hung out front—as I strain hard to hear the music of the past, then head cautiously down the wet, pebbled drive and stop before that gatekeeper's cottage.

The paint is flaking, the door still creaks, and I cross slowly over the threshold, within the echoing walls, pause, then tentatively mount the narrow stairs, fumbling my way along the dim-lit hall to enter the small, slanted bedroom—and, blinking in the rainy light, catch my breath as I stare and gradually become aware that above the black watch comforter raised to her chin is the bewitching grin of her erotic angel's face.

Then her gossamer image fades as I slump down on the bed and my thoughts go tumbling back to 1984, ten months after my crushing divorce, still trying to fill in Tory's loss, when I took Shay to the Museum of Natural History in New York and met Trisha Claire, her hair a lovely walnut gloss, who worked in the gift shop and played hide-and-seek with my son. And that was all I needed to begin a heated, three-week romance. She leaving soon for Guatemala on an archaeological dig, and so great in the hay, as well as with Shay, who was himself off a day later to Váncouver, then Ireland for the summer with Tory, Boyne, Tiki, and Rory, their bouncing baby boy. And my loneliness became unbearable (replaying Tory sex scenes, masturbatory dreams), so I called Trisha in Guatemala and, with her urging, flew down from New York. And she greeting me at the airport with, "We have to talk. I met someone I might be in love with." " 'Might be in love with'? Why didn't you tell me *before* I got on the plane?" "I wasn't sure, still am not." "So what should we do?" "Well let's just see what happens, Gene." And we went hitchhiking through the highlands, showering and sleeping naked together, but no sex, till after five days of blue-balled, climbing the walls, frustration, I couldn't take it anymore and told her I was going home.

That last morning I came sullenly down to breakfast, Trisha at the head of a long wooden table and me to her right, with other assorted guests, when out of the corner of my eye I spied a flash of raven hair, heard what seemed to be a Dutch accent—and glanced around to see that erotic angel's face with its turned up nose, Irish rose complexion, jade green eyes, proud breasts, and coltish thighs.

"Excuse me?"

"Pardon?"

"Might you be Dutch?"

"No."

"No?"

"Belgian," as she was served her steaming coffee and *huevos rancheros.*

"Ah. Well I'm Gene. And this's Trisha."

"Hello. I'm Gabrielle."

Her silky voice, face a vision, like a sunlit band in a forest glade—as I waited for the trees to sway—yet she remained.

And we went bouncing through the green hills of Guatemala in her party's van, with me flirting outrageously to piss off Trisha, till we parted near Tikal.

"Listen, why don't you give me your address and I promise that I'll write."

On the back of her deposit slip—her impish grin, no other paper in her purse—she wrote her name, Gabrielle Fleury, and her Bruges address.

And as soon as I got home:

August 21, 1984

Dear Gabrielle,

Remember that van bouncing through the green hills of Guatemala, with me on the floor and you seated above, all raven-haired and pretty, bewitching grin, before we parted and you gave me your address? And now I write to you, after liking what I saw of you, heard of you. Will you ever come to the States? I live outside New York City in a Crane Neck cottage overlooking the sea as a writer/teacher, typing madly away, producing unpublished novels, trying to sell stories to the movies, and raising, by myself, my four-year-old son, Shay. Please send me your picture and fill in the warm blurs. Then show up here, where I will wine you and dine you—and finally stop pining away.

3 September 1984

Dear Gene,

Yes, I remember us "bouncing through the green hills of Guatemala." It was such a nice surprise to get your letter. Didn't expect it. Find it kind of hard just to start writing about myself. It reminds me of those "unknown" penfriends I sometimes corresponded with years ago "to stimulate international contact" or something, having no idea who was on the other end of the line, wondering, asking for photos, teaching each other the language—Spanish in my case. Well, at least I know, **vividly**, how you look, how you talked. I remember myself curiously staring at you during that breakfast we had, and in the van, the square where we changed addresses, you with that brown-haired girl, me with my back turned to you, eyes in the back of my head.

And now back in Bruges, I have to get used again to a different view: soon enough a frozen canal covered with snow, people skating over uneven ice, birds and ducks fighting for the few pieces of bread they get outside my room in a studenthouse.

Will I ever come to the States? Probably not for a long time, not before you come to Europe . . .? End this year, beginning next, I have to

do research for my graduate study. I'm planning to do that in Mexico and to combine it
with some travelling around, maybe South America. I should love to go to Peru, Colombia—it's
all so open.

But lots of things I like to know about you.
Write me about yourself. I like your style
of writing. Do you also write autobiographi-
cal stories? Do you like to send some of your
stories?? I'm waiting.

Sept. 12, 1984

Dear Gabrielle,
How great to hear from you—in your small, neat,
slanted script. Recalling your lovely angel
face, impish smile, curious jade green eyes.

I'm back teaching Creative Writing at Stony
Brook University and taking care of my son.
I've enclosed one of my published stories (in
exchange for a photo of you?). I may be in
Ireland this summer. Meet me? So write soon.

23 September 1984

Dear Gene,
I liked your story, your sense of humor. You
write letters like you write stories (or the
other way around): a little impatient, short,
to the point sentences, full of emotion/feel-
ings—Hard to describe for me. I'm not a writer. Only started to appreciate **good** writing
three years ago or so, and since that time, I
only feel more frustrated in my attempts to
write papers and letters.

Hope you can decipher my "small, neat" (ha, ha) script.

Anyway, it's hard for me to decide **now** if I'll go with you to Ireland. The situation in my new lodgings still makes it difficult to make fixed plans.

My proposal: Why don't you come to Belgium before going to Ireland? If we still feel like it, then we can go to Paris, London, or wherever. All I can say now is that I'm pretty sure I'll be in Bruges through the fall, and maybe even all winter. **And**, that I'd really like to see you, I am really curious to see you! Of course we can also meet after your trip to Ireland. Well, just make sure that we meet somewhere, sometime.

· · · · · ·

Meanwhile, Shay and I during those amazing Indian summer days went veering by the shimmering blaze of Long Island Sound in my green Mustang convertible with the top down and the butter yellow bands of his hair fanning softly back like a fluted shell.

"Daddy?"

"Yes?" speeding through Crane Neck with its wealthy, gated homes.

"Why'd you marry Mommy?"

"Why?" under a canopy of rustling scarlet oaks, " 'Cause I loved her, still do, and you, too. But why're you asking?"

"Do you have to get married if you love somebody?"

"Not necessarily."

"Well, you know what *I'm* gonna do, Daddy?"

"No. What?"

"Get married, have a boy, then get divorced and keep the boy."

And approaching Setauket Harbor, a cluttered, briny bustle, all those sailboats, speedboats, and cabin cruisers resting forty to fifty yards offshore, rowboats moored along the dock to reach them, as, stepping down into a gently rocking one, I hoisted Shay aboard, and, pretending we were heading toward our own cabin cruiser, rowed out to the breeze of the bay.

Shay trailing his hand in the cool water and wondrously wide-eyed as I identified blue herons, ducks, geese, and herring gulls, bulrushes and spartina grass that we grazed and glided past—and he such a great, totally absorbed listener—as we neared the reedy shore.

"You know, Shay, nothing makes me happier than being here with you."

"Me, too."

The pure sungleam of his hair, Tory's Nordic cheeks like a shiny Braeburn apple, those mesmerizing hyacinth eyes, and long-muscled limbs like mine as a boy. And really, it wasn't 'cause he was beautiful that I loved him, but 'cause I loved him that he was beautiful.

• • • • • •

19 October 1984

Dear Gene,

The big news is that on the 25th of November I will leave for Sri Lanka! I think I told you that I have to do research for my graduate study, and that I planned to do it in Mexico or South America. Well, I changed my mind. Instead I accepted an offer to make a photo (and maybe film) reportage for the Dutch Royal Tropical Museum in Sri Lanka.

I'm really looking forward to go, and at the

same time, it scares me a bit: since the other side of me **hates** the academic life and doesn't see the use of all those anthropologists going into the field, to stay there for a while, and come back to that comfortable, rich Western world and write about how things would go so much better in the Third World if **they** only . . . and if *we* only. In short, I'm skeptical.

Do you still plan/hope to come to Europe? Of course I should like to see you, but I also should like to have the *time* and *rest* for it. Think about it—you are still welcome!

Well, maybe I will phone you one of these days (when you give me your number). I feel like doing it, but I just don't . . .?! Write me soon, please.

October 29, 1984

Dear Gabrielle,

Your trip to Sri Lanka sounds marvelous, but I want to go with you! And, PLEASE CALL (516) 751-6281! I appreciate and sympathize with your timidity, but damn it, I want to **see** you, **hear** your voice, **stroke** your hair—some **contact**, please!! There are no real women in my life at the moment. I'm sorry my letters are so short; I guess I'm just pithy, that's all.

· · · · · ·

And that was when Boyne came to the States one final time to try and get me and Tory back together. He urging to at least see her point of view, "Which I've always had an extremely difficult time myself in doing," that she'd felt she'd made a mistake with Pendragon, "And realize, Hagar, the importance of the past and how fleeting life can be"—as we zipped on by station wagons and vans toward Stony Brook's Christian Avenue, Shay remaining at home to play on the swing or down at the park at the bottom of the street with all the neighborhood kids. And the town not quite sure what to make of Boyne, the greatest painter since Picasso, keeping their proper distance like he was a Leper, E.T., or about to slice off his ear, but for those fearless few forging through for his priceless autograph.

"And strange to say, Gene, I've been missing that old notoriety lately—hell, used to be when Seamus Boyne talked, people listened; now, I've become defunct as E.F. Hutton. Anyway, today I'm going to treat you to my own special version of a 'ploughman's lunch': a hunk of home-baked bread roll topped with a large chunk of Irish Cheddar, Bermuda onion, beefsteak tomato, and a generous spoonful of Branston pickle!"

And we pulled into that sandy lot and went trotting up the creaky steps into Elmo's wood-shingled Cheese Shed filled with people and the feety aroma of Havarti and Danish Blue, Roquefort and Raclette, Wensleydale and well-aged Gouda. The customers all shuffling their timid soles toward a pretty, ponytailed clerk behind the counter, WPAT mood music softly playing above the air conditioner's drone, and a university student, backpacked, bespectacled, and straggly-haired, in ragged dungarees, sampling a sliver of Limburger, then grimacing, "Whoa, man, that is totally *awesome!*" his snaggletoothed grin aimed at the permed woman behind him. But she, after flashing a plastic smile, swiftly averting her eyes (for one does not share surprise in a proper Long Island town), while Boyne kept on talking about tempus fugiting, netting their timid stares and whispers, "That's him!" "I know, I know!" like little mice in their cheesy bin, when the Beatles' "Yesterday" came on over the radio, and be began humming along—more curious stares and timid whispers—then suddenly broke into song, booming it out, and spreading his arms wide for a big finish, *"Now I need a place to hide away, Oh, I believe in yesterday!"* Silence: gaping mouths, eyes fluttering away, but the snaggletoothed student raucously whooping and applauding, the pretty, ponytailed clerk giddily grinning, her hands raised to her mouth in child-like glee, as Boyne reeled off our order of Irish Cheddar and Gourmandise, paid in cash, received his cheese, then boldly strode, with his chin held high—the line parting like the Red Sea—out into the breezy air.

And what *did* I want then? What was I searching for in the autumn of '84 as a single man, single parent? Love? Romance? Fill in my loss of Tory? Or one exquisite girl to show that I was still thirty-three? A weekend of Sodom, a torrent of oral delights? Or a wife, to replace my wife, ex-wife, second wife? Whom I couldn't stop missing! Or someone with Tory's vivacity, Tory's capacity to humor and tolerate me? Someone to worship my words, my wand—in short, a dream-image of Tory? Another nightmare circle? Or just adolescent fancies after my repressed Great Neck childhood, few facts of life, no birds nor bees, and today, no glove, no love, no pill, no thrill—for I, Hagar, was once so shy, with crushes in my mind—and, suddenly alone again, was riding high on a wild rush of freedom, having always been, over the years, a rover, loner, lost in my literary life.

For bred as I was on movie dreams and magazine scenes of the face of Grace, butt of Brigitte, breasts of Raquel, I was hurrying to fill that void, Herr Hagar, a Humbert from behind, peeker round corners, four paces to the rear, waiting to spring and say—what? Words were on the lip, the tongue, stories were in the making.

But more often than not it was home alone to my nightmare bed and the thought that this was what I'd finally come to: no longer the dashing, donnish lover whose presence would rivet the gaze of girls, rather a forty-eight-year-old writer/college prof with his somber, tweedy walk, playing out his fading dream of being lost in a carnal maze. And whose legs could hardly catch 'em anymore, for how fast the girls did stride, especially the ones I taught, with pills in their purses and sex on their nubile brains, and used to aging lechers like me as I whirled right, darted left—Ah, but I couldn't go deep in the hole like Nomar anymore and slingshot a frozen rope to first. Trade him in, fans, for two players to be named later. Over-the-hill Hagar on creaky pins. Nonsense! I was still lithe on my feet in my fantasy mind, ranging far and wide and making the bare-handed pickup besides!

And strange how forty-eight now seems so young!

• • • • • •

November 21, 1984

Dear Gabrielle,

My Great Neck story was bought for TV this morning and I'm high as a kite, though the agents are still haggling over prices. It's been a long time in coming, and no guarantee it'll ever be made, but it's a start. Hope Sri Lanka is terrific for you—tell me more about it and when you'll be back in Belgium. Will you ever call? Please do. I'd love to hear your voice again—and I won't bite on the phone, promise. Also, I'm still hoping to get to Europe (and Bruges and you) sometime this summer. When, I can't exactly say, since this TV thing may interfere. However, if all is clear, I'm off! By the way, do you have a phone, in case I should decide to call **you**? Please send number and best time to reach you. Again, so far away, but we **will** meet—and strange, somehow, hardly knowing you, I feel so close to you.

5-12-84

Dear Gene,

Sri Lanka was very successful, and helped me over a lot of fears for my research. And it made me decide that I'm completely fed up with the university, so I plan to finish next year.

More than two weeks home now, and for the first time after having been away for a long time, I don't feel like leaving immediately. I'm tired of travelling. Now, I stay with my friend Todd till I find a place of my own. That will be hard given the number of people who look for a house here, and the number of houses available. Maybe I'll have to squatter again. Todd has a beautiful floor, enough space, a balcony, and we get along fine, but I feel I need my own house. I have this extreme need for independence, freedom.

How do you live? Do you have a house, an apartment? Do you live alone, together? I know you probably will not answer these questions, but I'll try anyway, you never know.

I am glad everything worked out fine with the TV movie. Very happy for you.

Maybe you are right, I should phone you. I guess that's the only way left for me to get you talking. I remember you as very talkative during our famous van ride!?

Well dear Gene, again I've been staring at the telephone for 15 minutes or so, but I'm too big a coward. Also, all those stupid thoughts cross my mind: Are we crazy? Dreaming? We met five months ago, *FIVE* months ago, and we hardly talked that time. I talked more to your girl-friend than to you . . . And now I'm supposed to phone you! Nevertheless, I enjoy the corre-spondence (and God knows why, since you never tell me anything), and I am *very* curious to meet you again. I have a good feeling about it, feel the same: hardly knowing you, though feeling close. Strange. So, nothing to stop me, except my shyness, I have to confess. But I have found a way out, so here is *my* telephone number: 011-32-50-258380.

Best times to phone are: Monday afternoon (till 17.00); Wednesday afternoons (till 17.00) and Friday (id.); at those times I'm doing courageous attempts to study. I hope you are an early riser, since it's six hours later here. Don't postpone phoning me as long as I did!!

• • • • • •

"Gabrielle?"

"Yes?"

"Gene."

"Well, well, well." Her lovely Belgian chuckle.

"I was afraid Sri Lanka might've swallowed you up in some steamy tropical rain forest, ravaged by man-eating tigers or nibbled by horny piranha fish."

A delightful laugh, "No, I'm just back in boring Bruges and Brussels again. You got my letter?"

"I did. And you sound good (I mean your tone), rather sprightly, bouncy, devil-may-care. I wish I were there with you."

"I know. So do I."

"Will we ever see one another? No, really, we *have* to spend some time together soon, we *will* spend some time together soon."

"I hope so."

"Also, please think of coming here when you've finished your studies, either on holiday or to do scholarly investigations of the Hagar species, Writer Erectus."

"The what? O," another lovely chuckle, "I see."

"And once again my phone number is (516) 751-6281 in Stony Brook, Long Island. And I'm still feeling close—no, even closer to you now than before."

"Me, too."

" 'Bye."

"Bye-bye."

• • • • • •

19 December '84

Dear Gene,

Finally your letters have a voice. A part of the Hagar puzzle. Writer Erectus. Strange to hear it. I had to get used to it. Even stranger it was to hear a voice that belongs to a face which I only vaguely remember. It made me realize that, since I cannot "fill you in," it is very hard to talk to you by telephone. Besides, that morning I got up late and I was still half-asleep when you phoned. Anyway, in August or September I hope to fill in the rest of your puzzle.

Now, my plans: This month I'll be in Bruges, then in March I'll leave again for Sri Lanka to finish my research. You are *also welcome* **there**.

It will be at least warmer than in Belgium now.
I'll stay there two weeks or so, then I'll
leave for Nepal, where I'm planning to hike
through the Himalayas, if my legs are willing
to carry me still.

Please write me before the 30th, so I can
make my plans. Or you can give me a quick call
about **when** (not if) you will come.

But I might be able to meet you in Paris in
April.

Hope your TV movie is going well. Are you
sure it is about Great Neck or Guatemala? (ha,
ha) Anyway, I think you should make a decision now. So go to the travel agency this very
afternoon and buy your ticket—you need a holiday. And if you postpone it any longer, you
will never do it.

· · · · · ·

"So, Hagar, you make your reservation?"

"Yes, but I'm having second thoughts, Seamus."

"Go."

"But I don't even know Gabrielle, met her for twenty minutes in
Guatemala, and now spending all this money—"

"Just go! You'll never remember the money. And you can even
stay at my apartment in Neuilly behind the Arc de Triomphe."

"I thought you were plumping for Tory and me to get back
together?"

"I am. But go anyway! I can hear it in your voice."

· · · · · ·

Then her plans changed again and she had to cancel our April in Paris.

And I got really depressed, the wind knocked out of my sails and nothing I could do, the movie delayed once more (welcome to Hollyweird!), but two days later, Gabrielle wrote to say that May was out but she could meet me in Paris in June:

> I will be coming from Brussels by train or hitchhiking. But for my own rest, I like to be clear to you, before you make your plans definite. It is hard to explain my fear—you call it pessimism, I rather call it rationalism, though I hate both feelings. Up to now I was under the impression that you would come to Europe **anyway**, and that meeting me was going to be **one** of the **many** things you were planning to do here. (Otherwise you could have come as well to Belgium). I thought it would be fun to meet you and was/**am** curious, so I didn't stop you, maybe even on the contrary. Now that I understand that you come **specially** for me, it feels much more "threatening" for me (if you excuse the word, I can't find any better in English). I got the idea that you have plans with me, and that scares me. I hope you can understand this feeling. Knowing that somebody comes specially to the other side of the ocean to meet someone gives one, at least **me**, the feeling we **have** to make something of it, or even more than that. It is a stupid feeling, a bad base to start with. Main thing is that I don't want to feel **obliged** to anything. This is mainly **my** problem, but I just want

to be honest about my thoughts, so you'll understand my nervousness, or "pessimism," as I have been honest about my **enthusiasm** to see you. I **am** looking forward to seeing you in Paris, though I don't know yet for how long I can stay, that will depend on my study, work, and **us**, of course.

Don't let yourself be scared away by this letter, but also don't fill me in with your **dreams** about me. I think part of my nervousness comes from the situation I am in now, having somewhat of a relationship with Todd. Maybe you'll understand that in this situation, I am not so open for new "adventures." Well, more than enough about this subject. I feel a little silly writing this. At the same time, it *is* important to me. Again, don't let yourself be scared away. I really like to see you in June.

· · · · · ·

And I picked her up amid the smoky bustle and clutter of the Gare du Nord with its palmlike pillars, she looking even lovelier than I recalled, tentative and shy, and with a nagging headache, before we taxied rapidly back to Rue Parmentier behind the Arc de Triomphe, made fumbling love, took a splashing bath together, walked and talked along the boulevards, with her hand snug in the back pocket of my Wrangler jeans (always envied guys whose girls did that), revealed our ages, she thirty-six, me forty-nine, and it was bliss, one of the finest times ever!

• • • • • •

July 10, 1985

Dear Gabrielle,

Still spinning inside—Paris timeclocks ticking, lovely images of you flickering past: the
sweet summer softness of you teasing and pinch-
ing, laughing and flinching—and six hours of
Air France back to New York and my son all warm
and bundly for me at home. It was all so right;
our first dinner of steak au poivre at Le Petit
Perigord, Bergerac wine, and hesitant love,
soaping, giggling in the tub, but far more,
just clicking—so rare in my life for it to be
such restful, mellow, relaxing fun, and caring
for your precious feelings, Monet's lily pads,
and Nabokov's prose, your hand snug in my back
pocket—so close, the joy and wonder of us. And
I *know* you felt it, too! How marvelously rare
to find our reality at the end of a 3,000 mile
fantasy!! (after all your aspirins and pain-
relievers and assorted headache potions finally
did the trick). And shy you, so lovely to my
eyes, realizing how lovely you can be in someone else's eyes, in your white Esprit jeans
and sneakers and maroon sweatshirt (unwashed
and reeking of you—I LOVED IT!!), bright you
and poetic you and zany, soft, and tender you
(Is he in midair, folks? *Certainment, mes
dames et monsieurs. O certainment!*) How I
loved that late-night soccer game we played in
the streets of Neuilly! I often imagine now

as I coach my son in soccer—your football—how
delightful it would be to have you out there
playing and coaching, too. I'd put you at
right wing for your sheer Bruges speed.

And wondering again when we'll meet??? Seems
so silly, doesn't it? 'Cause I don't believe
we'd ever grow bored or edgy or dulled by
day-to-day routine. If our process is right,
everything else falls into place. Please write
or call collect at any time—even if you have
nothing to say—your nothing is my something.

All my love.

· · · · · ·

"Gabrielle?"

"Ah! I hoped it was you!"

"Well I miss you *a lot* this morning—"

"Me, too!"

"—as once again Paris bloomed in my brain, washing away hot New York and the smoggy madness that surrounds my life, so I've been thinking of all sorts of ways to see you, maybe going to Belgium next Christmas or possibly Paris again—"

"I know."

"—or some small wooded enclave, some hidden nook, where I can snuggle and hug you, stroke you and make you laugh."

"And to think, *lieve* Gene, only two weeks ago we were *in* Paris. It seems unreal now and faraway. I am so glad, though, that I went, that I finally know who you are, about who I was having fantasies. Though these long distance calls always make me a bit nervous, like I have to hurry to say the things I want to say, and I always need some time to warm up. But nevertheless, I love it when you phone, and now your voice sounds so familiar and close."

"Close enough to kiss your tummy, nuzzle your nose, cup your breasts, bite your neck, nibble your toes, and in general make a feast of the taste and smell of you, the warm and lovely wonder of you, *mon petit et précieux chou?*"

"Well, just for starters, I guess."

"In fact, *your* voice has given me an erection."

"Just my voice?"

"Even had a premature emission. Anyway, I've got to go, take Shay to play school—but listen, soon I will zoom into Bruges unannounced or come storming into Sri Lanka, knocking various lovers hither and yon before ravishing you good and proper! I miss you very, very much, sweet *chou.*"

"Me, too."

"Bye-bye."

" 'Bye."

• • • • • •

And then, after another eight months of letters and phone calls and her traveling to Nepal and India and another stop in Sri Lanka, my movie was made, and we met in London in March of '86.

And it was even *better* than Paris! I was working on a new script about George Mallory, the legendary climber, who in 1924 (thirty years before Hillary and Tenzing) disappeared 700 feet from the summit of Everest, and she was there for her new job at CCI, the Cross-Cultural Institute, a policy think tank organization out of Brussels. We stayed at a lovely Tudor flat near Holland Park for five days of passionate love-making, heated intimacy, and dinners at Trattoo, Wheeler's, and the Cork & Bottle, before she rushed off in a taxi to a CCI meeting, staring intensely back at me through the cab's rear window, her jade eyes glowing, till she disappeared from sight like an old-time romantic movie, her Scorpio self so scared by this overwhelming vulnerability and flood of tender emotion.

But the major problems still remained of geography and timing:

she wanting me to move to Bruges, and no way I could then with Shay.

· · · · · ·

Friday, 29 March '86

My dearest Gene,

Back at work. Lots of things to do—thinking of you—the hell with work!

Did I tell you how much I enjoyed being with you in London? How sorry I felt that time was so short (I know, entirely my fault)? I felt so relaxed and comfortable. I liked talking with you, wandering through London with you. I loved making love with you (next time we meet I'll try not to be sick with a tremendous headache [Paris] or to be so tired [London], then it should be even better). I miss you, think about you a lot. Last night I was reading the Cummings poem you bought me on Monday, "somewhere i have never travelled," it's very beautiful, and then the book I bought myself, Sex Tips For Girls. I was reading the part about the diaphragm, and it felt good to know that I am not the only one struggling with the damn thing. Anyway, so much for the sexy and unsexy things (I should be finishing my Philippines conference proposal now: very unsexy).

If I go on a research trip next spring or summer to the Dutch Antilles, I'll come and see you, your cottage, your son, your writing room, and 1954 Royal Portable typewriter (if by then you'll not have settled down with some Hollywood bimbo). Would it be as good in N.Y., or is it the physical distance between us which makes it so special? What a crazy, frustrating situation—you in New York and Long Island, me in Brussels and Bruges, all tangled up with my new job—Todd and I broke up, we were fighting too much. It hardly makes sense. So, no promises, no expectations. **But**, you are very important to me, much more so than before.

Please send me more, much more of your work. And now, one last question: Why is it that I like you so much with your glasses on? And one more: Tell me about the most important loves in your life since or during your marriage. I know that's not a question, but a little essay will do.

Lots of love and kisses. I miss you, miss you, miss you!!!

· · · · · ·

So another year went by, I turned fifty, the Big Five O, without a blink, since I thought I still looked and felt thirty-five, and she finally came to New York, but this time with Filipino Paul (he to see his children from his first marriage), her new "friend" from CCI, who had moved to Bruges for a few months, before they left for Manila.

We had three and a half days together under Crane Neck's sweltering sun, played soccer with Shay, frolicked and gamboled ("Those are small towns in Suffolk County: West Frolic and East Gambol"), nuzzled and kissed at Bucky Friske's party, but that was the extent of our love-making as Paul called twelve times a day. And at the end of the week, I got her letter:

Dear Gene,

First, as you (hopefully) know, I always love seeing you, being with you: You have been and are a great friend for me in all my bad and better times. You have always been there, and that is more than I can say about myself. The realization of this makes me feel close and warm to you, and makes me hope that this will never change.

Having had lots of reason and time to think about my life the last couple of months, I have come to see that I want something else out of our relations than you do (I suspect). What I would like is a long-standing friendship, nothing more, nothing less. I like you, I love you, but, Gene, I'm not in love with you. And I don't think this will change. My anxiety is that you once again will be disappointed.

And there is another thing you should know, something which has developed only recently, and I am still trying to figure out what it means. It is, I fear, not something you will like, and I guess that is why I feel so hesitant writing you about it—fear of hurting you, fear of losing your friendship. Over the last six months that I got to know Paul, I have grown to like and love him, though I never really realized my feelings for him until recently. Only during my visit here did I start to understand what this could develop into, that it could be more than a good friendship, though we didn't do anything about

it. The time I have spent with him the last couple
of weeks, though, made these feelings grow. And
although I don't quite know where all this will
go and where I want it to go, I want to give it a
chance. I feel serious enough about it.

I think I know all the things you will
think and say: about me and Paul, about me
and you, about me. And yes, you are right: Up
to a certain point, I am very ambivalent in
my relation with him, I find it very hard to
commit myself, although I find it difficult to
figure out if that is so because a relation is
not satisfactory enough, or because I cannot
commit myself to anybody. It must run in the
family. My two sisters have the same "inde-
pendent, ambivalent" attitude, which certainly
doesn't make our love lives any easier. But I
think the time has finally come to try.

It is still my life, and I will learn standing
up, falling down, taking risks (as you always
tell me I should take).

Yet as soon as I write to you, I start to
doubt everything, and I want to see you again.
And maybe you are right that this means the
end of our contact. But I hope it won't be.
Maybe this all sounds so absurd to you. I don't
know what else to say. There is this continuous struggle inside me between my heart and
head. Somehow, these days, I tend to follow
my father's (bad) influence too much and choose
for the reason. Though I always feel very
mixed about that. God, I am so Belgian, so
Calvinistic!

```
               Don't hate me. Much Love,
                    Gabrielle

                      · · · · · ·
```

Two years passed, Shay now a trim and athletic nine and a half
(and a far better athlete than his father ever was at the same age),
Tory divorced Pendragon and went through a difficult time, lived
in Ireland for a while, before I heard from Gabrielle again:

```
                        Manila, October 25, 1988
Dear Gene,
WHAT IS THIS, A BOYCOTT??? Should I give up on
you or do you have a good excuse for not having
written me for two whole years? I hope nothing
is wrong; I also worry, you creep, now that I
have just turned forty!
   How is your Everest script coming along?
Will it be filmed in Nepal? In that case, I will
take the screen test. Or, don't you need the
expertise of an anthropologist who can tell
them everything they want to know about local
culture, customs, and climate? Who will be in
it? Paul Newman? Robert Redford? They are both
old but still cute. I don't mind taking a
screen test for them. Seriously, let me know.
   Still faithfully yours—and PLEASE WRITE!!!

                        January 12, 1989
Dear Gabrielle,
I finally sold my first novel, after breaking
the Guinness record for rejections at 162!
```

                              19 January '89
Dear Gene,

Just got your great news!!! Congratulations,
I'm so happy for you. You deserve it! I wish
I could be there to celebrate AND to see your
Irish book. Can I have a copy, please?
    Lots of love,
    Gabrielle

                    • • • • • •

We kept in intermittent touch, and then in '93 when Shay turned fourteen, he and I moved to L.A., driving my green Mustang across country, stopping to see some major league games, and he, who knew just about every rock lyric ever penned, started switching radio stations back and forth from Phil Collins's "Invisible Touch," Guns N' Roses' "November Rain," and U2's "All I Want Is You" to my "lamo" music, as he called it, whenever I sneaked in a moment or two of Sinatra's "It Was a Very Good Year" or Brubeck's "Take Five," "So weak, Dad!" before returning once more to hard rock, alternative rock, and "She has a built-in ability."

Finally, somewhere near Kansas City, I, too, began singing "his song."

"I thought you didn't like it, Dad?" he asked.

"It grows on you. 'She has a built-in ability. . . .' "

"Yeah?"

"Yeah what?"

"What comes next?"

" 'Built-in ability to'—I don't know, Shay, tell me."

" 'To take everything she sees.' "

" 'To take everything she sees.' . . . Then what?"

"Dad, you want to stop at a hospital and check for Alzheimer's disease?"

"OK, Shay, come on!"

" 'And now it seems I'm falling for her—' "

And three years later, this same son asked, "Dad, did you ever hear of Chet Baker?"

"Yes, I've heard of Chet Baker. I've got just about every record he ever made."

And the next year at eighteen: "Dad, did you ever hear of Sibelius?"

"You like Sibelius?"

And last month came the coup de grâce when I called him one night down at USC, and he sounded really depressed.

"Shay, you OK?"

"No, Dad, really bummed."

"Why?"

"Sinatra died."

"Don't tell me—"

"He's the man."

The two of us had settled in a cozy Liberty Canyon cul-de-sac, I ended up coaching him in basketball and JV baseball at Agoura High School, *Everest* was never made, but I kept on writing and teaching, Tory married Irish Simon McKenna, a year younger than she and part of the cast of *Riverdance*—and that, with a deep, protracted sigh at three on this misty Great Neck morning, brings me full circle back to the present.

June 1998 • L.A.

Part II

• • • • • •

"So, Hagar, how've you been, back from your 'fabbo' New York wedding, eh, boy?"

"Yeah. OK, I guess, though I keep feeling like I'm losing my hold on the moment, Seamus, that the present is swiftly slipping away."

"Why, what happened now? Not that Pepperdine cliff again?"

"No, no. Well, for example, I met this girl the other day at the check-out counter of the supermarket—you know, 'Paper or plastic?' with a sensual lilt—a fresh-scrubbed, Midwestern blonde. And I took my glasses off to appear, you know, more youthful, squinting hard at her name tag, it looked like 'Lynn,' and when I got home, I called the market and asked to speak to Lynn. 'Who?' said the manager. 'Lynn. She's a checker.' 'Lynn? Lynn? Sorry, we have no Lynn working here,' he says. And when I went back there, she was really friendly again, but this time I had my glasses on, and her name wasn't *Lynn* but *Tammy!* I'm telling you, Seamus, my sight, my hearing's going, coming apart at the seams!"

"So what're you gonna do about it?"

"Call 'Titsy Mitzi' Weiss, my old flame from high school."

"And how old is she?"

"My age, and now married to an Enron exec who just retired, drinks like a fish, no sex. She was the very first girl I ever danced with at the Great Neck Youth Center when I was thirteen. 'Titsy Mitzi,' with her perfect 34 Cs—and, as I told her, her breasts left a treasured impression forever on my chest."

"Now there's an image to savor on a dark and stormy Irish night. But, Gene, listen, are ya sure you're all right?"

"For the moment. No, I'm fine, Seamus, fine. And now Tory's arriving in L.A. on July 15."

"You looking forward to it, boy?"

"Honestly?"

"Honestly."

"Not really, but I'm still rubbing the belly of the Buddha."

"Right, well call me as soon as my daughter leaves."

"Do I have a choice?"

"Not really. 'Bye."

And I *have* stayed in pretty good shape for my age, and since I last saw her, at six feet, 185, work out every morning, lift weights, jog, have most of my hair, now silvery and curled over my collar, a beguiling smile, if I do say so myself (with partial removable bridge at the rear), and a twinkle to my blinking eye.

And thinking lately that maybe Tory and I *could* recapture that unbridled and carefree air of our courting days in New York when she was a blonde, glimmering girl, twenty years my junior, and looking so much like a young Stevie Nicks, as we whirled through the Village hurly-burly and roasting coffee aroma drifting under the awnings, the jubilation of her eyes, ponytail bobbing in the breeze, soft blonde hair that I loved to loosen and let tumble over her shoulders, the sun finding fiery strands and tawny, burnished bands. Then off to the Wicklow hills we flew, where she danced for me each morning or rode the white dream ponies along the seacoast of Connemara. Weeks of soaring highs, Irish skies, making love, and airy laughter, as well as favorite books and music: The Dubliners' "Wild Rover," Led Zeppelin's "Fool in the Rain," and Moody Blues' "Tuesday Afternoon" for her, and Sibelius, Bach, and especially Paul Desmond's incredibly pure and mind-blowing, driving solo on "How High the Moon" for me. She making me feel that gentle, glowing comfort I felt as a boy with my grandma—till I walled myself off in my writing room and ignored her, and her childhood fears flared in panicky waves, suburbia now stifling and boring, as well as the twenty-year difference in our ages, didn't want another father, or afraid I was having affairs, which I wasn't, projecting her own desires on me, before finally running away in '83.

And rapidly blinking today in this Indian tandoori buffet, while adjusting my squinting sight to Boyne's daughter, my ex-wife and mother of our son, who (unbelievably) will soon be forty-three and is still so pretty (though she has put on a few pounds) with her blonde hair bound as before in a loose ponytail and those wide eyes of a lovely hyacinth blue—that are currently staring intently at me as I listen with half an ear to her Hubby Three, Simon McKenna (with his harsh Belfast brogue and lean and hungry Nureyev look) talk about Michael Flatley and Jean Butler and the ups and downs of *Riverdance.* Shay passing me the Chicken Tikka and Saag Paneer as I nibble my Naan and sip my Kingfisher beer.

"And you're Jewish, aren't ya, Gene?"

"Indeed I am."

"Well ya know what kinda cigarettes rabbis smoke?"

"No, what kind?"

"Gafilter."

"O *Jeez!*" Tory wincing and looking askance.

"And with that, oy tink oy'll pop in the loo."

Shay standing, too, and pushing back his chair, "And I think I'll join you," shaking his head with a smirk.

"Sorry about that, Gene, but he's had a few beers—"

"No problem, Tory."

She pushing her combination plate aside, "You know I just learned that, like us, Freud's parents were married when his father was forty and his mother twenty."

"And see what that wrought?"

She smiling, "The Golden Sigi? Anyhow, Gene, are you tired?"

"No. Why?"

"Well you should be. You've been running through my mind."

"That's funny, Tory."

"No, I mean it. I *have* been thinking a lot about you lately, dreaming of you night after night and bringing myself off, how I'd drive you *crazy* in bed again, make you beg me to let you come."

"Yes, well—"

"I still love you, think I've made another mistake, so at least come visit. You'll have your own room."

"What about Simon?"

"Let me worry about that."

"Yeah, well . . . we'll see."

Simon and Shay now coming out of the bathroom, her eyes clouding over as I gently squeeze her hand. And realizing, however much I *still* love her, and always will, I could never fully trust her again not to betray me. And feeling so sad about that—as she glances up at her new husband:

"Simon, did you know I just recently read where women are attracted to the smell of a man who is similar—but not too similar—to their dads? Mating with someone *too* similar may lead to inbreeding, but mating with someone too different leads to the loss of desirable genes. Pun intended."

"And what, pray tell, do oy smell like?"

Shay grinning, "Chicken Vindaloo?"

And all of us guffaw.

Two days later, she and Simon fly back to Falls Village, Connecticut, where they stay in Tiki's old house. Shay will join them shortly for the rest of the summer of '98.

• • • • • •

"And what about your other Golden Oldie, Gene, 'Titsy Mitzi' with the 34 Cs?"

"Three down, Boyne, one to go."

"Why, what happened?"

"She said she's made her bed, she and her Enron exec now have a horse farm in Rhode Island, and that's her entire life."

"So what'd you propose?"

"That we meet in New York."

"And she said?"

"She said, 'No, I'm an old bag. You don't want to see me now.' And I said it doesn't matter. And she said, 'Yes it does. Just remember me like I was when you last saw me in '83.' "

"Well at least she's honest, boy."

"O that she is. No, she's really a terrific girl."

"Girl?"

"OK, woman, lady, gal. And I'm sure she's still attractive and extremely sweet—"

"So what was missing, Gene, that grandma glow?"

"Right, that gentle, glowing comfort."

• • • • • •

Shay dropping by on Sunday evening with his belated birthday present for me, a Gateway computer, and returning next weekend to check if I'm actually using it.

"You've got your e-mail address, Dad?"

"Got it."

"Good. But you still haven't used it, right?"

"Hardly."

"OK, well lemme see how it's working." And ten minutes later, he returns to the den, where I'm watching ESPN, highlights of Nomar homering over the Green Monster. "All set, Dad, and there's already one e-mail message on it for you."

"For me? From who?"

"Some girl."

And peering at the screen:

Manila, 07-25-98

Dear Gene,

I don't believe it—you have left the Middle
Ages and your 1954 Royal Portable!!! Is this
a serious attempt to enter the new millennium
or only your son's doing? Anyway, I write *lots*
of e-mails for those who respond. So, this
is going to be a staggered attempt to catch
up with you, to make up for all those years
of non-communication, and to try to make you
write me back.

It is going to be fun. Except that I am not
in a very good mood because, of course, your
long predictions have come true about my relationship: Paul is having a XXX affair, and we
are in deep crisis. This started already last
September and is still ongoing. Everyone else
knew, my friends, workers in my office. I was
the last to learn. I gave him till the end of
October when I return from Bruges. If it is
not finished by then, I will leave.

To show you how serious I am, I am already
scanning the internet ads for jobs in Belgium
and even (!!) looking at the dating services.
. . . At my age, what does a woman do who's
gray, skinny, and has lost 4 kilos since our
crisis?

So, how is that for a cheerful new beginning for the new millennium and our renewed
communication?

"Shay BABY!!" Leaping out of my chair.

"What, what's going on. Dad, what is it?"

And grabbing him in my arms and waltzing round the room, "She's finally *realized!*" and I keep on joyfully waltzing.

"Who?"

"The girl—the woman, *lady* of my dreams!"

And that night, I e-mail her back after several flubbed and fumbling attempts (like Nabokov, I'm almost completely mechanically inept. He could barely turn on a light switch without his wife Vera's help).

```
Dearest Gabrielle,
I sent this earlier today, but I'm still a
computer klutz, so I'll resend it: After all
the countless and passionate love letters over
a span of fifteen years, as well as untold
phone calls across distant seas, now you and
my son (and his birthday present—you sly devil,
I'm sure you were involved) have finally got
me on this fucking Internet!!! But I feel
your fears, your pain, your anger and current
frustrations. You don't need betrayal, eroding
your value and worth.

    You are so special! A joy and wonder. And
always remember the two big questions are:
What do I want? and What do I deserve? And
you deserve the best. Please excuse me sound-
ing like a teacher, but I am a professor, you
know. I will call you in the morning.

    Much love.

    Gene
```

• • • • • •

"Gabrielle?"

Her lovely chuckle, "A man of his word."

"On the lip, the tongue—"

"Stories were in the making."

"What a memory! And how are you, *mon petit chou?*"

"Ups and downs. Too busy with work, stupid reports that I have to submit to the Belgium government, too many deadlines, too many visitors from Brussels—How are you?"

"Well, just when I'd resigned myself to meeting you when we were eighty or eighty-five in an old age home, just dear friends for life, now you're only an e-mail away. God, whoever thought I'd say that!"

Her delightful laugh, "Certainly not me. And speaking of old, Gene, do you realize I will be fifty on October 24?"

"And I'll be sixty-two. And do *you* realize that I've loved you longer than anyone else ever has?"

"I do."

"Is this his first affair?"

"Paul's? No, O no. He had been having other affairs from the very start of our relationship, and this is only the latest."

"So drop him, get out of it! Why settle, accept heartache? He's not going to change, and sure as hell will do it again."

"You don't know that."

"I know that. How can you ever trust him again? Listen—"

"Look, Gene, if it is over, the first person I will call is you."

"Is it L.A. and being alone out here?"

"No, I'm not afraid of being alone in L.A."

"OK, well just know that of all the women in my life, believe me, you have made me the happiest—those few, precious moments, calls, and lovely letters—I wish I were there."

"You are very sweet. And thank you for always being there for me, for listening to me, really listening."

"Hey, my ex-wife said I never listened, so I've always tried to listen to you, learned how from my son. Anyway, do you know exactly when in October you'll be in Belgium?"

"Well things are very confused now, everything is confused now. You have confused me."

"That's my job."

"I know, and you are very good at it. Gene, I have to go. Big hug from me."

"I miss you, miss you, miss you. Sometimes I stutter in threes. But I'll be happy to fly to Bruges at the drop of a wooden shoe. 'Bye."

· · · · · ·

Wed, 12 Aug 1998 13:37:26
Dear Gene,
I started seeing a counselor today and that helped. Of course, she told me to separate for a while, and I guess she is right.
XXX,
G.

08/13/1998 9:10 AM
My dear sweet Gabrielle of my dreams,
Here I still am under a gleaming Southern California sun, and all I lack is you beside me to frolic and gambol (Remember West Frolic and East Gambol?)—and there you are in humid Manila (or are you currently climbing some Nepalese slope, Everest col, glued to the side of a Himalayan crest while acrophobic Hagar watches from far, far below?).

Wondering this morning what you remember of me. How you still see me in your mind's eye. (You have the benefit of that book jacket photo, I know.) But be specific. What did you like? Dislike? What was your favorite time with me? Our sex? Lust? Affection? Mellow, relaxing snuggles? And why didn't we work then? Geography and timing? Circumstances of job, Paul, or fear of intimacy? (Sounds like you're taking a final exam: Hagar 101.) Better yet, come to L.A. for your orals and I'll pay your way!

To conclude, a little astrology from Linda Goodman's *Love Signs*:

A Gemini man posseses the unusual and uncommonly appealing quality of seeming to remain eternally youthful . . . not rare, I suppose, for one who is reborn each day, but rare enough to attract the normally self-contained and cautious Scorpio female into wondering what makes him scintillate with such multiple colors of the mood spectrum. Now, when a Scorpio girl starts to wonder, there's no stopping her until she's satisfied her wondering with complete knowing. That means coming closer to him—and closer . . . and closer . . . until she suddenly looks around herself with alarm.

Can she cope with this introverted-extroverted soul, this full-of-gladness, filled-with-sadness little boy, this coldly cruel yet sensitive and tender man?

                              Fri, 14 Aug 1998 17:05:28
Dear Gemini Gene,
Can I cope with this full-of-gladness, filled-with-sadness little boy? Might be worth a try.

```
And I am so happy you are on-line now—for your
shoulder to lean (cry?) on, and, believe me,
I will consider your L.A. offer, although not
in the short-term, because, remember, I still
have a job that I like and that I will not
easily give up. Of course your astrologer is
right about what she says (mostly). And I feel
a bit better today, receiving many sweet let-
ters from friends, although you are the only
one who seems to have a direct interest (just
teasing). Anyway, I am incredibly busy.
    Kiss,
    G.
```

```
                              Thu, 03 Sept 1998 11:51:06
Gene,
Can't write much. I have been diagnosed with
Repetitive Strain Injury in shoulder and hands.
Can reach me on my cell phone: (63)9165327691.
Best in the afternoons, if possible, around 2
to 4 PM.
    Love,
    G.
```

• • • • • •

"Gabrielle?"

"Well, well, well, what a nice surprise!"

"How are you?"

"Overwhelmed with work, painful hands, very hard to type."

"I've called every doctor I know, diligently searching: One holistic guy feels B6 is good, but says remember you have to give it three months and no longer. Another M.D. feels you might try Vioxx, an anti-inflammatory drug that's proved very effective. Have you seen a specialist?"

"No, just a doctor here. They are not very familiar with it in the Philippines. I will see a specialist when I go to Belgium."

"Which is when?"

"Let me see: I will be in Brussels on 7 September, then in Bruges till the twenty-first."

"I'll be there."

"Well, I don't know, Gene . . . Are you sure?"

"Positive! No question now you need to be treated with some tender, loving care by Dr. Hagar."

"Yes, I am sure he does, even makes house calls. Anyway, I will be staying at my sister's, and her address in Bruges is 23, Ridder-sstraat. And my cell phone there is 31-610650029. But I wonder if you will even recognize me now."

"Why?"

"Because of how I look, all gray and wrinkled and tired. O, and I also am wearing reading glasses."

"All I recall is peering through the dark web of your hair one London morning after making love again, licking you all over."

"Well you could be disappointed, Gene—'specially if you knew me day-to-day."

"Never. For whatever happens, you'll *always* be precious to me."

"And you to me, but—"

"And you're still dancing away as my phone calls chase you round the world—so, please, Gabrielle, don't push me away again."

"OK, well . . . but call me first."

"I will. Love you."

"I love you, too. Bye-bye."

• • • • • •

"So, Hagar, how's our fil-um coming along?"

"What? O, fine, should be ready to start shooting it this spring."

"Ah, that's absolutely marvelous! Then they'll see the triumphant return of the explosive, tragic-comic, ever-embattled genius that is Boyne! And, meanwhile, I've been fervently studying Rembrandt's portraits of Titus, his beloved son, just to stay in shape. O, and sorry, of course, to hear about Tory, but happy to hear about Gabrielle, your girl of Flanders? . . . Gene?"

"What?"

"You OK? You sound sort of down today."

"Well I just got some bad news, a call from New York, and heard that Mitzi Weiss lost both of her breasts in a double mastectomy."

"Holy Mother of God! And this is the one with the 34 Cs?'

"Yeah, right. Poor Mitzi, so fucking awful!"

"No fun, boy, being a Golden Oldie."

· · · · · ·

The last blast of a summer squall whinnying through the chimney flue as I emerge from the bedroom dressed for my flight, and blonde Shay, smirking, shakes his tousled head.

"Dad, no!"

"What?"

"You're not wearing those jeans to go to Europe."

"Why?"

" 'Cause they're repulsive!"

"My favorite well-worn Wrangler's?"

· · · · · ·

"Ladies and gentlemen, will you please fasten your seat belts. We will be landing at Brussels International Airport shortly. *Mes dames et monsieurs*—"

My slowly loping, raincoat-flapping stride following along corridor after shining corridor with my one pouched flight bag, grim sigh, bleary eye—customs on ahead, crowds milling, no sign of her, searching the faces—*gray and wrinkled and wearing reading glasses?*—passport out of my pocket, old-photoed passport of years gone by. Where is she? Behind those silver railings? People waving, waiting, and none of them—

Gabrielle.

Still so lovely, with her jade green gaze and the dark blue tinge of her jet black hair, now shoulder-length and faintly threaded with gray—looking worn and thinner, smudged circles under her eyes—but smiling that same impish smile and frowning at me as I stare at her tan trenchcoat, the collar raised, still watching, waiting for me to pass through customs—Nothing to declare (except my genius)—and quickly out.

She coming forward as I bend to kiss—her still velvet cheek.

"How are you, Gene?" Nervous, glancing around, her Flemish accent so wobbling my joyous heart.

"Tired."

"Why, bad flight?" hitching her handbag's strap over her shoulder.

"Hardly slept."

"This is *all* your luggage?—You didn't? Not on the plane? This way. My sister's car is down below. We have to take the elevator." Muscular dents in her calves, hurrying on.

"No, I mostly read on planes, worry about crashing."

She looking back at me, "Yes, I know."

"Which car is yours, the Mercedes?"

"—The what? No, not very likely. The Peugeot."

"The French Mercedes."

"Yes, well put your luggage in the back. It needs a good washing," she coming around the side of this dark green 604, getting in, "O, I am sorry," and leaning across to open my door, "I too am tired. I had to get up at 6:30 this morning for meetings and I forgot what time you were arriving. I called but the airport lines were all busy and I thought you had said 9 A.M."

"How far is it to Bruges?"

The Peugeot weaving out of the basement lot and on up the ramp. "O, an hour or so, maybe a little more because of the weather—O God, it is *still* raining!" Her fast glance both ways, brushing the hair from her eyes. "We can take this road." Bumper to bumper as she drums her fingers on the wheel. "But you look well, though, except for being so tired."

"So do you," reaching out to knead the nape of her neck, so want to hold her, hug her, kiss her angel face, as the night traffic keeps crawling along through the gray falling rain. "How're your hands, your shoulder?"

"The same. Though today was worse."

"Did you see the specialist?"

"Yes."

"And?"

"I waited too long to treat it. I'll just have to live with it—*God,* how they crowd you in—" Veering sharply round a truck. "Get *over,* will you! Are you hungry now? No? Well we can stop for something, if you like. I have a few things at my sister's—O shut up! Where am I supposed to *go? Over* him? . . . Is traffic as bad as this in L.A.?"

"Worse! All over the world, it's one massive traffic jam."

"I know, and I think they have all come to Brussels tonight. We can get off here, we might make better time." Splashing through side streets, these narrow, twisting alleys. "And do I look as tired as you?"

"You look fine. What's happening with Paul?"

"Ups and downs."

"He gave up his affair?"

"He says he has."

"You believe him?"

Accelerating into the left lane. "We'll see."

"Does he know I'm here?"

"No. You are his greatest threat."

"O really? Haven't seen you in twelve years—"

"It doesn't matter, Gene."

"And how do you feel?"

"I don't know yet. The counseling has been helpful."

"You go together?"

"Together and by myself."

"Have you separated?"

"No, not yet."

· · · · · ·

And opening a dark brown fourth-floor door with her key, and down a long white hallway, past a small kitchen, bath, red curtain and hand-held shower, into a large room with a narrow beige couch, leather chairs, lots of bookshelves, throw cushions, and French windows looking out on black treetops, spires, falling rain—

"Where should I put this?"

"O, there. Anywhere. On the floor. You can unpack later, Gene."

"Can I sit here?"

"Yes, of course."

On the narrow couch.

"Would you like something? A sandwich, something to drink? Juice, a beer?"

"How 'bout a sugar-free soy vanilla latte?"

"A what?"

"No, I'm only kidding. Let me just relax," leaning back, my heart still pounding.

"Do you like it?" Watching her unbuckle her tan trenchcoat.

"The apartment? Yeah, except for the climb." White turtleneck sweater, blue cotton skirt, flats, and brushing her black hair from her eyes. "Gabrielle?"

"Yes?"

"Come here."

"Why?"

"Will you come here."

Staring at me but coming closer, her face now in shadow.

" 'Cause I want to kiss you. It's been twelve long years."

And reaching out, she stiffly takes my hand, and I ease her down beside me to gently incline her face toward mine, looking into her lovely eyes—jade green gaze shifting away—then stroke her raven hair, cup her face between my hands, and kiss her warm mouth, suckle her sensual lower lip—

"Gene, no," she abruptly standing, walking toward the tinsled window, and turning back to me with a sigh, "You can sleep in my bed, but I don't know if I will make love to you or not. I don't want to be like Paul."

And after I wash up, have some Swiss cheese and a red Delicious apple, I follow her into the far room, with its large king-sized bed and blue goosedown comforter.

Her back toward me as she strips off her white turtleneck and skirt in the hushed half-light, leaves her pale panties on, and slides under the covers.

"Would you scratch my back, Gene?"

The heat and silk, of her body, as sleek as before, as I continue down, stroking her still shapely bottom, and around toward her—

But she pushes my hand away and moves toward the edge of the bed.

I wrap my arms around her, nose her fragrant hair, till sometime later in the drizzled dawn, I wake to pee, list awkwardly down the dark hall, then get back in bed beside her, she still facing the wall as I clasp her round again, pulling her near, her drowsy murmur, kissing, caressing her hair, her nape—"Mmm, no, Gene, let me sleep." "Gabrielle?" "No," and she tucks herself into a fetal curl. And after a moment, as she settles in, wrapping my arms about her once more and just holding her, pressing against her . . . then turning aside, twisting free of this tangle of covers, to rearrange them, shift again, trying to find a spot, a comfortable niche in this new bed, her sister's bed, overtired, still so on edge, her sleepy breathing warm beside me, still beside me . . . keeping one hand on her, then pulling the comforter tight around me and tossing again as I try to fall asleep, weary myself to sleep, thrash and churn and toss asleep. . . .

Later on, I parade naked and woozy round the sunny apartment, "You *have* kept in very good shape, Gene," she in a wooly green robe sipping her café au lait, "And you as well, my dear," before taking a clumsy, lukewarm shower seated alone in her sister's tub, and decide to enjoy just being together and not pressure her at all—as I stand, sharply slip, clutching the shower curtain, and fall grappling with it as though locked in mortal combat with a grizzly bear.

She ducking her head in, "Gene, are you all right?"

"Fine," grinning, "still agile after all these years."

And quickly dressing and back into the kitchen.

"Well I've slipped in there myself. But here, would you like something to eat?"

"No thanks. I'll take you out, woo you with food," and turning around, "You like these jeans?"

"Those jeans? They're OK, a bit baggy on you. Actually you look better without clothes. Most men don't."

"Does Paul?"

She glances away, places her cup in the sink, "No, he needs clothes, definitely needs clothes."

"How can you ever trust him again?"

"Gene?"

"OK, OK, sorry."

"No, that's all right. I don't know if I ever can."

And off we go on a tour of her city, she showing me where she went to school, played soccer, first made love, first got drunk, strolling along the canals with their gliding swans, past reddish-brown brickwork, and under the lean church spires of charming medieval Bruges as I turn to her.

"You know, the comfort and ease, same dry sense of humor, play of ideas and sharing of insights we've had now for fifteen years is really rare indeed."

"Can you believe fifteen years we have known each other?"

"And I don't want to stay your distant romantic friend any longer. Time is fleeting, and I'm fading into the woodwork."

"You are sixty-two now, Gene?"

"Yes, and you're almost fifty."

"You had to remind me, didn't you. I thought I was forty-ten."

"Forty-ten?"

"That is what I say when someone asks my age."

"That's funny. And menopause, hot flashes?"

"So far I have been lucky, not too bad."

That night I meet her brother and two of her three sisters (Gabrielle the baby), then later some of her friends, Mario and Francois, Liliane and Liet, for a delightful dinner of *Stamppot Ardennaise met Worst,* a thick Belgian stew laced with spicy sausage, and a variety of beers, from weak to strong, light to heavy, sour to sweet. The conversation never-ending and covering everything from Clinton and Monica Lewinsky, the Philippine election and Northern Ireland, Salman Rushdie and the death of Linda McCartney, June Christy and Sarah Vaughn, to even Sammy Sosa and Mark McGwire.

Home at twelve-thirty, we crawl into bed with the same routine, scratching her back, she still wearing her panties and facing the wall in sleep—till I wake from a steamy sexual dream, erection tent-poling my sheets, bear hugging my pillow tight—absurd substitute for nibbling and licking her, tickling and kissing her throughout this sweaty night!

Silently I rise, slip into the living room, and stretch awkwardly out on the narrow couch, my raincoat flung across me. Hoping, praying she'll feel my absence, loss of heat, and draw me back for a night of fiery passion.

But not till early the next morning do I hear the floorboards creak and she appears in the room, as I continue feigning sleep, sits on the couch, touches me tentatively, and my bleary eyes flicker and blink.

"Why did you come out here, Gene?"

Yawning and looking up, ". . . Too painful to sleep beside you and not make love."

And, after sighing and shaking her head, she leans over and folds me in her warm embrace.

• • • • • •

She has meetings most of the day, she's sorry to say, but will get back as soon as possible. And after she kisses me briskly on the lips, I head into the bathroom for a long, gleaming pee, hands on hips, shaking the last drops free. But now what to do till she returns? Feeling so frustrated, so much left unsaid. Go out and pick up a young Belgian girl? Give her my usual line, "Were you a student of mine?" (in French, Dutch, Flemish? Or hope she speaks English?) No, not what I want now anyway.

So, following a half hour's nap, I decide to clean the apartment. Getting out the vacuum and whisking round the corners; putting all the dishes in the sink, this pink liquid, Ajax Amoniaque, rub-a-dub-dub, wash and dry; where the hell do the cups go? Opening door after—ah. And stepping back with beaming pride, giving myself The Good Housekeeping Seal of Approval, my dishpan hands, white-puckered, then back inside to dust her sister's books, a couple inverted, Joyce calling it a female trait: several volumes of *Duden*, Vondel, Bomans, orange and yellow copies of *Akzente*, a Jacques Brel album, before making the bed, plumping pillows, changing sheets, flapping quilts, and flipping throw cushions like Maravich behind the back or a fadeaway jumper from the far corner.

Most of the day now gone as I fling open the French windows: the twin spires of that Gothic church catching the slanting afternoon light, the huge, three-leaved swaying sycamore reaching to the terrace below, a view of chimney-potted and TV-antennaed Bruges, gulls shrillscreaming, cars careening down the sloping cobbled street—when the door swings wide.

Her jade eyes smiling, ". . . My God, what did you *do* here? Did you do all this?"

"No, I called an agency around the corner, got this sexy little maid to dust and mop—"

"No, really, Gene," she still shaking her head and smiling, "Well, someday you are going to make someone a very good wife," then moving into the kitchen, "Ah, you found the Ajax. The cups go in here."

"I thought cups go with saucers?"

"Not in her kitchen. Are you hungry, Gene? Because I am famished, even though it is early for dinner."

"Yes, and it's my treat. You name the place, your choice."

And walking side by side, arms around each other, on this dusky Belgian evening filled with an extravagant display of my public hugging, kissing her silky hair and cheeks, and buying her one perfect crimson rose.

"You know, I feel like the proudest man in Bruges tonight taking you out to dinner."

A marvelous meal at Paspartout, then home tipsy on wine and, resigned to it now, I get into bed for my very last night, scratch her back once more, kiss her nape, then turn away, move to the far edge, and drift off. . . .

When suddenly I feel her rubbing her groin into my butt— What's she doing? Pushing me off the bed? No—her arms circling me from behind, and I turn slightly, her hand sliding over my hip, across my stomach to take me, rock-hard, in her grip, stroking me up and down, and I twist fully around to kiss her, hesitantly, then passionately, suckling her lower lip, before kissing rapidly down her once-high breasts, but still firm, long, rubbery nipples, over her belly, so smooth, still flat belly, nuzzling into her fuzzy mound, along the fringe of her panties and hooking them, drawing them down, then licking the inside of her thighs as she sighs, and I tease her with the tip of my tongue, good, so good, swirling it round, till she's quivering, straining hard, and gripping my hair, my head locked within the vise of her thighs, before she pulls me forward, pawing at my swollen cock, then brushes the head—*O dear God!*—softly round her lips, and I straddle her face, she taking me deep in her mouth, silken lips, warm mouth, sucking, licking up and down, her fingers slipping under me, cupping me and gently squeezing as I moan—

"*Ohhh Jesus!*"

"What? Am I hurting you, Gene?"

"No, just don't stop!"

And she squeezing and sucking as I keep on thrusting—then out, shifting back on the sheets, and she raises her legs way up, knees touching her breasts, and I easily, O so easily and slithery, slide inside her, pressing her close as she gasps, and sighs in my ear, nails scraping my back, and on and on, barely moving now, no long strokes—And all these years I've waited, dreaming, wishing so for this, lovely Gabrielle lost in my arms, loving it as much as I, softly squealing and thrusting now along with me as she spasms, starts to come—and there's absolutely nothing better in the world than making the woman you love come—she grabbing my head, my hair, and lustily kissing me, her tongue deep in my sucking mouth—as, with a hoarse and shudding cry, I come again and again and again—

"O Gabrielle—"

"Shhh, don't talk."

"Christ—" tears filling my blinking eyes.

"No, just hold me, please, close as you can."

• • • • • •

And next morning, "Gene, I am sorry about last night, I don't know what is wrong with me. I'm as bad as Paul."

• • • • • •

September 21, 1998

Dear Gabrielle,

I kept tasting your kiss—mouth, lips, tongue—across 7,000 miles of Scottish shore, Irish Sea, Greenland glacier, and finally L.A.'s blazing sun. Everything in my house was a mess, had been gone through, sifted over—Shay even took to wearing my shirts—and now finally, after obsessively rearranging, I have some time to myself. You are so close to me now—deep within me, is what I feel—so precious to me, knowing you now so much better and loving what I've grown to know. Knowing how frightened or content I was to have it remain a long-distance

romance, heightened meetings in summer cities,
and then dance away—but no longer, no longer
afraid, totally accepting you, delighting in
you—even your pinches and pokes, nuzzles and
jokes (even with your panties on). I still
feel the heat and silk of your body arching
into me, silhouetted passionately together.

   I kiss your hands, hoping I can effect a
cure, wishing the hot flashes stay away, and
long for you beside me.

   Love,

   Gene

· · · · · ·

"Ah, Hagar, here I am in Ireland holding the phone while staring transfixed, with my soft, sable brush poised in midair, at this huge portrait of Rory, my splendid sixteen-year-old son, before applying a thick glaze of red to a white oil ground. And still filled with these debilitating, devastating fears that everything I paint now *continues* to look like *me* as I gnaw on, only draw upon, my sadly aging image!"

"Seamus, relax, calm down, I'm sure this too will pass, is only temporary—"

"Temporary, my Irish arse! For I *am* totally bald and snowy-bearded, turning seventy in the blink of a bloodshot eye, and being attacked even by those fucking tabloids now, the *Star* and *National Enquirer*, who claim I can't paint anymore 'cause I have MS *and* HIV! Good God, boy, 'twas only a short time ago that, like Turner and Picasso, I stood on the top of Everest and waved down at the smiling Sherpas!"

"You're still at the very top, by far the finest artist now painting—and this film will bloody well prove it!"

"Like Hans Namuth with Jack the Dripper, celluloid immortality?"

"Precisely."

"But Suffering *Christ*, Gene, my hand is *still* shaking, pacing about this skylit studio after the never-ending, nerve-rending shape and reshape—'cause I can't *crack* this fucking portrait! All I'm doing is masturbating, imitating others: Turner and Rembrandt—and now even myself! My vision blurry, hardly hear in my left ear, dyspepsia and arthritis gaining ground—"

"Seamus, I'll be there before you know it and I *guarantee* you'll crack it, be back in tiptop shape."

"You guarantee it?"

"Absolutely."

"From your lips to God's ear—and on the head of your only son, Hagar?"

"My first born is yours, Boyne, if I'm lying."

"Right, well I'm going to hold you to that, boy, for you have the art of Irish diplomacy."

"Which is?"

"Telling a man to go to hell so that he looks forward to making the trip! See you soon."

· · · · · ·

Sunday, October 4, 1998

Dear Gene,

I guess I postponed writing this letter because I didn't know quite what to answer. Well, maybe it is all very simple. I cannot leave the Philippines and live in L.A., not now, maybe never. Maybe there are too many miles between us, and I don't think I have the courage to cross them—unless I would "fuck up" everything here: my relation with Paul (we *are* trying to work things out), and my job (I still love my independence and the people I work with).

So, my dearest, sweetest Gene, what and where does that leave us? Friends? Penpals? Or just lovely memories?

Great letters I write! Why do I do this, cause both of us such pain? Maybe that is why my hot flashes started with a vengeance when I got home.

Still, much, much love,
Gabrielle

October 10, 1998

Dear Gabrielle,

I love you. I will always love you. And I would've loved you with support and trust and without hurt and humiliation. I know this to be true, for I learned how to provide that each day by raising my precious son. But I can't continue on any longer feeling as I do. I am glad for you, that you have sought help for yourself as to why you are part of a hurtful, destructive pattern. I am sad for you that you remain in this relationship. My words, alas, cannot make you whole, give you self-esteem, or make you see clearly.

Maybe you've been fooled by my sometimes flip and witty ways, but I was feeling excruciatingly vulnerable with you in Bruges, frustrated with the lack of love in my life, of not having someone near to share my joys and sorrows. You want to remain my penpal, a distant fantasy, far away from commitment, ever elusive and apologetic. But I ache inside now, Gabrielle, tears flooding my gut, for all we had in Paris and London, New York and Bruges. If you are truly working things out with Paul, why the need of a penpal? I feel time fleeting more than ever before. And last July, when you learned of Paul's affairs and you were giving it one last chance, I opened the door again (and you have to remember I've loved you longer than anyone) of growing old together.

For fifteen years I've been your friend and ardent lover. You will never leave my heart. But this decision is for my health, to get on with my life, and let you go. I wish only the best for you and thank you intensely for being in my life.

Love,

Gene

March 1999 • L.A.

Part III

"You OK, Hagar?"

"No."

"Gabrielle?"

"Yes."

"I'm sorry, boy, truly am."

"I tried, Seamus."

"I know you did, but Trisha was a ditz, Mitzi was ill, Tory wanted you back, and Gabrielle is still living with him. But I admire your courage with the odds stacked against you, I really do. So when're you coming to Ireland?"

"Next week."

"Heard from her at all?"

"No, and really don't expect to."

· · · · · ·

Seventy-year-old Seamus Eamon Boyne looking now like one of Picasso's late erotic satyrs, his gorgeous wife Tiki, redhaired son Rory, and ancient butler Symes constantly around him, and always near, helicopters hovering above his Irish castle, TV camera crews, carrying boom mikes and tripods, camped outside, and of course that horde of paparazzi hung like bats from the leafy branches as we somehow manage to complete our second week of shooting, then he and I adjourn to his basement screening room to watch the rough cut together and listen to his sonorous narration.

The scene is his cluttered, skylighted studio within his castle at Rathnew.

BOYNE (VO)

*And with my paintbrush still raised, I blinked lovingly
back at this portrait of my son—his face's luminous
texture (a red lake glaze) like the skin of one of
Cezanne's apples or the breasts of a Renoir nude—and
that he said looks just like me!—as I fired my bloody
brush clear across the room, bouncing off that picture
window, paint dripping down in a serpentine rimple
like a Jackson Pollock dribble.*

Boyne leaning over with a rusty whisper, "And, Gene, that was the
best thing I'd done all day! But look, you can cut out some of my
words if you want, may be too many."

"No, no, this is good, I like it."

"Well, actually, so do I."

Images of him now madly painting away with his left hand and
wearing his green beret, rugby-striped shirt, and stained seersucker
shorts as one shot dissolves into another.

BOYNE (VO)

*Still, over the next few days, as Houdini once said,
it was back to the ouija board as I went poring over
Rembrandt's portraits of Titus, his beloved son, or
pacing in frustration about my studio with the Bran-
denburgs (Marriner's version) grandly blaring, and a
glittery Irish sunshower falling into the sea.*

The camera moves in for a close-up of Rembrandt's portrait of
Titus at his Desk.

BOYNE (VO)

*And Jaysus, how the hell did he DO it? Capture the
bloody essence of his son, living, breathing, coming
alive? No artificially inspired light here, rather a
heartfelt, self-reflective glow shining deep from within
not from without: as simple and profound as that!
Father feeling what his son feels! And I couldn't even
get close to that!*

Boyne solemnly painting now, adding another stroke to his son's face, then making a bold slash with his palette knife, standing back, and angrily wiping it off with a tattered rag.

BOYNE (VO)

Well at least I could give it a final try—for as Pollock told me one time, the paint always has a mind of its own. All my vapor and glaze, painting up a bloody storm, stroking in a haggard shaft of daylight here, falling over Rory's nose and cheekbones there, his carroty mop of hair catching that reflected glow—And maybe, just maybe, like ichor filling my veins, I'd broken through, was on to something eternal!

Boyne, wild-eyed, now jigging before his canvas and painting non-stop with a stampede of energy, adding some swirling textures to the widening gyre of a flaming Turner background.

BOYNE (VO)

For what I was doing now was seeing and painting not from my point of view but HIS! Not me looking at him, but he looking at me! What Rembrandt achieved in that shattering breakthrough into true empathy, and the love of a father for his precious child! Such love, to see and feel through another's eyes!

Boyne stepping back and drying his hands, wiping his brush, blinking and sighing, then, with a grand flourish and a tear in his eye, signs the brilliant finished painting.

· · · · · ·

And all through this windy April night at Boyne's castle of Ballyduff, as I toss and churn with a restless sleep, his booming words on screen, "True empathy!" and "to see and feel through another's eyes!", are mixed with a tumbling host of shifting images of Gabrielle and *her* words: she saying to me years ago after beginning at CCI that "I really need to stay with this job to get rid of my inferiority complex. If I stop now, I will lose the little self-confidence I have." And now *I'm* feeling *her* gnawing self-doubts, shoals of despair, pain of Paul and fears of loss—when I awaken with a heart-thumping start to the phone stridently ringing beside my bed!

"—Yes, hello, hello?"

"Dad, it's Shay. Did I wake you?"

"Yeah, but it's OK." Boyne's large guest room slowly coming into focus in this misty Irish dawn. "What is it, what's going on?"

"There's an e-mail from that woman for you."

"There is?" Blinking, frowning. "From the Philippines?"

"Yeah. Should I read it to you?"

"Go ahead."

" 'Dear Gene, You were right. He did do it again. If you can, meet me in Paris on Saturday, April 24, at 8 P.M. at Le Petit Perigord. Gabrielle.' You gonna go, Dad?"

"I, I don't know. Everything OK at home?"

"Fine."

"Nomar?"

"The cat or Garciaparra?"

"Both."

"Great. He hit another homer tonight—Ho-mar by No-mar! And the cat caught another mouse."

"Terrific. I'll talk to you soon. Love you."

"Love you, too, Dad. When'll you be back?"

"I'm not sure now."

"Well good luck."

"Thanks. Hey, and give Nomar a big hug."

"The cat or the ballplayer?"

· · · · · ·

And following a raucous, drunken wrap party at Ballyduff on Friday night, Boyne pulls me roughly aside, his arm slung round my shoulder, "Even though I'm positively legless for the moment, boy, and feel awful 'bout you not choosing Tory, I still want all the best for you and your tattered heart, so Godspeed, Gene, for you and your Gabrielle!" Then I take a Saturday two-hour Air France flight to De Gaulle, landing at 6:05, rent a Ford Escort from Hertz, and drive swiftly along the Al into Paris, my fingers anxiously drumming the wheel—For will she really show, my dream come true, or find some new excuse, another *transitory enchanted moment,* then *poof!* gone before I know it? 'Cause she must have doubts of her own, not sure if I'll be there, taking a chance—coming from Manila, Brussels, or Bruges?

And entering the City of Light with twenty minutes to spare, *chestnuts in blossom, holiday tables under the trees,* and whipping up Boulevard Malesherbes (love that name!) and on toward Rue de Tocqueville, my mind and body warming to hugging and kissing her once more, and my mouth watering to the taste of steak au poivre crusted with crushed peppercorns and flamed in cognac, a bottle of Bergerac wine—haven't eaten all day, except for an Irish scone, or booked a hotel—and along this dark gray street down to 126 Rue de Tocqueville at five to eight, and Le Petit Perigord—

Not here? Must've taken a wrong turn. Check the name on the corner, putting on my glasses—No, it *is* Rue de Tocqueville. Swinging the car around. And no sign of her as I double-park, hop out, and stop this guy with my fractured French:

"*Excusez-moi, où est Le Petit Perigord?*"

"*O, Le Petit Perigord! Mais oui!*"

"*Oui?*"

"No longer 'ere, *monsieur.*"

"Where'd it go?"

"Out of beez-ness," and he shrugs and takes off.

O Christ, and now we'll *NEVER* meet! Frantically pacing back and forth, after eight, in this wild-goose chase! Too old for all this, a hollow ache in my gut. And she probably left, figured I wasn't coming.

No, wait, this other restaurant in its place: Belle Epoque. I'll just park my car and give it a try.

A small, bald Persian headwaiter greeting me with his oversized, over-eager smile, *"Monsieur?"*

"You speak English?"

"But of course!"

"Has a woman, a lady, come in here by herself?"

His smile growing wider. *"Oui,* she ees at thee back."

Quickly down these steep stone steps, nine or ten customers, a brown-haired girl with "I'm-a-film-student" glasses cackling with laughter, to an empty table at the rear, a bottle of Bergerac wine, a Sabena bag on that chair, and no sign of her!

What the hell is going ON?!

From behind, arms hugging my waist hard, "I was on the phone. I thought you weren't coming."

As I whirl around, "Well here I am," she in her tan trenchcoat and white Esprits, her jade green eyes shining through her glasses, then fiercely hug her back, and receive a long, passionate kiss—till she slips from my arms and starts walking away.

"You're not leaving *again?*"

"No, no," smiling over her shoulder, "I have to go to the bathroom. I've been waiting for you, holding it in."

And she stares into my eyes with that bewitching grin, before I sink down into this chair, and all I can hear, I swear, is "April in Paris" in my spinning, aging head.

Boyne at Seventy-five

Spring 2004

One

Within the swilling crowd, past Eros and down Haymarket, and quiet night shoppers wishing at windows as I scurry briskly across the bus-filled thoroughfare on this damp and gusty, bleak and blustery Friday eve toward the snug pubs of London, and these fierce April flurries wildly lashing and fluttering my hoary, bushy beard at ten after seven by those antique hands, leaving me twenty minutes to spare before I meet Rory, my Rhodes Scholar son, for a fatherly natter and gargle about his girlfriend Nicole—

Ah, and over there's that familiar watering hole on the corner, the Captain's Cabin, with its wealthy aroma of food and drink, and downstairs to the fashionable couples seated before their bitters, their Scotch and sodas. The grizzle-haired men of distinguished ilk and manner in blue pin-striped, doublebreasted suits and their wives in pastel linen, with tiny pearls couched on either lobe. And thankfully little or no recognition as to who I am in my belted black Burberry and raffishly canted beret as I order up the bitter brown foam of an almost cold Guinness, brewed in Dublin, less than an ass's roar from here. And this waiter, so nice and friendly with his paternal smile, filling my glass to the brim. And I have left the mad clash of Ireland behind, with everything abruptly falling into decline: like yesterday morning, scrub-a-dub-dubbing with a green-striped bar of Irish Spring in my vast tiled shower stall, and the pounding workman above repairing my castle roof—when suddenly crashing down came clouds of billowing plaster and splintering laths, and that terrified Dublin navvy:

"Beggin' yer pardon, sir—"

"*Jaysus!* What the blazes *happened?*"

"Laws a' gravity, Oy guess."

And shaking my battered head—what the hell else could befall me?—I let out a booming bellow, "Well don't just stand there, man, take off your clothes and join me!"

But he went quickly slipping and sliding out the door, probably assuming I was one of those flamin' poofters in the raw.

And this yet another graphic example of what's been occurring lately in my life, since I haven't painted anything worthwhile in four years or more—Washed up? Over the hill? Whose hill? Everest? Benbulben? Or a harrowing hill of my very own making? Can't seem to summon up that swirling teem of images anymore, recapture the elusive muse. No longer the blazing forge of thought in my magpie brain, when I was a windy blade and a bit at the top of the painting game!

And my gorgeous wife, Tiki, the one fixed point in my aging life, still Rubenesque with her melonous breasts, rosy, wind-bussed cheeks, and that lustrous mane of auburn hair (now tinted at sixty-five), storming about our Irish castle shortly before she left and shouting, "Seamus, you're absolutely impossible to live with anymore, everything has to be about you and your fucking ego—" "And *that's* why you're leaving?" "—you just totally ignore my needs or wall yourself off in your studio—Well, my brother did have a heart attack, you know?" "Sounds like you would've left anyway." "Right, I probably would have! And this's been all *through* our marriage, nearly twenty years, and now turning away from me more and more, our sex life down to those rare Saturday night slam-bam-thank-you-ma'am's and roll over and go to sleep—" "So then go, go! You wanna go, *GO!* Get the hell outta here!" "—and the last weeks I haven't been *able* to sleep, I hurt so much, looking at you and feeling so empty, wanting to talk to you, touch you, but what good would it do—and I can't keep *living* like this! I need some real sharing, someone who's supportive and understanding—" "So what're you telling me, Tiki, that you're having an affair?" "That's not what I'm *talking* about!" "You're *not* having an affair?" "Seamus!" "Well are you, yes or no?" "No, but maybe I will!" "Will when?" "Who knows, tonight, tomorrow, when I get to Vancouver!"

Living as I've been these last four years on my lifetime of laurels and my last successful "Rory" paintings, and now here in London at the height of my fame for yet another lavish fête of honors at the Tate, my seventy-fifth birthday this latest gala occasion—while, in actual fact, I *am* at the bloody end of my fraying rope, nearly suicidal, go mad or die, if I can't paint or draw every day just to prove I'm alive! Or find a new muse, another Ciara, Tory, Tiki, or Rory—

Like that fateful journey across the pond over fifty years ago: that first morning of land, the fourteenth of June, the gulls cawing madly, balanced as they were on air, then swooping down the long slide and back up to their tentative, poised hover. Spontaneously a thin shiver of earth out of the pitching sea, a lighthouse winking: Ireland. Green slice in a graygreen sea, and I was so excited to be returning again, four years after my father's funeral, drunk and awake all night with the gulls spearing my stale bits of cake that I let out a wild call from the side rail, my free fist pumping aside the air and shouting, "God bless Ireland!!" while I pointed my erection toward solid land. "There're only two countries left in all this barbarous woe—Ireland and Israel, and they'll fight it out between 'em!" when tiny, heeled feet began descending the stairway above, a white, pleated skirt coming slowly into view as I spun about, hard-on in tow, to greet her. She blinked. A startled gasp. She paused. Then, shrieking back up the stairs, she fled in the wake of my laughter—and two months later, Laura McCready Carlisle became my first wife, whom I ended up marrying twice!

Lamplight glowing across the frosted glass, night falling, maps and navy prints on the wall, and more men swaggering through that oaken door, collecting round the tables of this dark, cluttered pub. And as I strode about on this, my first trip to London for quite some time, from out the streets and shops came people into the pubs. Not only tourists but those from within. From Manchester, Nottingham, and Leeds, Cambridge, Swansea, Tourquay, and Cardiff, Blackpool, Perth, and Aberdeen, Dundee, Dublin, and Pittenweem, Port of Ness, and Skibbereen. All mellow names that—

"Sir, might I suggest adding a bit of something to your Guinness? We sometimes do here."

"Of course."

Whispering his suggestion to the bartender. Who nods, selects a bottle from the glittering row behind him, then adds a few deft splashes of the Jameson's to my dark and foamy stout.

"Here's the ticket, sir." Awaiting my reaction.

Sliding down my throat with a spreading hum of flame.

"Sir?"

Masking the bite, fumes across the eyes, and portholes on the walls.

"Bit too much whiskey, sir?"

"No-no, that's quite all right."

And that man over there has a wax moustache, and that woman is not his wife. Too young. The lean, acknowledged replacement in red spangled creation with wristlet baubles. Talking about me and smiling. Another gulp, another gargle. Fee, Fi, Fo, Fum, pink is the color of my Tiki's tum. And I'm getting slightly tanked, I can feel it. She's far too young for him, having spotted the muscles in my arm, the quiver in my white-whiskered cheek. She can't help herself. All in a moment, she'll rise and spangle over. "Excuse me, Mr. Boyne, but would you take me home this very minute? I've been watching you ever since you came in, and I'm afraid I can't help myself. O good God, here comes Godfrey!" "I say, what is all this rot, Cheryl?" Shuddering right cross softens his middle, judo chop crumples him to one knee. The entire bar aghast and standing, the waiter bowing from the waist at the knockdown. And Boyne escorting Cheryl home to her carefree flat in Chelsea.

'Cause, Tiki, my fleeing wifey number three, two can play this game—with you now 6,000 miles away in Vancouver hot in the throes of some full-blown affair! I'll have my *own* fucking affair! Famous as I am, I venture to say I shouldn't have any problems! A rattle of change in my raincoat pocket, and I'm going to leave this waiter an exceedingly generous tip. Fifteen pound six ought to cover it.

Out in the windy night air, my knees thick with stout, calves close to the pavement, and a rotating head of Jameson's as I approach this slim blue lamppost to give it the Astaire light step and spin, show 'em there's still lots of life left in my sprightly old frame: Whee! Around and around—and pop, pop the cane! Up the street with a burst of speed, the deceptive two-step-and-glide moving me right on by this sea of English cell phones—

And Guinness Time is 7:35. Christ, I'm late! Wait for me, Rory, please, be there in just a tick! Around this corner swarming with bald men and heavy women and into Duke of York Street toward the Red Lion, a marvelously preserved Victorian pub of etched plate glass and rich red mahogany as I wedge my way past plates of sausage-and-mash being gently handed across the bar—and there's Rory at that rear corner table with a pretty, pregnant girl (no, not Nicole) leaning near and urgently saying in his ear, "—Look, if you're that unclear, then you definitely *DON'T* have a baby!"

"Sorry I'm late—"

"O, Da!" Rory standing and giving me a robust, back-slapping hug. My lovely son, with his intense gaze, mother's halo of auburn curls, lightly freckled skin, and a day's growth of reddish beard. "And this is Pippa."

"Pippa Green."

And I shake the slender hand of this adorable, fluffy, chipmunk of a girl, with her broad Boston accent, and wearing a tassled, crimson shawl and glinting granny glasses.

"So great to finally meet you, Mr. Boyne. I really am truly honored."

"Yes, well, thank you very much. Have you been waiting long?"

"No, Da, not too long."

"O good, I'm glad. And where's Nicole?"

"With her mother, down from Leeds. But, here, what're you drinking?"

"Didn't mean to interrupt you, Pippa."

"No, Da, we were just discussing my quandary,.

"When're you heading up to Oxford?"

"Tomorrow morning, meet my tutor."

"What quandary?"

A waiter appearing.

"Da?"

"O, Guinness for me."

"And we'll have another round of the same."

"So what quandary, Rory?"

"Well, the fact is Nicole's pregnant."

"Hey, *mazel tov,* as they say in Gaelic!" And leaning forward, I take his face in my hands and kiss him, *smack,* on his freckled forehead.

"Yes, well, she's—*we're* not sure we should have it."

"Not *sure?* What're you talking about? Why on earth not?"

Rory glancing at Pippa, "Well, for one thing, I'm twenty-two and Nicole's twenty-four, and I'll, well, I'll be starting Oxford shortly—"

"So? What the hell's that got to do with it? Go on, Pippa, tell him about the joys of parenthood."

"I'm sorry, Mr. Boyne, but I'm afraid I can't."

"Why not?"

" 'Cause I think they *should* abort it."

"Are you out of your fucking mind! You never abort the bab!"

"Why not? Or are you pro-life, Mr. Boyne?"

"No, actually I'm pro-choice but anti-abortion. Why, would you abort *your* child?"

"I would if I could."

"Then you're a bloody loony, *absolutely* crazy! And who *are* you anyway?"

"Da—"

She removing her glasses, "I'm Nicole's best friend—"

"Some fucking friend!"

"—and Rory's not ready."

"But, Jaysus, no one's *ever* 'ready'."

"Sounds like a battery. Eveready? The rabbit?"

"We got it, Rory."

"Sorry. But, Da, listen, nothing's been decided on yet—"

"And the point, Mr. Boyne, is that if they're both unsure—"

"But are *they?* Rory, you really want an abortion?"

"I don't *want* it, Da, I just think for now it might be best for the both of us."

"Is that what Nicole thinks, too?"

"Well . . . no. But—"

"No 'buts,' Rory, this is your *child* we're talking about here!"

"I understand, Da, I'm not stupid."

"Whoever said you were? You're a bloody Rhodes Scholar, for God's sake, Yale, magna cum laude!" His cell phone shrilly ringing. "Jaysus, how I hate those blasted things!"

Rory snapping his open, "Hi, sweetie. Yes, he's here. Fine, fine. (Nicole says hello) . . . OK, OK, I'm leaving right now." And he snaps it closed.

"How come?"

"I have to pick her up at her mother's flat. Seems they've been having the exact same discussion."

"So when'll I see you again?"

"I'll call you Sunday, Da, some things I need to discuss. But, hey, I must say, you look pretty good for a man your age."

"Faint praise!"

"And your Tate thing is Monday, on your birthday, right?"

"Right, right."

"Never can remember if it's the twenty-second or the twenty-third. Well we'll definitely celebrate that. Pippa," he hugging her close, "talk to you soon," then me, " 'Bye, Da."

And watching him weave his way through the tippling Red Lion throng, I drain this small and portly, dimpled mug of stout as Pippa, her dark lashes fluttering, reaches for her fawn leather coat.

"And I'm afraid I have to go, too, Mr. Boyne. Here, this should cover mine."

"No-no, I've got it. And you can call me Seamus. By the way, how old are you, Pippa?"

"Twenty-five."

"And how many months pregnant?"

"Eight and a half."

"Are you an actress?"

"No, I'm a performance artist."

"Really? And where do you perform?"

"At the Hairy Boar in Soho."

"In your condition?"

"Well, 'my candle burns at both ends;/ It will not last the night—' "

" 'But ah, my foes, and oh, my friends—' "

"So you know Millay?"

"'It gives a lovely light!' "

"Right, and—O God, look at the time! I'm terribly sorry, Mr. Boy—Seamus, but I really must go. I have a show to do in twenty minutes. Though I feel just awful rushing off like this, would love to stay and talk."

"Don't worry about it, Pippa, it's happened before, many, many times, the damp, dark road, struggling on alone."

"No, really, I'm serious. Why, would you like to come along?"

"No, thank you, not tonight, but at least let me get you a cab."

And outside in the blustery night, my head dizzily spinning

with Guinness, and pregnant little Pippa waiting at the curb as I step boldly out into rain-drizzled Jermyn Street to flag down that slowing taxi, and reaching for the door—

WHACK!!

—go violently soaring head over heels through the air, my heart stopping, then—smacking this cold, hard ground—starting up once more as blurry Pippa kneels before me, *"Mr. Boyne?! Mr. Boyne?! O MY GOD! Are you OK?"*

Twitching my toes—which still function—Not in heaven, no, on my back, in the damp street, more people crowding noisily around, traffic screeching past. "What was it, a bomb?"

"No, you got hit by a car. Are you in pain?"

"Pain? . . . Don't think so." And gingerly sitting up, "Can move my arms, my legs," I stagger and sway to my feet, with the cabbie's and Pippa's assistance.

"Where were you hit?"

"Back here."

"On your butt?"

"Right, right, I was saved by my arse."

A short man stepping forward, "That bloody idiot must've been doing fifty miles per hour out of Regent Street, then took off—thought you were a goner. Say, but aren't you Seamus—?"

Another woman adding, "We'd better call 999."

"No, no, just take me back to my flat."

"I'll come with you."

"But your show?"

"I'll call and cancel it."

And gently inside we go.

"Where to, sir?"

"62 Cadogan Square."

"Righto."

And we're off with a puttering purr, my left leg a flame of pain.

Two

Splashing past Cadogan Gardens and pulling up at my high-windowed Georgian town house with its wrought-iron fence, stucco and latticed facade. And leaning on Pippa's arm, "Listen, I don't want to hurt the bab—" "Don't worry, you won't," I go slowly hobbling inside, by the brick, whitewashed walls of my wide, red-carpeted living room, and flick on all my tiffany lamps. "You know, for someone so small, Pippa, you're really very strong."

"I know."

"How tall are you?"

"Five-three."

"And weigh?"

"Now 140, but usually 115 or so, especially when I was swimming." And shaking out her floppy chestnut hair cut short like a teenage moppet's—as, keenly wincing, I sink down onto my gold brocaded sofa—she gazes all around with those radiant hazel eyes, "Wasn't this once an art gallery?"

"Yes, the Sligo-Moeran, my former patron's, and I bought it three years ago and had it thoroughly refurbished—*Damn!*"

"You OK, Mr. Boy—Seamus?"

"No!"

"Shall I call a doctor?"

"*No!* Just tell me what kind of car hit me."

"Looked like a Mercedes or Beamer sedan, but it all happened so fast."

"Color?"

"Black, I believe."

"Did it look deliberate?"

"Have no idea. Why, are you saying someone may've been *trying* to kill you?"

"Could be. It's happened before. And especially now."

"Why now?"

" 'Cause *everything's* falling apart, Tiki fleeing, navvys crashing into my shower, can't paint anymore—Though, actually, I thought a terrorist bomb went off. You know, Al-Qaeda?"

"Yes, I'm sure you did, that was one hell of a collision. And you never saw it coming?"

"Never saw it, never heard it," as I painfully take off my Burberry, and she removes her fawn leather coat, sitting across from me on that matching gold love seat in a long white T-shirt, gray vest, and snug black hip-huggers below her belly.

"How come you didn't want to wait for an ambulance or the police, have them file a report?"

"Didn't want the publicity."

"Are you gonna call Rory?"

"No, not yet, no need to worry him now," wincing once more, "I'll call him in the morning."

"You're really hurting, aren't you, Seamus?"

"Well let's just say I'm not quite up to a *Riverdance* jig. But I'm sure it's more shock than anything else."

"Would you like me to run you a bath?"

"A bath, a bath? Actually, that's not a half bad idea."

"Where is it?"

"Through that door. But wait, hold on a second, who *are* you?"

"Nicole and Rory's friend."

"I *know* that! But why're you doing this? You don't have to stay. I'm fine, really."

"No you're not."

"O Jaysus, I've found me a bloody control freak! Just what I need!"

"And I've found me another macho man! No, but really, Seamus, you take a nice, hot bath, a couple of Tylenols, and get yourself a good night's sleep."

"And you'll be watching?"

"Of course. Need some stimulation at my stage of pregnancy. Nothing like seeing a seventy-five-year-old man bathing in the nude!"

"How'd you know my—?"

"Rory told me. But, if it's all right with you, I can sleep on that sofa tonight, just to make sure you're OK."

"I *am* OK!"

"And I say you're not."

"You're a fucking shrew!"

"Hey, you noticed. Anyway, would you like your Tylenol now?"

"Whenever it suits you, Florence."

"Florence?"

"Nightingale. Before your time, Pippa."

"Well I am fifty years younger than you."

"Don't remind me!"

"So where's—?"

"In the bathroom cabinet, top shelf."

"And the bathroom is—?"

"Down that hall to the left," shifting painfully again on the sofa as Pippa grimaces and sighs. "*You* OK?"

"Yeah, just the baby kicking delightfully away. And *your* leg's still hurting?"

"That it 'tis. Figure it twisted, took the full force of the impact, since it was the left one that was planted."

"And how 'bout your butt?"

"Surprisingly fine. Why, Pippa, would you like to examine it?"

"Another time, when I'm in a hornier mood. Anyway, let me go start your bath."

And Jaysus, wait'll Rory and Tiki find out about this! as I hear the water running in my huge blue Harrods tub, and Pippa returns holding two Tylenol in her palm.

"You take water to wash it down or—?"

"Guinness'll do—In the kitchen, straight through those—"

"Got it."

And I take a few foamy swigs of stout with a Tylenol chaser as Pippa pauses before that walnut table to examine my sculpture of Poldy made of wood and white wool on an ebony marble base.

"This one of yours, Seamus?" I nod. "Is the dog still alive?"

"No, he died a while ago."

"It's really brilliant."

"Thank you. I did several of him."

"Very funky," and she sits back down on the love seat.

"They don't mind you canceling your show?"

"Yeah, they mind, but we're not exactly packing them in these days."

"Right," shifting awkwardly once more on the sofa, "So tell me, what does a performance artist do, Pippa?"

"Well, for one thing, I don't roll around in honey or chocolate on the floor like Karen Finley."

"So what *do* you do?"

"O, I read some Edna St. Vincent Millay, do a monologue on a current hot topic, like *The Passion of the Christ,* and the absurdity of God and the Ten Commandments, do a native dance—"

"Native dance?"

"Just joking, but it might well be an Indian or Irish dance, or even Swahili, though I'm not very graceful at the moment, occasionally strip and paint myself, or just strip and paint a mural, or have a light show, I don't know. It all depends on my mood and the mood of the crowd. I was thinking next week of doing a cooking show, and my first recipe will be Twelve Ways to Sauté Martha Stewart."

Laughing—and sharply wincing once more, "That's very funny," as I continue awkwardly shifting, "Can I come watch?"

"By all means. Come next Wednesday or Friday and see my water break."

"You really *don't* want this bab?"

"Read my lips," her hazel gaze now darkening to a brown and smoky pewter, "N-O."

And I slowly sip my Guinness, the Tylenol finally kicking in, "Did you go to college in the States?"

"Yes."

"Where?"

"Vassar."

"How'd you do?"

"OK."

"What's OK?"

"I graduated first in my class."

"Really?"

"No, I'm lying just to impress you."

"Well I don't understand why a brilliant Vassar grad becomes a performance artist."

"Or better yet gets pregnant?"

"So who's the father?"

"What is this, Twenty Fucking Questions? O, hold on, let me go check your bath—'and we'll be back after a word from our sponsor,'" as she hurries off, with a surprisingly sensual grace . . . then returns in a moment, "Be a few more minutes. I hope you like it hot, Seamus."

"Scalding. Anyway, tell me about the father."

"The father? The father? O, you mean Niall (Nigh-ell)?"

"Niall?"

"Niall Finch. What about him? He thought he was the world's greatest living unpublished poet, spent a year at Cambridge, and died of a heroin overdose four months into my pregnancy— though, as I told you, I never really wanted the child. Still, I nursed him, but I just couldn't save him—I know, I'm a regular Florence what's-her-name."

"So what was the attraction?"

"Well, let's see. For one thing, he was the first guy who ever went down on me."

"Good a reason as any. But why'd you get pregnant?"

"His idea. He was really into big families, was reading Blake's *Songs of Innocence* at the time."

"Was Niall that good a poet?"

"Well that's for you to judge."

"What's your opinion?"

"At first I thought he was amazing, but after the second or third time through, it didn't really hold up all that well. And now, I hate to say it, but I think he's probably among the world's worst poets, right up there with Maya Angelou—O hell, let me turn off your bath before it runneth over!"

And she comes jauntily back singing, *"We've only just begun,"* with an ear-to-ear grin on those plump and glowing chipmunk cheeks and reaches down to me, "You need a hand, Seamus?"

"Actually a leg would do."

"Then here, lean on me again."

And we step gingerly through these rising clouds of steam within my blue-tiled bathroom.

"Pippa, I think I can manage now."

"O, damn, and I was so looking forward to seeing you yummy in the raw."

"Well I can always draw you a picture."

And wincing once more with waves of pain, as, grinning again, she closes the door behind her, I ungainly shed my clothes, then slowly lower my life-saving arse into this scalding water.

Three

—Waking with a start in the pitch-black dark, and shrieking gales of rain rattling, rinsing the latticed panes, as her footsteps patter swiftly by my door—

"Pippa?"

And squinting at her silhouette framed before me in the harsh hallway light, my sight gradually clearing, and she only wearing that long white T-shirt and glinting granny glasses, *"What?"*

"You can't sleep?"

"No!"

"How come?"

"Well, hel-*lo!* How 'bout heartburn, back pain, constipation, needing to fucking pee every half hour, since the *bab,* as you so lovingly call it, pushes an elbow into my bladder! Otherwise, it's bliss out there on your sofa!"

"Well, I told you to go home. But if it'll make you feel any better, I can't sleep, either."

"Your leg, still?"

"That, and I keep replaying the accident over and over. Look, I've got a futon upstairs in my studio."

"O, now you tell me!"

"I'm sorry, Pippa, I forgot. How 'bout a glass of wine?"

"No, no booze, drugs, or sex allowed. I'll see you in the morning."

Four

Wild silence! like my perishable fame—followed by squalls of gusty rain shaking my Georgian timbers—as I fumble and grope to find the remote control and flick on my fifty-inch plasma TV.

One BBC channel after another, showing Mozart's *Don Giovanni,* then grainy Chaplin films, and the continuous world-wide news: Nothing about me thus far. Ah, and there's the ultimate oxymoron, President Bush, with his macho cowboy swagger and some memorable words of wisdom: "If we don't succeed, we run the risk of failure." Dubya (so far from my hero, JFK—and what might've been), with his unparalleled arrogance and lack of shame, undoubtedly the worst president in my lifetime, destroying the environment for decades to come with unquenchable neocon greed, the most dangerous man on the planet—But hell, flicking him off, got enough problems of my own, my leg still harshly throbbing! . . . And so drowsy now, my eyes fluttering, slowly sliding closed . . . the Tylenol finally working . . .

And Symes, my ancient butler, and I on the sunny beach at Rath-new, he, knobby-kneed in his pleated, puce Bermuda shorts, and me, in my red, hooded sweatshirt, sweatpants, and Reebok sneakers, breathing in deeply and flinging my arms out wide.

"Ah, Symes, could you possibly ask for a more perfect day, cresting breakers rolling in, Ireland in all its glory? So I propose that the two of us have a race!"

"A race, sir?"

"Precisely! Be the very thing to get the ichor flowing, shuck off the myriad effects of aging! Your trotters up to it, old friend?"

"My trotters are fine, sir. It's just—"

"For you were once a miler, and I a champion sprint man."

"But race to where, sir?"

Bridging my hand over my eyes and staring down the flat, deserted beach, "Well, let us say, O, down to Stag's Leap, that boulder just below it?"

"And you're truly certain about this, sir?"

"Without a doubt." Both of us bending and stretching, shaking out the torment in our ancient, aching bones, he then seventy-nine, me seventy-three. "On your mark . . . get set—GO!"

And gangly Symes bursting out of the starting blocks like an ungainly whooping crane, all knobby knees and quaking blood-hound jowls to take the early lead—but fading fast after twenty-five yards, gasping and wheezing and sinking slowly in the sand—as I pass him, leave him in my wake and—JAYSUS! grimacing in searing pain—having pulled a bloody muscle—as Symes guides me back to my castle, an arm about his bony shoulder, for a long, steaming soak in the tub and then the application of ice packs and Ibuprofen. . . .

Five

Outside, the rain still pouring, pummeling down in fierce, buffeting gusts, and Pippa standing, hands on her hips, in the doorway, wearing that same gray vest, long white T-shirt, and those snug, black hip-huggers below her gravid belly.

"So, Seamus, are you ever getting out of bed?"

"Never."

"Why not?"

"My father, Tim, used to say when things aren't going well, just pull the covers over your head."

"And you're sure you don't want a doctor?"

"No, no doctors."

"Did you call Rory?"

"Not yet."

"OK, then I'm going to fix you a totally awesome breakfast! You like omelets?"

"What kind of omelet?"

"Well, how 'bout a piping hot omelet filled with a dollop of chilled *tzatziki?*"

"Which is what?"

"A cold yogurt-cucumber-garlic filling. I just read this fabulous book by Tom Stone called *The Summer of My Greek Tavérna*, with these recipes in the back, and I guarantee you'll love it, I swear!"

"You've got all the ingredients?"

"Bought them all this morning."

"Need any help?"

"Shouldn't think so, but I'll give you a shout if I do. You mind if I put on some music?"

"Be my guest."

And swiveling slowly out of bed at 8:24 on this gray and stormy morning, I toss on my red terrycloth robe and a new black beret (lost my favorite one last night), my leg now stiff and still occasionally aching, and move into the living room, where the tiffany lamps are blazing, and Pippa is searching through my CD collection on the far, white-washed wall below the stereo equipment—and, a few moments later, Strauss's *Don Juan* comes blasting, booming out, bouncing off the ceiling.

"Do you know this piece, Seamus?"

Nodding.

"And the conductor?"

"Toscanini with the NBC Symphony Orchestra."

"Very good. You've got an amazing collection here."

"An even bigger one in Ireland, Pippa."

"I'm sure. But you know, it just *hit* me."

"What did?"

"That here *I* am on a Saturday morning in London talking to— to Seamus Boyne! *Unbelievable!*—the greatest painter going!"

"And *where* am I going?"

"To hell in a handbasket? No, I'm only teasing. You'll be fine, Seamus, just fine."

"From your lips to God's ear."

" 'What lips my lips have kissed.' "

"You're really into Millay, aren't you, Pippa?"

"Of course. It's why I went to Vassar."

And I follow her into my gleaming stainless steel kitchen, where, with *Don Juan* now building to that soaring French horn theme, she pours a bowl of already beaten eggs into a hot omelet pan, coated with cooking spray, vigorously shakes it above the heat, allowing the raw eggs to slide beneath, and then adds the cold *tzatziki* to the bubbling center, before lifting the pan off the stove, and, rolling the omelet over on itself, lets it fall gently onto my plate.

"There's also toasted pita bread and sliced tomatoes with oregano— and what would you like to drink? And don't say Guinness."

"Guinness."

"You're impossible!"

"But Guinness does for me what spinach does for Popeye."

"Fine, but how does black coffee sound?"

"Hum a few bars—No, I'll just add a splash of Irish whiskey to mine."

"Can you eat all of that?"

"I can eat anything."

Pippa grinning, "I'll bet you can."

And I take a hearty bite into this luscious-looking omelet, *"Holy Jaysus!"*

"What?"

"God's in his heaven—All's right with the world!"

"So Pippa passes?"

"With flying culinary colors! My hat—beret—is off to the pregnant chef!"

"Thank you, thank you. I'm also available for Muslim weddings and orthodox bar mitzvahs."

And sipping my morning stout as the rain beats steadily down, I sigh and lean back in my green wicker chair, "So, Pippa, how do you know Nicole?"

"I met her at Allegra Kent's dance class in New York, then she went home to England and I moved here two years ago and started performing."

"And that gives you enough to live on?"

"No, not really, but my mother left me some G.E. stock, I've always got just enough to muddle through, make ends meet."

"Your mother still alive?"

"No, she died in a car accident in Poughkeepsie, a hit and run, in 1999."

"O I'm sorry."

"And I hardly knew my father. He was a staff sergeant who died at Ft. Bragg, 82nd Airborne, his chute didn't open, when I was three."

"Any living relatives?"

"None. But anyway, as I said, I always seem to muddle through, and, hell, if I have to, I can always do British porn."

"You're not serious?"

"Well, it definitely would be a trip. I've got a pretty good body, though you'd never know it now. No, really, like Millay, who was small as well, five-one, but had surprisingly large and perfectly shaped breasts, though I'm sure my butt's a whole lot bigger than hers. Well, you can judge for yourself when you see me perform."

"I can't wait."

"See, I knew you were a dirty old man."

"And maybe then I'll even paint you—that's if I ever paint again. But when's your due date?"

"Who knows," she getting up with her plate, "could be any fucking day."

"Well, I must say you're glowing, skin like strawberry shortcake, pink and beautifully smooth, like my ex-wife's, second wife, Ciara's."

"Yeah, well, anyway, look," she rinsing out her cup in the sink, "I need to bathe and change my clothes, so I'm going home to my flat in Bayswater, and I'll be back later, so you get some sleep—"

"Yes, Florence. And then," wolfing down the rest of this savory omelet, "*I'll* make *you* dinner tonight. What would you like?"

"Whatever your heart desires."

"Right—O leave that, Pippa, I'll clean everything up."

"Thank you. And here's my home and cell phone numbers, and my address, should you need it, in Bayswater on Lancaster Gate."

"Fine. And there's an umbrella in that closet—no, the other one. There. And let me call you a cab."

"I've been called a lot worse in my time. No, thank you, that's very kind."

Six

And I'd best call Rory now. No, no need to worry him quite yet. But I will call Symes in Ireland.

"Good morning. Boyne residence."

"Symes, any unusual phone calls since I left?"

"None, sir, that I recall."

"And nothing strange has happened?"

"Other than that workman falling through the roof again. He's getting quite good at it, I must say. But why do you ask?"

"I was hit by a car—I'm fine, just a leg bruise, not to worry."

"Do you know the driver?"

"No. Nor did I call the police."

"Well I shall, sir, straightaway, contact my nephew Graham at Scotland Yard, just in case, to keep an eye on you."

"I appreciate that, Symes, and I'll speak to you posthaste if there's any further news."

Symes such a gem, a jewel among men—as I punch in Rory's cell phone number:

"Yes, hello?"

"Ah, there's m'boy!"

"Hey, Da, what's up?"

"Well, Pippa just left."

"*Pippa?* What's *she* doing there?"

"Nursing me."

"Nursing—You're shagging pregnant Pippa?"

"Rory, no—"

"Da, you're totally out of control!"

"No, that was the car."

"What?"

"I was the victim of a hit and run."

"*When?*"

"After you left the Red Lion."

"Are you OK?"

"Saved by my arse, so Pippa's been my nurse."

"Is that what they called it then?"

"No, really, she's been a godsend."

"Yeah, I'll bet."

"Rory!"

"OK, OK, but, Da, listen, we need to talk."

"How could you possibly *think* that?"

"Fine, Da, fine, then I'll see you Monday night at the Tate."

"Right, though I may, in fact, have to cancel, leg's still a bit gammy, but I'll let you know. You and Nicole decide anything yet?"

"About what?"

"The abortion."

"No, we're still debating. But promise you'll call if you need me. 'Bye."

Shaking my weary head and draining another Guinness before I sigh and screw up my courage to call Tiki in Vancouver (how soft in silk my Tiki goes). Let's see, area code 604—If it's 9:15 here, it's 1:15 in the morning there:

"... 'Lo?"

"Tiki, sorry to call you so late. Are you alone?"

"... Why, what does it matter?"

"Because I got hit by a car."

"You *what?*"

"I got hit by a car."

"You got hit by a *car?*"

"Is there an echo on this line?"

"Seamus, be serious. Tell me what happened."

"I met Rory at this pub, and was getting a cab for his friend after."

"Were you hurt? Did you break anything?"

"Luckily no, just strained my leg."

"And that's it? Where did it hit you?"

"High on my right buttock, saved by my—"

"Can you walk?"

"Bit gimpy, but I'm on the mend."

"Is Rory with you?"

"No, he's up at Oxford. And Nicole's pregnant."

"She *is?* Wow, all *sorts* of things happening there. But have you seen a doctor?"

"No, no need to. And Tiki, how's your brother?"

"Stable. They'll probably operate next Wednesday."

"Then you're coming home?"

"I don't know if I am coming home—O, I've got to go. Someone's calling me now—"

"Who?"

"—'bye."

And now really feeling blue—'cause maybe it is over after twenty years, the bond broken (though she has seen me through thick and thin, from eye operations, that carotid endarterectomy, to my furious mood swings, ego tantrums of aging—O I *do* love her so!), yet I damn well better protect myself—as I go hobbling over like Long John Silver to peek through these window blinds, the squalling, swirling rain having ceased for the moment, but still quite blustery out in the street—and the phone abruptly ringing (Tiki calling back to apologize?):

"Yes, hello?"

"Is Mr. Boyne there?"

"This is he."

"Ah, well this is Chief Inspector Graham Keane of Scotland Yard, and I just got off the line with my uncle, Hubert Symes, in Ireland, didn't want you to become alarmed, sir, when you see a short chap in a brown mac lurking outside your door. He's one of mine, Constable Eric Glassco."

"O, no, that's fine."

"And should you require any sort of assistance, please don't hesitate to call."

"I shall indeed. And thank you, Chief Inspector, thank you very much."

And limping back to the drizzly window, I peer out once again—no sign of him—as a black Mercedes sedan cruises slowly round the square. Scotland Yard? Or Al-Qaeda? Or who the bloody hell knows in these strange, terrorist times, like never before! And maybe if I hurry, I can catch a glimpse of his license plate if he comes around once more—as I whip open my front door, leaving it slightly ajar, into these slanting sheets of rain—and here's that black car cruising round again! Can't see the driver—but it's not the same, an Audi not a Mercedes that goes splashing swiftly past and—*O Mother of Christ!*—my flapping red robe flying wide open, exposing my willy to the world and that man from Scotland Yard across the road!—as I tug it tight—and, with my front door start-ing to close—gave Pippa the key, locked out in the street—make a wild lunge, stumbling and sliding, willy wagging, and—with some truly inspired agility—just manage to wedge inside!

Then panting, lock it shut with a click, my leg a raging ache—

Knock-knock!

". . . Yes?"

"Constable Glassco here, sir." His resonant Scottish burr. "Are you all right in there?"

"—uh, yes, just thought I saw—bit embarrassed by the wind—but, no, I'm fine, and thank you, thank you for inquiring."

"My pleasure, sir."

And watching him head around the corner out of sight before I shed my red robe and wet beret and go peglegging across the carpet—and suddenly thoroughly drained as I climb into bed and pull these covers over my head, wooly quilts and smooth, satin comforter, trying to ease my gammy leg into a more comfort-able—*Jaysus!*—position—swerving and shifting—There, that should do. My eyes so heavy-lidded—and drifting off, dreaming far more frequently now in my mid-seventies, grab a couple of hours through these fierce afternoon showers before Pippa returns. *We were very tired, we were very merry—/ We had gone back and forth all night on the ferry*—More Edna St. Vincent buzzing about my teeming brain . . . .

And Tiki, Rory, and I all intently watching that climactic wres-tling scene in the film Vision Quest *on TV, a few weeks after his sixteenth birthday, when he suddenly bounced straight up off his couch and challenged me to a match: "I can beat you, Da!" as I smiled and shook my head, but he kept persisting, "Come on, Da, you know you can't win." And Tiki, upset at the prospect, intervening with, "Rory, no, your father doesn't want to wrestle, let's just watch the movie." But he was unrelenting, "Come on, Da!" jazzed up by the scenes on the screen and accompanying driving sound track of Tangerine Dream, "I can beat you in basketball one-on-one," (which he'd recently done) "and I can beat you now in wrestling!" Tiki still trying to intercede—till, finally, I reluctantly agreed.*

And we began, with Rory insisting I start on top, quickly astonished at how strong he'd become at sixteen, twisting and skidding over the living-room carpet, burning my elbows and shins, locked in each other's arms, but no pins, getting him in a chokehold and having to break it—since it's illegal—then a full nelson—and having to break that, too, before Rory, grinning, claimed that he'd won—Tiki calling it a draw—but realizing if we'd kept on going, his strength and speed would've surely worn me down, his hands almost as strong as mine—

· · · · · ·

"O, Seamus, I'm really sorry, I didn't mean to wake you. And you look so sweet when you're sleeping."

"—Yes, well," rapidly blinking, "I was getting up anyway." And yawning and rinsing my blurry eyes with my fists, still so tired as I follow her stiffly into the living room, her bright chipmunk face looking freshly scrubbed, and she now wearing a baggy navy sweatshirt and navy knit pants with an elastic waist, as we sit on the gold sofa under the tiffany lamps, and the squalling rain continues to harshly rattle down.

"O and I checked all the papers, Seamus, and no mention of you, so at least you weren't shot three times in the tabloids."

"No, they got me in the buttocks, missed my tabloids. Sorry,

sorry, old joke." A feisty gleam from her hazel eyes. "No, but that's good news."

"Did you call Rory?"

"Yes. And he's upset that you're here."

"Get out! You're kidding? What's he think we're doing, the old nasty together, getting our freak on?"

"Who knows. But don't worry about it, Pippa."

"Did he tell Nicole?"

"I don't know, probably."

"Un-fucking-believable!"

"And I talked to my butler in Ireland and my wife in Vancouver."

"You've been quite busy, Mr. Boyne. Tiki, right?"

"Right."

"And what did *she* have to say? You tell *her* I was here?"

"No, not really."

"Yeah, well tell me about her, about Tiki."

"She's sixty-five, her face still as finely chiseled as a cameo brooch—and I absolutely adore her, love her madly."

"Does she know it?"

"I thought she did. But one's never sure with women—and I've been impossible to live with lately."

"I'm sure you have. Still, I'm jealous."

"Why?"

"I've never had a man speak like that about me."

"You will."

"You're sure, Seamus?"

"Pippa, believe me, you're 'barbarous in beauty,' as Hopkins says."

"You know Hopkins?"

"By heart."

"Give me a sampling."

" 'I caught this morning morning's minion, king—/ dom of daylight's dauphin, dapple-dawn-drawn Falcon, in his/ riding/ Of the rolling level underneath him steady air, and striding/ High there, how he rung upon the rein of a wimpling wing/ In his ecstasy! then off, off forth on swing—' "

"O God, that is so *cool!* Wicked poetry! But come on, more, more, give me more!"

"Later, Pippa, later, 'cause what I want *you* to believe is that *your* greatest poem or performance will be delivering this precious bab!"

"*OK*, Seamus—"

"No, hear me out. I know I'm a hobbled old codger, irascible bloody fool, but listen, I swear, it was fatherhood that made *me* a man."

"Which means what?"

"Which means that selfish, narcissistic Boyne finally began really caring about another human being, and it even made me a better painter!"

"O gimme a break!"

"No, really. For example, I was able to get inside Rory and feel, *really* feel what *he* felt—You've seen my Rory series?"

"O they're awesome, absolutely amazing, my favorite of *all* your work."

"Thank you, that's very kind. But back to the issue at hand: Pippa, you just have to commit to this child!"

"Why, 'cause you said so?"

"No, not only—"

She suddenly standing and wincing, then slowly sitting back down.

"Are you all right?"

"Just more interior shifting, football kicking."

"Then let me ask you this, are you worried it might be a junkie 'cause of Niall?"

"There is that possibility, however small, of defects, chance of deformity, but no, the real reason is I'm not ready."

"Eight and a half months and you're not *ready?*"

"You know, just for one day, I'd like a man to go through this just for one fucking day, see what it feels like, morning sickness, pre-partum panic attacks!"

"OK, fine, but you're not the only woman who ever experienced—"

"Just fuck off, Seamus! I'm gonna *have* it, all right? Are you satisfied? But that doesn't mean I have to want it, does it?"

"But the joys that are coming—"

"*Whose* joys? If my head isn't in it, how does that help the precious *bab,* as you call it?"

"But you'll be a *great* mother!"

"O really? And how do you know that?"

" 'Cause I see how sensitive and caring you are when you're nursing me, and you nursed Niall—"

"And see where *that* got me!"

"So you think you'll fail, is that it?"

"I don't know, maybe, being alone, raising it by myself— everything like that. Hell, I haven't even figured *myself* out yet!"

"Well I have."

"O have you now? So, tell me, who *am* I?"

"A brilliant, warm, sexy, loving, and exceptional bloody female! And a feisty maverick to boot. You like to prove others wrong, love the challenge, to show you *could* go to Vassar, graduate first in your class, then become a performance artist here in London, and now you'll surprise even yourself at what a fantastic mother you'll be!"

"You really believe that?"

"Absolutely!"

"Yes, well, we'll just have to see."

"That we will, Pippa, that we will. But for now, my dear, I'm gonna fix you an extraordinary Irish feast!"

"You're gonna cook?"

"Well the bab has to eat? O, and by the way, did you happen to see that small man in a brown mac lurking outside in the street?"

"I did indeed."

"He's a Scotsman from Scotland Yard, Constable Glassco, just keeping a keen eye peeled," and I go limping inside the kitchen, "Follow me," turning and ducking under these shiny brass and copper pans as I spin about, grinning before my stainless steel, six-burner stove, sink, and wide Amana fridge. "See, all the comforts of Martha Stewart! To slice and garnish, pickle and dice!"

"So what're you going to make?"

"O, drisheens in tansy butter, colcannon, or a Michaelmas goose, haha!—No, actually, I thought something simple might suffice, do a Piedmont style fondue," and opening the fridge to remove this bowl of Fontina cheese covered in milk that's been sitting for quite a while.

"Need any help?"

"Matter of fact, need some white pepper, in that cabinet above you, and one white truffle, which you have to slice paper thin. O, and while you're at it, slice up a lemon as well."

"Sure. You know you can squeeze more juice out of a lemon if you roll it between your hands before cutting?"

"I never knew that."

"See what you can learn from the young and pregnant."

And not long after, I watch Pippa dip into a steamy crockpot of my very own Fontina cheese fondue, sprinkled with paprika and thyme, and now thickly dripping from these luscious chunks of a crusty French baguette.

"I think you missed your calling, Mr. Boyne."

"You're not the first person who's ever told me that," and I pour some more of this superb and ice-cold RC Cola bubbling into her glass. "You know, Pippa, you don't have to stay here any longer, especially with Scotland Yard standing guard outside."

"O no, I'm actually beginning to enjoy it. And you *are* still sore, right?"

"Right. Well, it's up to you."

"Unless you'd *like* me to leave?"

"No, you're starting to grow on me."

"Yeah, like a goddamn vine!"

"No, really, you've been extremely kind. But, Pippa, that reminds me, I've been meaning to ask you, do you believe in God?"

"No, God's a total fraud!"

"And what bout Jesus?"

"Why, you really think he rose? I prefer the Jesus in D.H. Lawrence's *The Man Who Died*, when Mary gets him all hot and hard on the cross, and he says, 'I have risen!' It's all science fiction, really, sheer mumbo jumbo. Hell, that loony L. Ron Hubbard makes just as much bloody sense."

"And what if you're at death's door?"

"Utter rubbish! Like *The Passion of the Christ*, a masochistic, anti-Semitic torture flick about divine abuse! Why, you've seen it?"

"No."

"Totally gross! Just plain sick!"

"You have a problem with father figures?"

"No, just with God or God-like fathers. But let me ask you, when's the last time you actually read the Ten Commandments?"

"Not in the last sixty years."

"Well take a look at it sometime, Seamus. What you'll find is a vengeful, possessive, obsessive God, who's always talking about Himself in the third person, like some rock or movie star, and needing constant reassurance that there are no other competing gods. And then he gives Moses this long list of legal minutiae like enjoining us to kill witches, Sabbath violators, disrespectful children, and people who have sex with animals."

"Ah, so I shouldn't have fucked my sheep?"

"You fucked a—O you! Though I've heard it can't be beat."

"Yeah, well, don't knock it unless you've tried it. But, Pippa, listen, I'm sorry but I'm feeling really very tired again, all this Fontina fondue, so I think I'll run myself a bath."

"No, I'll do it, and get you your Tylenol chaser."

"What a woman!"

"I thought I was a bloody control freak?"

"You are, but an exceptional female as well. No, really, it's been a long and trying day, even stepped outside for a bit—but I'll fill you in on that later. For now, I shall require a hot, steaming soak in the tub, then retire to me bed with a tumbler of Tullamore Dew."

Seven

—And stumbling and woozily bumbling awkwardly around, I pause before these mirror images of Laura, Ciara, Tiki, and Pippa—as into the mirror strides my father, Timothy Patrick Boyne, with his patrician's face, of regal grace, and, gazing fondly at me with that wry and tender smile, a twinkle to his lilac eye, looks to be in his prime, like an elegant Leslie Howard in the film, The Scarlet Pimpernel, *when—O mother of Christ!—we go tumbling back in time! To Brittany in 1939 at the outbreak of World War II. He, a short-order cook from Valhalla, New York, who, crazed with grandiose dreams by the sauces he'd invented, thought he was Escoffier incarnate and strove for immortality, going mad for never attaining it. So loved to see him whipping up his own exquisite velouté, béchamel, or mornay, and that astounding Hong Kong curry, served in infinite varieties of mild, medium, and blast your bloody head off!*

But now, here in late summer France, I'm ten and a half, and he's thirty-one, gathering recipes for his precious cache, the Germans having already Blitzkrieged Poland, Paris soon under siege, and tomorrow we sail for New York—as on this, our last evening abroad, we have a farewell meal at a grand restaurant, with dancing, at La Baule, close to where French and British soldiers are encamped, some 200 or so having crowded within, and they begin to sing the "Marseillaise," when James Joyce (of course I have no idea who he is, other than my father telling me he is a truly great writer, just a thin, old man with glasses, wapper jaw, and patch over one eye) joins in, and gradually his voice, a thrilling Irish tenor, rises high above the mass of soldiers as they stare at this display, then lift him onto a table so he can sing it all over again. And after, he and my father share a bottle of white wine, and he says he admires my large hands and tapered fingers. My father tells him I'm a painter, and Joyce nods and wryly smiles.

O what a wondrous time that was, with dear Timothy Patrick Boyne, sweet father of mine, who died—Jaysus!—almost sixty years ago in that private Rhode Island asylum—a day after I shared his last meal with him, sneaking in some of his favorite Hong Kong curry, rather than that psychiatric gruel—O my father, now long dead father! same oval face as mine, though smaller and Van Gogh-eyed—But Christ, we're all fathers, and you don't love anyone but yourself if you're afraid to love your father. . . .

Eight

And, eventually, I come blinking awake, after staying in bed for an unbelievable *sixteen* hours, to rub these sleepy flakes from my eyes. Pippa not here on this chill and windy Sunday afternoon, the rain having fled and a bright blue sky drifting overhead with a scatter of tattered clouds—Glassco still manning his post outside—as I flag him a friendly wave—and my leg feeling much improved when I examine my naked self in the tall bedroom mirror, bruises on my stretchmarked arse, calf, and hairy thigh—and why, when you get to my age, does hair sprout in the most unseemly places?

I put a Bach Partita on, with Glenn Gould at the keyboard, then cancel the Tate tomorrow, to painful protests, then excessive solicitation, call Tiki once more, not there, before talking to Rory, and Symes again—when Pippa comes striding in:

"Ah, so Jesus has finally risen!"

"In more ways than one, my dear. No, I'm feeling a whole lot better, thanks."

"Good, Seamus, I'm glad. O, and check this out, I had a dream about you last night."

"Ya did, did ya? And, pray tell, what was it about?"

"You gave *me* a bath."

Exchanging a fast glance, "How old was I in the bath?"

Pippa laughing and quickly checking her wristwatch, "Anyway, I've got a party to go to tonight. So would you like to come along?"

"To a party? No. That's the last thing I need right now. What kind of party?"

"It's a rave, like a happening. They take over a whole house, this one's in Chelsea, on Astell Street, and people come and go."

"What kind of people?"

"All sorts. It's very Aubrey Beardsley, really, very sexual, very decadent, just great, sleazy fun."

"Sounds awful."

"Fine, then you can stay at home and remain a stick in the mud."

"Then you're going to leave me alone?"

"But you said—"

"How can I stay alone?"

"You're really such a big baby, Seamus!"

"But I'll be recognized if I go, need some sort of disguise. Don't forget I'm famous."

"So you want me to shave off your beard?"

"*Shave off*—No. Though, actually, that might just do, make me younger-looking, at least. Do you know how to shave a man?"

"I used to do Niall all the time."

"Right, and look what happened to him—No, sorry, that was uncalled for. But maybe I should just dye my hair and beard, you know, with that Grecian Formula crap, got some in my bathroom, never used it."

"Fine, whatever. But let's do one or the other, 'cause we should be going soon."

And ten minutes later, I keep staring hard into the mirror at a still wrinkled but now brown-bearded Boyne.

"I don't look like a geek, Pippa?"

"Not at all. Matter of fact, you look twenty years younger, very sexy, would definitely turn *my* head around."

Nine

And giddy Pippa chirping with glee as we enter the crowded rave. "That's Amphetamine!" "Amphetamine?" "Right, super funky!" The strident techno music rising high above the deafening clatter and din of chatter and pinging glass in this massive and bombastic Chelsea home, with its pot-heavy fumes, various dancers and exotic dress, very touchy-feely—and overhearing that garishly made-up woman, "And so off I went, can you believe at my age, in this Joan Bakewell miniskirt, black opaque tights, and flat boots—" A man sensuously stroking the embroidered flowers on the heaving bosom of her blouse as she prattles merrily on, "O and did I tell you who I almost ran into over the weekend?" "Who?" "Felicia." "The psycho bitch from hell? I thought she'd moved to Hampstead?" "I guess she hadn't just quite yet. At least not fast enough for my palate!" Nobody as yet recognizing me in this swilling, gyrating madhouse—looks like Elton John over there with those huge pink glasses—and my Grecian Formula seemingly holding. Don't need a *Death in Venice* scene, like when Dirk Bogarde's hair-black and make-up started running. "You OK, Seamus?" "Fine, fine, just feeling my way." Those two Edwardian-looking poofters wedged in a corner under a large hanging plant and probably nattering on about brie and chablis—as they turn the sly, gay glint of their lascivious eyes to scan me up and down. "Pippa?" "What?" "You know the definition of an Irish homosexual?" "No." "A man who likes women better than drink." "O I like that, I really do! I'm gonna use that in my show." The two of us trying to slide closer to the bar, walking a bit bowlegged now to compensate for my leg, where this John Lennon clone is leaning over a bare-breasted girl in pasties, "How's about we play Carnival, luv?" "Carnival?" "You sit on my face, and I guess your weight," as Frankie Valli keeps crooning, "*I love you, baby! And if it's quite all right—*" "Well, nice meeting you then, uh—" "Shirley. Shirley Curtis." "Nice meeting you, Shirley. Shirley Curtis." "Same here, Ross." "No, it's Ron. Ron Moss." "Ah, Ron. Ron Moss."

"Here, Seamus, just follow me." Gripping Pippa's hand firmly in mine as we pick and fumble our way around other lovers folded together, holding, I suppose, similar stimulating discussions. Her arm now slowly circling behind me as we pass Hugh Grant, swirling dancers, and a furry man standing atop a table in his full tartan kilt, and now flipping it up—nothing underneath but genitalia and a ginger fleece, and he shouting in a rich, Scottish brogue, "Marilyn Monroe, eat your bloody heart out!" Pippa and I smiling, and goading me to give her thickened waist a tickle—She jumps, heee, laughter trembling lightly through the crowded rooms, and subsiding in an echo down this long, black hall filled with awful art and shaggy tapestries, and up a spiral, iron staircase we go, with Liquid Bass now blasting, as this widely-smiling boy with dilated pupils accosts me with, "My right honorable friend, has anyone ever told you you look like Mick Fleetwood?" "Yes, Stevie Nicks." He hesitating a moment, before throwing back his head and guffawing, then moving closer, nearly cheek to jowl and constantly sniffing, he conspiratorially hisses, "Did you knock *her* up?" And Pippa intervening, "No, but I wish he had!" She grinning and tugging me on, where a rotund gnome of a man dressed as an English cavalry officer is yelling, "Impossible to get around town anymore, everywhere so bloody crowded, the tube, buses, and streets, London awash with Arabs, Slavs, and Pakistanis—so don't you insult my city, you fucking Muslim!" and he flings himself, fists high, at a swarthy man, twice his size—who deftly pushes him aside—so the gnome paces off several steps to the stuccoed wall and, charging, spurs clanging across the hardwood floor, attacks once more—and is easily subdued. Pippa now greeting a group of people she obviously knows—as this anorexic girl, with various rings on her lips, eyebrows, and nostrils, starts caressing my chest, arms, and beard, twining the latter through her fingers—and Pippa yanks me away, whispering, "Ecstasy." And smiling, I shake my head, "Not really." "No, Seamus, ecstasy, the drug. Most of the people here are on it. Come on," and we go squirming into an anteroom, where a chef-hatted man's kneeling and carving an enormous roast on the carpet, and an obese woman's exclaiming, "Roger's wife's foaled *again?*" "O, hallo, Pugsy! And have you seen where the *Irish Times* reported, 'Eight dead in Belfast, three of them seriously'?" "Ah, go on wid ya now!" "—And I never told you what Duncan did." "What did Duncan do?" "Brought a bouquet of flowers to my front door." "So what did you do?" "Lay down on my back and spread my legs, of course." "Why didn't you use a vase?"

And we emerge into a narrow hall, where two tall and scruffy toughs in camouflage fatigues and barbed wire tattoos on their bulging biceps jar Pippa hard, and the bigger, drunker one roughly mutters, "Hey, watch it, ya fat cunt!" and I whirl around, "What'd you say?" "You heard me, ya ould fart!" "OK, that's it! And you'd better be good!" "Shite! Oy'll *show* ya how bloody good Oy am!" And he lurches at me with a roundhouse right—that I snare in midair and squeeze savagely tight and into submission, "—*OK, OK, Oy give, Oy give!*" when Pippa steps between me and the other thug, "You really don't want to mess with him, mate, 'cause he just got out of solitary." And they both blink, pause, then slowly stagger off.

"Seamus, you want a drink?"

"No, but if you don't mind, I'd like to leave."

"I agree. Just follow me."

And with Phil Collins now singing "Against All Odds" from a kid's barely audible cassette, we wedge our winding way back down the stairs and outside into the chilly night air as the rising whine of a Ninja goes zooming past.

"Seamus?"

"Yes?"

"I have a favor to ask."

"Which is?"

"Will you be the godfather to my bab?"

Staring at her a moment more, then broadly grinning, "Of course." And in my best Brando, "Made me an offer I couldn't refuse."

And she leans across and kisses me on the cheek.

And I flag down a cab on the corner, "You coming back tonight, Pippa?"

". . . No, I think I'd better go home."

"Right, right." And in we slide, shifting my leg aside.

"And you cancelled the Tate tomorrow?"

"That I did."

"So what'll you do for your birthday?"

"I think I'll buy myself a Jaguar."

"Can I come along?"

"Absolutely. And Rory and Nicole are arriving tomorrow besides."

"Seamus?"

"What?"

"I wish you weren't so happily married."

" 'Happily'?"

"Well, whatever."

". . . So do I."

Ten

And will you please tell me what I'm *doing? Dreaming? . . . No, I really AM dreaming again . . . of the chilly night wind circling about us on our walk down to the park of St. James, Nelson overlooking his pillar, and way down there, by the end of the Mall, shimmering in violet light, is Buckingham Palace with its vaunted buildings and grounds—and maybe we'll just pop in for a nightcap to while away the hours:* I say, Philip, would you be so kind as to avoid any undue racket on the landing? Mr. Boyne, M.B.E., over on holiday, you know, seems to have quite exhausted himself in the park and he and his pregnant friend will be occupying the Groom Room this evening. I'm quite sure you understand. Splendid. Good show— *as more squalling rain continues falling—And now I'm painting, or trying and failing to paint Rory in Ireland—till finally the canvas catches fire, and I'm boldly stroking and slashing in a haggard shaft of daylight here, falling over Rory's nose and cheekbones there, his carroty mop of hair catching that reflected glow—And jigging before my canvas, I'm absolutely wild-eyed with wonder, for what I'm doing now is seeing and painting not from MY point of view but HIS! Not me looking at him, but he looking at me! What Rembrandt achieved with his son Titus in that shattering breakthrough into true empathy, and the love of a father for his precious child! Such love, to see and feel through ANOTHER'S eyes!!*

And I suddenly bolt upright in a lather of desperate, panting sweat at 1:17 on this dark and windy morning—and, fumbling, flicking on this light, reach for my sketchpad and pen and begin furiously drawing Pippa's adorable face—

NO, that's *NOT* it! Start again. Trying to get those lovely contours and cheeks—

JAYSUS, CAN'T! Violently squeezing the paper into a ball and flinging it furiously aside, letting out a primal howl! *So bloody AWFUL!* Not a spark of *life, heat,* or fucking *PASSION!* The elusive muse definitely not returning! Have to draw and paint every day or I'll go mad and die—just to prove I'm alive! Art the basic way I can impose order on my emotions, like Turner, Van Gogh, Pollock, and Rothko—

But here, let me try one more time—with this fine Picasso line, yes, along her elfin ears and chipmunk nose—

NO!! damn it, NO, NO, NO!!

Lost it, and *I CAN'T get it back!* And flinging this sketch, too, onto that rubbish pile—

The phone *STRIDENTLY* ringing—Pippa calling? Her water broke? Gave birth? Or God only knows—

"Yes, hello?"

"Seamus, where on earth have you *been?*"

"Tiki?"

"I've been calling and calling—"

"Well . . . I slept for sixteen hours straight, must've turned off the phone."

"And two or three hours ago?"

"Two or three hours ago? . . . O, went out for a bit."

"A bit of what? You might at least have the decency to—Seamus, what is going *on* there?"

"I can't bloody *draw* anymore is what's going on here!"

"Are you alone?"

"Alone? *Of course* I'm alone—unlike some people I know! And I just had this fantastic dream of painting Rory, got up, tried to draw, to sketch again—but I *can't,* I just can't fucking *DO* it anymore! Jaysus, the bloody well is dry, can no longer glean those teeming images!"

"O I'm sure they'll come back, they always have. Anyway—"

"O now, all of a sudden, you care, you're concerned?"

"Seamus, look, I don't need your sarcasm right now. I just called to wish you a happy seventy-fifth birthday."

" *'Happy'?!*"

"All right then, irascible, impossible, angst-ridden seventy-fifth!"

"Ah, Tiki, that's much better. And now you can get back to your lover!"

"O hell, why do I even bother!"

" 'Cause, like Everest, I'm here! And you're *there!*"

"Exactly!"

Eleven

And Pippa looking absolutely lovely today in a long, red-and-white-striped rugby shirt covering her pregnant belly, denim blue hip-huggers below, and that beige Vassar bucket hat pulled down low over her ears, while I, of course, am artfully attired in my black beret, green Lillywhites windbreaker, charcoal cargo pants, Reeboks, and a tassled, azure, cashmere scarf tossed poetically over my shoulder as I exit this funereal London cab that pulls puttering up to a posh Jaguar dealership not far from Regent's Park.

And carefully helping Pippa out, I feel, for some strange reason, the fugitive muse returning, as we enter this gleaming, circular showroom.

A door abruptly opening from the rear, and a large, portly man appearing in a suit of indigo serge, somber thumbs momentarily vested within his watchfob pockets. He removes them, haarumph. Maneuvers slowly forward, haarumph, haarumph, and with a final shift of his mountainous bulk, haughtily enunciates, "Sir?"

"Yes. We're interested in the XKR convertible, special edition."

"Special edition, sir?"

"Special edition."

"Yes. Well we might, possibly, sir, have one left, in salsa. I'll just have to see." Wheezing pompously over his ledger, pearl stickpin, and dark silk tie, as I gaze all around at these brand-new, glossy Jaguars and exchange another sly grin with cheeky Pippa Green. "Well, sir, we do seem to have one left. As I'm sure you know, only one hundred were made worldwide."

"And how much are they?"

"52,000 pounds, sir."

"Right, well I'd like to take her out for a test drive."

"By all means, sir. And Harold will accompany you."

"No-no, by myself."

"I'm afraid we can't allow that, sir, it's not permitted."

"Can't allow it, not permitted? Do you know who I am?"

"I'm afraid I don't, sir."

"You don't recognize me?"

"Can't say that I do."

"Seamus Boyne?"

A faint, flickering smile, "Sir, if I may say, you do look a good deal younger than Mr. Boyne."

"I've recently darkened my beard. But here, wait here. Where's your loo?"

"Through there. But, sir—"

"Be back in a flash!" Washing off most of the Grecian stain, a fast scrub, before rapidly returning, "See?"

"Yes, well, the resemblance is quite remarkable, but—"

"He *is* Seamus Boyne!"

"And here's my ID."

". . . Ah, well, you do appear to be—"

"I am. And I'll take your salsa XKR."

"Take it, sir?"

"Absolutely. And, moreover, I'll pay for it with a sketch. Be worth far more than the car in the long run."

"Mr. Boyne, I'm afraid this's most unusual."

"I *am* most unusual!"

"I'll have to consult with the owner."

"And here I thought *you* were the owner. Silly me."

And grabbing several blank sheets from this Xerox machine as the salesman departs, I sit Pippa down in a nearby chair.

"Seamus, what're you *doing?*"

"Just sit still for a moment."

And whipping off three delicate sketches of her with this ballpoint pen, like Picasso's Vollard Suite, the firm line having amazingly returned.

And the owner now appearing, a mousy little man in brown Harris tweed.

"O, Mr. Boyne, I'm *honored,* we're *all* honored! In fact, I own one of your Ciara paintings!"

"That's marvelous, Mr.—?"

"Foal, Reginald Foal."

"Well, here, Mr. Foal, are these worth a Jaguar?"

Foal examining the sketches with his shiny bifocals and a shaky, veiny hand, then sighing deeply, his eyes growing moist, "O these, my God, these are truly sublime! But would you kindly sign them just, well, just for verification?"

"Certainly, of course."

"And here are the keys."

"Thank you, Mr. Foal. But I do want to test drive her first. I'm sure you understand?"

"By all means, Mr. Boyne, be my pleasure."

And we follow him outside to this extraordinary-looking machine, "Does zero to sixty in 5.3 seconds." "Quite impressive," where I guide Pippa inside the leathery new car aroma, then slide gingerly in beside her.

"Seamus, you're incredible!"

"Whoever said I wasn't?"

"Where're we going?"

"Out for an English spin, put her through her paces, and see whether it's actually worth those three sketches of you!"

And we go speeding and weaving all round the Jaguar lot—with Pippa squealing!—then sleekly wheeling by Regent's Park, along Prince Albert Road, with me now grinning from ear to ear, "You know, just after World War II, Picasso bought a home in the south of France and paid for it with a single still life."

"And what'd *he* do for his seventy-fifth birthday?"

"Blew out seventy-five candles with three breaths on a seventy-five pound cake, then went back to painting."

"Well, I must say, Seamus, you don't look a day over seventy-four. No, really, even with the fading stain, you seem much, *much* younger today, could easily pass for a distinguished fifty-five."

"Which is definitely due to you, my dear, sweet Pippa, for hope still dances on a bald man's pate, and the muse may've finally returned."

"Well, I don't deserve the credit, but I do love the way you handled that fat, haughty asshole back there," as she checks her side mirror once again, and we go zipping up Primrose Hill, "Seamus?"

"What?"

"I think we're being followed."

"Foal?"

"Don't think so."

A fast glance in the rear-view mirror at that gray Cortina behind—"Glassco!"

"Why?"

"Precautionary, I suppose. But I think I'll lose him now, really let this beauty loose!"

"Seamus, easy, please."

And with a berserk snarl of the blown exhausts, we go rocketing off through Belsize Park, with Pippa still nervously checking behind, traffic looming up ahead—

"Think we may've lost him—"

"SEAMUS!!"

Narrowly avoiding an oncoming crash with that swaying cement truck as I shoot on past.

"Please slow down!"

Flashing by that veering traffic—

"I'm serious!"

—and accelerating into the clear—

"Stop, stop! Will you stop right *here!"*

"But why? What's wrong, what's the matter?" Swerving to the curb, and Pippa squeezing, heaving out of her leather seat.

"You could've killed my baby, caused a miscarriage!" And slamming the door, "Like Rory said," she goes storming off, "you always come first!" waddling down the street.

"Pippa, what're you—where're you *going?"*

Over her shoulder, "Away from you!" She disappearing round that far corner as, blinking and staring, I go cruising after—Where is she? Don't see her—then parking and hopping out as Glassco screeches to a stop beside me.

"Mr. Boyne, are you all right?"

"*Absolutely not!*"

Twelve

And neither of us ever find her. And she won't answer her phones, either cell or at home—And now someone's banging madly at my door—Pippa coming back?—as I promptly swing it wide:

"Happy birthday, Da!" and my smiling, windblown son, with his mop of carroty curls, clad in a navy pea jacket, and carrying a rectangular package wrapped in brown paper, gives me another backslapping hug and kisses me flush on my white-whiskered cheek.

"Is that my gift?"

"You could say. But how're you feeling?"

"Physically better, thanks, much better."

"Terrific," and Rory glances around with that intense blue gaze, Tiki's Nordic face, and places the package against the wall, "So where's Pippa?"

"Have no idea. But where's Nicole?"

"With her mother," and he sits down on the gold brocaded sofa.

"Why didn't Nicole come with you?"

"Well . . . to be quite honest, you, well, you intimidate her, Da."

"*I* do? Since when do I intimidate her?"

"I'll let *her* explain."

"No, come on, Rory."

"Well, she's English, doesn't like confrontation."

"Rory?"

"She thinks you don't approve of her."

"But I *do,* actually like her very much."

"Then tell her that."

"I will."

"But you never have."

"I haven't?"

"No."

"Then I certainly apologize."

"Wow, now there's a first!"

"O come on, Rory, you never heard me apologize?"

"Never."

"Not once?"

"Not once."

"Then I truly am an Irish ogre. Must've been hell having me as a father."

"And a great painter to boot. No, essentially you were a damn good father, but, well, in fact I was thinking about this yesterday up at Oxford, how hard it is to follow a legend, or, rather, probably impossible—"

"You want something to drink? Here, let me—"

"No, Da, I'm fine for the moment."

"But isn't that the struggle of all sons?"

"To some degree. To break free and become your own man, your own person."

"Well, I always felt the two basic things you can teach a child are first to walk and then to walk away."

"Precisely, Da. And that's the best thing you ever taught me."

"Ah, 'tis a wise child who knows his own father."

"Thank you," Rory standing and opening his peajacket, "that's nice to hear after all these years," before pacing anxiously round the room, "Anyway, I've—well, I've got some news. I'm—well, I'm not going back to Oxford."

"You mean tomorrow?"

"No, never, Da. I'm giving up the Rhodes."

"*What? Why?* 'Cause of Nicole?"

"No, it's not that, it's—"

"So what will you do?"

"Paint."

"*Paint*?"

"I've *been* painting."

"Since when?"

"O, for years now."

"And you never told me, told your—?"

"No, I wanted you to be proud of me—"

"But I *AM* proud of you! Always have been—"

"—and I didn't think I was good enough to show you—"

"—all you've accomplished, Yale, a Rhodes Scholarship, brilliant career ahead—"

"Da, listen, the world recognizes you as a great, great painter, a genius, and then along comes his son who also wants to paint, to please himself at the start, really as a lark, yet ultimately wants your approval, so I waited, couldn't *stop* painting, till I felt maybe I was good enough, at least to show it to you—"

"Does your mother know?"

"No."

"So you've been lying all these years."

"I never lied!"

"Then why didn't you *come* to me, share it with me?"

"I *couldn't* come to you. I wanted to be my *own* man, my *own* painter, not just the son of Seamus Boyne!"

"Does Nicole know?"

"Of course."

"And Pippa, too?"

"Yes. In fact, it was Pippa's idea to show you my work."

"*What?* Wait, wait a second, hold on, hold on, 'cause I'm starting to put two and two together here. Tell me, what's your *real* relationship with Pippa?"

"Da—"

"Are you the father of her baby?"

"O come *on!*" He turning toward the package.

"Come on what?"

"How could you even think that?"

"Ah, so it's *true?*"

He turning around, "I didn't say that. Anyway, you want to see my work, my painting?"

"No, Rory, why don't you just go *back* to Pippa or Oxford or Fuck-All-On-Thames and continue having your torrid artistic affair!"

"Thanks, Da, for your understanding." Tears filming his eyes as he heads for the door.

"Don't you want your painting?"

"No, it's my gift to you." And the door slams behind him.

"Well *FUCK* you, too, and your bloody gift!"

Suffering *CHRIST*, Pippa and Rory! Losing them both? So, good riddance! And firing this Poldy sculpture at the wall—missing it—and on through the latticed window, shattering, splintering glass—and now there's knocking at the door.

Who the hell's that? Rory come back? And flinging it wide: Glassco, in his dusty brown mac, with a worried smile—

"You all right, sir?"

"I'm fine, fine! But here, come on," throwing on my Burberry, "come along with me."

"Where to, sir?"

"To celebrate my fucking birthday!"

And off we go to the local round the corner.

Just in time for a couple of foaming cold lagers before closing. A richly hopped beer adding a brassy bite to the palate as I rant angrily on about deceitful children. The constable from Pittenweem nodding, he a father of two (one similarly estranged) but now a grandpa again, it seems. And this bartender is coming over to me, shaking my hand as though I were famous. "Jaysus! See, Glassco, *now* they recognize me!" And telling him of my Jaguar experience, then hilariously laughing together about me flashing my aged willy outside my rainy town house, "Thought sure you were gonna lock me up."

"Ah no, no way, Mr. Boyne," he draining his sudsy jar, "for as St. Augustine did say, 'Lord, give me chastity—but not today.' "

And the two of us go staggering back home, three sheets to the wind, arms looped around each other's shoulder, as I lead him on inside, "Glassco, old sport, I'll be leaving soon for Ireland, but thank you for all your time—and here, wait just a mo—" and returning from my studio, "Here, here's a sculpture for you and your newest, bawling grandbab!"

"O no, sir, I couldn't."

"You shall!"

"Well this is extraordinary, most kind. And what's that, sir?"

"What's what?"

"That package against the wall?"

"O that—That's, that's—Well, here, lemme see," my heart rapidly beating, thunder out there grumbling in retreat, "rip this bloody thing open—"

"A paintin', sir."

"*GOOD GOD!!*"

Thirteen

And, on this rainy, windswept morning, taking some Ativan for vertigo, and picking up this pen at 2:15 A.M. and letting out another deep, wheezing sigh, I glance out at that pitch-black, blustery London sky, then:

```
                              March 24, 2004
My dear, wonderful son,
   It's hard for parents to apologize, though it
really shouldn't be. And if you're a bloody
```

horse's patoot like me, it doesn't come any easier.

I suppose a large part of me will always want to see you as a little boy, like that time, which you captured so brilliantly in your work, when the two of us journeyed out to Benbulben, and I told you all about the legends of Queen Maeve and CuChulainn, Diarmaid and the great mountain boar.

No one could ever replace those memories or you in my heart. There may be some father somewhere who has a son like you, but if there is, I have yet to see it. You've grown into a splendid man, with a talent at your ripe young age that even I envy. I, of course, have had a hard time coming to grips with turning seventy (now seventy-five), or, in my case, $69.95, plus shipping and handling.

> Still, much love,
> Your Da

And rather than mail it, I'll give it to him when next I see him as I fold it in half and slip it in my bathrobe pocket. Then stare long and hard at his three-by-five-foot canvas done in tempera in a fragmented, smudgy Larry Rivers style, over bold Rothko tones of somber gray and Hockney blue, of an image of me (at least it looks like me) as a younger man being embraced by Rory as a child in front of Benbulben, and all these legendary figures, Queen Maeve and CuChulainn, filling the painting's misty sky—as I sigh once more, still so overwhelmed by his talent, such a truly exquisite talent! And I never knew, hadn't a clue—and I start acting like Lear! A bloody old *fool*, Boyne, is what you are, Lear-like in your blindness!

And feeling as old here on my birthday as Lear himself—Still, should I try Pippa again to get her side of the story? No, I *do* believe him, saw the truth in his fiery eyes. And he keeping his secret all these years—And now he and I competing? Saddled as he is with the name of Boyne—though I rarely used tempera, rather a thick impasto and glossy varnish myself.

But, Jaysus, what the blazes *DO* I know anymore? Though there was a time when I thought *all* my opinions were right, some even said sublime. *Everything has to be about you and your fucking ego!*

And now, here I am at an increasingly dizzy seventy-five, floundering, fumbling, forgetting, and stumbling—like when I walk into a room and can't remember why—or am hit by panicky waves of mortality at three or four in the morning (when I often pee), then sinking full fathom five, down, down, down, drowning in violent childhood fears—and beseeching the gods, my gods, Odin, Thor, and Zeus himself, to save me, help me, and just let me, with my large hands and tapered fingers, keep painting till I die!

For, face it, Boyne, you *are* aging, you *are* dying, and you are so full of sorrow, rage, arrogance, and pride, putting your work, your painting ahead of everything and everyone—*You always come first!*—and now losing Tiki, Pippa, and Rory besides!

Fourteen

And waking late on this strangely haunting Wednesday morning, with still no word from Pippa, I poke my sleepy head cautiously out the front door—and wince at this bizarre weather for March 24 of blinding sun, bitter cold, and, now, even a brief shower of hailstones!

So what does that portend? God only knows! as I call Rory to talk to Nicole—but his cell phone's forever busy. Then shunning a bath and wrapping myself in these warm, cashmere woolies, I toss the azure scarf dashingly over my shoulder and speed up to Lancaster Gate.

But Pippa's not at home. So I wait, spying round the corner for twenty minutes out of sight—Boyne now becoming a stalker!—then go zooming off, fuming with frustration, into—*Jaysus!*—London's infernal gridlock!

At five, I lower my bruised and creaky bones into yet another scalding bath, rinse out the remaining Grecian stain, put on my rakishly canted beret and plaid, belted Burberry, and point the purring Jag straight back to Bayswater.

· · · · · ·

And now here I am taking one nervous, raggedy breath after another before lightly rapping with this shiny, copper, first-floor knocker—

"Door's *open!*"

And stepping slowly through this pungent incense aroma into what looks like a fortune teller's parlor, with its iridescent-beaded curtains and ornate, leaded lamps and Karen Carpenter singing, *"Long ago, and O so far away,"* I stop short at the sight of Pippa seated naked to the waist and painting her bare breasts before a full-length, gilt-edged mirror.

"What the bloody hell are you *doing?*"

"What's it look like I'm doing? And why—?"

"Came to apologize." And carefully sidling beside her, I lean over and, cupping her upturned face in my hands, tenderly kiss her softly parted lips.

And she, sighing and shaking her head, *"Just a rainy day or two/ In a windy tower,/ That was all I had of you—/ Saving half an hour,"* grins and kisses me back. "O and Rory called. You thought *he* was the father?"

"I know, I know. But you knew about Rory painting. Why didn't you tell me? Why did everyone else know but *me?*"

" 'Cause he wanted to tell you himself, let you see for yourself."

"Yes, well—O but here, let me do that, Pippa."

"Do what?"

"Paint your body. 'Cause, really, that looks awful."

"It does, doesn't it. You're probably right. But please, Seamus, don't take too long, my show starts in less than an hour."

"OK, just relax and try turning more toward the light—There, that's good, perfect." And I begin gently stroking on these shimmering swirls of red and gold, over her lovely pregnant body. "Has anyone ever told you your breasts have the luminous warmth of a Renoir nude?"

"—No, not lately," and now she's giggling.

"What?"

"It just tickles."

"Sorry."

"No, don't stop, it's actually turning me on."

And a few moments later, she standing in front of the full-length mirror to assess my fleshy mural, twisting from side to side, "O, Seamus, this is *amazing,* totally insane! God, I'm *never* gonna wash it off! But how can I ever repay you?"

"O, I'm sure I'll think of a way."

· · · · · ·

And racing through dark and dusky Soho chafed with people till I find the first parking spot I see, then rush around to ease Pippa onto the curb.

"Now where?"

"Just along here, but, really, we must hurry!"

Bowlegged down Dean Street under the glow of lamps, past the slumberous line of parked cars, with Pippa swaying plumply by my side—and there are men passing by with envious, sly glances at her adorable, bustling stride and her ambling, shambling companion in carefree dishevelment as I guide her down this dark alley to the worn stage door of the Hairy Boar.

"Seamus, go take a seat out front and I'll see you after, 'bye."

Quick kiss, and she's gone inside.

And a short time later in this cramped and smoky den:

"Ladies and gentlemen, *mes dames et monsieurs,* the Hairy Boar takes great pride and pleasure tonight in presenting the one, the only . . . *Pippa Green!*"

And Bach's "Sleepers Awake!" comes roaring out of the loud-speakers, E. Power Biggs on the organ, over a smattering of applause from this small and chattering crowd—as she appears in a tassled fuchsia shawl draped about her bosom, and, delicately removing it with a wicked grin to astonished "oohs!" and "aahs!" at my shimmering mural highlighting her splendid breasts, she curt-sies, naked to the waist, then, pausing for silence, begins reciting her beloved Edna St. Vincent Millay:

"Just a rainy day or two
In a windy tower,
That was all I had of you—
Saving half an hour
Marred by greeting passing groups
In a cinder walk,
Near some naked blackberry hoops
Dim with purple chalk.
I remember three or four
Things you said in spite,
And an ugly coat you wore,
Plaided black and white.
Just a rainy day or two
And a bitter word.
Why do I remember you
As a singing bird?"

And *Suffering JAYSUS,* she's *leaking!* A small puddle spreading at her feet as she sways slightly, then sinks softly to the floor, Bach still booming over the applause—and I'm up on stage in a blink!

"Seamus, get some towels!"

"Where?"

"There's some in my dressing room."

"Right, right! And, hey, the show's over, folks!"

"This isn't part of it?"

Pippa trying to smile at the tattooed customer, "Sorry, no, there won't be a repeat performance."

"But here, *you*, lend me a hand!" Getting her to her feet, "Which hospital, Pippa?" wrapping the fuchsia shawl—

"Shaftsbury—it's not too far."

And with the help of the tattooed man, we guide her to the door—my damn leg's still so sore!—then outside, where I lift her, "I've got you, my dear"—the man arranging towels over the seat—and ease her on inside, "Thanks for your help."

I start up the Jaguar, "You still leaking?"

"Like a fucking faucet!"

"Which way?"

"Left on Shaftsbury Avenue, just past Charing Cross Road, on the right."

And *vroom!* we go speeding away, zero to sixty in 5.3 seconds!

"Seamus, what would I have done without you?"

"Had your soggy bab on stage!"

The hospital orderly greeting us with a wheelchair, and she goes rolling off to delivery.

And shortly thereafter, I call Rory—who's on his way with Nicole—then meet Dr. Nigel Kaplan, who is honored to make my acquaintance, and who also owns one of my paintings, and will let me watch the birth as I follow right behind him. "Where's the father?" "He's dead."

His nurse turning from the hospital bed, "Doctor, her torso is painted, so we have to wash it—"

"My *Lord!*"

"What, doctor?"

"This is *your* work, isn't it, Mr. Boyne?"

"Well, yes, I—"

"It's—It's *magnificent*, absolutely *brilliant!*"

"Thank you, that's very kind."

"So I can't *possibly* wash it off!"

"Well—"

"But I can *buy* her belly—No, really—Nurse, in my locker, there's a digital camera. Would you bring it straightaway?"

She nodding and hustling off as a blinking Pippa gazes up.

"What're you doing, doctor?"

"I'm going to photograph you, Ms. Green, at least preserve this treasure on film, then send it on to the Tate—Ah, there we are. Thank you, nurse."

And he starts madly clicking away from a variety of angles, Pippa and I both grinning—before the nurse washes off my fleshy mural, scrubbing Pippa all rosy and clean, though she continues bleeding slightly—

"Mr. Boyne?"

"Yes, doctor?"

"It might be awhile, contractions are rather weak, so you might want to wait outside. And I'll call you when we're ready."

And ten minutes later, Rory and Nicole arrive. He edgy, and she a willowy, wide-eyed ballerina, looking so shy, with her long black hair halfway down her back as I clasp her hand in mine. "Nicole, forgive me."

"For what?"

"Ever intimidating you."

"Rory!"

"All I said was—"

"I think my only son is an extremely fortunate man to have you by his side."

"Well . . . thank you, that's very kind. O, and you might like to know, Rory and I have decided to have the child."

"Ah, *mazel tov,* as they say in dear, dirty Dublin," and I kiss both of them, *smack,* on their foreheads. "And, Rory, here, this is for you," handing him my letter, "And your painting is absolutely amazing."

"Thank you. And how's Pippa?"

"Scrubbed all rosy and clean."

"Her water break on stage?"

"Right, to Bach's 'Sleepers Awake'!"

And a few minutes later, Dr. Kaplan coming out.

"We couldn't stop the bleeding, but the baby's on its way, so if you would, Mr. Boyne."

And I follow him back into the delivery room, where I grip Pippa's hand, she grimacing and glancing up.

"O, Seamus, to see all the love in your eyes for me—but listen, listen, if anything should happen, will you promise—No, *promise* you'll raise the baby?"

"Nothing's going to happen." The nurses scurrying about.

"But if it does, all this bleeding—?"

"I promise, I promise, but you're going to be fine—"

"O FUCKING CHRIST!"

And squeezing my hand hard as she keeps cursing and shrieking, arching her spine—and I whip my head around as out slides the wet and fuzzy head and then body of a perfectly formed baby boy! *May love and mercy/ Unclose his eyes!*

Snipping the umbilical cord, washing him pink and dry, then wrapping him up like a papoose, the nurse delivers him into Pippa's loving arms.

"Well, *hello,* Vincent!"

"Vincent?"

"Vincent Seamus Green!"

"Mr. Boyne, I'm afraid you have to leave."

"Why?"

And whispering, "The bleeding's started again."

"Will she be all right?"

"We're taking her into surgery—Leave *now*."

Rory rushing up, "Da, what happened?"

"She had a baby boy, but they can't stop the bleeding!"

"O no!" Nicole's hand covering her mouth.

And I can't stop pacing back and forth around this waiting room, nearly hyperventilating, then on down the hall—'cause Pippa *can't* die now, not after all we've been through, be a fabulous maverick mother—So small and helpless and totally alone in that cold and sterile room. Tears stirring and blurring—and I'm drying my eyes, then tracing my snowy beard as Rory and I continue striding side by side, and mumbling to myself, "—Lost Laura, my first wife, after marrying her a second time, to lymphoma, she aging twenty years, couldn't breathe, her spleen too large—And Ciara blown to bits by an IRA bomb meant for Louis Mountbatten at my Dublin show, at only thirty-one!—And, of course, my father, beloved father, Tim, dying of liver cancer in that grim Rhode Island asylum when I was seventeen, sharing his last meal on earth with me—and I felt like Turner when he lost *his* father, that I'd lost an only child!"

Rory now wrapping his arm around my shoulder as we keep on pacing—

"Da?"

"What?"

"Thank you so much for the letter."

Fifteen

And on this morrow of racing, hazy clouds, a silvery sheen, I'm already painting a full-length portrait of Vincent Seamus Green when—*Jaysus!*—the bloody phone keeps on ringing and ringing and ringing:

"—Yes, *hello?*"

"Seamus, what're you doing?"

"O—Tiki. Painting, can't *stop* painting!"

"And what're you painting?"

"This fabulous bab!"

"Whose bab?"

"Pippa's, the healthy, surviving mother, Rory and Nicole's best friend—and I'm the godfather, bab's got my middle name!"

"You're sure you're not the father besides?"

"Jaysus, Tiki, come on! But how's your brother?"

"He died early this morning on the operating table—"

"*O Mother of Christ!*"

"—there were complications—"

"Tiki, I'm taking the next plane to Vancouver."

"But what about your painting?"

"I'll finish it when I get home. It can wait."

Irish Climax

Christmas 2007

—*O Suffering JAYSUS,* will I ever come again? Never come again? Never *EVER* come again? Christ, I'm sounding so like a bloody broken record now in my dithering dotage, bones grown brittle with age and filled as I am with dyspeptic rage and mounting frustration at a bald and snowy-bearded seventy-seven—for women *MUST* have their gratification! And I've been unable to perform like in days of yore, growing so ashamed and soft. And tonight as usual, I began by nuzzling the smooth insides of her lustrous thighs and down to the mingling aromas of blossom and brine—

Yet the question still remains, as I continue frantically pumping away, how much longer can I keep it up, retain my former glory, and spill my Irish seed? For, face it, I'm no longer *brandy and ripe in my bright bass prime.* No, now like a top that's spinning to a dizzying stop, I'm at the mercy of *thieving time* that holds me aged and dying though I still sing *in my chains like the sea.* Chains of arthritis pain, headache and muscle pain, strange and fearful pain, deaf in my left ear, eyes at f/11, and peeing more than a dozen bloody times a day!

Yet even with my waning powers, each morning confronting my rising pharmaceutical tower of Omega-3, glucosamine, and chondroitin, a part of me still believes in my denial of death and dying, while ultimately outlasting 'em all, Rothko, Pollock, Rivers, and Willem, the fraud, de Kooning!

For I absolutely refuse to *go gently into that goodnight!* as I keep on pumping steadily away, with her under me, over me, her back to me. And the last thing dear, old Flynn said to me before he died, " 'Ah, well ya know now how Oyrish women hold their liquor, Boyne?" "No. How?" "By the ears!"—while outside my castle window and the dark-stained wainscoting, that new moon rages, a foghorn mournfully lowing from the Irish Sea, and the long vowels of wind through the slenderly swaying trees.

For denial's such a dominating, motivating force, like that JFK documentary, where I keep staring over and over at the back of Kennedy's head, hoping that the third shot'll miss, or the wound be healed, and Jack'll still be brightly smiling—as opposed to that T-shirt I just saw in Dublin of Bush's Dumbo-eared, smirky face in the crosshairs, and the caption: "Lee Harvey Oswald, where are you when we need you?"

A onslaught of winter wind out there and the rhythmically calming crash of the sea's evening waves, while beneath me once more, her salaciously female wiggle, a randy wriggle, wamble as it were. To twist, writhe, roll, and wiggle about; to wit, wamble, as it were. And recalling now in a rush of lusty memory all of my wives: the voluptuous, passionate Tiki and our unbridled bliss in the Ardmore loo; or the fairhaired Ciara and I playing naked hide-and-seek in my castle's boxwood maze; or the day I was painting madly away, and Laura, almost telepathically, heard my lustful plea and tiptoed nude into my studio to catcurl at my knees and unzip my fly, her tongue grazing over my thighs and rising passion, taunting and tickling, sucking and licking, as, flinching backwards, I writhed with delight, my eyes squeezed tight, gripping her head, her hair till I was bone-dry—then soft, rabbity kisses bye-bye.

And boom, in a blink, I was in need of Viagra, Levitra, Cialis, my already imposing member swelling (I thought) to mythic proportions. Though Dr. Hafiz claimed it was all in my mind. And with Levitra, the fear of going blind, blurry vision, heated cheeks red as a beet, as well as sweating, heart-pounding vertigo. Yet once I was so shy, afraid to let a girl touch me, then became ram, goat man, anything goes, though always a late-developer, physically, athletically, sexually—but not artistically, never artistically, before eventually battling through coyness and impatience, girdles and garters, fingernails and pleading to explode my urgent need.

And now needing energy more than ever, and praying to St. Rafka of bodily ills for a blessed orgasm, having had for dinner tonight only a bowl of avgolemono soup and a bottle of Newcastle Brown. And, surely, I'll bang my tankard high in heedless revelry if I finally spill my seed and fall into that rapturous sleep, or the chromatic snooze it induces, while I keep desperately holding on now for dear life, for the *rest* of my rollicking life, to what is most important, family and friends, loved ones, flesh and blood, and my amazing, scattered brood: Tory teaching dance now in Boston; Rory in his studio up in Oxford, shows last month in Berlin and Prague; Hagar and Shay, now twenty-seven, in L.A., making a fil-um out of *Irish Wine;* Symes now eighty-nine, close by in the Rathnew house I bought him after Moira died, with his round-the-clock nurse and caretaker; Pippa hosting her BBC cooking show and raising Vincent Seamus Green, that obstreperous rogue, now almost three; same age as Geordie, Rory's adorable rascal; and all my Samoyed doggies, Poldy, Sinjin, Brady, and now, Poldy's great-grandson, the wily, six-month-old and perpetually horny Fitz-Grady.

And I've painted each and every one of them again and again and again. For few passions're as powerful as the protective love for those nearest and dearest, and nothing sends my gorge rising faster through the roof than a threat or abuse to those I hold close to my heart.

And last week, I, painter and patriarch, flew to London to receive a Knight Commander of the Most Excellent Order of the British Empire, casually clad in a slouchy khaki blazer over a green-striped polo shirt, and spoke in a quiet rasp with an air of devilish glee as I told the assembled media, "You have permission now to call me Lord of lords, or your demigodness'll do. But I definitely expect you to kneel," while those genteel critics and reporters rattled on about the astounding urgency of my art "that remains absolutely riveting."

Riveting, me Royal Irish Arse! For as Pollock once told me,

"Painting's no problem. The problem's what to do when you're *not* painting!" Cézanne on his deathbed calling out the name of the museum director who rejected his paintings. And poor Van Gogh only thirty-seven when he died, same age as Raphael, Caravaggio, and Watteau. And Picasso living fourteen more years than I am now, dying at ninety-one in '73 and working on his last painting, *Man with a Sword*. And my sword, my veritable caber, now grown rusty and filigreed with age, but still holding up as I raise her shapely, tapered legs round my neck for far deeper penetration. And like me, Pablo always painting women, women, and more women, voluptuous women, tempting women, orgasmic women, with their breasts high, thighs spread wide—but at the end, no men on canvas anywhere in sight, and no more copulations, while the women remained waiting moist with desire—so he began distorting them, disjointing them, crushing and violently breaking them into shards and twisted pieces—which I never did or will ever do.

But when he was my age of seventy-seven, his brilliant Blue Period *Mother and Child* brought only $150,000 in New York. His entire estate ultimately valued at $240 million. Jaysus, today that's roughly the equivalent of six—no, probably five of my works, or maybe a whole lot more!

Our sexual shadows swaying on the bedroom wall as I keep squeezing and stroking her exquisite satiny arse, kissing her lips and wind-bussed cheeks as—*O Jaysus!* I'm starting to flag, to wither and die—*NO!* No-no-no, there's my Christmas gift, that prayed for tickle, that heated rasp and prickle on my phallic seismograph! Pumping harder now and side to side—and dear God, so want to please her, make her pleasure last—"Come with me now!" "I already have, Seamus, *twice!*"—and Holy Mother of Christ, please don't let me die again, just come one final time—as I slam my stroke home, harder and harder, faster and faster, her eyelids fluttering, thighs high and wrapping me tightly round as

I grip her sleek, succulent rump, she still clinging and crying out, her feathery fingers lightly tickling (licking?) my balls— But how could she—?

"*O SUFFERING JAYSUS—YES!*" I scream, shout, bellow to the raging moon and surging Irish Sea, "*YES, YES, YES!!*"

Still coming and pumping—But how could she possibly lick 'em when she was below—? "*GOOD GOD, FITZY!*"

"Seamus, what, what is it?"

His smiling Samoyed face and snowy ruff, plume tail happily swishing. "Fitz-Grady was licking me bollocks!"

And Tiki bursts out laughing, "Well, whatever floats your boat, lucky it wasn't your goat," as my little doggie, with his round brown eyes and fine white lashes, keeps on blinking and panting, before trotting out the door on his furry puppy paws.

"You know, love, you're absolutely right, so." Shouting, "God bless you, Fitzy,," and snuggling into my wife, "and to all a good night!"

· · · · · ·

Dick Wimmer is the author of *Baseball Father, Baseball Sons, Irish Wine, Boyne's Lassie,* and *The Irish Wine Trilogy.* He lives in Southern California.

Printed in the United States
by Baker & Taylor Publisher Services